a sweet celebrity romance

Lovestruck

DANA LeCHEMINANT

To those who are left behind and continue forward anyway.

Lovestruck:

overcome by intense feelings of love toward someone

Hollywood Hot Scoop

Dennie on the Rocks?

Buckle up, readers, because Hollywood's hottest couple may be calling it quits. That's right, Derek Riley and Bonnie Aiken could be done for good. One of our favorite sources witnessed a lovers' quarrel early Tuesday morning outside Champion Studios, and neither big screen legend looked happy when they parted ways. We've been rooting for the dynamic duo since their first appearance on screen over a year ago, but it looks like Bonnie is ready to break another heart in search of her next spring fling. If poor Derek needs a shoulder to cry on, I volunteer as tribute!

Vote below on who you think the starlet will go for next. My money's on rugby star Cole Evanson now that he's split from his longtime girlfriend, but Bonnie and music sensation Liam Connolly have been spending a lot of time together, with *and* without Liam's girlfriend, Kasey. Could Liam be two-timing our favorite delivery girl-turned screenwriter? Or maybe Cole and his perfect bod are the reason Derek looks ready to give up on this whirlwind love story. Share your thoughts below and stay tuned for your next *Hollywood Hot Scoop*! XO

CE CREAM

Chapter One

BONNIE

"WHAT DOES A GIRL have to do to get someone murdered around here?"

Derek chuckles, far too calm about the stupid tabloid article that is about to make our lives far more difficult than they need to be. "If your charm hasn't worked so far," he says without looking up from his phone, "I'm pretty sure nothing will."

Easy for him to say. I don't think he's ever been in a situation where his charm hasn't worked. The man *oozes* charm. Besides, he's not the one who has the whole country speculating about his dating life. At least not to the same degree as me.

No one is voting on *his* secret love affairs.

I glance out the limo window to see how close we are to the Dolby Theater. I was already nervous about tonight, and this article dropping a few hours ago isn't helping anything. How am I supposed to walk the Oscars red carpet when my whole relationship with Derek is in question? Sure, our relationship isn't real, but the world doesn't know that.

Our publicist, Fran, must read my question in my face because she clears her throat and pulls my attention to her at the other end of the limo. "Here's the plan," she says, glancing between us.

We must be quite the sight right now, with me sweating so badly that I'm going to be nervous about lifting my arms even a little on the red carpet, and Derek stretched out in his seat and scrolling through a new script on his phone like he doesn't have a care in the world.

He doesn't. No matter what his relationship status, he has always been popular since the first time he smiled on camera. Even as an unnamed background character, he was stealing hearts with his dark hair and baby blue eyes, and now he's one of the most sought-after actors in Hollywood. He could date a garbage can and still be an Oscar nominee like he is now.

Derek's life is and always has been perfect, and he's too good of a guy to realize how easy he has it.

"The plan?" I push when Fran doesn't continue.

She blinks, pulling her eyes away from Derek. I'll accuse her of drooling later. "This latest article is trending more than we'd like, so tonight you two are going to prove to the world that you're absolutely committed to each other."

I glance at Derek, who purses his lips. "And how do we do that?" I ask. "We've been together for a year and a half. If that's not a sign of commitment, then what—"

"Eighteen months is hardly a blip," Fran argues. "Maybe in Hollywood that's a long time, but the fans who love you are the ones who believe in happily ever after."

It's the curse of only being cast in romantic movies, even though I've loved the movies I've done. Everyone expects my relationships to be fairy tale worthy. "Okay, but what does that have to do with me and Derek? How do we fix this?"

"Derek could propose."

Derek chokes, his phone slipping from his fingers. "Derek could what?"

Fran smiles, showing off her unnaturally straight teeth. "Propose. On the red carpet."

Sitting up straighter, he glances at me for a split second but keeps his focus on Fran. "Do you really think that's a good idea?"

"Of course it is. It's the best way to help you both."

This is what we get for sharing a publicist. Fran is great, she really is, but lately she's only been seeing us as a pair. It's like she forgets Derek and I are two different people with different trajectories. He's in the big leagues, ready to change the world one story at a time, and I'm just happy to get roles. I don't care what they are.

A proposal would help me—I know it would—but I can't see how it would benefit Derek. Especially because I know what Derek's ideal future looks like. A highly public marriage to me isn't it. This has been true since the beginning, but it's been getting harder and harder to think about going back to just friends.

I've gotten too comfortable being his girlfriend, which is dangerous.

"We can't get engaged," I say, putting my hand on Derek's arm. I feel his gaze shift to me, but I don't let myself look at him. If I do, my resolve will break. "Fran, this relationship is already hard enough, and we're not ready to get married."

"It doesn't have to jump right into a marriage," Fran says with a scoff. "You know how these things go. As soon as this *Hot Scoop* thing blows over, you can carry on your merry lives and keep this engagement going indefinitely."

"Until the next gossip column forces our hand," Derek says roughly.

Finally I look at him, and I can read his expression clear as day. He not only doesn't want to marry me, but he *can't*. Not without breaking certain promises. Derek will only marry once, and it's going to be to someone he really loves.

I take a steadying breath, though my fingers have started shaking. I'm not ready for this relationship to end, but there are only so many directions things could go. Either we ramp things up, or we end it and move on. Our careers won't let us coast along like we've been doing.

I've known this for a while, but I've been trying not to think about it. I'm terrified of what's coming when Derek finally realizes he's let our pretend relationship go on for too long.

"We're not getting engaged," I say as firmly as I can. "We'll just be madly in love tonight and hope for the best."

Fran's mouth pinches. "You know I don't like relying on hope."

"Then you shouldn't be working for Bonnie," Derek says. He takes my hand, lacing our fingers together before lifting my hand to his lips. I know what he's silently telling me. *Thank you.* He knows as well as I do that Fran isn't wrong about how beneficial a proposal could be, but we're in this together. What affects one of us will affect the other.

Besides, Derek is too good of a man to be saddled with me forever. He deserves something real and lasting, which isn't something I can give him. That means we are more than likely going to "break up" within the next week, and I'll be on my own again. I already feel uncomfortable just thinking about it.

When it's finally our turn to step out onto the red carpet, we've both put on our best smiles as the cameras start flashing. The reporters pelt us with question after question about our relationship and if we're breaking up, and we deftly avoid answering any of them, only speaking when someone asks about Derek's nomination or our upcoming movie. And when someone from *Hot Scoop* asks for a picture of the two of us together, Derek pulls me in for a kiss that would have anyone believing we're head over heels.

But it feels more like a goodbye.

I've never been more glad to go to an after party, though technically this would be considered an after-after party, since we already spent the last couple of hours in a hotel penthouse suite hosted by the director of Derek's Oscar-winning movie. *This* party is going to be way better than the last because there won't be anyone to impress. After a night of plastering on a carefree smile, I'm ready to let loose and stop pretending. I'm exhausted—and over-the-moon happy for Derek—but I wouldn't miss this for the world.

Derek holds my hand as we make our way to the front door of his luscious Malibu house, nodding at Bruce, his home security guard. Bruce glances at our hands but doesn't say anything, though I can tell he's itching to make a comment. He probably read the article this afternoon and is wondering how much longer our relationship is going to last.

"Who's here?" Derek asks, pausing before he opens the door.

Bruce smiles. "The whole gang."

I perk up. "Even Freya?"

"Flight landed this morning."

Derek gives my hand a squeeze, matching my grin because he knows how much I adore Europe's sweetest princess. "After you," he says, pushing the door open and guiding me inside.

Voices pull us to the back of the dimly lit house, to the huge lounge that overlooks the ocean. The room is my favorite in Derek's house, not only for the view but because it's full of the most luxurious couches and chairs I've ever sat in. At the moment, two of the three couches are occupied by our four best friends, though it doesn't seem like anyone has noticed us yet. They're too busy watching highlights from the Oscars and making snide comments.

"I would never be caught in something like that," Freya says, pointing to the TV with her LaCroix.

Next to her, Liam snorts a laugh and puts his feet on her lap as he stretches out across his girlfriend, Kasey's, lap as well. "That's because you don't have Kate Winslet's bod. You wouldn't be able to pull it off."

Freya shoves his legs away and seems to be considering dumping her drink over Liam's head. I think the only reason she doesn't is because of Kasey beneath him. "How dare you say such a thing to royalty?"

Cole chuckles, taking Freya's side, as he always does. "Better watch yourself, Liam," he says, shaking his head.

"Freya," Kasey says with a lifted eyebrow, "you literally told us ten minutes ago that you hate when people give you special treatment."

She sniffs. "Special treatment is not the same as avoiding insults."

"Admit it," Liam says. "You would be a total frump in that dress."

"I would look fabulous, but pink is not my color."

"That is absolutely not true," I say, grinning when all eyes swivel our direction.

"Derek!" Liam bounds from his seat and nearly tackles Derek as he leaps onto him in his usual greeting. "How does it feel to be an Oscar-winning actor, my man?"

Though Derek struggles to hold him up—Liam isn't small by any means—he clearly loves the attention as he laughs. "Probably about the same as being a Grammy-winning musician, so you tell me."

"I am so angry there are no awards for government officials," Freya says right before she slams into me with her own hug. "Hi, Bon! Did you miss me?"

"Always." And I mean that. Freya may be the heir to a freaking *throne*, but she's one of the best friends I've ever had. She and Kasey, who is a recent addition to our gang, are crucial to my sanity. "I didn't know you were flying in this week!"

Freya pats my cheeks like I'm a child and she's my elderly grand-mother, even though she's only a few years older than my twenty-nine. "I would not miss celebrating with Derek!"

Derek untangles himself from Liam, who seems to have been trying to put him in a headlock instead of hugging him, and pulls Freya into a tight embrace. "Thanks, Peach. That means a lot. I wasn't even sure I was going to win."

"Of course you were going to win." Cole hasn't moved from his spot on the couch. He's usually more enthusiastic than this, and though he seems happy for Derek like the rest of us, I can almost feel his underlying sadness. It's been five months since he broke up with his girlfriend, and he hasn't been the same since.

Though I really want to hurry to the bedroom Derek keeps for me so I can change into pajamas—I spend more time here than I do in my own apartment—I make my way to Cole's couch and sit on his legs, which are stretched out along the couch. "Hey, Evanson. Why the glum face?"

He fixes on a terribly fake smile. "I don't know what you're talking about."

Holding out my hand, I wait until he grabs it, and then I smile at him. "Wanna talk about it?"

He shakes his head, which I expected. He and Sage were going to be forever, and Cole even had a ring ready to go for months before the breakup. He said he was waiting for the right moment, but now that Sage has split, I'm wondering if he knew something wasn't right. Cole's not really a talker, though, unlike the rest of us. He'll never admit to being heartbroken, even if we can all see it.

"We're here to celebrate Derek tonight," he says, squeezing my hand.

"And apparently the end of your relationship," Liam throws in, flopping back to Kasey's side and pulling her into his arms. "Tough beat, Bon."

I look up at Derek, who frowns as he joins Freya on the third couch. "Guess we didn't sell it tonight?"

"Don't get me wrong," Liam says. "Clearly you two have chemistry, and I will be taking notes from that kiss you did for *Hot Scoop* tonight."

Kasey smacks him.

Though my face lights on fire, Derek chuckles. "It was just a kiss."

"That was not *just a kiss*," Liam counters. "If that was just a kiss, Bonnie wouldn't be looking like a tomato right now."

I press my hands to my cheeks, but I've never been able to hide my blush. It's kind of a problem when I'm in the middle of a romantic scene and not supposed to be reacting that way to the man across from me. "You know that's called acting, right?" I say to cover my tracks anyway.

But Derek has a frown now, like he knows exactly why I've turned so red. He probably does. We've known each other long enough that he can probably read me like a book, and he doesn't like the idea that I might have felt something on the red carpet tonight.

It wasn't real, he seems to be saying, though I hardly need the reminder.

I shoot a look back at him that says, *Let's talk later*, and then I throw a pillow at Liam. "Apparently I'll be dating you next, Liam. You or Cole, according to *Hot Scoop*."

Liam groans. "I'm sort of taken, Bon."

"Sort of?" Kasey asks, giving him a withering look that makes him grimace.

"Completely," he amends. "And happily so. Man, I hate that site. How has no one taken it down yet?"

"Because your country believes in the freedom of the press," Freya says with a haughty little sniff that sounds ridiculous coming from her. She's never been haughty in her life, probably because her country is tiny. Just a little island in between England and Denmark with more sheep than people.

Cole rolls his eyes. "Candora is no different," he reminds her, as if she might have forgotten the laws of her own country.

"Maybe, but we do not have gossip sites wasting their resources on silly celebrity stories."

"Yeah, except *Hot Scoop* loves talking about you, and you know it."

"We're getting off topic," Liam says, tossing the pillow back to me. "Are the two of you officially over, or what?"

I don't need to check my phone for messages from Fran to know the answer to that question. I think she knew what she was saying when she suggested Derek propose tonight. "I think we're done," I admit, and Derek nods to confirm it. "It was fun while it lasted, right?"

"You are the only two people I know who would be okay with being in a *fake* relationship for eighteen months," Liam says, shaking his head. "And even if I wasn't madly in love with a perfect woman, I still don't think I could date you, Bon. It would feel like dating my sister. I don't know how you did it, Derek."

Cole clears his throat, squeezing my hand again. "If you need...I could..."

I shake my head, though I love that he's offering. "No, it might be time for me to take a break. I'm filming that mystery romance in Colorado next week anyway, so there's no point in setting up a new relationship until I'm no longer on location." Especially because I want to do well on this movie. It's different from my usual, which will hopefully get me taken more seriously. I've gotten some prominent roles, but never anything that showcases my actual skills.

Plus, the movie is based on a book written by one of my all-time favorite authors, and I'm *really* hoping for a chance to meet him while we're filming. At least that way one of my dreams would come true.

We go quiet after that, and Liam eventually turns on an episode of *Jeopardy*. Game shows and HGTV are the only things we can watch together because movies and sports hit too close to home.

After everyone goes to bed—they all have rooms here whenever they want—Derek and I stay up and talk, like we've done a million times. Since the day we met, we've been great friends, and yes, I love kissing him. He's exceptionally good at it, just like he is with everything else he does. But even if I might have felt something tonight, I know it isn't anything real. It's just the anxiety of something ending and the reality of being on my own again, without a guaranteed person to be at my side.

I've never allowed myself to have a deep connection that would come from a real relationship, and I don't see that changing anytime soon. That's not something I need. But I really don't like being alone.

"I'm sorry things are ending this way," Derek tells me as we sit side-by-side next to the firepit on the back patio and watch the world slowly wake up around us. We've done this a lot over the last couple of years, when our jobs and our fame get overwhelming. There's something peaceful about being awake when the rest of the world is still and quiet. Mostly we've been talking about inconsequential things tonight, but I knew we would inevitably get here. "You'll be okay, right?"

I'm exhausted, and not just from putting on a show at the Oscars. Sometimes I feel like my whole life is a show, and I never get a chance to exist without performing. But I chose this life, and I can't imagine doing anything else. "I'll be fine," I tell Derek and smile at him.

Though he frowns, clearly not believing me, he kisses my forehead and then rests his cheek against my hair. He's tired and should get some rest before Fran starts planning our breakup. It'll be public, most likely—Fran loves generating good buzz—and Derek is already getting started on his next project, so he needs all the rest he can get.

Sighing, I settle in against him and close my eyes, feeling sleep tugging at me. This is for the best, no matter how much I don't like it. Derek will always be one of my closest friends, but it's time we start living our own stories.

CHAPTER TWO

HANK

I AM SO GLAD I'm not living my own story right now. It's alarming how many times I've had that thought, but it comes with the territory of being an extremely empathetic writer who sometimes forgets to separate fact from fiction. My currently racing heart is a testament to how poorly I distance myself from my work, and I force myself to stand and take a lap around my house to calm down.

It's not a big house so it's not a very long lap, but it's enough to pull me out of the moment I was writing. Enough for me to move back to my computer, though I don't sit down. Grabbing my mug of tea, I squint at the screen and look over the last couple of paragraphs.

My heroine was just about to uncover the murderer's location when someone wrapped a cord around her neck from behind. I'd known this moment was coming, but something isn't feeling quite right. She didn't have enough warning to save herself, and unless I write in someone to come save her, she's going to suffocate at her desk. I suppose I could have her scratch her nose right before it happens so she has a hand beneath the cord?

That's a little too, uh, on the nose. I need something more deliberate, something that readers won't expect but is still plausible enough to keep Gabrielle alive long enough for her to catch the villain.

I take a sip of my drink, grimacing when cold tea reaches my lips, and then I look down to find three other half-drunk mugs on my desk. I probably grabbed the wrong one, but none of them look especially warm.

"Maybe it's time for a break," I mutter, grabbing all four mugs and heading to my little kitchen. I'll wash the dishes from last night's dinner—okay, from the last two days of meals—and maybe go for a quick walk to get my mind moving again. This is the third time I've written Gabrielle into a non-win situation in this book, and it's starting to get annoying. I don't usually have this much difficulty getting through the first draft, but there's something about this book in particular that is proving to be especially frustrating.

With my dishes washed, dried, and tucked away, I head back to my computer, telling myself that I can only work for an hour before I fix myself lunch, even though it's already three in the afternoon. Better late than never. But right as I sit down, someone knocks on the door.

I freeze, just as I always do when someone appears at my house. Now that my only neighbors have married and moved away, this lane is always quiet, and it's far enough from town that I never get salesmen or someone asking to borrow some sugar. Which means whoever is on the front porch, they're here specifically for me, and they were smart enough not to call first because they know the only way to get in touch with me in person is to surprise me.

That means I'm not going to want to open that door.

The person knocks again, and I slowly inch to the window, hoping to get a glimpse of whoever it is through the curtains without them noticing me moving the fabric aside to get a peek.

I reach out a finger and nudge the curtain to the left.

A big brown eye greets me.

Cursing, I stumble backward just as a deep, feminine voice says, "I know you're in there, Hank. Open the door."

"I'd rather not," I call back. Not with my agent on the other side with a request I am not inclined to agree to.

"You've been ignoring my emails, Hank. That's in breach of your contract."

Maybe I should look into self-publishing. I've heard it's gotten easier over the last few years, and I've made enough of a name for myself that I could probably make it work. It's not like I need the money. I just need to write.

"I can practically hear your thoughts in there, Hank, and whatever you're thinking, it's a bad idea. Just let me in and we can talk. Good gracious, is that a spider?"

Mariah Harvey is a good woman and an even better agent, but she has never understood my desire to stay under the radar. My reasons for keeping to myself are legitimate, if unhealthy, but she shouldn't care as long as I keep giving her books that will sell.

"My deadline isn't for another two months," I remind her, glancing around my house as if I might find a place to hide. I won't. My house has all of two bedrooms, one of which I never enter and never will, and the kitchen and living room are collectively five hundred square feet. Emphasis on the square. I don't even have a coat closet to duck into; all of my coats are on an old-fashioned coat rack by the door.

Mariah knocks again, as if I might open the door now that she's done it thrice. "You know I'm not here about the next Gabrielle Frost book, Hank, though I'm excited to read it."

"You and me both," I mutter, glaring at my computer. Assuming Gabrielle doesn't suffocate and end the series, of course. Maybe I could have one of her fictional fans step up to finish what she started, like the intern at the police station. Start something new, with a different main character.

An ache settles in my chest at the thought, and I shake my head. No, I can't stop writing Gabrielle. She's the whole point.

"Hank, just let me in before this spider jumps on me and sucks me dry. You should really get this place sprayed."

I can't help but smile as I finally open the door, though only enough to poke my head out. "Her name is Heather."

Though Mariah looks like she was about to shove past me and into the house, my comment catches her off guard. She stares at me, slack jawed, until her eyes go back up to the spiny red and white arachnid nestled above my door. "You named a spider Heather?"

"She's a Gasteracantha cancriformis, and she and I have an agreement."

Mariah takes a step back, probably thinking I'm crazy. "An agreement."

"She protects the house from moths because I hate moths, and I don't take down her web. Simple symbiosis."

She tries so hard to smile and pretend she understands, but then a shudder runs through her and she tucks her blazer tighter around her body as she eyes the orbweaver overhead. "Hank, just let me in. I don't want to have this conversation through the door."

Sighing, I step back and open the door wide enough to let her inside. I'm already uncomfortable as she fills my small space with her big city presence, even if she isn't necessarily a large human. Her personality fills the largest of rooms, and I am too used to being the only one in this space.

The last time anyone was here was a year and a half ago, when I watched my neighbor, Hope's, kids when her husband got caught in a bear trap. And yes, I get a weekly visit from my friend, June Harper, the only person in town I can stand, but she never comes inside. She's perfectly content to stand on the porch and chat for a few minutes before handing over my groceries. Delivering is not her job—she runs the hardware store—but she says she likes the excuse to come out this way.

I know she's really just checking up on me because she promised Hope she would.

"You know," Mariah says as she takes in my house, "when I pictured your place, I pictured it a little more..." She waves her manicured hand around, clearly at a loss for words.

When I close the door, shutting off my only escape, I can barely swallow the nerves building in my throat. Why couldn't this have just been an email? Oh right, because I haven't checked my email in weeks, knowing I needed an excuse to avoid this exact conversation.

I gesture to the large armchair that serves as my only seating outside of my desk chair. "Let's get this over with."

Mariah scoffs as she sinks—literally—into the chair. It's probably time to replace that one, but I haven't been able to bring myself to look into something new. It's been a slow process, updating things, and the chair will likely be the last thing to go. If it ever goes.

"Hank, you're acting like this is some torturous thing I'm asking of you."

"And you're going to pretend I'm wrong," I counter, settling at my desk.

Her eyes snap to the screen, though she's too far away to read anything. "Is that Gabrielle?"

I click the screen off. "I'm not doing it, Mariah."

"You're not doing what?"

"I'm not going to let you parade me around to a bunch of people who don't actually care who I am, just that I'm going to make them a lot of money."

She laughs. "Oh, honey, they'll make the money with or without you. The book is already a bestseller and filming is underway."

"Then why do you keep asking me to show up on set?" I fold my arms, belatedly realizing I should offer her some tea or something. I've only ever seen her in person once, when I reluctantly drove to the nearest city, Sun City, to sign my contract, but I distinctly remember Mariah having a ridiculously complicated coffee order that was mostly made up of sugar and cream. I doubt my limited options will appeal to her.

Though she has been speaking with an authority in her voice, she's back to inspecting my house with concern. The front curtains are closed, but the back are wide open, giving us a spectacular view of the forested hills behind my lane. Enough sun shines through to illuminate the dust motes floating in the air, but I keep my house relatively clean. (Unless, of course, I'm on a writing streak. Which is not now.) The north wall is lined with bookshelves on either side of the hallway leading to the bedrooms, and I'm rather proud of my collection. I have several first editions and out-of-print books that I found in used bookstores back when...

Well, back when I still left the house. Finding rare books on the internet isn't quite as exciting as making a discovery on a dusty shelf.

When Mariah finally fixes her gaze back on me, she's adopted a sort of pitying smile that I really don't like. "Hank, you shouldn't spend all your time cooped up in this little house. It can't be good for you."

I've lived here alone for the last four years. "I'm perfectly fine."

Her expression only turns even more pathetic. "Honey, you're afraid of meeting a few people on a movie set."

"I'm not afraid of—"

"Great. Then I'll expect you to be there Tuesday morning because it's part of the contract you signed. I'll even send a car for you." She gets to her feet, brushing her pencil skirt as if everything is settled.

I wish it weren't, but she's right about the contract. I've managed to avoid book tours by finding loopholes over the last couple of years, but I doubt I'll find a way out of visiting the set now that Mariah is here in

Laketown. They are making a movie in my hometown, adapted from my first Gabrielle Frost book, so it makes sense. But knowing I won't have a choice is exactly why I've been avoiding Mariah, and a pit forms in my stomach as she heads for the door.

"I have a car," I mumble. I may not have driven it in six months or so, but I think it still runs.

Mariah pierces me with a stare, her hand on the doorknob. "I know you have a car, Hank. What I don't know is if you'll show up on Tuesday unless I do everything I can to ensure it happens, so I'll be sending a car. Wear something less..." She gestures to my pajamas, which I honestly didn't realize I was still wearing until now.

Not finding a word again, she sighs heavily and then heads out, peeking up at Heather as she passes the round web overhead.

I don't move until the sound of her car is gone, leaving me in a thick silence that doesn't normally bother me. In fact, I generally crave the quiet, which is exactly why I live in a tiny house in the middle of nowhere. But for the first time in years, the lack of noise is almost heavy, and my breaths come with some measure of difficulty. It's just the anxiety. The thought of having to interact with strangers. I can do it, and I used to have no problem talking to people I didn't know. I had all sorts of friends and reasons to be out and about.

But that was *before*.

Now, I just want to be left alone.

Hollywood Hot Scoop

Derek and Bonnie Split - The World in Mourning?

IT'S TRUE. OUR FAVORITE pair is no longer. But let's be real. We're all secretly glad that Derek is back on the market, am I right, ladies? Bonnie clearly didn't appreciate what she had, and anyone who can turn their back on the likes of Derek Riley doesn't deserve him.

The duo was seen calling it quits only days after Derek's well-earned Oscar win, and we've got exclusive footage of the tearful goodbyes. Make sure you subscribe so you don't miss our coverage of what was said once our lip reader gets a chance to figure out all the details!

No one knows yet if Derek and Bonnie have worked out who gets to keep their shared friends, but even if they manage to come to an agreement over who gets which holidays, I think they're all better off without Bonnie. Rugby star Cole Evanson needs his best friend while he deals with the aftermath of his breakup last fall—stay tuned for more juicy info on that front—and Her Royal Highness, Princess Freya, needs to keep her standards high as she gets closer to her Candoran election campaign later this year. With the way Bonnie got in the middle of music sensation Liam Connolly's romance with the love of his life, Kasey

Graham, it stands to reason Derek's friends are all going to be on his side going forward.

We'll be there to support Derek as much as he needs!

We here at *Hot Scoop* are hard at work getting an interview with the elusive Derek Riley, so be on the lookout for his side of the story as we expose what really went down with the end of Dennie. Keep scooping! XO

CHAPTER THREE

BONNIE

"Wait, Henry McAllister is *here*?"

Katie sighs, holding her makeup brush in front of my nose and looking at me like I'm a toddler who can't sit still.

I can't help it if I'm wiggly. I'm always nervous at the start of shooting a new project and have a lot of pent up energy and nowhere to put it until I'm on set. But I just heard that the man who *wrote* Frosted Peaks *is here in Laketown and coming to set*, and she expects me not to move? Meeting *the* Henry McAllister has only been my dream for years!

Honestly, I liked the sound of this movie even before I knew the title, and then I realized it was an adaptation of one of my favorite books. I made my agent set up an audition immediately, forced Derek to run lines with me and help me nail down the character, and put my full energy into getting this role. I've never wanted anything more.

I've been in love with the Detective Frost series since the first book came out a couple of years ago. McAllister is an utter genius, and he has created the most kick-butt heroine I've ever read. Gabrielle is *real*. She's not written like a man but with boobs, like many "strong" female characters are. She's fierce and doesn't take crap, but she's also vulnerable and feminine in a non-ick way. At first, I wondered if maybe Henry McAllister was a pen name and the author was really female because he managed to write her so beautifully. Especially because there aren't any pictures of him anywhere.

"Do you realize what this means?" I ask Katie, who hasn't resumed her makeup routine because I'm not sitting still.

She sighs again. I've worked with her several times before, and she clearly doesn't have much patience for me today. I shouldn't alienate her, given how nice it is to have a friendly face sometimes. "What does it mean, Bonnie?"

"It means I'm going to be one of the few people who know what Henry McAllister looks like! And he never does events or anything, so no one ever gets to meet him."

"Cool." The way she says it, it's clear she thinks it's anything *but* cool. I guess she's not really a mystery reader.

"No, listen." I grab her wrist, sending a dusting of powder onto my lap. "This guy is legendary. He didn't start publishing until a couple of years ago, and he already has four books out. That's so rare in traditional publishing! He was a number one *New York Times* bestseller for like six weeks in a row with his last book."

"It was only three weeks."

Katie and I both jump, turning to the door of the makeup tent where a woman watches me with raised eyebrows.

"But I wouldn't bring it up with him," she says. "He gets touchy when you mention the *Times*."

Okay, so I don't love the idea that McAllister might have an ego, but I'm still stoked about meeting him. As Katie finally starts my makeup, I hold out my hand to the woman. "Hi, I'm—"

"Bonnie Aiken, I know." She glances at my hand but doesn't take it, instead letting her eyes wash over me in an appraising way. I'm used to looks like that, but coming from her, whoever she is, it feels like there's a lot more judgment than usual. "I'm Mariah Harvey, Mr. McAllister's agent."

Oh, so she must know him really well! "What's he like?" I ask. I'm wiggling again, and Katie is starting to look murderous. I shoot her an apologetic glance before focusing back on Ms. Harvey.

Settling in a vacant chair, Ms. Harvey speaks more to her phone than to me. "Pretty much how you'd expect him to be," she says with a shrug. "He's a mystery writer, after all."

I've always pictured him as a silver fox, distinguished and full of wisdom. In my head, he's solid and sturdy, with bright blue eyes that have an icy hue, but not in a cold way. More of a shrewd way. Like Neal McDonough, who seems to look straight through your soul. I will absolutely be intimidated by McAllister just as much as I will be fangirling so hard.

"When can I meet him?" I ask, biting my lip in anticipation.

"Oh, that's not likely to happen. He's busy speaking with the director. I doubt he'll have time to—"

"Bonnie, I'm not finished yet!" Katie's shout follows me out of the tent, though it takes me a second to realize I'm on the move.

Apparently, I hear the words "not likely to happen" and my sub-conscious brain takes over. It happened once when my high school classmate told me I would never be able to beat him in a footrace, and I totally kicked his trash before I was even aware I was running. And one time, when Liam said I wouldn't be able to fit ten jumbo marshmallows in my mouth at the same time, the next thing I knew I was choking on one. Freya's bodyguard had to give me the heimlich, and Derek banned us from making s'mores after that.

I don't always look before I leap.

I turn a corner, hoping to take a shortcut past catering to get to the director's trailer, but I run smack into another person and crash to the ground in a heap. "Ow."

"Sorry," he says, scrambling to grab his glasses from the dirt before hopping to his feet. "Didn't see you."

I take the hand he offers me and then grimace at the dirt streaked across my white pants. *Dang it.* It's all over! The costume director is going to kill me. "I am in so much trouble," I mutter, fruitlessly brushing my thigh as if that will get the dirt off. "You wouldn't happen to have the world's biggest Tide to Go on you, would you?"

He chuckles. "Sorry. No. Did I hurt you?"

Yes, but I'll be fine. I don't have time to stick around and chat anyway. I refuse to lose my chance to meet McAllister, even if I'll be covered in soil when I do it. "I'm fine. Guess I should look where I'm running."

"You and me both."

I'm about to apologize for my part in the collision when I finally look his way and get my first glimpse of the guy. Whoever he is, he's cute in a dorky librarian kind of way, complete with a green cable knit sweater and canvas boots beneath khaki pants. He must be one of the extras or something because he looks like he was made to be in a small town. That, or he actually lives here in Laketown, where we're filming, and he's sneaking around on set.

I narrow my eyes, which makes him take a step back in surprise. "What were you running from?"

He lets out a quick breath. "What were *you* running from?"

"I wasn't. I was running *to*. Are you even supposed to be over here?"

He glances around the production tents and trailers, his ears turning red. "No, but—"

"Do I need to call security?" I don't have my phone. I don't even have a loud voice. But I could probably scream or something, and someone would come to catch this guy. My security team is around here somewhere, and it's a miracle no one saw me leave the makeup tent in the first place.

Sighing, the guy brushes some dead grass from his sleeve and shakes his head. "No. I was just in a meeting with Beckett Perretti. I needed to get some air."

Beckett is the director. Yeah, okay, pretty much anyone who knows what movie we're filming would know the name of the director, but the guy sounds genuine. Maybe I should believe him.

Wait.

I grab his arm, making him tense up. "You were just in a meeting with Beckett? Was Henry McAllister there?"

He furrows his eyebrows, glancing down at my hand before meeting my gaze again. "Uh, yeah."

I squeal. "You got to meet him?"

"Sort of?"

"Is he still there?"

"Not anymore."

I deflate, dropping his arm and doing my best not to pout. From the sounds of things, McAllister won't be coming back to set anytime soon. He'll probably fly back home as soon as he drives to Sun City, the closest airport, and then he'll disappear and I will never get the chance to meet one of my idols. I don't like to cry over spilled milk, but this feels like a whole gallon of spillage. That must be worth a few tears, right?

"Were you hoping to meet him?" the guy asks. He studies me, and it's like he can't figure out what my deal is. He also doesn't seem to recognize me, which is a strange feeling. I can't even go to Walmart in sweatpants and no makeup without someone figuring out who I am. Not that I do that. Often.

Sighing, I fold my arms and will my tears to stay in my eye sockets. My one chance to meet my favorite author... "Yeah. He's kind of my hero."

"Why?"

I don't like the way he asks that question so incredulously. Huffing, I glare at him as I say, "He has written my all-time favorite female character, and there is no one who puts the same level of heart and soul into a book the way he does. You'd think a male mystery writer would turn his heroine into a chesty blonde with enough kick-buttery moves to take down guys twice her size, but the way he wrote Gabrielle is just so real, you know?"

He fights his smile as he folds his arms to match me. "Kick-buttery?"

I know he's making fun of me, but I don't have a better word for it. Not one that I'm willing to say out loud, at least. "Yeah. And yeah, Gabrielle totally kicks butt, but she has real human flaws and quirks that make her feel like she could really exist. It's not often a writer can put someone so genuine on the page like that, and I was really hoping to tell him that."

"I think he knows."

"No, I know. People probably tell him that all the time." I sigh, feeling silly now for going off like that to a stranger. "But I wanted him to know that *I* knew it, you know?"

"I know." He holds out his hand for me to shake. "I'm Hank. Hank McAllister."

It's not until I've pumped our handshake three times that it clicks, and I freeze. "Hank," I repeat, my eyes opening wide. I probably look like a crazy person, but I don't care. Mostly. "Hank as in Henry."

He nods once.

"You're Henry McAllister."

"Hi."

I scream and then clap a hand over my mouth to shut myself up when he winces. "Sorry," I whisper through my fingers, only now realizing that I'm still holding on to his hand. I let go, even though a part of me wishes I hadn't. "Sorry for screaming. And for spewing all that fangirl stuff at you." He probably thinks I'm a nutcase.

But he smiles, stuffing his hands into his pockets as he looks around the area again. So far, no one seems to have noticed the two of us standing here in between the tents, but it's only a matter of time before we're discovered now that I've screamed. "It was nice," he says with a shrug. "Not the screaming part, I mean. The, uh, other part. I had no idea if anyone even liked Gabrielle's character."

"How could you not know? She's the best!"

Another shrug. "I've never talked to anyone who's read the book."

Well, that's just straight crazy. He's been way too popular over the last couple years to have never talked to anyone about his books. "Weren't you just in a meeting with Beckett?"

"He hasn't read the book."

I gasp, and for a second it feels like something has wrapped around my heart and given it a firm squeeze. "That's every bookworm's nightmare," I whisper, as if speaking it at full volume will make the truth worse. "How has the director not read the book? This movie is going to be a travesty if I don't do something." And how did I not know this before now? We've already started filming, and it never came up in any of the table reads or discussions.

I knew the script was questionable, but I figured Beckett had a plan to make it all work.

Hank's eyes do a quick head-to-toe of me before jumping back to my face. I have no idea what he thinks about me other than the uncertainty in his eyes. "I didn't catch your name."

So he *really* doesn't know who I am.

I hold out my hand again, giving him a broad smile. "I'm Bonnie."

Though he was reaching for my hand, he stops halfway and goes still, his eyes locked on my hand and barely any emotion in his face. "You're Gabrielle." It isn't a question, and there's not enough inflection in those two words for me to get a sense of how he feels about it.

I fold my arms again, suddenly feeling self-conscious in a way I haven't in years. "Yeah, I guess I am. I don't know how I got lucky enough to play her, but—"

"You look like her."

Holy mama, that's some intense eye contact. But it's almost like he's not really seeing me, like he's looking through me and seeing his detective heroine standing in my place. Heat floods my face, and I feel like I need to touch him or something to break the connection. So I do, reaching out and wrapping my fingers on his arm near his elbow.

"It's an honor to portray her. Seriously."

He blinks, coughs, and then stuffs his loose hand back into his pocket as he drops his head. "I'm sorry. It's surreal, thinking about my book becoming something different."

"Well, prepare yourself for it to turn out terrible."

He smiles. "I'm sure you'll be great."

I can't stop the laugh that breaks out of me. That isn't what I meant—not at all. I'm a decent actor, better when I have good costars, but I'm no Audrey Hepburn. "Even if the director hasn't read the book?"

Hank shrugs once more, highlighting just how different he is from the man I imagined when picturing Henry McAllister, writer extraordinaire. He's just a little taller than me, probably five foot nine or ten, with dark brown hair and eyes the color of espresso, and I'd guess he's somewhere in his early thirties. Everything about him is warm, from his smile to his soft gaze, and it's hard to imagine someone like him writing about murder in such detail. It's a testament to his skills as an author, I suppose.

He's not at all what I expected, but I almost like this version of him better. Maybe because this version is real. Real people are always better than imagined ones.

"I should..." Hank scuffs his boot in the dirt, hands still firmly tucked in his pockets. "I should probably head back before my agent sends a search party after me. I only got away because she went looking for coffee."

Not sure why she ended up in the makeup tent, but whatever.

I should really be going as well and figure out my pants situation before I have to report to set, but it's hard to want to leave. This could be my only interaction with the amazing Henry McAllister, and I need to make the most of it. Kasey is going to freak out when she finds out that I met him, and I need to send her some kind of proof.

"Could I take a picture with you?" I ask, only to remember I don't have my phone.

Hank grimaces anyway, clearly uncomfortable with the idea. He doesn't even have his picture in the back of his books, so he's probably a super private person. "Sorry," he says, and I'm pretty sure he means it. "It's not you. I'm not..."

I shake my head. "You don't have to explain. It was insensitive of me to ask."

That gets a chuckle out of him. "You'd know better than anyone how it feels to have people ask for a picture with you, wouldn't you?"

"Comes with the job."

"It was nice to meet you, Bonnie. Good luck with filming."

"You too!" I cringe. "I mean, it was nice to meet you too. Not good luck with filming. Because you're not going to be in the movie, obviously. Could..." My cheeks are flaming now, and I let all my breath out at once. "You can say no, but could I have a hug? I'm a big hugger, and you're, like, the coolest person I've ever met, and I'm friends with a princess."

Great. Now he's going to think I'm bragging about being friends with royalty. "You know what? Never mind."

"Bonnie?" Hank gives me a crooked grin as he slowly pulls his hands from his pockets. "I'd love to give you a hug."

"Really?"

He holds out his arms.

I slip right into his hold, probably holding him too tightly but not really in control of anything happening right now because *I'm hugging Henry McAllister*. And he is *really* hugging me back. I meant it when I said I was a big hugger, but this is the hug to end all hugs. I wouldn't have pegged Hank as a physical contact kind of guy, but he sure had me fooled. To paraphrase Jack Callahan from *While You Were Sleeping*, this is a whole body leaning situation, and I am never letting go.

"Thanks," I squeak when he finally pulls away, and the little smile and head shake that Hank gives me before walking away might be the cutest thing I've ever seen. And considering I once did one of those puppy interviews with Buzzfeed, that's saying something.

Hollywood Hot Scoop

Bonnie's New Beau

Filming is underway for the heavily anticipated adaptation of *Frosted Peaks*, but we've got juicier news than male lead Jonah James's Vegas losing streak last month. That's right, Bonnie Aiken has already found her new boy toy, and you'll never guess who it is.

While Derek Riley has been lying low since the breakup, Bonnie has wasted no time, and if you thought "Dennie" was a cute couple, you are *not* prepared for "Benrie." Our favorite source has learned that Bonnie's new beau is none other than Henry McAllister, author of *Frosted Peaks* and the whole Gabrielle Frost detective series. Check out that chemistry in these photos, Scoopers! Talk about swoon!

Little is known about the elusive mystery writer, who up until now has kept his identity a secret, but never fear, my beloved fans. Keep those phones at the ready and be sure to turn on your notifications so you don't miss any Benrie news as we get you the next *Hot Scoop* in Hollywood. XO

CE CREAM

CHAPTER FOUR

HANK

Junéé finds me in the backyard, a loose term for the wilderness that exists beyond my house. I'm not sure how long I've been sitting in the dirt watching the clouds roll over the hills, but it must have been longer than I'd like because my body is stiff and chilled when her footsteps pull me out of a daze.

"Whatcha doin', Hank?" She drops down into the dirt next to me, leaning back on her hands and crossing her legs. I'm still not sure how we became friends; she's a recent transplant to Laketown and used to work for a DA in Denver, two things I don't like. But June is the only person who actually makes an effort to talk to me anymore. Even if it's only because someone else asked her to, I appreciate her occasional company. I may like being alone, but loneliness isn't my favorite thing.

"I'm thinking," I tell her, stretching out my legs and groaning when my muscles complain. "And getting old."

"Tell me about it."

She's got two years on me but still has a youthful shine about her, not that thirty-four is really that old. My thirty-two is nothing compared to some, but I feel each and every one of those years every time I think about the passing of time. Especially lately.

Time to change the subject. "It's not grocery day."

"Nice to see you too."

My phone starts ringing in the house behind us, and we both glance back. It's been doing that all morning, and I've been tempted to yank the cord out of the wall. It's probably Mariah with another contract exploitation. My visit to the set yesterday was pointless, no matter how much she told me it was crucial that I make an appearance. Beckett Perretti barely spoke two words relevant to me, instead droning on and on about some sort of new camera technique he was going to make famous in this movie, and my anxiety ramped up until the only thing I could do was run away.

The only good thing to come out of my excursion was meeting Bonnie, even if I still haven't recovered from that interaction.

When the phone stops ringing, June nudges my shoulder with her own. "Have you been on the internet today?"

"Why would I be on the internet?" The only reason I even *have* internet is so I can email my manuscripts to my editor, though I've been tempted to buy myself a bunch of flash drives and start mailing them instead. It would take longer, but I would have a great excuse to ignore Mariah.

The phone starts ringing again, and I wince.

Sighing, June reaches into her pocket and pulls out her cellphone, swiping to some sort of news article before handing it over to me. "That's why."

It's some stupid celebrity gossip. I roll my eyes, wondering why June would think I would have any interest in something like this. But then my gaze catches on my name, and my heart starts to pound the longer I read.

Oh good lord, there are pictures.

Three of them, taken from a good distance away and zoomed in, but they're a lot clearer than I remember paparazzi pictures being back when I sort of paid attention to celebrity news. It would be impossible not to recognize my own face smiling at Bonnie next to me. My lungs constrict as I stare at the picture of the two of us hugging. Bonnie's smile is wide and warm—one of the features that caught my attention yesterday—but combined with the article, this *Hollywood Hot Scoop* website is implying...

"Breathe, Hank," June says, tugging her phone out of my hand, which is fine because I'm shaking too much to hold on to it anyway. "I'm sorry for springing that on you, but I wasn't sure how to prepare you."

I shake my head, forcing a breath and holding it in my lungs until I start to feel dizzy. I let it out too quickly and try again, this time managing to slowly exhale and gaining a little control back. This panic isn't new, but it's been a while since I had to deal with the helplessness that comes from it. "You couldn't have pre..."

June starts rubbing my back, which isn't helping but I'll let her think it is. "Hey, it's just a stupid tabloid. It doesn't mean you're actually dating Bonnie Aiken."

"Ha!" I tuck my head between my knees and start counting sticks under my boots. "Dating. Right."

"Oh come on, you could totally date a movie star if you wanted to."

"Wanted? No. Dating. No."

June mumbles something that sounds a lot like, "I don't understand you, McAllister."

Most people don't.

After a few focused breaths, I'm feeling less untethered, though my ringing phone isn't exactly helping the situation. I can at least sit up straight again, even if my thoughts are jumbled up and knotted together.

"When did...?" I nod toward her phone.

"The story was posted last night. I'm surprised you actually went on set." She spits the word 'set.' Not many people in Laketown are happy about the movie filming here. Life in Laketown is usually pretty quiet, but as soon as the first semi rolled in and crushed one of the flower pots on Main Street, most of the Laketownians turned their noses up at the film crew. (That's what June told me, anyway.) Sure, it's bringing money into the town, but that's not exactly a thing people care about here.

They don't want things to change, and we all know it will. Even if changes to the town itself are temporary, this movie will put Laketown on the map. People will actually come here instead of leaving things quiet and simple. It will be a lot harder to hide, and it's my own fault.

I shouldn't have patterned the fictional town of Glacier Falls after my hometown. The first time Mariah came to Colorado, when the studio initially bought the film rights, she realized the connection immediately and made sure to tell every executive she could to ensure the movie was filmed here. In her words, it would be a marketing goldmine.

For me, the impending fame of my town is a nightmare.

Suddenly exhausted, I roll back until I fall into the dirt, sprawled in the weeds and tempted to never leave this spot until the forest swallows me up. I'll be eaten by mushrooms before winter sets in. "I didn't have a choice," I tell June. "My agent made me go to set."

"But you seemed to enjoy yourself."

I glare at her amused tone. "Being friendly doesn't mean I enjoyed myself."

As my phone takes up its next vigil—honestly, I would have expected Mariah to show up at the house by now—I consider my options here. It's just a stupid celebrity site, and eventually the world will forget about the pictures. I could easily wait this out. Or I could get my lawyer on the phone and ask him to sue anyone who is perpetuating the story. I don't think that one will work, but the idea makes me happy.

My favorite idea is the one I speak out loud. "Well, it was nice knowing you, June, but I will be moving to Alaska this afternoon."

I'm on my feet before she grabs my hand, stopping me from going inside and tearing my phone from the wall. "Come on, it's not that bad."

I know she doesn't believe that, otherwise she wouldn't have shown me the story. I could have carried on in ignorant bliss until it all became buried beneath the next invasion of privacy for someone more interesting than me. Yes, I've written a couple of books that have sold relatively well, but that doesn't make me famous.

Then again, Bonnie seemed to think I had all sorts of fans. Her reaction surprised me, as did the physical response that came from seeing her. I've seen pictures, of course, but an unfiltered Bonnie with no makeup jarred me. She looks so much like Shelby.

It felt like I was looking at a ghost.

"June," I say, already regretting the question that is working its way out of my mouth, "how popular is that article?"

Cringing, June puts her hand over her pocket, as if trying to hide her phone.

I groan. "So a lot of people have now seen my face."

She nods.

"They know where I live."

"I don't think so. The story doesn't say anything about Laketown, and I doubt the studio is broadcasting the filming location until after things wrap up. Bonnie Aiken is popular enough that she would draw a crowd if anyone knew where she was. And you can count on the Laketownians keeping it all a secret because as soon as someone opens their mouth, the town will be overrun. It'll be worse than when the Taylor clan shows up in the summer."

I shudder. The Taylor family usually only comes to Laketown for a week, but there are so many of them. If one of them wasn't my old neighbor and a decent guy who knows I like my privacy, I would dread their annual family reunions even more than I already do.

"So you should be safe, is what I'm saying," June finishes.

That makes me feel a little better, but I don't like knowing there are millions of people who could now pick me out of a crowd if motivated enough. My anonymity is one of the few things that have kept me sane over the last few years.

Writing is another, and I should really get back to work. After I unplug my phone, of course. "Hey, I need to save someone from being choked to death."

June hums as she follows me back to my house, though I know she won't come inside. She'll need to get back to her hardware store, and I'm just now appreciating the sacrifice she made to come all the way out here and tell me about the article. "Hands?"

"Phone charger."

"Yeesh, that's brutal. What if it breaks? I've had about a million charging cords break on me, stupid things."

That could work, and it fits in with the humor I try to sprinkle throughout my books. If they get too heavy, I get dragged down with them, so a balance is crucial. "I'll try it." I open the back door and turn to give her a grateful smile. "Thank you."

She lifts a hand. "I'm always down for brainstorming."

"I mean for telling me about the article. And for being my...uh, friend." I feel childish, thanking her for that, but when I was fully prepared to live a solitary life, knowing someone cares about me has brought a light into a world that has been ever increasingly dark. "Have you talked to Hope lately?"

"Couple days ago, though she was pretty brain-fried. I hear that the newborn stage can be brutal."

I'd forgotten about her baby, and guilt starts seeping into my chest. Hope only lived down the road for a few weeks, but she and her husband, Chad, worked their way past my defenses over the course of a snowy weekend. When I have few friends as it is, I should really be better about keeping in touch.

"Hey." June touches my arm. "I'll tell her you asked about her, okay? You've got bigger fish to fry."

If by 'fish' she means dealing with the aftermath of getting caught by paparazzi, then she's right. "Maybe I'll come by the store sometime soon," I tell her. It's the same lie I tell her every time she comes out here.

She grins. "No, you won't. See you Thursday with your groceries, Hank. Good luck!"

Luck. Luck is not a thing I possess, unless you count my books. Even then, I don't attribute their success to luck. It's all Shelby, and as I cross the front room to yank the phone cord out of the wall, I glance at the second bedroom. I haven't opened that door in years, and that isn't going to change, but sometimes I wonder...

The house goes silent as soon as the cord is free, but my ears keep ringing. What is it they say about ringing ears? Someone is talking about you. In my case, it's half the country, and I can't help wondering what Shelby would think about all of this.

If she was still alive, she probably would have laughed and told me how lucky I was to be dating a superstar. Then she would have kissed me until the sun came up and blamed me for keeping her awake. And I would have smiled, not caring one whit what the world thought of me because all that mattered was her.

CE CREAM

CHAPTER FIVE

BONNIE

"How does it feel to be replaced so soon, Derek?" Liam says.

"If you need a shoulder to cry on, I'm here," Cole says.

"I really thought Cole had a shot."

"Nah, Bonnie clearly has a type."

Liam laughs. "I'm sorry, but since when has her type been nerdy chic hipster? And in what universe are you and Derek not the same type?"

"In the universe where I'm way bigger than him."

"No, I saw his abs in *The River Crossing*. Man's a beast. Derek, show Cole your abs."

"I'm not doing that," Derek says without hesitation.

"Gentlemen, please!" Freya claps her hands in front of her camera, breaking up the boys' back and forth. "We must stay on task."

Honestly, I'd stopped listening as soon as Liam and Cole started joking about my new "relationship." This weekly video chat we do is usually full of joking around—Liam can't survive without a good joke every few minutes—but never has it all been so centered around me. My friends' humor is one of the things I love about them, but I'm not loving it so much today.

I can't stop thinking about how *Hollywood Hot Scoop* has decided that my friends are going to cut me out now that Derek and I aren't a couple. Thinking they would turn their backs on me is irrational, and I know it, but that doesn't mean the fear isn't there.

Freya looks straight at the camera so I feel like she's looking at me. "Bon, it has been a couple of days, and the story is not dying down. What are you going to do?" Her accent, which rests somewhere between British and general Scandinavian, is oddly soothing today and keeps my focus on the current topic: Hank.

I shift on my bed, glad to have the privacy of my trailer right now. I've been filming all day, and I'm exhausted in the way I always am at the start of a shoot. I'll get used to the long days eventually; I always do.

"I'm not sure what I'm going to do," I say, which is true. "Fran has been trying to get Hank to come in so we can have a meeting about it."

"Where would he be flying in from?" Derek asks.

"Vermont," Liam says with unfounded confidence. "All great writers live in Vermont."

"That explains it," Cole says. "I wondered why you never became a great writer."

Liam pulls his phone absurdly close to his face to glare at Cole. "Hey, I am an excellent writer. And what are you trying to say about Kasey? *She's* not from Vermont. And lyrics are different from novels, anyway!"

Freya clears her throat and gestures to the camera. I'm assuming it's meant for me.

I give her a grateful smile, though I'm tempted to latch on to the subject of Kasey and the screenplay she just sold so I can get the attention off of me. I would so much rather celebrate her success. "He actually lives here in Laketown, where we're filming," I say slowly. I may have slightly freaked out when Beckett told me that. Henry McAllister is only a few minutes away from where I'll be for the next month.

I have been so tempted to ask Derek to use the random connections he seems to have everywhere to figure out exactly where Hank lives so I can talk to him again, but I know better than to be invasive like that.

"Why has it been so hard to get him in a meeting?" Derek asks.

I wish I knew, though I suspect it might be because I fangirled too hard when I met him. "He's probably just really busy," I say, shrugging.

"Sure he is." Liam pulls off his shirt as he speaks. At some point in the last couple of minutes, he moved from his kitchen to his pool, and he props up his phone before slipping into the glowing water.

Freya groans. "I do not understand why you always insist on taking off your shirt when we are discussing serious matters! You already have Kasey's affection; you have no one to impress."

Liam rests his arm on the edge of the pool and drops his chin onto it. "Because it's a million degrees in Malibu."

"It's sixty-seven," Derek argues. "Where is Kasey, anyway?"

"Bachelorette party." He looks miserable about the idea, even though Kasey has a right to celebrate her best friend's upcoming wedding. I never would have expected the likes of Liam Connolly to settle down so easily, but he and Kasey instantly clicked last fall. It makes me wonder if there's someone I'll click with like that, but it's unlikely.

No one ever sticks around.

"Bonnie," Freya says, "let us go through some hypotheticals."

I grin, adjusting my laptop on my stomach. "I love hypotheticals." It's my whole job description, trying to decide what I, as my character, would do in any given situation. And in this case, the character is me.

"Let us assume your cute writer friend never comes to set to discuss the possibilities."

"You think *he's* cute?" Liam asks.

"Adorable," Freya and I say together. I'm sure Kasey would agree with us.

I purse my lips. "I would be pretty bummed, honestly. I barely got to talk to him about his books, and I would love to hear where he gets his inspiration from."

"But that has nothing to do with a relationship," Derek points out. He's been on this side of Freya's hypotheticals enough times to have a good grasp of where she takes things. "Does that mean you're not interested?"

I shrug. "I didn't really think about it. Haven't thought about it since."

"Lies," all four of them say at once. It's our group's way of acknowledging that someone is clearly hiding behind untruths, which is valuable when our lives are so readily available to the public. In our own ways, we've all gotten too good at wearing masks, and we collectively decided that our friendship could only thrive if we were honest with each other.

Still, I roll my eyes. They seem to think there's more to this than there is. "I've only thought about it because of the *Hot Scoop* thing. And because I'm trending in a good way, which hasn't happened in a while."

Derek grimaces. Our relationship was supposed to help me trend, and it did. For a while. But we kept it going too long, too comfortable in our friendship without any real romance, and the end of the ruse did the opposite of what we wanted. Derek, of course, is perfectly fine. I was the one who looked like a jerk for leaving him, even though Fran arranged for Derek to do the dumping. He's too well-liked for the internet to accept that he could be in the wrong, so I got labeled as a heartbreaker once again.

For some reason, the internet loves the idea of me being with Henry McAllister, and I'm clinging to that with everything I've got. It's so much better than them deciding I'm going to be alone forever while my friends leave me behind.

"Let's say, hypothetically, that I think starting a fake relationship with Hank is a good idea," I say. "I really don't think he would agree with me."

"How well do you know the man?" Freya asks.

"I *don't* know him. That's why I think he wouldn't go for it. He's an incredibly private person."

"Not anymore," Liam throws in. "The guy has been memed. He'll never be private again."

I feel so bad about that. I ambushed him on set the other day, and now people are using his adorable smile as a reaction image for anything good in their lives, putting text of those good things on my back. Things like "my cat when he stretches" and "sleeping in on the weekends." It could have been a whole lot worse, all things considered, but I have a feeling Hank isn't thrilled about being a headliner.

Otherwise he would have at least responded to Fran.

"If I knew exactly where he lives, I would go talk to him in private instead of making it a whole thing," I say. But then I let out a short laugh. As if anyone would let me leave set on my own. Katie was instructed to tackle me if I ever try sneaking out of the makeup tent again, and my security detail has doubled in the last two days. For once, I thought maybe things could be chill for this movie, but I forgot what movie this is.

Frosted Peaks is going to change my career for the better. I can feel it.

I would feel it more if I didn't have to worry about the internet's obsession with Hank and me together.

"Hypothetical," Freya says. "Let us assume McAllister agrees to a mock relationship."

"If only," I mutter.

"Assuming he does, and you start to feel something more for him... What will you do?"

I want to laugh and tell her that I am not a serious relationship kind of gal. Even with Derek, who's my best friend, I rarely felt more attached to him than I do to any of the others on the screen in front of me. I've never been serious with any of my boyfriends because I have never been willing to put my heart on the line. That's asking for heartbreak.

But my laughter sticks in my throat, and I grimace. "I don't do love," I say, and the words sound as true as they've always been. But they don't *feel* true.

"Lies," Freya and Derek both say. Cole and Liam are frowning, as if they suspect the same.

"Bonnie, you are like a sister to me," Freya says. "And I know you will not always be content with shallow relationships. Deep in your heart, I know you want real connection, just as we all do."

Derek picks up his phone, typing something while I let Freya's words sink in. Of course I want real connection. Who doesn't? And I've had enough deep and vulnerable conversations with Derek to come to the realization that I want it more than most. A childhood of financial struggle spent home alone with always working parents can do a number on a girl.

But no matter how much I want connection, it also terrifies me. The harder I cling to something, the more it hurts when I lose it.

That's probably why the latest *Hot Scoop* article about the breakup spooked me as much as it did. I wouldn't have survived without my friends, and there's no way I would make it very far without them and their support. My connection with them is dangerous enough, and I don't need to be throwing romance into the mix.

My phone buzzes, and I lift it up to look at the text Derek sent me.

Derek:

> Don't let past failures dictate your future. Things couldn't work between us, but that doesn't mean you aren't worthy of being loved.

Tears fill my eyes, and I shift my computer for a second so no one sees. I think, if Derek and I hadn't started in a fake relationship, we might have been something, but we spent too long telling ourselves it wasn't real. He wants a family—roots—and I never would have been brave enough to give that to him, so keeping things casual worked for us. Sometimes I wondered if he wished things were real between us, like I did when I was feeling especially lonely, but even though Derek was the best boyfriend a girl could have asked for, I never felt like I gave him as much as he gave me.

He deserves the world. Someone who loves him without hesitation. He's so good at taking care of everyone else that he needs someone who is strong enough to take care of him.

"We are talking hypothetically," Freya reminds me. "What would happen if you started to fall for your writer?"

I don't hesitate with my response. "I would end up brokenhearted." Nothing good ever lasts, and I'm not the person anyone truly loves. Never have been, never will be. "Once the internet got bored, Fran would stage a breakup and find me a new fling to keep up interest, and that would be that. It's better if I don't put Hank in that position, especially because it won't start by his choice either."

Better for him, yes. But is it better for me? I think Freya might be right. Even if I never think I'll get it, I do want the kind of love that makes me feel safe and wanted. I'm loved by fans across the world, but none of those people know me. Is it really crazy for me to dream of someone choosing me over everything else?

That someone won't be Hank McAllister, but maybe my person is out there somewhere. The guy who will make my life complete.

"What if *you* don't have a choice?" Cole asks.

That's the real question, and I already know the answer. I don't, and I rarely do.

CE CREAM

Chapter Six

Hank

"Hope, your baby is amazing." And I mean that, even if I'm halfway to an anxiety attack right now. My smile, as much of it as I can see in the little square of my face on June's phone, looks strained, though I don't think Hope has noticed.

My used-to-be neighbor is too focused on her two-month-old daughter to pay attention to me.

June puts a steadying hand on my shoulder. She just about had a heart attack when I showed up at her hardware store and asked to borrow her phone, but I appreciate her support. "How are the kids doing with having a new baby around the house?" she asks, leaning closer to me to be in the frame of the video chat.

Hope looks up, a bit of surprise in her expression. "The kids? Wait, what time is it? I think I'm supposed to be picking them up from school soon."

Before either of us can say anything, her husband appears, wrapping his arms around her and kissing her cheek. "I'll get the kids," Chad says gently. "You've literally got your hands full. Hank? Is that you?"

I know he can see the hardware store in the background and is probably wondering why I've ventured outside of my property limits. Technically, we're only neighbors when he brings his family to Laketown for a vacation, but the guy knows me better than most. He knows this is out of character for me.

I try another one of those 'definitely doesn't look real' smiles. "Trying to get out of my comfort zone," I say, my voice cracking. *Nice.*

Chad raises an eyebrow. "Why?"

Hope smacks him. "Be nice, old man. Not everyone is a homebody like you."

"Hank is."

"I'm..." I swallow when the words stick. "I'm trying not to be." Heaven knows why.

I got Gabrielle out of her choking situation, using a broken cord like June suggested, but I've been thoroughly blocked for two days. Mariah showed up at my house yesterday—I ignored her—and my email is so full since I unplugged my phone that I'm afraid to open it to see what's waiting for me in my inbox. The house was getting too quiet, and the second bedroom was looming in a way it never has before, so I grabbed my keys before I could overthink things and here I am.

Trying to breathe like a normal human doing normal human things like going into town to talk to a friend. Or three.

Honestly, I'm glad Chad is around. If anyone knows how hard it is to stray beyond the comfort zone, he does. He went from a long-term relationship that ended terribly to marrying a woman more than a decade younger than him in the space of a few months, inheriting her niece and nephew in the process.

"Speaking of comfort zones," Hope says, "what's all this about you dating my brother-in-law's ex-girlfriend?"

I blink. Either that new mommy brain is failing her, or I missed something. "Uh, what?"

Chad rolls his eyes. "Bonnie and my brother Houston used to be a thing. Briefly. Were those photos artificially created or something?"

"No, they're real," June replies. "Hank visited the movie set the other day." I can't decide if she's trying to be helpful or making sure I don't lie about the whole situation.

"It was a contractual thing," I mutter. "We don't have to talk about me. I want to know about Link and Zelda."

"The kids are still genius troublemakers," Chad says, narrowing his eyes at me. He used to be a private detective before he took on full-time parenting, and I'm going to guess he hasn't lost his investigative touch. He knows there's more to this. "So wait, are you actually dating Bonnie Aiken?"

"Aww, I wanted you to date June!" Hope whines.

June and I glance at each other, both of us grimacing.

"June is awesome," I say at the same time she says, "Hank is great."

"But?" Hope prompts.

Is she expecting us to start listing each other's flaws or something? June's my best friend; I'm not about to do that.

June, on the other hand... "But if I were to get back into the dating game, I'd need a man."

"Hey," I complain.

She shrugs. "Like I said, you're great, but you're not exactly Mr. Muscles, are you?"

Never have been, never will be. "And no," I say to the phone, "I'm not dating Bonnie. I've barely had one conversation with her."

"Excuse me? Mr. McAllister?"

June and I both turn to the door, which opened without us noticing, and June's phone slips from my fingers when I realize it's Bonnie Aiken standing there, flanked by one of the burliest men I've ever seen. The kind that would be June's type, were she to give up on her self-imposed dating ban.

Bonnie bites her lip, glancing around the little shop before turning her focus back to me. "Sorry to just show up like this, but Katie from makeup heard from Calvin in catering that someone said one of the extras said that their mom heard that you were here at the hardware store."

I open my mouth to reply, but my mind gets tripped up on what she just said. "What?"

Bonnie shrugs, turning pink. "Someone in town saw you, and it eventually reached me. I was hoping we could talk."

June bends down and picks up her phone, gingerly making her way to the door behind Bonnie. "I'll just take my lunch break now. Hank, lock the door when you leave?"

I nod once, though I know this is not a conversation I want to have.

Bonnie waits until the door shuts behind June before she comes over to the counter that separates us. Though I'm glad for the barrier, it does sort of make this all feel more awkward. Especially because the big guy stands by the door, looking menacing.

"I'm assuming you saw the article on *Hot Scoop*?" Bonnie asks.

I nod.

"Sorry you got dragged into that. You seem like a fairly private person, and you're probably not used to that kind of stuff."

Another nod. It's about all I can manage right now because the longer I look at her, the more I realize she's in costume. I may be talking to Bonnie, but she looks like Gabrielle. She looks like *Shelby*. Well, Shelby with perfect hair and a thinner face. And three inches taller. And her eyes are too blue. And—

And I need to stop comparing her to Shelby if I want to be able to speak like a functional adult. They're clearly not perfect reflections of each other, but the similarities still make this conversation diffi-cult.

I tuck my hands into my back pockets, focusing on the stained wood on the counter between us instead of her. "It isn't your fault that those photos were taken," I manage to say.

"But it is my fault that I'm here to ask for a teensy little favor."

My eyes jump to hers again, my heart already racing. She's not really going to ask me what I think she's going to ask me. Is she?

Bonnie glances at the door, turning a bright red. "That wasn't your girlfriend, was it?"

She's going to ask. "No," I say, even though a lie would probably save me from the impending favor.

Her hands stretch out over the counter, fingernails painted electric blue. "I don't have a lot of time—we're filming a scene on the other end of Main Street in a minute, but I wanted to see if you might be willing to be my boyfriend."

I drop onto the stool behind me but miss. Instead of sitting so I can process what she just said, I crash to the floor. Bonnie yelps, but I'm back on my feet before she makes it around the counter to help me up. That doesn't stop her from grabbing my hand, which paralyzes me.

Her eyes go wide. "Oh! Sorry, do you not like being touched?" But she doesn't pull her hand away.

Correction: she *tries* to pull away, but for some reason I'm holding on tight.

I blink, matching her confused expression with one of my own. I don't have anything against being touched, and I'm not sure why she thinks I might. But that's not what has me baffled right now. "You want to date me?"

Her face blossoms with color. "Not for real! Of course not really. That would be presumptive of me. I just... Okay, so, my public image hasn't been stellar lately. Not that I've done anything wrong, which I guess is part of the problem, but people have gotten bored so I'm not all that popular. Not that being liked is important! Okay, yeah, it is in my line of work. Being popular is super important in the film industry because if the public likes you, studios like you, and you get better roles and things. Not that I'm complaining about getting to play Gabrielle! This movie is a dream! But I want the movie to do well, so I want people to be interested in me, and right now all of their interest is in you. With me. Like, the world wants me to be with you for some reason."

Her eyes go wide as she realizes what she said. "For lots of reasons! You're obviously super cute in an adorably nerdy way and the fact that you're the author and I'm playing the lead is like internet dynamite, you know? So my publicist thought—I thought—maybe if we pretended to be in a relationship for a while, it would be good for us both."

She finally closes her mouth, biting the inside of her lips as she waits for me to say something.

I'm still processing all of that, but I got the gist. Swallowing, I slowly let go of her fingers and stuff my hands into my pockets again. "You want to trick the world into thinking we're a couple so you can boost public opinion."

Bonnie nods, looking too hopeful for my liking. "I know it doesn't sound great, but it will ensure the movie does well. That will get you more money, right?"

I shake my head. I don't actually care about getting more money. I could retire tomorrow and be good for the rest of my life, though I would go insane in a year or two without something to keep me busy. "The studio bought the film rights from my publisher," I mutter. "Kind of a flat rate deal for me, so..."

She deflates, biting just her bottom lip this time. It makes her look young, like a kid who is realizing she might be in trouble. How old is she, anyway? She has the kind of face that makes her look timeless, like she'll always be a Hollywood knockout even when she's old and gray.

"A relationship wouldn't benefit you at all, would it?"

Nope. Probably the opposite. I barely manage my anxiety as it is, and a relationship with Bonnie Aiken, fake or otherwise, would force me into the public sphere. Exactly where I'm too scared to go. I couldn't even come to a barely frequented hardware store to see my best friend without my chest getting tight.

Bonnie sighs. "Sorry, Mr. McAllister. I shouldn't have even asked. I'm sure *Frosted Peaks* will do just fine because the story is amazing. Sorry to bother you! Eli, we can go."

To my surprise, she actually leaves, followed by the big guy. I expected her to put up a fight. Have a whole bunch of reasons why I should do it. Offer me a lump of cash or a vacation home in Hawaii or something I don't need.

I didn't even tell her no...

But it's not like I can tell her yes. Keeping up a friendship is a task, and I haven't even held a woman's hand in years. A relationship, however fake, would require more than that, and there is no way I would be able to mimic chemistry with someone so similar to Shelby.

"Why are you talking yourself out of something that is a non-issue?" I ask out loud, running my hand through my hair. Bonnie already left and dropped the idea because she could tell I wasn't going to agree.

I just need to go back home and get to writing so I can meet my deadline.

There must be something in the air because when I step outside the store and lock the door, I don't head straight for my car. On the rare occasions I come into town, I always take care of whatever needs doing and do everything I can to avoid lingering. Laketown is small enough that everyone knows who I am and *why* I am, and no one passes up an opportunity to talk to the town hermit if I make an appearance.

It's a nightmare, and the longer I stand here, the higher my chances of being cornered.

I glance left, where the road is blocked off so the film crew can do their thing. I got the same form letter that everyone else got, offering me a chance to be an extra in the movie, which means there will be Laketownians beyond the big trailer blocking my view of the filming. I'd guess people in town would also show up to watch, even if they're not playing an extra.

Another great reason to hurry home.

But when am I going to get a chance to see Bonnie in action? They wouldn't have cast her if they didn't think she's a good actor, and I've watched one or two of her Hallmark-like romances since learning she got the part. She can play make-believe with the best of them. But can she be Gabrielle? It's more than just looking the part, and my heroine has a lot of deep and heavy baggage that drives her motivations.

Bonnie is a bubbly and spunky person, not exactly the personality type I would pair with my no-nonsense detective. What if she comes across as disingenuous and ruins the whole movie?

I tell myself that I'm doing myself a professional favor as I turn and head for the set. Not that I'm curious about the filming, even if that's the real truth. My steps get heavier the closer I get, but I force myself to keep moving so I can tell Mariah that I'm doing my duty as the author. Maybe she'll stop heckling me to show up to things. Maybe I'll even try to get a picture taken with Bonnie so I can at least help a little. A relationship is out of the question, but I would feel guilty if I didn't do *something* to help her after she asked so nicely.

I mean, technically her asking nicely was just a lot of rambling, but it was endearing in a nerve-wracking kind of way.

"Hank!" June is kind enough to whisper-shout my name when she sees me, rather than drawing unnecessary attention my way. She waves me over to where she's sitting on the back of one of the Main Street benches. A few people from town are loitering nearby, but they're all pretty focused on the scene that is apparently happening in the middle of the street.

June bumps her shoulder into mine when I sit next to her. "This is a fun surprise, seeing you out here."

"I won't make a habit of it." I frown as I try to decipher what's happening in front of me.

Bonnie is sitting in the street in front of a black SUV, though she's listening intently to the director, Beckett, as he talks with wild gesticulations. Her costar, Jonah James, is studying what I would guess is the script as he leans against the driver side door of the car.

"Wait," I say when it clicks. "This is the meet-cute?"

June snickers. "I think it's so funny when you use book terms. It's not exactly cute when Gabrielle first meets Logan, is it?"

"No, I know, but meet-awkward isn't a term." This is weird, seeing a scene from my book set up like this, and I tense when the crew starts moving, the director going to his chair and Jonah handing off his script and climbing into the car.

"Quiet on set!" someone shouts, and then they start going through all the checks to begin rolling.

"Action!" Beckett shouts when everything is good.

Apparently Gabrielle has already been hit, because Bonnie is still on the ground, and Jonah stumbles out of the SUV in a panic, rushing to her side.

"Whoa, are you okay?" he asks, dropping next to her and grabbing her arm. "You came out of nowhere."

Bonnie rolls her eyes and blinks up at Jonah. "I'm fine. I tripped. Bad timing, I guess."

"You tripped into the street?"

She shrugs. "Clumsy?"

Jonah laughs, his grin too wide. "I can't be mad about that. I'm Logan." He holds out his hand, all charm.

Bonnie hesitates before taking it and letting him help her to her feet. "Gabby. Thanks for braking, by the way. That could have been a whole lot worse."

"What can I say? I've got good reflexes. Can I buy you a coffee?"

"I'd like that. You can let go of my hand now."

Jonah somehow grins wider. "But I'm worried if I do that, you'll disappear. I'd rather keep you right where I want you."

"How about that coffee?"

"Cut!"

I jump when Beckett stops the scene, and it's then that I realize I've gotten to my feet and taken several steps closer to the set. My hands are in fists at my sides, and I feel like someone has been slowly cutting off my oxygen supply without me realizing.

"Mr. McAllister?" It's Bonnie who notices me first, her eyebrows low as she takes a step toward me before stopping herself.

I look at Beckett. "What was that?"

He raises an eyebrow. "What was what?"

I gesture toward Bonnie and Jonah. "That."

"That was the meet-cute."

"But it was wrong."

Sighing, Beckett starts looking around as if trying to find someone who can drag me off set. "Mr. McAllister, that was straight from the script."

"Verbatim," Jonah adds unhelpfully. He's a good physical fit for Logan's character, but I don't know enough about him to care right now.

I fold my arms. "I don't care if that was in the script. It was entirely wrong."

"Hank," Bonnie whispers.

I ignore her, keeping my eyes on Beckett. "That wasn't like the book."

He groans. "Oh good. A purist."

"It's not about purity. It's about taking out one of the most crucial parts of the story. Gabrielle should be *pushed* into the street, and then she's supposed to chase after the guy."

"How is she supposed to meet Logan if she runs away?" Jonah asks, and he puffs out his chest as if proud of his argument. Something tells me he didn't read the book either.

What kind of director—or actor, for that matter—doesn't read the source material for the project he's doing? That's just stupid.

Turning to face Jonah, I try to keep my voice even. "Logan follows Gabrielle."

"They chase the guy together until they lose him around a corner," Bonnie adds quietly. "It's the only reason she trusts Logan so quickly, because he runs faster and nearly catches the guy." Then she looks at me, giving me a grimace. "For the record, I think our version is too romcom."

That's exactly what I was thinking. Turning back to Beckett, who looks ready to throw his tablet in the air and give up for the day, I raise my eyebrows at him. "You do know this is a mystery suspense, right?"

"It's a love story," he argues.

"Woven in through a murder investigation. Gabrielle almost dies in the third act."

"Spoiler alert," Jonah grumbles.

He can't be serious.

"You haven't read the whole script?" Bonnie asks him in alarm.

Shrugging, Jonah points to the crewman who is holding on to his script for him. "I just need to know the scenes we're doing today."

"But how are you supposed to know the mood of the scene or how your character is going to react to something?"

I'm no actor, but even I know Bonnie is in the right here. So when Jonah says, "That's what the director is for," I suddenly feel sick.

I shouldn't have given in to my curiosity. Ignorance would have been so much better than knowing this movie is going to be a total disaster.

I have a feeling I'm not going to have any influence over anything that happens on this set, so I shouldn't even try. If any of my other books get optioned, I'm making sure my feedback is part of the contract or I'm not selling.

Wait, do I even have the right to refuse? I should probably check with my lawyer…

"Mr. McAllister," Beckett says wearily, "as much as I would love to do a perfect page to screen, that's not how movie adaptations work. I can't cram four hundred pages into two hours."

I never expected that, and I knew things would have to be cut or changed, but—

"Beckett," Bonnie says, her voice suddenly sweet and gentle. She's now doe-eyed and mesmerizing, and I'm not the only one transfixed. "What if we try something in the middle? I get pushed, but when I try to chase after the guy, Jonah grabs my arm and stops me because he's worried that I'm injured? It won't take a new scene setup, but it would help lay the groundwork for the big plot twist."

Beckett rubs his chin thoughtfully and then gestures for one of the women behind him. They start whispering, which I hope is a good sign.

"Oo," Jonah says, rubbing his hands together. "I love a good plot twist. I can't wait to find out what it is."

I have never had the urge to punch someone before, but I kind of want to hit him for being the idiot who didn't read the whole script. "Logan is the bad guy," I tell him.

His jaw drops. "Wait, what? I am? Since when?" He hurries over to grab the script and starts riffling through the pages while saying something to who I assume is his assistant.

I swear Bonnie breathes a sigh of relief. After checking to make sure Beckett is busy, she comes over to me and puts her hand on my arm. "I thought Jonah was upping the charm to compensate for Logan's real motivation, not because he thought he was actually the love interest.

And there are so many things about the script that I hate, but I'm not a screenwriter, you know? I'm just a pretty face saying the lines they give me."

"It's not your fault no one paid attention to the actual plot." I sound grumbly, but I can't help it. "I kind of wish I hadn't come so I wouldn't know how badly that scene was written."

"It's not just that one." Bonnie grimaces. "I tried telling Beckett that we needed to tweak things, but he wouldn't... He says he has a good grasp of the story." She shrugs, her cheeks flushing red as she does her best to look unbothered. Apparently she can only act when she's in front of a camera because I don't believe her for a second. She is *incredibly* bothered.

Beckett is still deep in discussion, and Jonah has a hand over his mouth, like he just read the part where Logan turns on Gabrielle and reveals that he's been working with the other antagonist all along. I should probably go, but I feel bad about leaving Bonnie on her own.

"Thank you," I say, ducking my head. "For suggesting a compromise."

Bonnie grins wide. "I am so good at compromises. Like, last summer Derek wanted to go to the wilderness of Alaska for our public vacation, and I wanted to go on a Caribbean cruise, so I suggested we do an Alaskan cruise so we could both win, and that way the photographer didn't have to sleep on the ground and trudge through the moose-infested woods with us."

When she started that sentence, I did not expect it to end up where it did. I'm not even sure what to ask first. Slipping my hands into my pockets, I go back through what she just said and pick out the important parts. "Derek?" I start with.

She blushes. "My ex. Derek Riley."

Oh. She dated the biggest star in Hollywood. One of the few celebrities I've actually heard of. That's...cool?

"What is a public vacation?" I ask.

She blushes even more deeply, tucking her arms behind her back as if embarrassed. "Well, you can't tell anyone, but Derek and I are really just friends. But the world thought we were dating, so we had to get pictures of us together to keep up the charade."

Why does everything this woman says catch me off guard? "How often do you get into fake relationships?"

She laughs as if I just said something funny, but when she realizes I'm not laughing with her, she stops and turns a shade of red that can't be healthy. "Oh. Um. Pretty constantly?"

"Why?"

"Because that's what the world wants." She tucks her arms around herself now, and a part of me wants to hug her again. I haven't stopped thinking about the way she held me when we met, which is dangerous. But right now, she looks like she could use the support. "Look," she continues, "I know that sounds awful. It's always been mutually beneficial, you know? Out-of-the-box marketing, in a way, like acting in a different medium. My relationships make a lot of people happy."

I should have gone home so I wouldn't have to think about how this genuinely sweet and naturally beautiful woman has been in constant fake relationships in order to please a bunch of strangers, and she doesn't even seem to think it's strange to live her whole life for someone else. What about *her* happiness?

I can't stop my next question from coming, though I know I'm going to regret asking. "Why would you let someone else control your life?"

A sudden and incredibly loud pop makes everyone in the nearby vicinity duck and scream. Bonnie leaps into me, nearly knocking me over. A few people—Laketownians, mostly—take off running as if it were a gunshot, but everyone else looks over at the front tire of Logan's SUV, which seems to have spontaneously exploded.

"Can I get props over here?" Beckett says into a megaphone. "Everyone take a break. Bonnie, Jonah, let's run through the blocking again."

The street bursts into movement, everyone hurrying to complete whatever job they have. Though Jonah passes us, muttering something about how he's been playing Logan all wrong, Bonnie doesn't move.

I'm not even sure she realizes I'm holding her.

"You okay?" I ask. It's a dumb question, considering she's hiding her face in my sweater and trembling. My hands itch to stroke her hair and offer some sort of comfort, but my elevated heart rate tells me I can't handle that level of contact. "Bonnie?"

Stepping back, away from my arms, she laughs weakly and tucks her hair behind her ears. "That didn't scare you?"

Maybe, but I was so focused on Bonnie jumping into my arms that it barely registered. "Of course it did," I lie. "My heart is racing." That part's real.

Her warm smile almost makes the lie worth it. "Oh good, so I'm not the only one who doesn't like loud noises." She licks her lips and glances around. "By the way, I know it's strange that all my relationships have been staged."

"I didn't say that."

"Your face did. And celebrity romances are fake all the time, publicity stunts and stuff, but I know I'm the weird one who has never really been in love. I'm fine with it that way." She squirms when she says that, so I'm not sure I believe her. But I'll let her keep talking. "And I really shouldn't have asked you to be my fake boyfriend. I guess I hoped it would help the movie."

I appreciate the sentiment, but there's no way I could do this with her even if I wanted to. "Bonnie, a relationship isn't going to make the movie better. But I think you can. You probably know the book as well as I do."

That gets her laughing and blushing at the same time, and my chest grows tight as I watch her. There's something so warm about her, a genuineness I've never seen before. "No way. I've only read it, like, five times."

I have to clear my throat before I can get any words out. "That's five times more than most people. Most people haven't read it."

"That math only works if most people have read it once."

I tilt my head. "Honestly, based on my sales, they probably have."

"Or they're like me and own all the different editions."

Alarm spreads through me, like a delayed reaction to the blown tire, which is currently being replaced. She's kidding, right? "Why would you have more than one copy?"

"Because they're all so pretty!"

"That's like owning both the DVD and the Blu-ray," I argue, still baffled. But I also feel like laughing, which is such a foreign feeling that I don't know how to sit with it. I shift my weight, like I'm no longer comfortable in my own body, but I'm not *un*comfortable.

Bonnie laughs, touching my arm at the same time and leaving me overheated. "No one uses hard copies anymore, Hank. It's all streaming. What are you, fifty?"

As I stick my hands in my pockets, trying to give myself a sense of normalcy, I glance over to see Beckett flipping through the script while Jonah watches us with unveiled interest. It's probably time for me to leave before I get any bad ideas. "No, I'm not fifty," I mutter, "but I also don't own a TV, so it doesn't matter."

"Seriously?"

I shrug. "Not really my thing. I used to have one, but it broke six months ago and I didn't bother replacing it."

"You are a strange man, Hank McAllister." She claps a hand over her mouth, her eyes going wide. "I didn't mean that how it sounded."

I find myself smiling a real smile for the first time all day. The fact that I am aware that this is the case worries me a bit, but I've gone plenty of days without smiling. This isn't anything new. So why am I noticing it today? Because Bonnie smiles so much that the differences between us are impossible to ignore. "I am strange," I agree and gently tug her hand away from her face. I'm tempted to hold on to it, but I let go and take a step back. "And I'm pretty sure I'm holding up production, so I should head home."

"Do you live nearby?"

"Good luck with the new scene, and good luck trying to fix the script. I'm sure you can make it so much better." I turn to head back to my car, then stop dead when I see what looks like a hundred Laketownians staring at me from the sidewalk. It's about a hundred people more than I'm comfortable with. I can practically hear their thoughts.

Hank left his house. He's talking to someone. He actually smiled. It's like they thought I would spend the rest of my life hidden, and now they're wondering if I might actually give them the answers to their questions. The questions that have haunted me for the last four years.

For two seconds, I feel dizzy. Then there's nothing but darkness.

CE CREAM

chapter seven

BONNIE

WHEN THE AUTHOR OF the book you're turning into a movie faints out of nowhere and prompts the medical team to storm the set, it kind of kills the mood to film. Beckett doesn't look happy, but with the combo of the tire exploding and Hank's collapse, he makes the smart choice to take a quick break.

I follow the medics to the medical tent. This really isn't my place, but I feel like I'm partially to blame for Hank's current state. Even if he doesn't want me hanging around, I have to make sure he's okay.

"Excuse me?" I say, poking my head into the tent.

Hank is already sitting up between the two medics and holding his arm out for a blood pressure cuff. He's pale, his glasses askew, but he looks relatively unharmed. That's a relief, and probably more than enough reason for me to mind my own business. But my feet remain planted.

"What happened?" I ask, probably barely loud enough for anyone to hear me.

The two medics, a man and woman I haven't met and therefore don't know names of, glance back at me and share a look. Then their attention goes right back to Hank without acknowledging me.

Hank looks at me, though, focusing on me over Boy Nurse's head. "I'm fine," he says breathily. But his expression is saying anything but. He looks almost panicked.

"We'll tell you if you're fine," Girl Nurse replies. She spouts some numbers off to Boy, who writes it on a notepad. "Your blood pressure is pretty high, Mr. McAllister."

Hank lets out a shaky laugh as he looks down at his arm. "I'm not surprised."

"I'll get a second reading just in case. Are you on any medications that—"

"No. It's just anxiety." His eyes flit to me again, his ears turning red. "I don't, uh, I generally don't leave my house."

"Agoraphobic?" Boy guesses. "Have you thought about—"

Girl clears her throat, eyes darting back to me. "If you don't mind, Miss Aiken."

Right. I shouldn't be standing here in the doorway and listening in on a conversation like this. "Sorry," I whisper and turn to leave, but something in Hank's expression holds me back. He still has that panicked look, but now there's more desperation in his eyes.

I can't read minds, but it's not hard to guess that he doesn't want me to leave him alone with these two. But how can I stay? I lick my lips and glance behind me, making sure no one outside is near enough to hear me. "Do you want me to stay, honey?" I ask, trying not to sound as hesitant as I feel.

Hank's eyes widen ever so slightly, understandably confused by the pet name. He takes a slow breath as both nurses turn to face him, and then he nods and holds out his unencumbered hand toward me. "Please."

Boy and Girl meet each other's eyes but say nothing as I step forward and take hold of Hank's hand. His fingers are cold but soft, and his grip is stronger than I expected.

"Huh," Girl says, looking down at the blood pressure device in her hand. "Not so high…"

"Like I was saying," Boy says, ignoring her, "if you suffer from agoraphobia, you can—"

"I don't." Hank swallows. "I don't get anxious when I leave the house. I'm *generally* anxious. But I manage it."

"Then why did you—"

"Enough, Boyd," Girl says with a roll of her eyes. "Not every invisible condition is mental. Mr. McAllister, were you feeling lightheaded before you passed out?"

Boy—or Boyd, I guess—rolls his eyes right back at her and grumbles, "I was just trying to help him, Gayle."

Wait, Boy and Girl are actually named Boyd and Gayle? I bite my lip to hold back a snicker.

Instead of looking at the two nurses, who both stare at Hank as they wait for an answer to Gayle's question, Hank looks at me, more life in his eyes than before. "Thank you," he says, almost soundlessly.

I frown. "For what?"

His answer comes in a squeeze of his hand.

Before I can say anything, the tent flaps fly inward and Beckett fills the small space with his large presence. There are way too many people in this tent right now, but he doesn't seem to notice. "Bonnie, we need to get back to filming before we break for lunch."

My body tenses, like it often does when I'm around Beckett. He's a brilliant director, but I would never call him a people person. I keep my eyes on Hank, as if he might keep me calm. "Can you give me just a few more minutes?"

"We already wasted enough time talking about changing the scene."

I spin to face him. "We're going to change the scene, right?"

Letting out a heavy sigh, Beckett folds his arms and pins me with a steely stare. He hasn't even spared a glance for Hank or the medics, which is more irritating than his scowl. "Bonnie, we've talked about this. If we change the scene, we'll have to change the whole—"

"You heard Jonah. He's playing the character wrong because he doesn't know—"

"Who is directing this movie, Bonnie? It's clearly not you. Now get back outside so we can move on to the next scene."

I shouldn't be surprised that Beckett turns and leaves after that decree. It's not like he listened to me before, so why would he today? Pasting on a smile, I turn to Hank and return the hand squeeze he gave me earlier. "I'm glad you're okay," I tell him and pull my hand free.

Or, I would have, but Hank holds on tight. "Is he always like that?"

My eyebrows dip down. "Is who like what?"

"The director." He frowns. "Does he always ignore you?"

Something bubbles to life in my chest, though I can't quite name what the feeling is. It's warm and comforting, whatever it is. "Oh. Um. I'm sure he knows better than—"

Hank drops my hand and rips the pressure cuff from his arm, ignoring the protests of the nurses who were silent while Beckett was in here. Once Hank is free, he gets to his feet and grabs hold of my hand again like it's the most natural thing in the world. Tugging me with him, he follows Beckett's path out onto the set and over to the canopy where Beckett is just arriving at Jonah's side.

"Mr. Peretti," Hank says, his voice coming out clearer than I've ever heard it. "I think you need to change the scene."

Beckett barely glances back. "I told you, Mr. McAllister, I can't—"

"Most of your audience are going to be my fans, and they can be brutal. Have you ever met one of them?"

Though he clearly doesn't want to have this conversation, Beckett turns to face us, his jaw tight. His eyes slip down to my hand locked with Hank's, but he keeps his focus on Hank's face. "Can't say that I have."

"You're wrong." Hank pulls me a step forward. "Did you know Bonnie's a fan?"

Oh, this is not where I thought this conversation was going to go, and it takes all my skills as an actor to keep from running away screaming. I force a smile, trying to come across as shy and humble. How Beckett wants me to be. "Maybe a casual fan," I say.

"She knows this story better than I do," Hank argues. "And if you don't want to become a pariah at the hands of Gabrielle Frost fans around the world—if you want a chance to make a second movie—you might want to listen to her."

The foreign feeling in my chest grows, and I look at Hank like I'm seeing him for the first time. There's nothing quiet and reclusive about the way he's talking to Beckett right now, and it's like I'm seeing a whole different side to him. A side that's...defending me? I don't think anyone outside of my friends has ever done what he just did.

He doesn't even know me, and I've brought him nothing but trouble. Why would he help me?

Beckett's jaw clenches even harder as his eyes jump to the production crew gathering around us. Clearly our conversation is more interesting than their jobs, and I can't help but think about how I'm standing in plain sight, holding Hank's hand. He may not want to be in a relationship with me, but holding my hand like this isn't going to do him any favors.

"Bonnie's right, Beckett," Jonah says, script still in hand. "Some of this stuff doesn't make sense without the change she suggested."

Beckett sighs, softening as he glances back at Jonah. I know they've worked together before, and it seems like there might be some friendship there too based on how Beckett and Jonah have a silent conversation.

"Fine," he growls, and I feel like cheering. *Thank you, Jonah!* "We'll change the scene. Now, can we get back to—"

"It's not just that one," I say, though some of my confidence dwindles when Beckett's eyes jump to me. "There's a lot about this script that could really use some work."

"We're in the *middle* of production," Beckett says, the words strained. "And we're already over budget and behind schedule. There's no time to—"

"I'll fix it." My eyes go wide. I don't know how to fix a messed up script!

Laughing darkly, Beckett shakes his head. "Did you forget that you're an actor, Aiken? Not a screenwriter. You can't do both."

I can feel the words he doesn't say: *so choose.* He would rather have me behind the scenes than on the screen, and I know it. But this is the first time he's even considered one of my suggestions, so I don't want to lose any ground I've gained thanks to Hank and Jonah. "I can if I fix the script off the clock. After we're done filming for the day." I'll probably have to enlist Kasey to get it done, but I'm sure she would love to help me fix the mess that is this screenplay.

Beckett sighs again. "Is this because you're dating the author?"

I glance at Hank, who seems to be silently telling me that my response is my call. He'll follow my lead.

No one's ever done that before.

Fighting inexplicable tears, I lift my chin and shake my head. "This is because I want this movie to do well."

"And what, pray tell, gives a movie success?"

"Chemistry." It's Jonah who says that, once again softening Beckett's stance when the director turns to him. He lifts his eyebrows high, like it should be obvious. "Not going to lie, I don't think Bonnie and I have it. Not with the way I was playing Logan. There's no surer way to make fans hate something than by leaving it empty and emotionless."

Pinching the bridge of his nose, Beckett looks like he might be at the end of his rope. "Jonah, are you telling me my leads can't make this work? I knew I should have picked—"

"I'm telling you Bonnie and McAllister have chemistry in spades, so the problem clearly isn't her. I've been doing this all wrong, and if anyone can fix this movie, she can. I think you should trust her."

Heat floods my face, and I'm almost too afraid to look at Hank. "Chemistry?" I parrot back. With Hank? I mean, obviously there was something, or that photo of our hug wouldn't have gone viral the way it did, but I don't even know Hank. And he certainly doesn't know me. "I mean, yes! Chemistry is crucial to a movie working."

"Think about it," Jonah says with a shrug. "Your lead actress is dating the guy who is the whole reason we're even here filming this movie, so she's going to know exactly what the scenes need to really work like they're supposed to. *And* she just offered to do someone's job for free."

Oh, I did do that, didn't I? Is this going to put someone out of a job? But no, the screenwriter already did his part. This is additional work. Work that will hopefully make this movie better than the nightmare it's been so far.

Beckett's eyes shift to me once more, and though his gaze is cold, I can practically see the dollar signs behind it. If letting me adjust the script changes this movie from a bomb to a blockbuster, he'd be an idiot to argue.

"I can fix it," I whisper as one last plea.

Dropping his arms to his sides, Beckett grumbles something to himself and then says, "Fine. But if this starts delaying production and gets us even further behind, we're scrapping it and sticking to the old script. Understand?"

"Yes," I breathe, nodding wildly. "You won't regret this, Mr. Peretti."

"Pretty sure I will," he mutters back. Looking at his watch, he lets out a few curses and picks up his megaphone. "Let's break for lunch!"

Though I'm still holding Hank's hand, I throw my other arm around Jonah's neck. "Thank you!"

He chuckles. "This is my career too, Aiken. If you can prevent this movie from taking me down with it, I'm all for it. Ah!" His eyes brighten when his assistant runs up to him, a book in hand. "Perfect."

I stare down at the familiar cover. "*Frosted Peaks*?" Hank's book.

Jonah nods, flipping through the pages. "Thought it might be a good idea to figure out exactly who my character is, so I have home-work tonight." He looks at the title page before quirking an eyebrow up at Hank. "You didn't sign everything in the bookstore here?"

Hank's lips twist into a grimace. "Not my thing."

"Too bad." Gaze dropping to our hands for a few seconds, Jonah smiles at us both and then heads to the trailer we use during our breaks.

I figure it would be best to get everything out quickly. "He thinks we're dating," I whisper, turning to Hank.

Hank's eyes are on the sidewalk behind me, where I'm assuming there are still a whole bunch of Laketownians watching us like they were before. "I think everyone thinks we're dating," he whispers back.

"I'm sorry. I couldn't think of another way to get them to let me stay in the med tent."

He shakes his head. "I'm the one who grabbed your hand when we left."

"You don't have to do this, Hank." But I want him to. Partly because there's something about him that makes me brave. More than *something*. He stood up for me in a way no one ever has, and his confidence in me sparked Jonah to jump in too. I know it's a bad idea to let myself get used to something like that when I know it can't last, but I've never felt anything like what I felt during that conversation with Beckett.

Like I matter.

Taking a slow breath, head bent, Hank lifts our clasped hands and presses a kiss to my knuckle. "If I don't help you with this," he says slowly, "are things going to get worse?"

They are now that he kissed my hand like that. But even if he hadn't, there are too many people who believe in the relationship now. It's more than just a rumor based on a single hug. "Probably."

Hank winces. "I don't want that for you, Bonnie."

The fact that he even cares is enough to pierce the shield I've put around my heart. That's dangerous. "I can handle the gossip, Hank."

"But you shouldn't have to. I can't promise anything, but..." He meets my eyes for the first time since talking to Beckett. "I want to help you if I can."

My heart soars, but I tamp it down before I get any bad ideas. He wants to *help. He's not telling you that he might fall for you. Besides, you don't want him to fall for you!* I'll have to leave him behind when things die down and Fran decides I need a fancy new boyfriend to keep my popularity where it needs to be.

"Thank you, Hank," I say softly and hope I'm not making a huge mistake by letting him into my life.

Hollywood Hot Scoop

Benrie Confirmed: Hollywood's Hottest New Couple

You heard it here first, folks! Bonnie Aiken and Henry McAllister are *officially* a couple. Multiple sources spotted the couple getting cozy on the set of *Frosted Peaks* this afternoon, and I don't know if we've ever seen anything cuter! From the looks of things, Henry is absolutely smitten with our favorite leading lady, and Bonnie clearly returns the regard. Can we blame her? While Henry may not be a Derek Riley, the novelist sure is scrumptious. I just want to eat him up!

Be sure to subscribe to be the first in the know when it comes to Benrie news. We here at *Hollywood Hot Scoop* are always ready to reveal the romance as it unfolds, and you won't want to miss any of it! XO

CE CREAM

CHAPTER EIGHT

HANK

Maybe it's weird that I brought June with me to this meeting, but as soon as Bonnie mentioned the word *contract* when it comes to our pretend relationship, I knew I needed someone who could understand what I was signing. True, I could have asked my actual lawyer to look over it, but I trust June more. Plus, it will be helpful to have someone on my side who knows that none of this is real.

None of this is real. It's a reminder I've had to give myself multiple times since leaving the set yesterday, but it has done nothing to settle my anxiety.

"Why did I say yes?" My steps falter as June and I walk onto the field where the bulk of the production staff are set up just outside of town. I'm getting a strange déjà vu, even though the last time I was here felt nothing like this.

The last time I was here, I met Bonnie and got myself into this mess. The last time I was here, I could have sworn I felt... But no, I don't even want to think about what I felt when I was talking to Beckett.

June grabs my arm, pulling me to a stop. "The fact that you just asked that question out loud has me worried, Hank. Why *did* you say yes?"

I swallow and stuff my hands into my pockets, trying to look calm even though I'm anything but. I can feel several pairs of eyes on me, and I probably shouldn't stand here for long, especially not with June. If the internet can create an entire relationship based on one photo, I can't imagine what they would do if they saw me with another woman. Reluctantly, I gesture with my head for us to keep walking.

"I'm not sure I have much of a choice," I mutter. "And I want to help her." I do. I wish I could help her in some other way, though.

Hot on my heels, June is quiet for nearly thirty seconds before she says, "Fine. You want to help Bonnie. How is this helping *you*?"

It's not. From the minute I met Bonnie, my life has been flipped on its head, and every wall I've put up to protect myself seems to be crumbling. That, or there are people throwing up ladders and climbing to the top to look down on me with binoculars.

"Hank," June says when I don't answer, and her voice is full of warning.

"I know," I say back and then knock on Bonnie's trailer door before I can chicken out. I can barely stomach the thought of what I'm about to do, but neither can I abandon Bonnie. I'm in between a rock and a hard place.

Bonnie greets us with a megawatt grin when she opens the trailer door. "You came!" Her eyes linger on June, a bit wary, but she waves us both inside. "Make yourselves at home."

I pause just inside the door, taking in the small space. She lives in here? As far as trailers go, it's incredibly nice, but if I thought my house was small...

"Feel free to sit," Bonnie says to me. Her hand brushes mine as she passes to the bedroom area at the back, sending a shock through me that isn't entirely unpleasant.

I settle next to June on the surprisingly comfortable couch and try to find some sort of confidence so I don't spend the morning sounding completely pathetic. "Uh, Bonnie, this is June."

"June Harper," June says, reaching up and grasping Bonnie's hand with a firm handshake. "I'll be representing Mr. McAllister."

"Repre..." Bonnie blinks a couple of times before it clicks, and her eyes go wide. "Oh! You're his lawyer!"

June looks a little too mischievous right now. "I'm his friend," she corrects. "But I also know law. I'm just here to make sure you don't wind up hurting him."

"Trust me, that's the last thing I want. That's why I have my publicist, Fran, here." Bonnie grabs a laptop and sets it on the table in front of us, showing us the woman on the other end of a video call.

Fran lifts a single penciled eyebrow as she takes me in. "Mr. McAllister," she says, holding her hand toward the screen. What, does she expect me to try to shake it? I'm so nervous that I almost lift my hand and try. "I've been trying to get a hold of you for a couple of days now."

"My internet is out," I say quickly. It's not technically a lie, though it's only out because I unplugged the router last night. I've been slowly descending deeper and deeper into hermithood over the last few years, but this is more cut off than I've ever been. If something ever happens to me, no one will find my body for weeks. Well, one week. June would figure it out pretty quickly.

Humming to herself, Fran types a few things before adjusting her cat-eye glasses and popping her gum. She has this look about her, like she belongs in the fifties as a nosy reporter, and I already don't like her. "Well, Mr. McAllister," she says, "you've caused quite a stir with my little Bonnie, haven't you?"

I tuck my hands under my thighs to keep myself from fidgeting. "I suppose."

"In his defense," June says, leaning forward, "he and Bonnie were just talking. Whoever took that first photo alleged a lot of things, and it's the media's fault Bonnie and Hank are in this mess."

Lifting her other eyebrow this time, Fran studies June for a moment. "And you are?"

"June Harper, Mr. McAllister's representation."

"Ah. Well, Ms. Harper, as I'm sure you know, public opinion is a very difficult thing to control."

"But that's your job, isn't it?"

Fran smiles a pinched sort of smile that contains more irritation than amusement. "It sure is, hon. That's why we're having this meeting. Now, where's Bonnie?"

"Right here," she says, sliding onto the couch next to me. It's a bit snug with the three of us, and my heart rate spikes as soon as her hip presses against mine. "I figured we could go pretty standard with this one, Fran. Nothing too crazy."

"Please," I say before I can hold it in.

"And I would like to point out that Mr. McAllister has not agreed to anything at this point," June says.

I can feel Bonnie's eyes on me, but I keep my focus on the computer. I don't need her doe-eyes convincing me to agree to anything and everything that would help her, no matter how difficult. I don't want to make any promises I can't keep, but the fact that I'm here at all is proof that Bonnie's skills of persuasion are stronger than I would like.

She didn't even have to try. Just being around her has made me protective of her.

Fran huffs a quick laugh as she studies June. "Aren't you a peach?"

"What do you recommend, Fran?" Bonnie asks.

"Daily appearances, of course," Fran says, immediately making my breath catch in my lungs. But she's not done. "You'll need to go out around town a few times, probably make an appearance in LA, do some lives on Insta, that sort of thing. Nothing too complicated starting out."

That's starting out?

"As Mr. McAllister doesn't have an online presence, it's difficult to say where this will go and how much we'll need to put into it," Fran continues, obviously talking solely to Bonnie even though I'm sitting in the center of the camera's view, pressed between the two women. "I suggest taking it one day at a time. For now, I will slip a confirmation to the press beyond *Hot Scoop* that you are, in fact, in a relationship, and I'll let you handle the rest. You've been through this enough times to know what to do, Bonnie."

"I think that sounds reasonable," Bonnie says, looking at me again. My eyes slip to my thighs as I focus on breathing. "What do you think, Hank?"

I think I'm in way over my head. The internet may want me to be with Bonnie, but none of that stuff sounds like things I'm capable of. What if I only make things worse?

"Mr. McAllister," Fran says, waiting until I look up at the computer again. "I know this sounds daunting, but I need you to consider the repercussions of killing this relationship before it has had a chance to blossom."

I'm not going to like this. I can feel it. But my voice is stuck in my throat so I can't tell Fran that I don't want to hear what she has to say.

"Bonnie is already on unstable ground with the media," Fran says. "Her recent breakup with Derek Riley, while necessary, stirred up some negative feelings among her fans, and her career needs a win. If we can't prove to the world that Bonnie is capable of holding a relationship with someone unconventional like you, she may lose whatever credibility she has gained over the last few years."

I frown. I'm pretty sure Bonnie has been acting for almost a decade. Did she not have credibility before that? Even if that's the case, could one failed relationship be enough to ruin her?

Before I can ask, Fran keeps talking. "And I'm not sure you fully understand what's at stake for you, Mr. McAllister. *Hollywood Hot Scoop* and countless other websites have set their eyes on you, and you don't want to underestimate the power of their followers. If you turn your back on Bonnie, it'll be my job to try to protect her. That means placing blame on your head."

"Is that a threat?" June asks. Her words are so sharp that I flinch away from her.

Fran smirks. "It's a fact, Ms. Harper. And it's nothing personal."

It feels personal. But can I really blame her for protecting Bonnie when Bonnie has proven she's skilled at letting people walk all over her? Without Jonah stepping in—without *me* stepping in—she would have suffered in silence and let the script remain a mess. Beckett was never going to listen to her, and it's obvious Fran knows Bonnie isn't going to fight for herself.

In a strange way, I admire the gumption Fran has in being upfront about things. Even if I don't love the threat she just made. As much as I wish things could go back to the way they were, it's becoming more and more clear that that isn't an option and never will be.

"Hank," June says, back to that warning tone she had before.

I look at her, my eyebrows pulling low as I consider the fact that I may not have a choice here. "What would you have me do?" I whisper, hopefully so Fran can't hear me. Bonnie's too close to avoid, but in a strange way I trust her to keep her thoughts to herself until I've made a decision.

June scowls at me. "Don't you care what this will do to your life?"

"What life?" My own question feels like a slap to the face as reality settles in around me. "I don't know if I can call what I have living."

Yes, I'm terrified by the idea of this pretend relationship. I'm terrified of what it'll mean for the solitude I've built for myself. I'm also terrified of sinking into complete obscurity. But more than anything, I'm terrified of what will happen to Bonnie if I don't step in and help because I'm too focused on myself.

This much terror and guilt isn't good for my blood pressure.

June puts her hand on my arm. "Hank, I think this is a bad idea."

"How about this?" Fran says. "I'll send over the contract, you can look it over to your heart's content, and you can either sign it or sign the NDA I will also send to make sure nothing bad happens to Bonnie. Good? Great." She ends the call before any of us can respond.

"NDA?" June says in a growl.

"I'm sure it's nothing," Bonnie replies, speaking over me as I stare at the blank screen in front of me. "Just a way to protect us both."

"I don't think your publicist has any interest in protecting Hank."

"I'll make sure he's fine."

"Is that really up to you, Bonnie?"

"What is that supposed to mean?"

I can't breathe. It feels like the trailer is getting smaller—an impressive feat—and their arguing isn't doing anything to slow my racing heart and racing thoughts and racing breaths because I can't pull in enough air with everything closing in around me.

I jump to my feet, desperate to get outside and get some air and get a chance to properly think this all through because I can't—

An umbrella topples over in my path right before I reach the door. It's an old-fashioned one, with a curved wooden handle and red fabric stretched taut along the ribs. Red with white polka-dots.

The whole world stills. Grows quiet. Calm.

It feels like I just jumped into a cool lake in the middle of summer, leaving the heat of the sun and the sounds of the world behind. I pick up the umbrella, running shaky fingers along the smooth handle.

"Oh, I forgot I stole that from set the other day," Bonnie says gently, coming up behind me. "One of the things I love most about Gabrielle's character is all the little details that make her feel like a real person, you know? Like her favorite umbrella being so spunky when she's supposed to be this hardened detective. It's such a unique quirk."

Swallowing, I gently rest the umbrella back in its spot and turn to face Bonnie.

She gives me an apologetic smile, and there's so much worry in her expression. It's an expression I haven't seen on her. "Are you okay? That didn't go how I wanted it to go. Fran isn't usually so..."

"Horrible?" June supplies from the couch. She watches us with narrowed eyes.

I grab Bonnie's hand and tug her outside, closing the door between us and June. While I appreciate my friend's protective nature, this is a decision I have to make myself. Out in the open air, I can breathe easier, but I stopped panicking as soon as I saw that umbrella.

Funny. I would have expected the opposite.

"Fran is just trying to do her job," I say after a few deep breaths. "I'm glad you have someone on your side through all of this."

A smile flashes across Bonnie's face, but it's short lived. "I'm glad you do too. June is right. Fran was kind of horrible to you. But I mean it when I say I'll make sure you're okay, no matter what you decide."

"We should do it." Though the words seem to strangle me for a moment, they mostly feel right. I need to help her. "If a relationship is the best thing for you, for your career, I'll do it."

As she practically vibrates with the smile that blooms across her cheeks, I can tell Bonnie is doing her best not to look overexcited. "Really? Hank, you have no idea what that would mean to me."

I might have an idea, and my body seems to relax more the longer I stand next to her and soak in her joy. "What was Fran saying about instant life something?" I ask, rubbing my arm as a brisk wind rolls across the set. I wore a flannel, since we're only just getting into spring, but Laketown sometimes surprises me with how long it takes to warm up. Still, spring is coming. I can smell the change in the air.

Bonnie frowns for a second, but then she brightens again. "Oh, you mean the Insta lives? It's just filming live videos on Instagram. Nothing special."

I wince. "Live videos? How many people usually watch those?"

"I don't know. A few hundred thousand, usually? But the videos always get uploaded for people to watch later if they don't see them live. Time zones and all that."

I knew Bonnie was famous. It would be difficult *not* to know that. She's a Hollywood starlet who has starred alongside some of the most celebrated actors in this century. But I guess it never really computed how many people would bother to see what's going on in her life on a day-to-day basis.

Could my decision really have that much of an impact on someone like her? I'm not going to back down—not when I saw her relief when I agreed—but I still wonder if her situation is as dire as Fran seemed to think. If people got to know the Bonnie I've seen these last few days, surely they would love her no matter who she's with.

I start talking if only to stop myself from asking my questions out loud. I need to stay focused on the tasks at hand, including the whole live video concept. "So...hundreds of thousands of people, maybe millions, are going to start paying attention to me. My personal life will be up for debate and dissection by people who didn't even know I existed until the other day when they saw my photo. That's...fine."

It's not fine. It's anything but fine. But it has to be fine because otherwise I'm going to hurt Bonnie's career and possibly destroy mine in the process depending on how Fran handles the situation. My identity is out there—that can't be changed—so I should embrace this change and see the positives, few though they may be. I might get more readers from this, which means more profits, which means more money that I can donate to underfunded police forces around the country.

But this really isn't about me, so I tuck those thoughts away and turn my focus to Bonnie. "What is our relationship going to look like?" I ask, looking down at our hands together. I didn't even realize I was still holding on to her. I shift so our fingers interlace, which better fits a romantic relationship. The gesture feels foreign and familiar all at once. "What do we need to do to keep convincing people that we're a couple?"

Bonnie waits until I look up and meet her gaze once more, and then she smiles in a way that makes me feel like I've downed an entire cup of fresh tea. I'm suddenly warmed all the way through. "I don't think it will be hard to sell it, honestly. You're already my hero, so as long as you don't look at me like I disgust you..."

"That's impossible," I murmur and then cringe. I probably need to explain that one. "I mean you're beautiful, Bonnie. No disgust here."

Her cheeks tint a lovely pink. I didn't notice before that she has some freckles that dot her cheeks, faint speckles beneath her makeup. I wouldn't have guessed something like that, with her dark hair, but her skin is fair enough. I wonder if her freckles get darker in the sun. My stomach hitches; I shouldn't be wondering that.

"Mostly I want to make sure you're comfortable with all of this," she says, and it's like she's suddenly embarrassed as she ducks her head. "If you want to hold my hand and nothing else, that's fine by me."

"What if I want to kiss you?" I don't. At least, I don't think I do, but I also haven't kissed anyone in four years. I'm for sure out of practice, and I don't know what would happen if we *did* kiss. I don't anticipate blurring lines, but I'm a writer. I know the tropes. As soon as the couple in the fake relationship kiss, everything turns real.

I can't afford that. I'm already looking at her in a way I shouldn't.

"You can kiss me if you'd like," she says to the ground. I honestly can't tell if *she* would like that or not. Not that it matters.

Clearing my throat, I shake my head when Bonnie looks up at me with curious eyes. "I don't want to come across as a jerk," I say carefully, "but I'm not planning on this being anything but a way to keep your publicity in a good place. I won't—can't—catch real feelings at any point, so I want to make sure we're both on the same page. I would hate for you to get hurt."

Jonah's conviction that we have chemistry might be accurate to a point, but we could never make this relationship real. *I* could never.

Thankfully, Bonnie's expression barely changes as she studies me. "You don't have to worry about that on my end, Hank McAllister," she says easily. "Real feelings and I have never mixed. I've had enough fake boyfriends to know that I'm not going to fall for you, no matter how cute you are."

"Cute," I repeat, though the word gets stuck in my throat. I'm blushing, and blushing hard, but I can't help liking the idea of someone as effortlessly darling as Bonnie Aiken thinking I'm cute. "Well, thanks. And if you're not worried, then I guess we..." I try to imagine the two of us kissing, but no matter how much romance I put into my books, I can't picture it.

"We can just take things as they come," Bonnie suggests. "And if we need it, I can grab the chemistry coach at any point if we think we can't make a kiss look believable. Assuming that's where things go."

Somehow I forgot that this woman's job is kissing various men in front of a camera, which means she must know all the rules in the book. Wait, are there actual kissing rules? Is movie kissing different from real life kissing? Why am I suddenly unable to think about anything *except* kissing?

I clear my throat again, pushing my glasses up my nose and forcing myself to sound aloof and unconcerned. "I have a deadline coming up." Good heavens, I sound like a robot. It's been way too long since I asked someone on a date, and I'm pretty sure I shouldn't be this nervous when she will contractually have to agree. "Maybe one of these nights we can go to the ice cream shop in town and brainstorm the next Gabrielle book? It will count toward one of those outings Fran wants us to do, and it'll be easier to get out of the house if I can do some work at the same time." *Ha! Nice one, Hank.* I sound like a pig, and even if the date wouldn't be real, that's no way to ask a woman out.

Still, Bonnie's eyes light up. "Wait, you want to brainstorm with me?"

"Not to be presumptuous, but you did say you were a fan."

"I am *absolutely* a fan! And I would die to know more about the next book before it comes out. You'd really let me help? That's a literal dream come true, Hank."

I didn't expect so much enthusiasm, and regret builds in my stomach. Maybe it will be less of a dream when she realizes how thoroughly stuck I am in this book. "I warn you, it's not as glamorous as it sounds. I might even have to scrap what I have and start all over, and you might hate this series by the time our relationship is over."

By the time our relationship is over. That's a strange sentence I never thought I would say. I've always been a *forever* kind of guy.

Forever ended a lot faster than I thought it would.

"I think it still sounds fun," Bonnie says. "I could probably get away on Thursday, but we'll have to have Eli with us. My bodyguard. He'll just blend into the background, so don't worry."

I can't imagine the Herculean bodyguard blending into anything, but I'll take her word for it.

"Thursday sounds great," I tell her, even though it sounds awful because the whole town will probably show up as soon as someone realizes I'm there. It's not like I'm going to be able to avoid them anyway.

Why did I agree to this? That's a dumb question because I already know the answer. When Bonnie smiles at me, I get this strange sense of hope that I won't completely fade away. She's the first person who has ever convinced me to willingly leave my house more than once, and that has to mean something.

"I'll pick you up here at eight," I say, and it takes me a second to let go of her hand. It's been so long since I held anyone's hand that it almost feels like I've forgotten the mechanics of it.

Bonnie smiles, but there's something off about it. And she's focused on something behind me. I turn to look, but she grabs my shoulder and pulls herself in, planting a lingering kiss on my cheek. "I think I saw someone with a camera," she whispers to keep me in place. Not that she needs to try.

If I thought holding someone's hand was foreign, this is worse. What am I supposed to do? Kiss her back? No, that's weird. I could hug her? I try that, though it feels stiff and awkward, and I can feel her tension in her body as she tries to adjust to my hold. It's not like I haven't hugged her before, so why in the world am I struggling this much?

"Uh, turns out it's been a while since I was in a relationship," I admit, keeping my voice low. I doubt someone with a camera would be able to hear us unless they're closer than I'm thinking.

Bonnie frees her arms so she can wrap them around my neck and make this embrace less chummy and more romantic. At least, I think that's what she's doing. If nothing else, it's more comfortable. "Maybe we should talk to the chemistry coach tomorrow."

I'm already out of my comfort zone here. A chemistry coach sounds like my worst nightmare. It was a hug that started this whole thing, so I just need to do what I did then. "No. No, we can figure this out. *I* can. I'll be better on Thursday." And if I can't, then maybe I'll try the whole coaching thing. "Is the photographer gone?"

Bonnie chuckles. "No, but hopefully they got enough of a show to be satisfied. I'll let you go." She does, but slowly. Like she doesn't want to part ways. And she gives me this heated look that makes me shiver.

Maybe she hasn't been in many blockbuster hits, but Bonnie Aiken can act. She almost has me fooled. "See you Thursday, Hank. I can't wait."

"Yeah."

By the time I drop June off and head back home, the weight of what I agreed to has fully settled on my shoulders, leaving me exhausted. I haven't even had to do anything yet. But I know my choice was the only one I could have made. I knew it even before I said yes. I knew it the instant that umbrella fell into my path.

As I step inside, my eyes stray to the coat rack in the corner by the door. It's nothing special, and neither are my coats. But the big red umbrella with white polka dots tucked behind it?

I don't believe in signs, but this one feels too in my face to ignore.

"Shelby, what in the world are you trying to tell me?" I whisper, holding my breath in the silence that follows.

As if she might actually answer.

CHAPTER NINE

BONNIE

HANK KNOCKS ON MY trailer door right on time, which is unfortunate because I am in no way ready. I open the door just enough to poke my head out—I'm only halfway dressed and wrapped in a robe—and give him a smile. "Do you mind waiting, like, two minutes?"

"Better make it ten," Derek says in my earbud.

Hank nods, his hands in his pockets as he stands there looking adorable in his sweater and chino pants. "Take all the time you need. I'm in no hurry."

I'm pretty sure he means that.

As soon as I close the door, I shush Derek even though no one else can hear him. "You know how much I have a hard time choosing what to wear, and filming went long today," I complain. "What about this?" I hold up a seagreen, ruffled sundress with off-the-shoulder sleeves.

Derek squints through the phone, which I've propped up on one of my shelves. "Isn't it like forty degrees there?"

"Good point." Though it's vastly different from home, I kind of love the weather here, and the crispness in the air is making it easy to feel like

I'm truly living in Gabrielle Frost's world. The only thing that would make it better would be fall instead of spring, but I won't be picky.

Tossing the dress on my bed, I grab a cream-colored cashmere sweater and some high-waisted jeans.

"Better," Derek agrees. Then he amends his response by saying, "It's perfect," probably knowing I would take *better* to mean I should keep trying. He knows me too well. "Why didn't you ask for Freya's help, by the way?"

"Because it's like four in the morning in Candora." I pause, counting the hours to make sure I'm right. I think I am. Unless it's five? Regardless, it's way too early to call her.

"Kasey?"

I laugh. "I love Kasey, but she has gotten far too used to wearing Liam's clothes."

"Got it," Derek says, though a wrinkle has formed on his brow as he looks at me. "And you're sure this is a good idea, dating the author?"

I quickly get dressed off screen, talking as I go. "I'm not really dating him, and my popularity has already gone up since the latest round of pictures surfaced. People love Hank."

Derek grumbles something I don't understand, and then he says, "I'm sure they do. It's not him I'm worried about."

Over the years, Derek and I have talked a lot about our future goals. His have never changed, though neither of us have figured out a good way for him to settle down and start a family while still doing what he loves. Constantly filming on location, as he tends to do, doesn't lend itself to putting down roots. My goals are less certain than his. For a while, I just wanted to be in as many movies as I could. A star on Hollywood Boulevard would be nice, maybe a couple of Oscars. But I've never had a real dream. Something I could fight for.

At the same time, it feels like I'm always fighting for my place, and I'm getting tired. Even here, as I rework the script after hours, Beckett pushes back on any changes that aren't directly related to Gabrielle's character, like he can't accept that I might have good ideas for the other characters as well. I've had to recruit Jonah to back me up, and while I'm grateful he's willing, I hate that I need him in the first place.

If I have any goals in life, they're simple. I just want someone to listen to me. To not want to change me. To *choose* me. Even if I know it'll never happen.

Fluffing my hair and checking my phone to make sure my set makeup still looks decent, I consider my words carefully before I talk again. "I know you think I'm lonely, Derek, but I'm fine. I promise."

"I know you're fine. But you should want more than that. You can't keep hiding behind fake relationships forever, Bon."

"What's that? You're breaking up. I'm losing you, Derek."

He rolls his eyes. "Fine. I'll leave it alone. But please don't get heart-broken over this guy when it ends. I hate seeing you unhappy, and this one feels...different. I'm worried about you, Bonnie."

I know I told Hank that I wouldn't get attached, but Derek's speaking my fears out loud. Hank is so different from any of the guys I've dated, and I already admire him so much. It will only get worse as soon as he starts talking about his next book. What if I forget that none of it is real and I let myself hope?

Then I'll end up hurting when Fran decides I need to move on. Or when Hank gets tired of all the pretense. He was very clear when he said our time together would never lead to something real.

I groan, grabbing my phone so I can properly glare at Derek. "Will you stop getting in my head and making me overthink this? I'll be fine. Love your guts!"

I catch one last eyeroll before I hang up on him and stuff my phone into my purse, and then I swing the trailer door open with too much enthusiasm. The door tugs me with it and I go flying, crashing right into Hank.

"Oof!" I'm not sure whether that's me or him grunting in pain, though he gets the worse end of the deal as I land on top of him.

"Sorry!" I scramble to free him, though I'm doing a terrible job and keep slipping right back onto his chest.

Hank grabs my arms, holding me in place as he grimaces. "You okay?"

I laugh, feeling way more awkward than I should be. I've been on a million dates, so I don't know why I'm blushing right now. "I should be the one asking if you're okay," I say.

Hank's eyes flit upward, and I follow his gaze to see Eli standing there, one arm stretched out like he's about to come to my rescue. When I look back down at the man beneath me, I realize he doesn't have his glasses, which means I have an even better view of his brown eyes than I usually do. And they're the warmest eyes I've ever seen. A deep amber with a ring of molten gold around the edges.

Hank clears his throat and slowly pushes me upward until he can free himself and sit up. He finds his glasses in the grass and puts them on, and then he looks at Eli again and holds up his hands, as if trying to prove we're both unharmed.

"We're fine, Eli," I tell the bodyguard. At least physically, anyway. I'm mortified, so I can't say the same for my pride. I smile at Hank, trying to loosen the tension in the air between us. "I promise I'm not usually this clumsy."

"It was the door's fault," Hank replies.

I snort a laugh and scramble to my feet. "Ready to head out?"

He shrugs. "Sure."

Eli drives us into town, and while I'm used to being chauffeured, tonight I feel like I'm in high school and on my first date with Josh Franklin. His dad drove us around and made several comments about how I was such a "pretty young thing" and so nice to say yes to Josh, who had apparently had to work up the courage to ask me. That whole date was a disaster, and not just because Josh was too intimidated to do anything but sit rigidly at my side during the movie. I wasn't even famous then.

While Eli isn't going to make inappropriate comments about my appearance—I asked him his opinion once, and he said I wasn't his type—Hank is all sorts of stiff and stoic in the seat next to me.

He hasn't smiled once since showing up at my trailer, and I'm trying not to read into it. Maybe he's rethinking his decision to agree to this? He signed the contract that Fran sent him, which means technically he can't back out and has to keep this up for the next few weeks at minimum, but I'm sure I could find a loophole. If not me, Liam has a killer lawyer who could help Hank.

Grabbing the door to the teeming ice cream parlor, Hank stands there for a second and takes a few deep breaths. He's gearing himself up for this, though I don't think his internal pep talk is working. Not based on the terrified expression he's failing to hide.

I should probably help the guy out. He is new to the fake relationship scene, after all.

As soon as he pushes the door open, knocking the bell overhead and signaling our arrival, I tuck my arm through his and lean in close as I pull us inside. "I didn't realize going out with me was such a chore," I whisper to him.

Hank immediately turns a bright red. "No, it's not... I'm not worried about being out with you. I'm worried about *them*." He throws a subtle nod to the room at large as we get in line, though he didn't need to gesture. The whole place went silent as soon as he spoke, as if everyone had simultaneously realized who just walked in.

I don't usually go out to public restaurants like this, especially without an entire security team behind me. Most often, it's a private club or Eli has cleared the place before I ever arrive. Even so, I'm used to getting stares if I'm in a place where people can see me. But this feels different.

This feels like an entire town has collectively come for the sole purpose of getting a glimpse of me.

Hank's arm is rigid, just like his clenched jaw, and he is doing his best to keep his eyes locked on the menu. A drop of sweat beads on his temple, further illustrating his discomfort.

This was a bad idea.

"We can go back to the car and let Eli get our ice cream for us," I suggest, though I feel like everyone can hear me now that all the conversation has stopped.

Hank tugs his arm free of mine, and my heart sinks, but then he grabs hold of my hand, all without shifting his gaze. Impressive, considering the gasp that runs through our audience. I guess everyone knows who Hank is. If they didn't before, they certainly do now that he's dating me.

"They'll talk either way," he says, louder than I expected. A few people even flinch from his assessment and turn their attention to their ice cream. "Besides, I want to show you Laketown."

I smile. "I would love to see Laketown with you." And I mean that. Fake relationship or not, Hank intrigues me, and I'm pretty positive that he based the small town in *Frosted Peaks* on Laketown. Coming here was like stepping into the book, and I've only seen a few parts of it so far.

The small family in line in front of us places their order with many backward glances from the parents, and then it's our turn.

I make a show of checking out all the flavors, even though I'll probably go for whatever has the least amount of sugar so my nutritionist doesn't get angry with me. "They all sound so good!"

Hank relaxes as he leans closer to me. "My personal favorite was always the mint chip," he murmurs.

"Was?"

"It's, uh, been a while."

There are so many mysteries I want to solve right now when it comes to Hank and his antisocial tendencies. He's not an awkward guy by any means, and he handles conversations with finesse, for the most part. Everyone in this town seems to think it's some miracle that he's here, and I'm starting to think they're not shocked because I'm his date. At least not entirely. This is mostly about Hank.

But it's not like I can flat out ask him why he's a shut-in, now can I?

"I'll take a single scoop of the mint," I tell the teenager behind the counter.

It seems to take him a second to remember that he's at work, and then he does his best to get my scoop without looking away from me.

Hank clears his throat. "And a scoop of cherry chocolate," he tells the kid, giving him a scowl.

I laugh. "Already feeling possessive?"

Hank doesn't say anything, but the red that rises up his face is enough of an answer.

I nudge his shoulder. "You're pretty cute when you're jealous, Hank McAllister."

Until now, I'd never met anyone who blushed as much as me. It's nice to know I'm not alone in my inability to hide my embarrassment.

By the time we get a seat in the corner, courtesy of Eli intimidating a couple of teens into finishing their ice cream quickly and heading out into the growing darkness, Hank finally seems more at peace with the situation. Though he keeps glancing around as he eats his ice cream, he's way more relaxed than he's been all night. I plan to keep him that way.

"Okay," I say, pointing my spoon at him. "I only have so much time before I have to be in bed, according to my assistant, so if you were serious about brainstorming your book, I suggest we get to it."

Hank's eyebrows rise for a moment, as if he'd forgotten that part. "Right. You sure you want to help?"

"Hank, there is nothing I love more than a good story. Especially a Gabrielle Frost story. *Please* let me help you."

His little smile makes the begging worth it. "Well, if you're serious, you should know that I'm completely stuck."

I've never been much of a creator, so I can only imagine how awful that must feel. The closest I've probably come to writer's block is having to take a poorly written character and figure out how to act as her in a way that audiences would enjoy. But that's probably nothing like this.

Liam was blocked last fall, and it was Kasey who helped him out of it. Maybe what Hank needs is someone cheering him on.

"How far into the book have you gotten?" I ask, placing some ice cream on my tongue. Hank was right about this being delicious, though I wonder why he got the cherry chocolate instead when he said this was his favorite. He doesn't seem all that interested in his cup.

Hank grimaces. "Gabrielle has already solved the murder, and she just has to catch the guy. But I'm only halfway through the book, and I'm not sure what direction things need to go."

"Maybe she solved it too fast," I suggest, smoothing the surface of my ice cream with my spoon. "I mean, crime shows always wait until the last minute to solve the murders because that's how they keep their audience interested."

Frowning, Hank takes a small bite and doesn't say anything until long after he swallows. "Everyone always focuses on solving the crime. Those shows never talk about who is left behind."

There's something about that comment that catches my attention, though I'm not sure what or why. Whatever it is, Hank feels dimmer than he did a moment ago, and I don't like it. Derek gets that way sometimes, when he thinks too hard about the life he might have lived if he didn't get cast as the hero in an indie action film that went viral. He gets stuck on the things he may have missed and forgets that he's doing something he loves.

I don't want that for Hank.

"So you want to tell the story that happens after the dust settles?"

Blinking, Hank looks up and shakes his head. "No. That doesn't make for a compelling story. And it would take the focus off of Gabrielle, which goes against the whole point. The story can't go on without her, and she needs me to keep her alive."

I'm sixty percent certain one of the fluorescent light bulbs has burned out above us because there's an even darker shadow hanging over Hank now. Whatever reason this story is stuck, it is really bugging him.

Digging into my ice cream, I quickly search for a way to get his creative juices flowing. It takes me longer than I'd like to admit. "Is Gabrielle finally going to get with Captain Stacey in this book?"

Hank blinks, his mouth open as he stares at me. "Stacey?"

"Well yeah. You've been teasing those two for four books now, and I'm dying for them to realize they're madly in love with each other!"

"They're not..." He stops, closing his mouth as his eyes narrow. "They're not in love with each other."

I burst into laughter at the indignation in his tone, which is probably not a great thing because it pulls everyone's attention back to us, but I can't help myself. "You're kidding, right?"

His frown deepens. "No."

Oh my goodness, he actually means that. My jaw falls open. "Hank. Stacey is desperately in love with Gabrielle, and everyone knows it."

"I'm sorry, but who wrote the book? Because I'm pretty sure it was me. And he's not in love with anyone. That's the whole backbone of his character."

Where in the world is this sass coming from? I kind of love it. "When was the last time you actually read one of your books, Hank?" I retort. "Because you can ask any one of your fans, and they'll agree with me."

Scoffing, he shakes his head at me but seems to be fighting a smile now. "You're telling me there's a slew of delusional people out there who think *Stacey and Gabrielle* should be a couple? You're all insane."

"There is fan art of the two of them! Fanfiction galore. People even dress up as Stacey and Gabrielle at cons and things because they're just so perfect together."

"Stacey is a hardened cop who is incapable of feeling affection."

"Stacey is guarded. There's a difference."

"He's a side character."

"He's endgame!"

Hank snorts a laugh at the same time a broad smile breaks free, and something shifts in the room. No, something shifts in *him*. Even when I've seen him smile before, it hasn't looked like this. He's always been weighed down and subdued, but this grin seems to bring him to life.

Reaching across the table, I grab hold of his hand and hold his gaze as I lay out my final argument. "Hank, Gabrielle can't be alone forever. Logan was a baddie and that movie critic didn't appreciate her like he should, and sooner or later she has to realize that Captain Stacey has been by her side since the beginning. Not to mention he needs her as much as she needs him after losing his sister in the last book. The poor man is grieving, and he's all alone. No one should have to live like that."

However I expected Hank to respond, it wasn't his smile disappearing. It wasn't with tears. They're barely there, just a glimmer of moisture behind his glasses, and I'm not even sure he notices. I notice. How could I not? I just made a man tear up, and I have no idea why.

Hank lifts his lips in a tiny smile and then picks up my empty ice cream cup. "I should get you home. Er, back to your trailer. Wouldn't want you to get in trouble for being out too late."

It's not even nine o'clock. I'm not sure what I said wrong, but I've clearly offended the man.

I slap on a smile to make sure no one thinks I'm not having a great time with my new boyfriend, and I watch as Hank deftly ignores everyone who watches him cross the parlor to the garbage can and throws our trash away. Hank only ate half his ice cream, and I'm sure at least one person took notice of that. It'll be interesting to see what direction Fran has for us tomorrow after this first excursion in public.

For my part, it didn't go nearly as well as I would have hoped. For one small moment, Hank seemed like a different person. Like he had woken up for the first time in years. Whatever I said, it flipped a switch, and he was back to being quiet and muted. Hank is great no matter how animated—or not animated—he is, but I feel like I got a glimpse of someone...more.

There is more to Hank than the man I know, and I have a feeling he's been hiding for a long time.

Everyone has their comfortable levels of vulnerability, but Hank looked happier when he opened up a moment ago. There was no trace of the anxiety and tension he always seems to have, and I'm almost desperate to pry him open again and let that other Hank free.

With how wary his expression is as he returns to our booth, he seems to realize the same thing. And he's terrified. Still, he holds out his hand to me and smiles when I slip my fingers into his. "Ready?" he asks gently.

"You're still coming to set tomorrow, right?" We never established that, but I'm desperate to ensure this relationship doesn't die before it starts. If not for my sake, for Hank's.

Though Hank blinks in surprise, he recovers quickly and nods. "Of course I am." Then he surprises me—and everyone else in the packed parlor, for some reason—with a kiss on the cheek that leaves my heart beating faster.

CE CREAM

CHAPTER TEN

HANK

I WAKE IN A cold sweat, angelic laughter echoing in my head. I didn't mean to fall asleep in the broken armchair—I hadn't intended to sit in it in the first place—and it feels like the seat is sucking me in, making it impossible to get up. My dream is already slipping from my consciousness, but my heart pounds like I'm still running.

Chasing something I can never catch.

I almost caught her this time, but then she faded into the darkness, laughing at me. I've been having this dream for four years, but this time it felt...real.

I glance at my watch and groan. It's only a quarter after two, which means I only slept for about an hour. I already know I won't be able to fall asleep after dreaming about Shelby, so I might as well go back to work.

My novel is right where I left it, otherwise known as the same page I've been stuck on all week. I'd really hoped Bonnie would have found a good way for me to move things along, but then I went and ended things way too early. I wouldn't be surprised if I have an angry publicist to deal with when I show up on the set later today. Or even an angry Bonnie.

I told her I could handle everything the relationship entailed, but I never anticipated she would focus so much on Captain Stacey.

John Stacey was the character I never meant to create. He was simply a background authority figure, a way to keep Gabrielle from going too far outside the bounds of the law. But with each book, he always seemed to have something more to say, and then the victim in the third book ended up being his sister. I tried to change it multiple times, but the story refused to cooperate if I deviated from that outcome.

And then Bonnie went and told me about how people thought Stacey and Gabrielle should end up together, and I haven't been able to think about anything else since.

Okay, it's been less than six hours since she mentioned it, but still. The idea is in my head now, and I'm not sure it's going to go away. She was so certain...

I scroll up a few pages to remind myself of the scene—I've been stuck here for days, so it's not like I've forgotten—and then I pull my keyboard closer, considering what this scene would look like if Stacey hadn't come to the hospital just to check on Gabrielle's health after her almost-suffocation. As I have it now, he came as her boss and nothing more, but maybe... My books so far have been limited to Gabrielle's perspective, but I wonder what Stacey would be thinking right now.

I start typing.

After his years on the force, John Stacey had always considered himself a hardened man. He had seen too much violence to believe there was still good in the world beyond basic human kindness, and not everyone possessed even that much. What was the point of letting himself feel when he knew it would only lead to heartache?

But as he stood outside Frost's room, telling himself that he was only there for her protection, something inside him ached with a feeling he hadn't allowed himself in years.

"I know you're lurking out there, Captain." Frost's voice was quiet, strained. Understandable, given what she had endured less than an hour ago. It tugged Stacey to the door, and he couldn't find the will to ignore it.

Someone had tried to strangle her at her own desk, but Frost still managed a smile as soon as she saw him in the doorway. She looked awful and beautiful all at the same time.

Stacey shifted his weight. Beautiful. *He shouldn't be thinking that. She was one of his detectives—his best detective—and that was only one reason why he couldn't be looking at her the way he was right now. There were so many others, reasons he couldn't find the will to name.*

Frost chuckled, wincing as soon as she did. "Do I really look that bad?"

Stacey hadn't had time to go through the security footage from the precinct yet, but he already knew it had been a brutal fight. He could see it in every cut and contusion. Frost had been caught unawares, but she would have gone down fighting even without the phone cord snapping and ultimately saving her life. She had always been a fighter, and yet she still saw good in the world.

"How do you do it?" he asked, his voice coming out just as ragged as hers.

She didn't seem to understand. "Do what? Lose so badly?"

"You're alive. That's a win in my book."

"Could you..." She winced, shutting her eyes. "Could you come inside? I don't think I can talk loud for long."

Stacey couldn't bring himself to move at first. Keeping his distance had always been the best strategy, with anyone he met. It was the very reason he had fought so hard to become captain. The authority of his position put an invisible barrier between him and anyone he encountered, and that barrier was the only thing that made it possible for him to remain alone.

But this was Frost. And he'd almost lost her.

Doing a quick sweep of the hallway beyond the room, Stacey stiffly stepped inside and closed the door behind him, cutting off the sounds of the relatively quiet hospital. It felt safer, somehow, though he wasn't sure if the safety was for him or her. Each of his footfalls was heavy as he slowly made his way to the bed, and he could feel Frost's eyes on him as he approached.

He lowered himself into the chair that had only recently been occupied by Frost's artist friend, the loud one who sometimes did witness sketches for the precinct. The only reason Stacey tolerated her was because she made Frost smile, which was problematic in itself. He shouldn't care whether Frost smiled as long as she did her job, and yet...

He sighed. All of this had been so much easier when he could pretend he was at the hospital as police protection, but now that it was just the two of them alone, he couldn't bring himself to look at her. He feared if he did, something in him might break.

The strongest stones are the hardest to break. *It was the mantra he had been telling himself for years, and he wasn't ready to let it go. If he didn't let himself feel, he couldn't get hurt.*

"We're going to find the man who did this to you," he said, keeping his eyes on the worn linoleum beneath his feet. He felt something crack inside him at the same time his voice broke as he forced himself to keep talking. Keep pretending this was a normal case. That he wasn't falling apart. "Hansen is going over the footage, and O'Hare and Bowyer are sweeping for any witnesses. It won't be long before—"

"John." Frost's hand found his, her battered fingers wrapping around his.

It was as much his name on her tongue as it was her touch that snapped his tenuous hold on his emotions. His careful calm finally broke, almost violently, and he hunched in on himself as the pain broke free. "I almost lost you, Gabby." And he wouldn't have survived if he had.

I stop when I can no longer see my screen, though I don't know if it's the lack of vision or the shock of knowing that I'm crying for the first time in four years that halts my progress. I probably shouldn't be surprised, given how this series started, but I hadn't realized until now that Captain Stacey is me.

I can already hear what June would say: "No duh, Einstein." She's probably even tried to tell me as much during one of our brainstorming sessions, but why would I listen? I am way too good at pretending my life is perfectly fine the way it is despite knowing deep down that I should have been in therapy from the beginning.

He needs her as much as she needs him. That's what Bonnie said about Captain Stacey on our date last night. Our *date*. Which I botched because I let her get in my head. Bonnie's not even the type of person to get inside someone's head; I can't imagine her being anything but selfless and sweet. Then again, I know next to nothing about her because, idiot that I am, I haven't asked.

Some boyfriend I am.

Wiping my eyes dry, I plug in the internet router and wait for my computer to connect, and then I pull up a search engine. I know I'm going to hate this, but I type in my name anyway, holding my breath as it loads.

The first few results are pictures from the other day, when we were standing outside her trailer. Bonnie is practically glowing as she smiles at me, and even I look relatively happy beside her. *Relatively* being the key word there.

I scroll down a bit to find some pictures from the ice cream parlor, and I know I messed up even before I read the headline.

Small Town, Small Feelings: Is Bonnie Ready to Move On?

I look miserable in these photos. And Bonnie may be smiling, but not even the actress could fully pretend she was having a good time last night. Basically, if I didn't know better, I would agree with the person who wrote the article that it looks like we're already calling it quits, and that's a problem.

This relationship is supposed to last until Bonnie's done filming, and there were parts of the contract I signed that suggested an even longer term in order to continue promoting the movie until it is released in theaters in the fall. If I can't even last a week, Bonnie is doomed.

Is that really the kind of man I want to be?

I push myself out of my chair and start pacing, accidentally glancing at the umbrella in the corner even though it's currently hiding beneath one of my coats because I couldn't stop looking at it. Maybe it's time I snap out of this isolated life I've been living for the last four years.

That's a long time to grieve.

My pacing stops in the middle of the room as a wave of anxiety rolls over me. "Maybe I should ease into things," I mutter out loud, as if that might help convince me.

Phantom laughter, an echo from my dream, makes me flinch and turn on another light. I don't believe in ghosts, but hearing laughter at three in the morning isn't exactly a calming experience. I know it's all in my head, but...

My eyes travel around my front room, taking in the tiny space and reminding me how alone I am out here. If it wasn't the middle of the night, I would probably call June just to hear another voice. But I don't have a lot of options right now.

Flipping on the porch light, I grab a jacket and tug it on as I head outside.

The trees that surround my house sway in the breeze, which helps the world feel less silent, but it's too dark for me to see anything, so that's creepy. I try to picture the area to ground myself in the moment. Most of the trees are evergreens, but there are a good number of aspens and oaks to brighten up the landscape in the fall. We'll be getting wildflowers in a month or two, though they won't be at their most colorful until July, and we got a pretty decent snowpack this winter so the taller peaks to the west will still be white until July.

I've always loved this place, since the day I bought the house seven years ago as a vacation home.

I just never thought I would call it *home*.

Settling myself on the porch with my back against the house, I look up and smile when I find Heather finishing up a new web in the corner. The spider first appeared a few months ago, and her circular webs really are breathtaking. "You've outdone yourself this time, Heather," I tell her. "You've got a long way to go before you reach Charlotte's talent, but you're getting there."

I'm pretty sure talking to a spider is a sure sign of madness, but I need to talk to *someone*, so I'm working with what I've got.

"Let me lay it all out for you," I say, crossing one foot over the other and getting myself comfortable in case this turns out to be a long chat. "I am in a manufactured relationship with Bonnie Aiken, one of the most beautiful women I've ever seen. She's an actress, and a good one, and she's currently playing the role of Gabrielle Frost. You know, the detective in all my books? Not sure if you've read those or not—not judging if you haven't. They're not as good as everyone seems to think."

Yeah, I've lost my mind, but already the tightness in my chest is easing. So I keep talking.

"The thing is, I'm not sure I remember how to be in a relationship. Even a real one. Not since..." I take a deep breath. I need to get this out, and Heather is the only person...spider...who isn't going to judge me. Even if she is, she'll have no way to tell me as much unless she learns how to spell.

"I was married once," I tell her, and the words seem to tug something loose inside me, leaving me feeling unsteady. Unmoored. "Hard to believe, I know. What kind of crazy person would want to be with a loner like me? Well, Shelby was...she was definitely crazy. In her own way. The best way. And I wasn't always like this. Especially not with her.

"I'm not sure I even remember the old Hank," I admit. "I think... I think he died when Shelby did."

I'm probably imagining it, but I'm pretty sure Heather shifts in her web, like she's getting closer so she can hear me better.

"Yeah," I say with a sigh. "She died. Four years ago. We used to live in Denver—me in a big city, I know—and she left for work one morning. Never made it home."

I breathe in slowly, letting those words sink in. This really isn't the kind of conversation I should be having with a spider, and I'm not sure if there's anything else I can say on the Shelby front. What happened to Shelby isn't the reason I came out here to talk to Heather. I came out here because it feels like the world is tilting on its axis and I've forgotten how to balance.

"See, that's why it's hard to imagine myself dating someone, Heather. But I gave my word to Bonnie—signed a contract too—and all I've managed to do so far is fail. What if I can't help her? She needs me to boost her public image, but I'm worried I'm only going to make it worse."

Heather wiggles her legs.

"I don't know what that means, but I appreciate you trying to help. I think... What if I'm too far gone to be of any use to anyone?"

When I think about the person I have become over the last four years, it almost feels like I don't actually exist. I've been living in a shadow, simply surviving. I'm empty, as much of a ghost as the laughter from my dream, and I'm not sure how I'm supposed to come back from that.

How does anyone live again after their whole world is ripped away?

A moth suddenly flies in front of my face, and I shriek, diving away from it as if that would actually save me from the bug. Thankfully, it doesn't seem very interested in bothering me and flutters up toward the light. Sprawled on the porch, I hold my breath as I watch the moth get closer and closer to the large web, wondering if I'm about to witness a gruesome murder.

Sure enough, the moth gets tangled up in the web, and though it puts up a valiant fight to free itself, Heather descends with lightning speed and starts doing her thing, wrapping it up until it stops squirming.

My stomach churns—I really didn't need that visual tonight of all nights—but I can't bring myself to look away.

"Look what it did to your web," I murmur as soon as I'm sure I won't vomit into the bushes. There's a giant tear in it where the moth struggled, and Heather just barely finished making it look so nice. She's going to have to repair it after she's done eating. "Why go to all that trouble of fixing it if it's just going to be broken every time you catch your next meal? All that work..."

I groan, dropping onto my back and shutting my eyes tight. "Seriously?" I ask the universe at large. I already feel like I'm losing my mind by talking to a spider; I don't need a life lesson out of tonight's conversation too.

Still, maybe the universe is on to something. I've spent the last four years protecting myself from pain, pretending I'm happy living alone and avoiding any deep attachments. Yeah, Heather is going to have to rebuild her web because of that moth, but that moth is going to keep her alive for a long time. She probably doesn't care about all the work in front of her because she couldn't have gotten such a good meal if she didn't put in the effort before.

I've been hiding in a corner for so long, waiting for things to feel okay again. But how am I supposed to catch anything good if I don't accept that life comes with risks? If I don't put in some effort to turn my life into something more than simply surviving?

I lie on the porch with Heather until the sun pokes up over the tops of the trees, the whole time wondering if I can relearn how to build my own web. I only know one thing for sure: I need to start with Bonnie and fix the holes I created last night.

CHAPTER ELEVEN

BONNIE

I WAS LOOKING FORWARD to harness day. With most of my career being in romantic comedies and generally lighthearted movies thus far, I've never had the chance to do anything remotely close to a real stunt, and Derek always talks about how much he loves doing his own stunts because it makes him feel that much more connected to his character and what's happening in the scene. So today was going to be one of the fun days. Maybe even a boost to my career.

"Don't worry, Bonnie!" my assistant, Trevor, shouts up to me. "We'll get you down from there in no time!"

"Take your time!" I shout back. Not sure I necessarily mean that, though.

We're shouting because something went wrong with the rig. I was supposed to jump from one roof to the next after an explosion, but when we did the first take, the mechanism went haywire and pulled me all the way up to the top of the crane holding me in the air, leaving me dangling forty feet above the ground. And apparently no one can figure out how to get me down.

"At least I'm not afraid of heights," I mutter to myself. Derek saw to that, since he's a bit of an adrenaline junky and convinced me to go skydiving *and* bungee jumping with him.

Okay, so maybe I'm still a little afraid of heights, and this harness is *so* not comfortable.

I don't know what happened. I watched my stunt double do this half a dozen times this morning, and it worked perfectly every time. She ran across the roof, and when she got the cue for the explosion, she leapt over the gap between the buildings and glided smoothly to the other side. Every. Single. Time.

My friends are going to find this hilarious, so I'm going to do my best to never let them find out.

At least I've got a cool view of Laketown, which is seriously tiny. I knew the main street was small, but I figured there would be a lot of streets stretching out beyond the heart of the town. I thought it would be sort of like Lake Tahoe, but honestly I don't even know where the lake is. I'll figure it out eventually, I suppose, though it's not like I'm granted a lot of free time. Maybe I can convince Hank to take me.

Ha! After last night, I'm pretty sure Hank is going to be begging for me to get him in touch with Liam's lawyer so he can get out of the contract he signed.

"Hey, Bonnie?" Trevor waves his arm to get my attention again, but he has a megaphone now. He must have borrowed it from Beckett. "We're going to try to toss you a walkie talkie, okay?"

My coordination skills are minimal at best, but I'll welcome any chance at having a conversation while I wait. Especially because I'm pretty sure this means I'm going to be up here for a while.

It's my stunt double, Anne, who comes into the alley beneath me. She seems to be judging the distance and prepping for the toss. What happens if I don't catch it? It'll go flying back down, and no one will want to snatch it out of the air when it's going that fast. It'll smash to pieces!

Which means we've only got one shot.

"No pressure," I tell myself, which is the universal phrase to mean *all the pressure.*

"Ready?" Trevor asks on the megaphone.

I give both him and Anne a thumbs up.

Anne bends down and then swings her arms up, and the little radio shoots upwards. I'm tempted to grab it as it comes up, but my gut tells me to wait. Miraculously, it reaches the top of its parabolic peak right in front of my face, and all I have to do is reach out and wrap my fingers around it.

The little crowd on the ground cheers, and I breathe a sigh of relief.

Pushing the talk button, I say, "Way to go, Anne. That was a perfect throw."

It's a male voice that responds. "You okay up there, Bonnie?"

My heart, which was calming down after my catch, jumps right back into overdrive. "Hank?"

Honestly, I wasn't sure if he was actually going to show up after the awkwardness of last night.

"I'm glad you're here," I tell Hank, and I really mean that.

Where is he, anyway? I'm not so high that I shouldn't be able to see him, but none of the people down below look like they could be him.

"Look up," Hank says.

Look up where? I look at the crane behind me, wondering if I might find a firefighter coming to rescue me.

"No," Hank says, laughter in his voice. "Across the street, on top of the general store."

I gasp as soon as I see him sitting on the roof, legs dangling off the edge. Even from here, I can see his adorable little smile, and I nearly drop the walkie talkie at the sight of it. No way am I going to lose this little lifeline, so I adjust my hold and make sure my grip is tight before I speak into it.

"What are you doing up there?"

He shrugs. "When I got to set a few minutes ago, they told me what happened, and I wanted to make sure you weren't alone up there. June provided the walkie talkies."

"That's surprising."

"Why?"

"I'm pretty sure June doesn't like me."

"She's just protective." Hank looks down at the sidewalk below him, where June is in conversation with Jonah, of all people. Jonah looks happy, but June keeps looking up at Hank.

I have no reason to be jealous of whatever relationship she has with Hank, but I am. June may not be dating Hank, but she's close enough to him that she wants to protect him. That probably means she knows a lot of his secrets. The things I want to know.

I hug the walkie talkie a bit closer as I swing my legs to keep my circulation flowing. "I was going to blow you away with my awesomeness today," I tell him. "That clearly didn't happen."

"I don't know. You still seem pretty awesome. You'd never catch me in a harness like that."

"Are you afraid of heights?" I would hope not, given the way he's sitting on the edge of a building right now. It's not a tall building, but he's still twenty feet up.

Hank chuckles. Not into the walkie talkie, but I almost think I can hear it from here. He lifts the radio, looking more at ease than I've ever seen him. "I didn't like heights until I did the Mürren via ferrata in Switzerland and found myself walking on the side of a cliff wall."

"Oh, I've heard of that!" I'm pretty sure Derek has been there. He's been everywhere, though, so it's not surprising. "I didn't really peg you as the adventurous type," I tell Hank.

Grinning, he shakes his head. "I'm not anymore. But I used to be."

"What changed?"

"A lot of things."

I shouldn't be disappointed that his answer is so vague, but I am. For a second there, I thought maybe he would finally open up again, but I guess I shouldn't push him right now. Especially because he's the only thing between me and freaking out about being stuck up here. He makes for a good distraction, and I'm not going to risk losing that by making him uncomfortable.

We both push the talk button at the same time. I laugh and try to tell him to go first, but I'm pretty sure he tries to tell me the same thing at the same time and we both laugh again.

I tuck my radio against my chest to show him that I'm happy to listen.

He smiles and slowly lifts the walkie talkie to his mouth. "I used to go on adventures with my wife before she was murdered four years ago."

I drop my walkie talkie.

It sails in a smooth line to the ground and shatters when it hits the pavement. And when I meet Hank's gaze and see the truth of his words in his sad expression, I'm pretty sure my heart shatters too.

It takes twenty more minutes to get the crane working again, and another twenty to get me down to the ground because no one is willing to take a chance with my safety. I'm not mad about that. What I *am* mad about is my stupid hand letting go of the only means I had to talk to Hank, because heaven knows the man wasn't about to grab a megaphone and explain himself in front of the entire film crew.

Nope. We both just sat there, staring at each other for almost half an hour without any words between us. Plenty of thoughts, though. Oh boy, do I have thoughts.

As soon as my feet are on the ground and I'm free of the harness, I hunt for Hank. He disappeared from the roof about ten minutes ago, while I was focused on the people getting me down, and if he left after a bombshell like that, so help me…

"Bonnie!" Trevor hurries up to me and throws his arms around my shoulders. He's not generally an affectionate guy, but I'm guessing he saw his career flash before his eyes and was frightened by the prospect of having to find someone else to work for.

"Where's Hank?" I ask him.

He frowns. "Hank?"

"You know, my *boyfriend*." I practically push Trevor aside so I can start searching the crowd of people who all want to tell me how glad they are that I made it down to the ground. Technically, Trevor hasn't met Hank yet, which is a bit of an oversight on my part, but everything about this relationship has been a bit of a mess from the start so that's a minor detail.

"Bonnie!" Hank's voice, while not as frantic as Trevor's, cuts through the crowd easily.

Relief hits me so hard that I almost start crying. What in the world? Ignoring my strangely emotional reaction to learning he didn't leave me, I hurry toward Hank's voice and find him doing the same from the other side of the street, turning this into a rather epic sort of reunion that would make for a darling scene in a romantic movie.

I slow down when we reach each other. Hank does not. He crashes into me, arms wrapping around me in a tight embrace that feels a hundred times more secure than the harness I just escaped.

"You're okay," he breathes. One of his hands moves to the back of my head, holding me close. "I got worried for a second there at the end."

I'm not really sure how to react right now. For one thing, he's holding me in a way he hasn't held me before, and I have never been this comfortable in a man's arms before. Let me repeat that: NEVER. Derek might be built like a superhero, but I was never desperate to stay in his hold for the rest of my life. Not like this.

For another, I'm still reeling over Hank's little—nay, enormous—revelation while I was in the harness, and I don't know how I'm supposed to demand that he explain himself.

"You know," I say because I don't know what else to say, "it's too bad there probably aren't any paparazzi here right now to chronicle this moment."

Hank's arms tighten around me, the rest of his body going tense. "Well…"

I tilt my head back to look at him. "What?"

"I may have asked June to film this for us."

Oh. Okay, so none of this is real. He's just really good at hugging. And I shouldn't be this good at being disappointed.

I shift my gaze away from him before he notices that disappointment, watching the way Jonah is still focused on June despite her phone pointed in our direction. He seems to find something about her interesting, though she isn't matching his energy. At all.

Hank tucks some hair behind my ear, pulling my attention back to him as his eyes travel my face. "I'm sorry," he says, his words soft and low. "About last night. I told you I could make this all work, and I clearly failed. But I want to do better."

As his thumb brushes my cheek, a blush blooms to life across my face. "You're already doing better," I breathe, hating that I'm this affected right now. I've always been so good at distancing myself from the emotions of a relationship, and yet I can't seem to tamp down my interest with Hank. If he was anyone else, this would be easy, but there's something about this man that keeps pulling me in.

Hank smiles, and one of his arms snakes around my waist to pull me flush against him once more. "And I'm sorry for what I said when you were stuck up there. I shouldn't have dropped that on you like that, but I thought it would be easier to get it out if I didn't overthink it."

"I get that. I really do. But if you think this is the end of that conversation, then you—"

He presses his thumb to my lips, shutting me up easily. "It's not. If we're going to spend all this time together over the next few weeks, I want you to understand why I am the way I am. But not here." His eyes dart to the side, where half a dozen crewmembers are unabashedly watching us.

I have to grab his hand to free my mouth, and I don't especially mind the chance to hold his fingers. Despite our audience, I'm perfectly happy where I am right now, and he doesn't seem too bothered either. Maybe we should give them all a show and see what sort of chemistry we're working with. Unless I'm mistaken, Hank seems okay with the idea of testing out a kiss as his eyes trace the features of my face.

"Miss Aiken! We need you in the med tent." Gayle the nurse appears at our side, her eyes darting between us with interest. "We need to make sure you didn't get any injuries while you were up there."

I don't bother holding back my groan. "I'm fine."

"Liability," Boyd the nurse replies, showing up on our other side, as if he thinks I need to be cornered before I'll comply. "We are legally obligated to give you a full check before we can let you get back to, uh, work." His eyes rove from Hank's head to his toes, like he's sizing my boyfriend up to see if he fits the requirements for dating me. Then he grunts and holds out his arm to me. "Shall we?"

I glance at Gayle, who looks ready to strongarm me rather than taking Boyd's gentle approach.

I groan. "Fine. Hank, I'll see you later?" I really should have gotten his phone number at some point so we can coordinate our appearances more easily; I'll have to ask Trevor to grab it from him, since I can't ask my boyfriend himself. That would be a great way for people to start questioning our relationship.

Hank reluctantly releases me and nods. "I'm glad you're safe, Bon," he says, and there's genuine concern in his eyes.

I might like that a little too much.

Deciding to be daring, I lean in and brush a kiss against the corner of his mouth. I don't linger, as much as I want to, but tuck my arm through Boyd's, and I feel Hank's eyes on me until I disappear into the med tent.

CHAPTER TWELVE

HANK

I SHOULD PROBABLY GET a cellphone. I told Trevor, Bonnie's assistant, that I didn't have one when he said he would text me Bonnie's number, and the poor kid stared at me like I was speaking a foreign language. I could have given him the number to my landline, but that almost feels worse than not having a phone to begin with.

I got rid of my cell when I left Denver because there was no one I wanted to get in touch with. All of my friends were Shelby's friends, and I never had any family to stay connected to except for those on her side. Cutting myself off from my old life felt like the easiest way to survive after she died.

For the first time in four years, I'm thinking about getting a phone again, which is why I'm standing in front of the general store on Main

Street while filming continues down the road. I haven't worked up the courage to go inside, but I'm debating. That's new for me.

Except, right now I'm pretty sure I'm losing the debate, and my hands are on my keys, ready for when I make a run for it.

That's how June finds me, hyperventilating in front of the general store with my fist wrapped around my keychain.

"You doing okay, Hank?" A pair of hands take hold of my shoulders. "Maybe you should sit down." She directs me to a bench and forces me to sit, and then she crouches in front of me, her face twisted in sympathy and frustration.

Across the street, a few Laketownians are staring at me like they've seen Bigfoot. They've probably been watching me for longer than I'd care to know, and before long the whole town will be talking about how I'm out and about yet again.

I rub my face, sliding my hands underneath my glasses to cover my eyes. "I hate small towns."

"You and me both."

"Why do you live here?"

"Why do you?"

She already knows the answer to that question, just like I know why *she's* here. Laketown is a great place to escape reality and relationships that weren't meant to last. June left an abusive fiancé; I left a ghost.

I sigh, dropping my hands. "I told Bonnie about Shelby. Up on the roof."

June looks like I just slapped her. "You did what?"

Nodding, I sit up and lean against the back of the bench. I'm exhausted. I shouldn't have chosen to do all this on a day when I didn't get any sleep, but I was worried I would chicken out. "I didn't get a chance to explain it all, but I told her my wife was killed."

That's not what I told her. I told her that Shelby was *murdered*, which is the truth but sounds a whole lot more horrific.

I press a hand to my chest and take a deep breath. "I don't know why I told her," I continue, since June is still too stunned to speak. "I mean, I do, but I don't have a good reason to want to open up to her. It's not like our..." I shut my mouth before I say something about the nature of our relationship that someone might overhear. "I think I'm just tired of living under a shadow, and I wanted Bonnie to know why I am the way I am."

"Hank, that's huge." June moves from the sidewalk to the bench next to me. I know she wants to take my hand because that's her default gesture, but she's smart enough to know we're being watched. The internet would love to think I'm cheating on my famous girlfriend with a small-town nobody. Hey, maybe being the victim would give Bonnie a huge boost and I would be able to go back to my lonely life of solitude.

But I don't want that. It's just like I said to June the day we talked to Fran about the contract. My life isn't much of a life. Solitude doesn't fit right anymore, as evidenced by my middle-of-the-night conversation with an orbweaver. The last four years have been a slow descent into madness, and it's time I stop my downward spiral before I've gone too far to be saved.

I look around to make sure no one is close enough to eavesdrop on our conversation, and I drop my voice just in case. "I've spent the last four years hiding from my past, June. That's not something I can just get over, as much as I want to."

"I know that. But I also know you're a lot stronger than you think you are. And while I don't like this thing you have going on with Bonnie, I do like that she's sparked this change in you, Hank. I mean it when I say this is a huge step, but you have to remember that it's just steps. Not one giant leap. How did she respond when you told her?"

I grimace. "She didn't. I mean, she didn't really get a chance, and now she's filming again so I'll have to wait until they're done for the day, whenever that is. I was thinking I might..." I pause. As soon as I say it out loud, I'll have to do it. "I was thinking I might get a phone to make it easier on her."

June's eyebrows fly high, and she glances at the general store behind us. "Like, a *cellphone* phone? Really?"

"Steps, right?" I say. My eyes catch on Jonah, who is walking closer while chatting with his assistant. I should probably watch what I say unless I want the whole world to know my issues. "And don't think you're getting my phone number. I'm worried you'll stop bringing my groceries if you can talk to me whenever you want."

Chuckling, June shakes her head and gets to her feet right as Jonah walks past.

"You'd better not stand me up, Harper," the actor says, pointing at her.

June narrows her eyes, but her smile contradicts any true irritation. "I don't back down from a challenge, James."

He grins, clearly pleased by that response. "Neither do I." Winking, he continues onward.

As soon as he's out of earshot, June turns to me with a scowl and points a finger at me, though she's a good deal more threatening than Jonah was with the gesture. "Not a word."

I'm more likely to laugh than anything, and I am so glad for this change of subject. "I wasn't going to—"

"He asked me out to lunch, and how could I say no to something like that?"

Pursing my lips, I lift my shoulders in an exaggerated shrug. I don't think I've ever seen June blush, but she's bright red right now. "What happened to your dating ban?"

She groans. "It's one date. That's it. Go get your phone, and don't worry about giving me your number because you must think I have a pretty high opinion of you if you think I would actually call you,

McAllister." She pats my shoulder. "Let me know if you need anything, Hank."

"Thanks."

"And good luck. I hope Bonnie listens to you."

I hope so too. June's one of the few people who know the full story with Shelby, mostly because she did a bunch of research on her own and then forced me to fill in the blanks. She doesn't give me pitying looks because she knows that only makes it all worse. Hopefully Bonnie can understand that I don't want pity when it comes to Shelby. I don't want people thinking I've overreacted to her death. I just want Bonnie to hear me and recognize my entire life changed when I lost the love of my life.

And I can never go back to who I was.

It takes two hours to buy a phone and get it activated, mostly because Steven, the guy who runs the general store, had no idea how to get me on a plan because everyone in Laketown has always driven to the nearest city, Sun City, to get their phones over the years. But he was eager to help make all the phone calls and get it figured out for me after I promised to name a character after him in my next book. He didn't care if the character ends up dead as long as his name is in there, so I happily accepted his offer. Mostly so I wouldn't have to be the one on the phone.

Strange how much a person can get out of the habit of something. I used to talk to large groups of people on a daily basis. Now I get anxious thinking about making a call to get my barely smart phone to work.

I would have gone for a non-smart variety of phone if Steven had had one. But he didn't. Apparently the world doesn't believe in holding on to the basics anymore.

As I step back out onto the street, feeling weirdly connected to civilization, I am torn about what to do now. Part of me wants to toss the phone in the trash and pretend I never took this step, and the other part of me wants to hunt down Trevor and tell him that I fixed my phone problem and can now text Bonnie.

That's the part that wins out. The Bonnie part. I'm terrified to continue our conversation, but June was right about taking steps. And it feels a whole lot easier now that I've taken the first one.

Filming is still underway when I reach the other end of Main, so I linger at the back of the set and try to figure out which part they're filming now. I'm pretty sure they don't film in order so they can efficiently use their time and space, so it could be anything, and I'm not in a great spot to see what's going on. Where is Bonnie?

"Psst. Hank."

I jump, even though the whisper was quiet, and turn to see Trevor waving at me from behind a small white trailer. Since he seems to be gesturing for me to follow him, I duck behind the couple of people watching with me and hurry over to him.

"Bonnie's over here," Trevor whispers, almost inaudibly. I would imagine those microphones they use pick up on a lot of sound, so I keep my steps light.

He takes me around a computer setup that seems to be where Beckett is watching the footage as they roll, and then we stop at the edge of a rack of clothing.

From here, I have a much better view of Bonnie and Jonah as they walk down the sidewalk and talk while the camera moves ahead of them. Bonnie's in Gabrielle's signature leather jacket and combat boots, her hair up in a pencil bun, and it's still surreal to see her like that. She fits the character so well, even if she's nothing like Gabrielle in real life.

"I'm just saying it's strange that the father won't talk to you," Jonah says, his voice calm. "Don't you think that's suspicious?"

Bonnie scoffs. "Oh, and when did you become an expert in murder investigations? I thought you worked in finance."

Jonah shrugs, but there's something in his body language that is far from calm. How he manages to *look* frustrated without *sounding* frustrated is impressive. It makes him look unsettling in the most subtle way. "I do work in finance," he says, "but I'm also good with people. And I think he's hiding something."

"I think he was just told that his daughter is dead and he doesn't know how to process that." Bonnie stops, putting her hands in her jacket pockets and looking around at the extras who walk past her. "Look, Logan, I know you want to help, but I really can't have you poking around my case."

Jonah clenches his jaw. "Someone tried to kill you two days ago, Gabby. Pardon me for being nervous about letting you wander around when there's a killer on the loose."

A little smile makes its way onto Bonnie's lips, more smirky than anything I've seen on her before. "Are you saying you're worried about me, Logan Banks?"

Jonah steps in closer, his frustration quickly shifting into desire as he looks down at her. "I might be saying that."

"You only met me two days ago."

"What can I say? You made an impression when you hit my car."

"I think your car hit *me*, technically."

Jonah goes in for a kiss, but Bonnie presses a hand to his chest and holds him back. "Easy, tiger. I've got work to do."

"It can wait an hour, can't it?"

Bonnie bites her lip, her smile growing as she slowly lifts up on her toes.

An arm nudges me, making me jump. Trevor widens his eyes. "It's not real," he mouths.

"I know that," I mouth back, but I realize how much I'd been frowning when my eyebrows relax.

I turn back to the set as Bonnie brushes a kiss against Jonah's cheek and smirks at him when he groans. "I'll see you tonight," she tells him and continues walking, leaving him standing there with an expression that is so hard to read that I wonder what's going through his head right now.

I should know the answer to that, but I don't because this scene is so different from how it was in the book. That doesn't mean it's bad. It just means I don't know what to expect.

"And cut!" Beckett shouts, sparking the crew into life as everyone hops forward to reset everything while he turns to the monitor next to his chair to replay the footage.

"Hank!" Bonnie skips over to me, her smile bright and warm and so different from the look she was just giving Jonah. "I didn't think you would be back here today."

I grab her hands, though I'm not sure why. "You were amazing."

She rolls her eyes. "That wasn't even a difficult scene, and the lines were so easy. Anyone could act that."

But I don't think anyone could make me jealous like she just did. I'm not even dating her, and I didn't want to watch her flirt with Jonah like that.

Clearing my throat, I nod toward Jonah, who is studying the script. "He's surprisingly good."

"I know, right?" Bonnie's eyes go wide. "Ever since he found out Logan's real motivation, he's been killing that part. That's a good thing," she adds when I frown. "It means this movie might not suck after all."

"I don't think it was ever going to suck. Not with you in it." I love the way she blushes, even though I blush right along with her. Apparently *I'm* getting flirty now, though I can already tell I've maxed out my non-awkward lines. "Uh, I got myself a phone, by the way. So we can plan things more easily." I pull it out of my pocket to show her, realizing there's still the protective cover over the screen. I peel it off and stuff the sticker in my pocket.

Bonnie lifts an eyebrow. "Did you not have a phone before?"

I shrug.

"Well, I'm glad you have one now. Hopefully it wasn't expensive, though you could totally send my team an invoice and we could—"

"Bonnie." I find myself mirroring Jonah's movements in the scene, stepping closer to her and giving her a smile. "I can pay for my own phone. Just know that you're going to be the only person who has my number because I'm not all that fond of people."

She bites her lip. "I've noticed that. You must like me if I get to have it."

"I guess I like you a little."

"Oh. My. Goodness." Trevor interrupts our moment, eyes bouncing between the two of us. "You guys are totes adorbs. But Bonnie, you're needed for the next take. I'll handle the phone stuff."

Bonnie sighs, but her smile speaks louder than her apparent frustration with being taken away. "It's good to have you here, Hank. Talk tonight?"

I nod, watching her walk away. Tonight. I can do that.

Right?

Hollywood Hot Scoop

Benrie's Tearful Reunion after Accident on *Frosted Peaks* Set

Don't worry your pretty little heads, Scoopers. Bonnie is alive and well on the set of this year's most anticipated movie, and we here at *Hot Scoop* can't be mad about our daily dose of Benrie. After a mechanical malfunction that left our beloved Bonnie stranded a hundred feet in the air, Henry came to her rescue by scaling a building to get to her. Derek who? We've got a true hero on our hands! And once they were both safely on the ground, our new favorite couple were quick to make up after last night's disagreement.

I don't think we'll be seeing any more tension between these two, unless you count the good stuff. I don't know about you, but I want to find myself a Henry to look at me like that. Talk about swoon! That's a man in love, no doubt about it.

Be sure to subscribe so you don't miss any future Benrie features. Based on that jealous look in his eyes, Henry might be out for blood when it comes to Bonnie's heartthrob costar, Jonah. Seems the mystery writer isn't big on sharing. I smell a love triangle in the future, and I know who I want to win. Vote below on which man you think Bonnie should choose! XO

CHAPTER THIRTEEN

BONNIE

HANK IS QUIET AS Eli drives us down a dark, winding lane with nothing but trees on either side. Hank has barely said anything to me since showing up at my trailer fifteen minutes ago, and I've done my best to match him. I'm generally a talker, so it's been killing me a bit. I'll have to tell Freya that I managed to keep my mouth shut for more than two minutes, though I have a feeling she won't easily believe me.

"Take a right up here," Hank says, leaning forward to give Eli the quiet direction. "It'll turn into a dirt road, but we don't have to go far."

When he sits back, he grabs hold of my hand, though he seems just as confused as I am when he looks down at our fingers. Eli knows this thing is fake, so we don't need to pretend for anyone. Hank also looks terrified.

"If you're bringing us out here to kill us," I say, trying to lighten the mood, "you might find it more difficult than you anticipated."

He chuckles. "I can take Eli, though I'm worried about you."

Even Eli laughs, shaking his head as he navigates the dirt road.

"There's a really nice meadow up here, and the skies should be clear tonight. We get a few more stars in Laketown than you do in Los Angeles."

"You're taking me stargazing?" Why does my heart rate kick up at that thought? It's not like I haven't seen stars before. And I won't let this turn into more than I bargained for with this relationship, so nothing is going to happen.

Then again, Hank *is* holding my hand when he doesn't need to. Whatever he's thinking, it's edging dangerously close to the line we both said we wouldn't cross.

Telling Eli to pull over on the side of the road, Hank looks at me in the light from the dash. "This was always one of my favorite places to go when I would visit Laketown," he says quietly.

"So you haven't always lived here?"

He shakes his head and slips out of the car. A moment later, he opens my door and offers his hand to help me out. "I've got some blankets in the back. There's one for you too," he tells Eli with a small smile.

I'm not sure if my bodyguard knows what to think about Hank, but he takes hold of one of the blankets, handing Hank the other.

Though we only walk a little ways into the dark clearing, we're far enough away from Eli that I feel like we're entirely alone. I genuinely don't remember the last time I was alone with someone other than Derek or another of my friends, and normally I would start to get nervous. But something about Hank is so calming. So far, he has never made me feel like an obligation even though that's exactly what I am, and I don't have words for how much I appreciate that.

He lays out the blanket and sits first, gesturing for me to decide where I want to sit. I settle close enough to him that I won't give him the impression that I'm avoiding him, but I still leave a little distance. I figure he'll appreciate the space, given his private nature, and I'm not about to give him any reason to clam up. I'm *desperate* to hear what he has to say.

Leaning back on his hands, Hank lifts his eyes to the sky. I'm more interested in watching him, but I follow his example. Then I gasp.

"I've never seen this many stars before!" And while it's not like I didn't *know* there were a lot more stars than what we see in LA, I wasn't prepared for seeing the sky like this in real life. "I always thought the movies exaggerated what it looks like," I say reverently.

It's too hard to keep my head tilted back like this, so I lay down on the blanket, sighing as an unfamiliar sense of peace washes over me. "I can see why this is your favorite spot." I could lay here for hours and never get bored.

Settling beside me, Hank laces his fingers together and rests them on his chest. I'm weirdly disappointed that I can't hold his hand because of it. "*Used to be* my favorite spot," he says.

I've been good at holding back my curiosity since this morning's revelation, so I feel justified when a question bursts out of me. "Did your wife really get murdered?" Well, I felt justified until I hit that last word, and now I feel like a jerk. Clapping a hand over my mouth, I beg the universe to turn back time five seconds so I can try that again. "I'm sorry," I say, since time manipulation isn't a thing. "That was insensitive of me."

Hank chuckles, which is about the farthest thing from what I expected after that hideous question of mine. "It's not your fault. That's what I told you. And..." He swallows, and though I can't see much of his face in the moonlight, I can practically feel his tension. "Yes. She was murdered. Four years ago, when we lived in Denver."

What's a girl supposed to say to something like that? Probably not what I say. "By who?"

"I don't know," Hank replies. "It's a cold case."

I want to know *everything*. Maybe it's morbid of me, considering this is a real person connected to someone I know, but I want to know all the details so I can know Hank. This is the kind of thing that sticks with a person.

He must feel my curiosity because he sighs and keeps talking, his words strained. "Shelby left for work on a regular Tuesday morning but never got to the gallery where she was a curator. She wasn't found until late that night when someone called in a tip about a body in an alley several blocks away. Any leads the police had all led to dead ends, and eventually they gave up."

I shouldn't ask, but I do it anyway. "How did she die?" And when Hank doesn't say anything, I reach over and steal one of his hands so I can hold it between both of mine.

"She was stabbed," he says slowly, as if he found some strength in my hold. "According to the autopsy, she was probably pulled out of her car and tied up before they killed her; her car was abandoned a few miles from where she was found. The police think maybe it had something to do with an art piece at the gallery—maybe a ransom or something—but no one was ever contacted. Nothing was missing. They left her phone, purse, everything in the car. There was never any reason for anyone to..."

"Oh, Hank." I squeeze his fingers as my eyes well up. I can't imagine how hard it is to say all of this and relive something so awful. "That's horrible."

He swallows thickly. "Losing her broke me. I couldn't stay in our house without being reminded of her, so I sold it and ran away from the life we'd built together. Cut myself off from our friends. Quit my job. Left the city that took her from me. I came to Laketown to sell our vacation home, but once I got here, I couldn't bring myself to lose my last connection to her. We'd been coming here for years, to spend a long weekend or take a vacation away from the grind."

His lungs fill slowly, his eyes still locked on the sky above us. A breeze rustles through the meadow grass, the only sound in the silent night, and it feels like something shifts in the air with that breeze. I've never been somewhere this quiet, and while a part of me wants to stay in this silence forever, I'm desperate for Hank to keep talking.

He does, his words growing quieter than before. "Shelby loved coming out here. She said it was the only place she could recharge, and she was always so *alive* here. Especially in this meadow. I'd never seen a person frolic until the day Shelby first discovered it, and sometimes it felt like she would spend hours dancing through the wildflowers. I haven't been back here since she..."

For the first time since he started talking, he moves, his hand tightening around mine as he turns his head to look at me. "She's the reason I wrote the first Frost book."

"Oh!" My exclamation comes out way louder than it should have, and I wince. But it's all falling into place now, and maybe I'm too excited given the heavy conversation, but I can't help it. "You wanted to solve her murder!"

He nods. "I holed myself up for over a year in a house where everything reminded me of her, and I was in a dark place. I kept going over her case, combing it for any piece of evidence they might have missed, but there was nothing. I was losing my mind. So I wrote down how I wished it had happened, just to give myself something to hold on to. I never planned to turn it into a book, but then Gabrielle started speaking to me."

"Gabrielle was inspired by Shelby, wasn't she?" When Hank nods, I sit up, still holding on to his hand because I'm afraid he might fall apart if I let go. Lying down feels too intimate, but at the same time I want to stay close to him. "That's why she feels so real. Because she *is* real! But you flipped the script so she wasn't the victim anymore. And—oooooh." It's all coming together now. "*Frosted Peaks* is about a young museum curator who accidentally walked in on an art heist and was stabbed, just like..."

I swallow my comparison to Shelby, wincing when I meet Hank's sorrowful gaze. *Oh.* My stomach twists painfully as tears fill my eyes. What am I even saying? "I am so sorry, Hank." That's not really enough to convey how deeply I feel that, so I keep talking. "I have this problem where I get too caught up in the story of something and forget that it's real life. I'm not trying to be insensitive, I just think it's incredible that you gave yourself closure in your book by letting Gabrielle solve the murder. You're sure it wasn't her friend at the gallery like in the book? The one who wanted her job?"

Hank sits up too, his gaze now fixed on our hands. "No. Kelli—her coworker in real life—was almost as broken up by the whole thing as I was, and she isn't an art thief like in the book. Nothing was ever stolen, and she wasn't dating anyone so there's no equivalent to Logan's character either. I just needed a way to solve the murder that made sense so I could breathe again. And you're not being insensitive. This is exactly why I wanted to tell you. I hoped you would understand why it took me so long to agree to this relationship and why I've been a terrible boyfriend so far."

Guilt threads through me, thick and hot. "Hank. I should never have—"

"You didn't know." He quirks his lips up in a small smile. "Maybe if you had, you would have found a better person to play this role with you."

I snort a laugh despite the gravity of this conversation. "Are you kidding? After that harness debacle, you're being hailed a hero. I almost hope we get even more set disasters so you can keep coming to my rescue."

"'*Even more* set disasters'?" The alarm in his voice sends a shiver through me, though that could also be from the crisp breeze that picks up around us again, this time strong enough to make the trees sway. "How many disasters have there been?"

More than is normal, though I probably won't tell him that. Although, I do like the concern in his eyes. Even in the darkness I can tell he's worried about me. "Oh, the harness has been the worst so far. And you were there for the tire exploding. It's just been little things, like props going missing and Jonah getting stuck in his trailer a couple of times."

Hank grips my hand tighter. "Is that normal?"

Now that I know what Hank went through with his wife, I'm not about to stress him out. "There's always something that goes wrong when filming, no matter what it is, and action movies like this one are more involved, so it stands to reason more things will happen. It's kind of exciting, the way it all keeps you on your toes."

"You and I have different definitions of exciting."

"Says the man who walked across a cliff in the Alps."

His smile is extra adorable after all that sadness. "Shelby was the adventurous one. Hank on his own is boring."

"You are far from boring, Hank. And thank you. For trusting me with your pain. I know that can't have been easy."

Letting out a deep and weary sigh, he looks up at the stars again as if they might contain the answers to the universe, though I'm not sure either of us know how to read them if they do. "I'm tired of hiding from the world," he says, his words heavy with truth. It reminds me of what he said to June when he was still deciding if he wanted to help me. *I don't know if I can call what I have living.* "I've spent so long pretending that I don't need to let anyone into my life, but then…"

"But then you met me," I finish for him, fighting my grin. "Your crazy fan who inadvertently roped you into becoming one half of the country's most popular couple."

Though I can't tell for sure, I'm pretty sure he rolls his eyes. "Then I met a woman who doesn't bat an eye when talking about murder and somehow manages to make me want to leave my house and face a town who all know Shelby died but don't know how. Laketown loved Shelby whenever we came to visit, and they've spent the last four years trying to get me to face the world, mostly so they can get answers from me, I'm sure. They don't actually care about *me* outside of being the town's most mysterious hermit. And yet you've still gotten me into town more than once."

I could be wrong, but I would guess this town likes Hank just as much as they liked his wife and want to see him happy again. How could they not adore him? I can understand why he would want to hide from all the pain, but even if I still have a lot to learn about this man, I already know he's worth knowing. Laketown—and the world—would be better off with him a part of it.

"I hope you won't resent me for this relationship that got thrust onto you, but I'm glad I got you out of the house, Hank. People need people, and you shouldn't be alone." Though I'm already holding his hand, I let go so I can offer him a handshake. "I know you already have June, but could I be your second official friend?"

He chuckles. "Technically you would be my fifth friend."

"Oh?"

"My neighbor, Chad, was my first friend. Then Chad's wife, Hope, followed by June. And there's Heather, but she's a new addition."

"I haven't met Heather." And yet I'm already jealous of her.

Hank smiles. "She's great. I think you would like her." Then he takes my hand. "So if you're okay with being my fifth official friend..."

"I'll take anything you give me, Hank McAllister. You're already my boyfriend, but I would love for you to be more than that."

"We're doing everything backwards, then?"

"No one ever said relationships have to happen a certain way. Besides, I like friendships way more than all that love stuff. That stuff gets messy, so I tend to avoid it."

"Why?"

Well, there's a million-dollar question. I would answer it if I could, but the night is getting colder, and I would imagine Eli is eager to get me back to the safety of my trailer. I would love to keep learning about Hank, but now that it seems he's going to try to flip the switch, I should retreat. Unlike him, I don't have any good reasons to avoid love other than general fear of what comes when it ends.

Lying back down, I shiver and glance at my phone. It's barely nine o'clock, and I don't want my time with Hank to end. I also don't want to talk about myself.

"Do you know any of the constellations?" I ask, moving my eyes to the stars.

He takes a second to answer. I wonder what he's thinking. "Some of them."

"Will you teach me?"

For the next half an hour or so, Hank points out the constellations he knows and tells me their stories. I try to listen, particularly because he's an excellent storyteller, but I can't stop thinking about what happened to his wife and how hard that must have been on him. I've never lost anyone like that, but part of that is because I've never been close to anyone like that. The sympathetic heartache that I feel for this man is painful enough, and I'm glad I haven't set myself up for that kind of pain.

Eventually, I sit up and let out a sigh. "I should probably get back before Trevor sends out a search party. I think he and my makeup artist are in cahoots and hate it when I don't get enough sleep."

Hank frowns as he gets to his feet and pulls me up next to him. "Do you always do what your makeup artist tells you to do?"

I laugh. "It's not like she controls my every move." That's Trevor's job, though I suppose he's usually doing whatever Fran tells him to do. And if not Fran, my agent is the one telling me where to go and when, and the director decides which scenes we're doing and how I should act them.

As Hank gathers up the blanket, I consider his question more seriously. I have to wonder if he wasn't really asking about the makeup artist. When was the last time I made a choice for myself? Do I even want to make my own decisions? Historically, my choices have rarely turned out well for me, and I much prefer relying on the expertise of others. My life has been infinitely better that way.

"Bonnie?" Hank holds out his hand, the blanket tucked over his other arm. "You okay?"

Instead of taking his hand, I smile and tuck myself up against his side, hugging his arm as we walk back toward the car. "I'm processing a lot of things tonight."

"Sorry."

"No, I'm so glad you told me about Shelby. I feel like I understand you so much better now."

"I know our relationship isn't real," Hank says, "but I'd like to think our friendship is. I thought it was time I trusted you."

We meet Eli at the car and continue our silence as he drives us back to the production area. I'm not sure why Hank is quiet, but I'm worried he's expecting more from me. He was incredibly vulnerable tonight, and I love that he trusts me. But he doesn't have a public life. He can trust more easily than I can.

It's not like I expect Hank to sell all my secrets to the press when it would only damage his own image and privacy. But that doesn't mean I can share all my woes. I don't have many woes to begin with, but sharing them would only lead to heartache when this all ends.

The more I give of myself, the fewer pieces I have to hold on to. If I'm not careful, soon there will be nothing left of me.

I'm not willing to risk that.

Chapter Fourteen

Hank

Everything is strangely sunny when I step onto the front porch in the morning, even though it's barely dawn. Or maybe it all just looks lighter because I can breathe more easily. I spent another night wrestling with my book, but I feel awake today. I feel *alive*.

"It's probably delusion," I tell Heather as I watch her break down her web to build it again. I'm not sure why she's destroying it when it looks perfectly fine to me, but I'm also not a spider expert. As long as she isn't packing up and moving, I'm fine with whatever she decides to do with her time.

I sip my tea, enjoying the experience of a hot beverage that is actually hot because for once I'm not too distracted to drink it right away. I feel like I've suddenly inhabited someone else's body, and I can't fully decide one way or the other if it's a good thing. "I'm probably so exhausted that my brain has been tricked into thinking it's functioning how it should," I tell the spider.

Something buzzes in the house, and it takes me longer than it should to realize it's my phone. I perk up. That will be Bonnie, since she's the only one with my phone number.

Though I'm tempted to keep watching Heather do her thing, I slip back into the house and grab my phone where I left it in the kitchen. But it's not Bonnie's number at the top of the text. It's not even her assistant, Trevor. I set my mug on the counter as I read the message.

Unknown Number:

> Hey Hank, I wanted to tell you thanks for looking out for Bonnie yesterday. I told her she didn't need to do the stunt, but she insisted it would be better if she did it herself even though she hates heights. She's too stubborn for her own good sometimes.

I frown, reading through the text a couple of times. Obviously it's someone close to Bonnie. And someone she must talk to often, if they know me as Hank rather than Henry. But how did they get my number, and why are they texting me?

Though I would really rather ignore the message, I send a quick text back.

Hank:

> Who is this?

Unknown Number:

> Right. This is Derek.

I grab my keys and head out the door without really knowing what my plan is. I don't like the idea that someone like Derek Riley has my number. One, it means Bonnie gave it to him, and I feel more exposed than I would like. Two, he's her ex-boyfriend. It may have been a fake relationship, but from everything I've seen online, Bonnie is incredibly close to the guy.

Too close.

By the time I get to the production area and slip past the security guard, who nods at me, there's a strange buzzing sensation running through me. It's not anger, but it's not a positive feeling either. If this pretend relationship I have with Bonnie is going to include her famous friend, I probably need to set some boundaries.

I hear Bonnie's voice before I reach her trailer, her words pulling me to a halt out of sight.

"You know why I can't tell Hank any of that."

My stomach twists, and I inch forward as another female voice responds, though it sounds like it's coming from a phone or something.

"No, I do not know, Bonnie. And quite frankly, I am hurt that I am only just now hearing all of this, and only because Derek decided to share."

There he is again. *Derek Riley*.

"I only shared," Derek says on the call, "because I know you're bottling it up again. You can't keep it all to yourself, Bon."

"I'm fine," Bonnie says, clearly frustrated.

"You do not look fine," the other woman argues. "You are wearing yourself down."

This isn't the kind of conversation I should be listening to, so I step forward and into Bonnie's view.

She squeaks when she sees me, and both her friends say her name with worry coloring their words. "Hank," she says, her eyes fixed on me. "What are you doing here?"

"That's probably my fault," Derek says.

Without offering my own answer for Bonnie's question, I move until I'm standing next to her and have a view of the phone, mostly so I can see the guy who thought it was a good idea to send a stranger a text like the one he sent me. Derek looks pretty much like he does in all his photos, bright blue eyes set against dark hair and beard. I can see why he's popular, but at the moment he's not exactly on my list of people I like.

"Hank?" Bonnie says, her eyes on me rather than the phone.

I take in the blonde woman on the call, who looks intimidating and impossibly beautiful at the same time, and then I wave. "Hi," I say, mostly to her, though I suppose I'm saying hi to Derek as well since he's on the call. "I'm Hank."

"Freya," the woman replies with a warm smile.

Bonnie's arm touches mine as she moves closer to be in the frame with me. "Freya Alverra," she says to me. "Crown Princess of Candora."

The blood rushes from my face. Princess? "Oh. Um." What is a person supposed to do when meeting a literal *princess*?

Freya waves, amusement in her expression. "There is no formality here, Hank."

"You're one of us for now," Derek adds.

For now. I didn't miss that distinction, and Derek knows it. His eyes are narrowed, and he's studying me the same way I just studied him. I'm glad we're not meeting in person for the first time because he would look far more impressive than I ever could.

"Derek, will you stop?" Bonnie says. "What do you mean you're the reason Hank is here?"

"He texted me," I say before Derek can make an excuse.

All three of them wait for me to say more, but that was the reason.

Frowning, I fold my arms against the chill of the morning. "I would prefer my phone number to stay between us," I murmur to Bonnie.

As color rushes into her cheeks, she shifts the phone so we're no longer in the camera. "I'm so sorry, Hank. Derek said he wanted to thank you for something, and I thought—"

"It's fine." It's not, but there's nothing I can do about it now. And Bonnie's guilt is somehow making *me* feel guilty. "As long as no one else has it," I add.

Bonnie turns even more red.

Oh boy.

"None of my friends will share it with anyone," she says, and it almost looks like she might start crying.

My guilt builds, settling heavy in my stomach. "It's fine," I say again, but this time I mean it. I can only imagine how Shelby would look at me if she knew how curmudgeonly I've gotten since losing her, and that's not who I want to be.

Derek clears his throat, and Bonnie pulls her phone back up. "Hank," he says, "I was going to tell you that I'm glad Bonnie has someone looking out for her while she's out there."

Bonnie scoffs before I can say anything, though I don't know what I might have said. "I don't need someone looking out for me."

"You were up in the middle of the night," Freya says sternly. "If that script is keeping you awake, then—"

"It wasn't the script." Bonnie's eyes dart over to me for half a second. "Besides, *you guys* are the ones preventing me from working on the script this morning."

"Just let Kasey handle it, Bon," Derek says. "You're doing too much."

Something flashes in Bonnie's eyes. Anger? I'm not sure she's capable of anger, but there's *something* there. "Derek, I offered to fix the script. I'm going to do it."

"At the expense of your health? You're exhausted, and you shouldn't..."

I stop listening, turning my focus to Bonnie. As much as I hate the way Derek is talking to Bonnie like she's incapable of looking out for herself, he's right about one thing. She looks like she barely slept last night. A good chunk of that is probably my fault—anyone in her position would lose sleep over what I told her last night—but I'm guessing she doesn't have a lot of free time around her filming schedule.

Interrupting whatever dumb argument Derek is saying to Bonnie, who is looking more and more furious, I grab Bonnie's hand and say, "Will you let me help you?"

Bonnie's attention immediately shifts to me, and I feel a strange sense of triumph when I catch a glimpse of Derek's frustrated scowl before Bonnie drops her arm to her side, phone and all. *That's right. She's listening to* me. "What?" she says, her eyebrows pulling low.

I have no idea how to write a script, and whoever this Kasey person is, she can probably do it. I don't think Derek would suggest her if she couldn't. But Bonnie's going to need some convincing to let go of the task, and Derek's way clearly isn't working. "Can I help you with the script, Bonnie?"

"Thank you," she says, "but I can fix it."

"I know you can. But don't you think it will go faster if you share the load?"

She blinks, staring at me like I just said something revolutionary. "Oh. I don't...yeah, it would."

I slip my hand into hers. "So can I help you?"

The smile she gives me warms me way better than a cup of tea ever could. "Okay. Thanks." Then she seems to realize her friends are still on the video call, and she lifts her phone with wide eyes.

Derek's lips are pursed, but Freya is grinning. "I am eager to know you better, Hank, but alas, I am late for a Council Meeting."

"No, wait!" Bonnie says in alarm. "We didn't even get to talk about your hunky new bodyguard."

"We might have if Riley did not decide to interrupt," Freya says, throwing a glare to her camera.

Derek glares right back, but I don't think it's real. "I just wanted to make sure you were okay after yesterday, Bonnie," he says.

"You can check on her on your own time," Freya replies. "Besides, my bodyguard is *not* hunky."

"He looked pretty hunky to me," Bonnie argues.

Freya lets out a stream of words in a language I don't understand. "He is hunky, yes, but he is going to last no more than a month. Not even Gregor likes him."

"This is the third bodyguard you've had in as many months," Bonnie says. "Are you sure you're not driving them away?"

"If I am going to have someone a step behind me for the rest of my life, I must be able to trust him. Not a single one of these men has shown me I can do that."

Bonnie snickers. "I'm not going to argue. But you can't honestly tell me you don't think this latest one is attractive. He's a beautiful Candoran specimen with a smile that would distract anyone who might be attempting to harm you. He's like a Norse god."

Freya snorts out a laugh but stifles it with her hand. "I will be certain to tell him you think so. I was unaware that Norse god was your type, Bonnie."

I shouldn't be feeling as jealous as I am. Derek is one thing, but a questionable bodyguard who seems only distantly connected to Bonnie? Something is wrong with me, and yet I want to ask if Bonnie thinks *I* am attractive. There is no way she would ever call me *hunky*—my metabolism doesn't lend itself to bulk, even when I've tried in the past—but I want to know if I have at least a little something going for me. Otherwise, the only external image I have of myself will be from June, who doesn't consider me a *man*.

Not exactly a confidence booster.

"He can be attractive without being my type," Bonnie says.

"I feel like I shouldn't be a part of this conversation," Derek mumbles, and then he's gone.

Freya snickers. "It serves him right. But I really do have to go." She blows a kiss to the camera. "Please try to get more sleep if you can, Bon. I know you want to do your best work on this movie, so you must take care of yourself. Hank, I will neither text you nor share your phone number, so you have nothing to fear from me."

I groan, but a smile plays on my lips at the same time. "That's going to follow me, isn't it?"

"Most likely," Bonnie says. "Good luck with your bodyguard woes, Freya!"

Freya blows another kiss and hangs up, leaving Bonnie and me on our own.

I decide to ask my most burning question before the awkwardness builds. "I know I shouldn't ask, but what did Derek mean when he said you were bottling things up?"

As she tucks her phone into her pocket, Bonnie bites her lip. She deflected last night too, so I don't know what I expected. "Hank."

I duck my head. "Sorry. Like I said, I shouldn't have—"

"I don't trust easily."

"June's the only other person who really knows what happened to Shelby." I wince as soon as the words leave my mouth, mostly because they make no sense in the context of our conversation. "I mean, I get it. Not trusting people. It's hard."

Bonnie squeezes my hand, reminding me that I'm still holding on to her. The feel of her fingers between mine has apparently become comfortable enough for me to forget they're even there. Strange, considering how long it's been since I was in a relationship or even around other people.

"No one else knows?" she asks.

I shake my head. "Before she moved to Laketown, I was entirely alone."

"Being alone is awful." Whether or not Bonnie meant to say those words out loud, she seems to regret them as she turns her focus anywhere but on me. She can't hide her blush, though. "Um, I should probably change. I have a meeting with Jonah and the chemistry coach pretty soon."

After what I saw on set yesterday, I have no idea why they need a chemistry coach. They're perfectly fine. Too fine. But instead of fixating on how much I hope I don't have to watch Bonnie act any more scenes with Jonah, I shift our conversation back to what she first said. It's a risk, but I'm feeling bold this morning. As someone who has spent a significant chunk of his life alone, it's impossible not to wonder how anyone could let someone like Bonnie Aiken feel alone when I know she hasn't been single in years.

"Is that why you've been in so many relationships? So you're not alone?"

Fully crimson now, Bonnie tugs me up the stairs and into her trailer. "They haven't been real," she says and drops my hand, heading for the closet farther back.

"I know that, but I didn't want to call them fake in case anyone outside was listening."

That gets her to pause and look over at me. "Oh. Smart. I wasn't..." She shakes her head, like she's trying to shake something out of it. "I need to be more careful when I'm outside or Fran's going to murder me." She gasps and covers her mouth. "Oh, Hank, I'm sorry. I didn't mean..."

Surprisingly, nothing about what she said hit me like it might have a week ago. I don't know if that means I'm numb or healing, but it certainly feels better than the ache I've had for the last four years. Smiling, I settle myself on the couch. "It's okay, Bonnie. It's getting easier."

She watches me for a long time, and so many emotions cross her face that it's impossible to guess what she might be thinking. I hold my breath, hoping she'll trust me enough to open up to me, even if it's only a little bit. Yes, I told Bonnie that our relationship would only ever be fake, but we agreed to be friends last night. Friends share their burdens with each other.

Besides, the longer I watch her in return, the more I'm worried my heart is starting to lean in the wrong direction. I took a step by talking about Shelby, and now it feels like I can't stop walking. I have been at a standstill for so long, and I'm over it.

Please let me in.

"Yes," Bonnie says after a long time. "Yes, that's why I've been in so many relationships. Partially, anyway." She starts sorting through the clothes hanging in her closet. "More than anything, they were calculated decisions for my career."

Like ours. If she thinks I didn't notice the shift in her tone, then she doesn't know me very well. Which, admittedly, is true. But I'm pretty sure I'm now watching Bonnie the actor, not the real Bonnie, and I don't know how to bring her vulnerability back. I've gotten lucky, so I probably shouldn't push. But I do anyway. "Will you tell me about them?"

She glances at me. "Why?"

Because I want to know you, Bonnie. But I don't say that, because I'm a coward. What I do say sounds ridiculous and like something a guy like Derek would say. "Because I want to know how I measure up."

She laughs and shakes her head. "There's no need to compare yourself to anyone, Hank. You're all different."

And she's good at deflecting. "Please? I would rather hear about them from you than have to look it up online."

Sighing, she turns her attention back to the clothes in front of her. "Are you sure you want to hear about all this?"

"I wouldn't ask if I didn't."

"I believe you. You are one of the most sincere people I've ever met, Henry McAllister."

The only reason I don't feel like an idiot for blushing is the fact that she's refusing to look at me, so my embarrassment—and maybe pleasure—go unnoticed. "So? Are you going to spare me from the horrors of the internet?"

"My first boyfriend was Jeremy O'Hara."

"Am I supposed to know who that is? I've been cut off from the world for four years, and before that I only paid attention to whatever Shelby was into, which was mostly artists and poets."

Oh, that makes me sound like I didn't have a life. I did, but I'm the sort of guy who has generally been content to follow.

Her hands begin sorting through the clothes again as she talks, and she sounds like she's talking about the weather instead of her love life. "Jeremy played for the Seahawks. Tight end. A bit handsy at times—I was brought in to try to fix his bad boy reputation—but he got me a lot of attention in the beginning, so that was nice. Before that I'd just been doing little films and TV shows."

I try to say something but realize my jaw is clenched too tight. I force it open. "What do you mean by handsy?"

She laughs as she pulls out a pink sweater and holds it up to her body. "Nothing terrible. He liked to put on a show more than anything, but our contract kept him from doing anything he shouldn't."

I really don't like that a piece of paper was the only thing protecting her. Nor do I like how she brushes it all to the side. So far, this is doing nothing to break through the actor mask she's put on, but I'm not ready to give up. "Why did it end?" I ask, my voice strained.

"Jeremy got bored and hired a, well, *some company* one night and got caught by the paparazzi. I got to stage a tearful reaction video, which caught the attention of a director, Michael Bobby, and that's how I got into one of my first big roles. He's an amazing director, so all the stuff with Jeremy was totally worth it." She puts the sweater back in the closet and resumes her browsing.

I don't even have words. Maybe it's because I was with Shelby for eight years and she was my only significant relationship, but I can't wrap my brain around how casually Bonnie is saying all of this. Does it not bother her at all that she offered up a piece of her heart, however small, only to have it disrespected so horribly?

"After that was Michael, of course."

I regret asking. "Michael, as in Michael Bobby? Your director?"

"Yep!" Bonnie pulls out a different sweater—blue this time—and then shimmies out of her fleece jacket that she was wearing. "That relationship turned out to be a double-edged sword. Some fans loved the idea because of our business relationship, and others hated it because he was about twenty years older than me, so it didn't last very long. My publicist had me start dating a YouTube star pretty soon after Michael thought we should part ways."

I can't stop the surge of protectiveness that keeps building as she talks. She makes it all sound so normal, like pretending to date people to boost their images is no big deal. I know she is smart enough to see the dangers in this sort of thing, and I can't help but wonder if this is the same thing I encountered when I offered to help her with the script.

She could have said no to all of these relationships, but she chose not to. How much of her life has been spent doing what's best for everyone but herself? "Bonnie, maybe we should—*what are you doing*?" I turn my head away from her, but she already has her shirt off. I'm facing the other end of the trailer, but I cover my eyes with my hand anyway. Just in case.

"Oh! Sorry. I wanted to change, but I forget sometimes that not everyone is used to seeing me."

"Why is *anyone* used to seeing you?" And why am I so tempted to turn around? That's a dumb question, though I'm surprised by the attraction sparking to life in my chest. I thought that part of me was broken.

"Makeup and wardrobe have seen plenty of me," Bonnie replies with a tittering laugh, as if it's no big deal. "Sorry to scandalize you, and it's okay if you don't like what you see."

"It's not that. I don't want..." My words falter, and my face blazes hot. Yeah, definitely not broken.

Bonnie sits on the couch next to me and takes hold of my arm. She waits until I cautiously look her way—thankfully she's wearing the sweater now—and then she smiles at me. But it's not a real smile. It's a nervous smile, with a healthy dose of wariness and fear behind her eyes. "You don't want what, Hank? We made our rules, remember? You should always be comfortable in this relationship."

Is that what she thinks this is? Adjusting my glasses, I take a moment and study her face, hoping she'll be willing to show me more than the surface again. "Are *you* comfortable?" I ask her, looking down at her hands circling my forearm.

She snickers. "Hank, I dated the stuck up son of an oil tycoon. You're about as tame as they come."

"I didn't mean with me, though I hope you'll tell me if you're ever not. I mean with all of this." I gesture to the trailer, hoping she knows I mean everything beyond it as well. "With your public life. Never having any privacy."

She smiles, and at first it seems like she's going to brush my question away. One of her hands even lifts in the air as if to wave it all off. But then she pauses, her eyebrows slowly dipping lower, and it's like she's finally cracking a window into the real Bonnie again. Somehow, she looks even more tired than she did when I showed up, and the urge to pull her into my arms rises to the point where I almost wrap my arm around her by the time she speaks.

"Trust me," she says quietly. "A lack of privacy is worth it."

I frown. "Why?"

"Because it's better than being totally alone."

There it is again, only this time she keeps her eyes on me. The acting mask is gone, leaving a woman who desperately wants me to see her but doesn't know how to let me in. I know exactly how that feels. I may never heal from Shelby's death, but I can't keep hiding from the world either.

"Have you..." This could be my riskiest question yet. "Have you ever had a real relationship?"

Something changes in her expression, and it's as much sadness as it is happiness. "Houston."

My heart stumbles in my chest as I remember the conversation I had the other day with Chad and Hope in June's store. "Houston Briggs?"

She nods. "I didn't take you for a baseball fan."

"I'm not. I... His brother, Chad."

Recognition sparks in her eyes, bringing a smile to her face. "One of your five friends?"

"He owns a house down the street from me."

"What a small world!"

Not small enough. If Houston is anything like his brother, I have to wonder why that relationship ended. Sure, Houston is famous, but Chad has always spoken highly of his pro pitcher brother. "How did you end up dating a baseball player from New Mexico?"

She turns a bright pink, which I don't especially love, given the fact that her relationship with Houston is the only real one she's had in the last who knows how long. "We met at a party in California. He and a few of his teammates decided to crash it after a game, and he was too charming to ignore."

I've never been accused of being charming. Even Shelby told me more than once that I had the charm of a sea slug. "It's a good thing you're cute," she would tell me right after and then kiss me senseless. How is a guy like me supposed to compete with a professional pitcher?

Wait, do I even *want* to compete? This relationship isn't real and has no potential to *become* real. I shouldn't have to keep reminding myself of that.

"He's getting married at the end of the week," Bonnie says, and for some reason that seems to disappoint her. Which only makes me feel worse. Of course the relationship she's the most sad about is the only one that wasn't orchestrated for her. I don't think anyone could truly be happy about having people thrust on them as romantic interests. "Are you going to the wedding?"

I got an invite, though I'm pretty sure Chad knew I would ignore it. I've never even met Houston, though I have no doubt Chad and Hope have both spoken to their family about me. Given the enigma that is a man in his early thirties living life as a hermit, I wouldn't blame them. "No," I say, answering Bonnie's question later than I should have. But then something sparks in my mind. "Are you?"

"Yeah. It got worked into the schedule before we started filming. Beckett's not happy about it, but what can he do?"

I hate that my mind is scrambling for a way to convince Beckett that he has to do something to keep Bonnie here. I don't have any right to be jealous, but I am. "It's not common for people to go to their ex's wedding." And that sounds like I'm being rude, so I add, "That's nice that you're still on good terms with Houston."

Bonnie smiles, shaking her head. "We were always more friends than truly attached to each other romantically."

Why do I get the feeling that that's a lie? It's like that cracked window keeps opening wider, and the longer I look at her, the more I can see the nerves she's trying so hard to hide. This woman is an actor. A good one. But I'm starting to see through the sheen and find the woman underneath.

And I'm pretty sure she's been hurt more than she'll ever admit.

"What if..." I swallow, trying to hold back my thoughts, but the words are going to keep coming whether I want them to or not. "I could come with you. To the wedding." *What in the world did I just say?* I don't want to go to a wedding! Sure, it would give me a chance to see Chad and Hope, but I've barely managed to find the will to leave my house. There's no way Houston's wedding will be small.

But even as my anxiety rises, something in me wants to go with Bonnie and make sure she's okay. She's so good at pretending she's happy with the way her life is, but I've started getting glimpses of the truth. No matter how strong she is, she's been passed around from man to man, and it doesn't sound like any of them valued her like they should. Not even Houston.

If he did, he never would have let her go.

Bonnie seems to think I was joking about going to the wedding—her smile hasn't changed—but the longer we look at each other, the more her expression turns to confusion. "You want to go to Sun City with me?"

I absolutely do not. My heart is already racing at the thought. I nod anyway, trying to smile. "I think people would be concerned if I didn't. Houston is famous enough that there will be plenty of attention on his wedding."

"And plenty of people expecting to see you at my side," she finishes for me. "I didn't think about that. But Hank, I know you're not big on public events."

"I can manage." Hopefully.

"Besides, I'm flying to Los Angeles for a couple of days right after the wedding to do an interview with Derek about the latest movie we're in together."

Oh, this just keeps getting better. "I could go to California." *Keep breathing, Hank.* "If you want me to." Keeping calm is a struggle, but based on the way Bonnie's expression turns grateful, I know I can't take back my offer. In fact, she looks downright relieved by what I'm saying.

That's a bad idea. What if I mess everything up like I did with our ice cream date? This scenario would be so much worse.

It's one thing to spend time alone with Bonnie as I get to know her better, another to wander around my small town and the watchful eyes of my neighbors. But Los Angeles? That's a completely different situation and far from the baby steps I've been taking.

That's a leap over a chasm too deep to see the bottom. A jump from an airplane with no idea if I have a parachute.

Bonnie grabs my hand, her eyes bright with what I'm going to have to assume are happy tears. "I would love that, Hank. I'm not going to know anyone at the wedding outside of Houston and his family, so it would be nice to have a friend. Derek was going to come with me originally, but..." She shrugs with a laugh that isn't at all believable. Whatever acting skills she had earlier are gone. "I can't believe you would be willing to do something like that when you have already done so much with this relationship. I'll need to find some way to pay you back."

If only she knew how much she has changed my life in a few short days by giving me a reason to wake up and live again. Even if she hadn't, I'm getting the sense that Bonnie is used to doing what's best for everyone but herself. I'm not social in any sense of the word, but Shelby was. And I know even Shelby would have hated going to something like an ex-boyfriend's wedding by herself. I'm sure Bonnie can make friends anywhere, but she's too well-known for anyone to treat her like a regular person.

No wonder she's felt so lonely.

I put my other hand over hers. Hopefully this unexpected adventure won't send me scurrying back into hiding when it inevitably overwhelms me. "I'm happy to go, no repayment necessary. It's been a long time since I've been...anywhere, really. And I wouldn't mind seeing Houston's brother. It's been a while for that too."

Bonnie grins. "Well, then it's a date!"

Great. I'm glad I could help her feel more comfortable about her trip. Knowing she has a date seems to have lightened the weight on her shoulders.

The problem is I'm starting to think I want that date to be real, and that's not going to end well. Bonnie doesn't do love, and I think I might be in danger of falling right into it.

CHAPTER FIFTEEN

HANK

"From the looks of it, Bonnie's version of the script isn't bad. It just needs rearranging so it better fits the bones of the book." Kasey, Bonnie's screenwriter friend, is sitting outside with a view of the California coast behind her, and I haven't yet figured out how someone as young as her could have a view like that. Bonnie said something about her having a screenplay picked up, but I have a hard time believing that would be enough for her to be among the rich and famous. Then again, she *is* friends with Bonnie.

When Bonnie went to meet with Jonah and the chemistry coach—a meeting I was tempted to try to be a part of—Trevor set me up in a spare trailer with a laptop so I could take a look at the script. I have no intention of actually working on it if I can help it, considering I'm a novelist who is not known for his brevity, but I figured it would be a good idea to touch base with Kasey over video chat before handing the project off to her.

I need to know I can give this project to someone who will get it done, and fast. Otherwise, I'll feel like I've broken Bonnie's hard-earned confidence. And right now, I'm struggling to trust Bonnie's friends, mostly because of Derek.

As I was getting situated, he texted me again despite my hope that he would have figured out not to, like Freya did.

Derek:
I owe you thanks again for taking on the script. Bonnie was overworking herself.

My response was less gracious:

Hank:
You know you're not her boyfriend anymore, right? I've got her.

Kasey seems nice enough, but I'm withholding judgment for now.

"I take it you've read the book," I say, hoping she says yes.

Kasey smiles and nods. "When Bonnie first got the role, we both fangirled about it. She's more of a die-hard than I am, but I'm a fan."

"I would hope so." I clear my throat, hearing how vain that sounds. "I mean because you have an idea of how the plot should work. I'm in over my head with this."

"Smart clarification," a male voice says from off the screen.

Unease winds its way into my belly as Kasey rolls her eyes. "Liam," she says to someone behind her computer, "you were supposed to stay out of this."

"That would involve staying away from you, and I don't like that." The owner of the voice comes into view and kisses her cheek. He looks like the perfect stereotypical Californian, with messy blond hair and a considerable lack of clothing as he leans on the back of Kasey's chair and flashes a wide smile at me. "So this is the adorable author you all are fawning over?"

Kasey smacks his bare chest. "Liam, this is Henry. Or do you prefer Hank?"

I'd rather this Liam guy didn't know either name, but that's not exactly polite. Bonnie's friends are really pushing my limits today. "Hank. But I don't want…"

"Oh, don't even worry," Liam says with another brilliant smile. "Kase and I had a fun run with the paps a few months ago, and we totally understand the value of anonymity."

"I'm not sure *you* do," Kasey teases him. "You love the spotlight."

"Not as much as I love you."

"Could…" I wince when they both look at me. "Could we get back to the script? If we don't get these scenes fixed, Bonnie's going to do it herself."

Liam's smile shifts into something softer. Less flashy. Moving his arms so they're around Kasey's shoulders instead of the chair, he looks right at the camera. "I'm glad she's got someone looking out for her. We've been getting worried the last few days, and I swear Freya is two seconds from flying in from Candora and using her diplomatic prowess to force Bonnie into taking a break."

"Bonnie hasn't said anything," Kasey adds, "but we can all see she's getting tired. From the sounds of it, that movie set is a mess. It's not just the script but the whole production seems to be falling apart."

That's news to me, though I think Bonnie might have hinted at something last night when she mentioned disasters on set. "Bonnie seems like the kind of person who feels personally obligated to fix everything," I mutter, almost to myself.

"Bonnie is one of the best people I know," Liam replies. "And you're right. She's also not the sort of person who admits when she needs help.

Derek's usually pretty good about seeing it, but Bonnie's also good at hiding it. Especially when she thinks she'll inconvenience someone else."

Before I can respond, Trevor steps into the trailer with a tablet in his hands, and he comes straight for me like a man on a mission. "Hey, Mr. McAllister, Fran wants to talk to you."

Liam whistles low. "If you're getting summoned by Fran, you must have done something wrong."

"Is that Liam Connolly?" Fran's voice rings out loud and clear from the tablet as Trevor hands it to me. She looks annoyed to be in the same room—so to speak—as Liam. "You'll recall I fixed your little problem last year, Liam, so I would keep your disdain to yourself."

"Technically *I* fixed our problem," Kasey argues.

"And Ethan," Liam throws in.

Fran scoffs. "Yes, well—"

I clear my throat loudly, scowling at both screens. If I had my way, I would end both these conversations and go back home, but it's clear I won't be doing that anytime soon. Especially knowing Bonnie is probably going to need some help at some point, whether she admits it or not. I get the feeling I'm about to spend a lot more time on set. "Can we not?" I say.

Liam chuckles, but Kasey grimaces. "I'll go through the scenes that need reworking," she says. "Sounds like you have more important things to do, and I've got plenty of free time."

"You're welcome," Liam says, kissing her cheek again. Whatever that means. "I will reluctantly leave you alone so you can work. Fran, lovely to see you as always." I can't tell if that is genuine or not, but his smile looks real.

As soon as they hop off the video call, I feel like I can breathe again. I don't necessarily want to talk to Fran, but I'm pretty sure listening to her is part of the contract I signed.

I should really look more closely at contracts when it comes to interacting with bossy people.

Leaning the tablet against the laptop screen, I try to keep my expression cordial. "You wanted to talk to me?"

She gives me a smile that is far less real than Liam's. "Yes, I wanted to discuss the arrangement. Are you alone?"

I look up and meet Trevor's gaze.

He shrugs. "I know all the things."

Okay then. "What do we need to discuss?"

Fran's grin turns almost wicked, which is not the kind of look that helps an anxious man feel great about what's coming. "While we have had some good moments, the people of the world are...dubious. You're going to need to put in more effort."

I was afraid of that, and I'm sorely tempted to hand the tablet back to Trevor and go home before this can turn into something I'm not going to like. "What kind of effort?" I ask instead.

Fran rolls her eyes. "You have to actually act as if you like Bonnie."

"I like Bonnie." I don't think I've ever given the impression otherwise. Okay, so our first date wasn't great, but I hoped I made up for that after the harness debacle.

Tutting loudly, Fran waggles her finger at the camera as if scolding me, and I really don't like the way she's looking at me. I know she has Bonnie's best interest at heart, but there's a lot I don't like about this woman. "Henry, darling, I don't mean *like*."

"Then why did you say it?"

She ignores me. "I mean you have to show the world that you are *in love* with Bonnie Aiken. This little cutesy routine isn't working, and we all know it isn't Bonnie who's afraid of a little intimacy."

Of all the words, why did she use that one? She'd better not be implying what I think she's implying. "Fran, I hope you don't expect me to—"

"Oh, honey, you are so sweet and naive." She clucks her tongue again. "Bonnie may have been in a lot of romance movies, but they weren't *that* kind. I am simply saying the world wants a kiss!"

I've come a long way since the day I met Bonnie, and I've done a lot of self-discovery and healing. I even might be falling for my co-conspirator. But I'm still taking baby steps here. A kiss may be innocent for a Hollywood star, but for me... That's asking a lot. "Fran, I'm not sure if—"

"Henry, sweetie, your contract says you will do whatever it takes to sell this relationship. If you're not willing to plant one on Hollywood's darling, the world is going to start to wonder. Besides, I hear you will be joining Bonnie at the Briggs wedding, and that is the perfect place to demonstrate your devotion."

I blink, processing. "Wait, you want me to—"

"Bonnie's with the chemistry coach right now, isn't she, Trevor? Perhaps, Henry, you should go join her and learn a thing or two about acting before this relationship fizzles and ruins Bonnie's career. I would hate for that to be on your head. You need to—"

I click the screen off before she can continue, glancing up at Trevor, who lifts his eyebrows high as if waiting for something. The thought of kissing Bonnie has been there from the beginning, but it was always a *maybe*. Now it feels like an order, and my heart starts pounding in my chest. "Do you think she's right?"

He shrugs again, though his bunched up grimace speaks pretty loudly. "I don't think a kiss could hurt. Bonnie has always been pretty..." His face splotches red. "Free," he finishes. "She's a kisser. Most people know that about her."

My stomach twists itself in a knot as my mind starts picturing her with the many men she's been attached to. "Ah." Apparently that's all I can say, and it doesn't seem to give Trevor any confidence in my ability to do as Fran suggested. *Ordered.*

"Like with Houston Briggs," Trevor continues, unbidden, "it only took about ten minutes after meeting the guy before she was all over him."

Houston was the one relationship that was real, which means that was the real Bonnie. *She's a kisser.*

Shelby and I kissed the first time we met, but it wasn't because *I* made it happen. She was nineteen, I was twenty, and she came to a party at my fraternity. When she found me reading a book by myself on the back porch, she did everything she could to convince me to go inside and join the party. When I declined—I was only part of the fraternity for the free rent—she said she would bring the party to me and plopped herself down on my lap. She asked me to read to her, and I agreed because she was beautiful and energetic and captured my attention entirely, like she put me under a spell. I was three chapters deep into *Brave New World* when she pressed her hands to my cheeks and kissed me.

It was awkward and messy, and we both ended up laughing in the middle of it, but I fell in love almost immediately.

I haven't kissed anyone else.

"So…" Trevor wrinkles his nose, which probably means I'm not going to like what he's about to say. "I was talking to Fran on the way to find you, and she didn't get the chance to say the most important part of this kissing thing before you, uh, hung up on her."

This kissing thing. Like it's no big deal. "What is it?"

"Fran thinks you need to be the one to initiate it. Everyone knows Bonnie isn't afraid of public displays of affection, so if you really want the country to believe you're in love with her, *you* have to show them. I'm sure Bonnie's already gotten this instruction, so she'll keep her hands to herself."

"No pressure, then," I murmur.

Trevor laughs nervously. "Is it really that awful of an idea to kiss someone like Bonnie Aiken?"

"It's not her I'm worried about." It's the fact that I've barely been able to stomach the idea of being away from my house like this. That it was only last night that I told her about how Shelby died. That I am only just starting to imagine opening up my heart to someone new after it was broken so completely by Shelby's murder. How can I move on when I never got to say goodbye to her? Never got closure?

"Bonnie's still with Clyde, if you want to get some help with the whole thing."

I frown, pulled from my increasing anxiety by that comment. "Bonnie's with...Clyde?"

"Yeah. The chemistry coach. His name is Clyde."

And apparently Trevor is too young to know about the infamous bank-robbing duo. When did I get so old?

"So I should go find Bonnie and Clyde?" I ask, chuckling at the pairing. It's almost as funny as Boyd and Gayle the nurses, a pairing that seemed to amuse Bonnie as much as it did me.

Though Trevor gives me a weird look, like he can't figure out why I would be laughing, he nods and takes the tablet from me. "Jonah's trailer is just two down from Bonnie's."

"Thanks."

Several pairs of eyes follow me as I trek across the production area, even though I'm pretty sure they're filming a bunch of side character scenes right now and have no reason to be standing around watching me. Maybe Fran's not so crazy if even the people who have been around us the whole time are starting to wonder enough to give me searching looks.

I just need to kiss Bonnie. No biggie.

When I reach Jonah's trailer, I hesitate to knock. Who knows what they could be doing in there with the chemistry coach? The longer I stand here, though, the more people will start to whisper, and I need to show some confidence for Bonnie's sake. I may be doing better with this relationship, but I clearly need more work.

My phone buzzes in my pocket. Then again. If it's Derek, I may need to consider blocking his number before this becomes a thing. I'm not about to be his eyes and ears when it comes to Bonnie, even if I do plan on keeping an eye on her to make sure she's taken care of as much as she seems to take care of everyone else.

I glance at the texts, rolling my eyes as soon as I read them.

Not likely, but he texts one more time before I turn my phone to silent and shove it back into my pocket.

Ignoring the unease building in my belly, I reach up and knock on the trailer door.

It's Jonah who answers, a knowing look in his eyes. "Wondered if you would be showing up here at some point."

"Fran?" I guess.

He nods and steps back to let me in. "Honestly, I'm glad I don't work with her, but she's a force to be reckoned with. I warn you, though, Clyde is pretty excited to work with you, and he's his own kind of a force."

I stop with one foot on the steps and look up at him. It's none of my business, but I ask anyway. "How was your lunch with June?"

He grins wide. "She doesn't like me."

I have a feeling that's not going to stop him from trying again. Thankfully, June can take care of herself, but as I head inside, I make a mental note to check up on her from time to time while filming is underway.

I don't know what I expected from a chemistry coach, but a little old balding man wasn't it. He looks like someone's ninety-year-old grandpa came to visit the set, and despite his broad smile, I'm instantly uncomfortable. *This* is the person who's supposed to teach me how to find more chemistry with Bonnie? He looks like he hasn't experienced romance in twenty years, since the day his wife passed of old age.

"You must be Henry!" he says, holding out his hand. I'd thought he was sitting next to Bonnie, but he was actually already standing, which puts the top of his head at the level of my chest.

"H-Hank," I correct, though my name comes out stammered because Clyde has a surprisingly strong grip. "And you're Clyde?" It's a question because I'm honestly not sure at this point.

Clyde guffaws. "Yes, sirree. Have a seat here next to Miss Aiken, and we'll jump right in."

I fall onto the couch rather than taking a more graceful approach. What does he mean by 'jump right in'? My heart rate spikes as I watch Clyde struggle to get himself into a chair across from us. Jonah, I notice, finds himself a stool so he can watch. Great. What happened to Bonnie and me already having tons of chemistry?

I don't think I want an actual answer to that question because it probably has something to do with me and my many issues.

Still, I don't think he should be here for this.

Bonnie nudges her shoulder into mine. "Jonah knows our relationship is fake," she says, reading my thoughts.

I frown. "Why?"

"Because Fran put me on backup in case things fail between you two," Jonah answers for her. When I look at him in alarm, he wrinkles his nose. "I don't like it any more than you do, McAllister, but it's part of the job."

"Fine, but why are you *here*?" I sound rude, but I almost don't care. This meeting is going to be bad enough without a witness.

Chuckling, Jonah shrugs and looks around the trailer. "Technically, you're in *my* space. Besides, I'm curious."

Definitely don't like that.

Touching my arm, Bonnie pulls my attention back to her. "Just ignore him. And everything will be fine with our relationship. Did Fran talk to you?"

About kissing Bonnie in front of as many people as possible? "Yep," I squeak.

Clyde lifts an eyebrow as he settles in his seat across from us.

"And did she tell you what we need to do?" Bonnie asks.

She's speaking so gently that I feel pathetic for making a big deal out of this. Our relationship isn't real. Bonnie doesn't *want* it to be real. A kiss won't mean anything, so I should really stop panicking.

That's easier said than done. My one and only first kiss was twelve years ago.

I clear my throat again, trying not to look anyone in the eye. "She said I need to kiss you."

"Are you okay with that?"

It is strangely emasculating to have a beautiful and intelligent woman ask if I am comfortable with the idea of kissing her. Everyone is entitled to their levels of comfort, but I was *married* for six years. It's not like I am new to any of this.

"Perhaps we need to take a different approach," Clyde says, and he sounds more like a therapist than a chemistry coach. Not that I know what a chemistry coach is supposed to sound like. "Hank, why don't you tell me about your first love?"

My eyes jump to his in panic. "What?" I look at Bonnie, trying to understand why she would tell anyone about Shelby when she knows how difficult it has been for me to talk about her.

Bonnie's eyebrows pull low as she looks at me. "Was there no one before Shelby?" she asks, almost too quietly for me to hear.

I shake my head as I clench my hands in my lap. I keep my words quiet, but I'm not ashamed of my past. It is what it is. "My parents were too young when they had me and left me with my grandmother. My grandma was too old to be a parent but looked after me to the best of her ability before she died soon after I turned eighteen. There was never time for dating because I was always looking out for her. Shelby was my first...everything."

She was the person who helped me feel like I could be a part of something. The reason I switched my major from business to literature halfway through college because she thought I had a "professor vibe" and should look into teaching, which was the best career move I could have made because I loved it. Shelby was the guiding light in my life to make me think a family was the best dream I could ever have despite never really having one of my own.

I still have parents. Technically. But I have no idea where they are, and I've never bothered to find out. They didn't do anything to shape me into the man I became. Not like Shelby did. And when I lost her, I lost everything about who I am right along with her. How am I supposed to sum up a relationship like that?

"Hank?" Bonnie takes hold of my hand, pulling my gaze back to her. "You don't have to talk about her."

"Ahh," Clyde says, scribbling something in a small notebook he produced out of thin air.

"She was the first person to really see me," I say to the trailer at large, despite what Bonnie just said. We're never going to get through this if I don't say *something*. "She never judged me for what I was, but she always pushed me to do better."

Bonnie smiles. "My first love was a boy in the second grade. His name was Stevie, and every girl was in love with him. One time, on Pet Day, his mom showed up and surprised him with a puppy, and I knew he and I were meant to be."

A smile cracks through my melancholy. "Because of a puppy?"

She nods. "I always wanted a puppy. Desperately. But my parents didn't think I could take care of one, even after I used the excuse that having a dog at home with me would be way safer than being by myself."

"By yourself?" Shock runs through me like a bolt of lightning. "You were home alone in the second grade?"

Shrugging, Bonnie tucks one slender leg over the other. "Pretty much my whole childhood. They both worked, and daycare was too expensive."

No wonder she doesn't like to be alone. And no wonder she struggles with asking for help. She's used to taking care of herself. "I'm so sorry," I whisper, adjusting our hands so our fingers are laced together. "No one should have to be alone like that."

"Says the man who just spent the last four years holed up in a house by himself."

"Exactly. I know what I'm talking about, and I wouldn't wish it on anyone. Especially not you."

"This is good!" Clyde says, making us both jump. He's grinning like he just won the lottery. "Emotional intimacy will almost always lead to physical intimacy, though the same can also be said for the other way around." He throws a wink to Jonah, who finger guns him back.

I'm not sure I want to know what that means.

"Hank," Clyde continues, "I want you to tell me three things you appreciate about Bonnie's appearance."

I wrinkle my nose.

Clyde laughs. "We'll get to the better stuff after this. Three things."

Shifting in my seat, I take a second to admire her. Though she's filming later, her makeup is minimal right now, leaving her looking natural and younger than she appears on screen. She's tall and slender, as many actresses are, and her dark hair has a slight wave to it. A small blush warms her cheeks, and her eyes fall when she seems to decide I've looked for too long.

I smile. "I like your freckles, Bonnie." I reach up and brush my knuckle against her cheek, bringing her gaze back up to me. "And your smile when you think no one is looking. I like the way your eyes are a shade of blue I've never seen before and seem to see way more than anyone realizes."

Bonnie blinks as her cheeks turn a deeper pink. She's not smiling now, as much as I wish she would, but those deep-seeing eyes of hers are saying a lot. This is the most open I've ever seen her.

"Now," Clyde says loudly, and I'm starting to wonder if he knows what he's doing because he's really killing the mood. "Bonnie, what are three physical things you admire about Hank?"

Immediately I'm uncomfortable.

Grinning, Bonnie wraps her other hand around our clasped ones and jumps right in. "I like your glasses," she says, "and the way they make you look as smart as you really are. I like that you wear what's comfortable, not what's stylish." She laughs when I frown at that one, and then she wipes my expression clean off my face when she runs a hand through my hair and sends a chill through me. "And I like your messy hair. It makes you look approachable and kind."

"Bonnie, name three non-physical things you like about Hank."

"What if I want to go first?" I ask without looking at Clyde.

He laughs but doesn't respond.

Bonnie bites her lip as she scoots closer to me. "Hank, I like the way you treat everyone as equals. I like the way you're unafraid to show emotion, even after everything you've been through. And I like that you didn't immediately jump at the chance to be in a relationship with me."

While everything she just said hits me hard, that last one feels more like a gut punch than a compliment. "You...you *like* that you had to beg me to do this?"

Bonnie snickers. "I like that you gave it a lot of thought and weren't tempted by anything but the chance to help me. You're here because you want to be."

I don't wait for Clyde to give me directions this time, jumping right into my own three things. "I like that you accepted my answer when I first told you no. I like the way you act with your whole heart and seem to be more of a vessel for Gabrielle to tell her story rather than a person pretending to be her." I lift our hands up to my lips and press a kiss to her knuckle. "I like the way you care more about other people than you care about yourself, even if I don't like the pressure it puts on you. Not many people in your position are so outwardly focused, and you are inspiring. It's no wonder the world loves you."

That...was not where I planned for that to go, and panic courses through me when a tear slips from her eye when she blinks. I didn't want to make her cry!

"They don't love me," she whispers. "They only ever love who I'm with."

"That is absolutely not true." I say that, but maybe it is true. Maybe Bonnie has spent her whole life fighting for attention but never getting it the way she wants it. Even Houston, her one real relationship, only lasted a little while, and I can't imagine how it feels to be constantly watched and critiqued by people who have no idea who this incredible woman really is. Does anyone even really know her?

I lean in and press a kiss to her forehead, tucking her hair behind her ear. "You are worth loving, Bonnie. No matter what the world thinks, that is unequivocally true."

"You promise?" Bonnie looks like she's on the verge of really crying, which is so out of character for the always cheerful woman I've known so far.

I move my hand to her cheek and brush her tear away with my thumb. I want to pull her into my arms and show her that she's not alone like she was as a kid, but something holds me back. "Promise."

Bonnie's lips curl up in a smile. It's the one I love, only softer. Warm, uninhibited, and simply Bonnie. It's the kind of smile I can easily picture myself kissing.

Jonah clears his throat, and the sound hits me like a slap in the face. I turn to glare at him for interrupting, only my eyes snag on Clyde first.

The old man winks at me before clapping his hands together. "Well, I'd say you don't need much help from me at this point. Remember, intimacy is about vulnerability. You two have a lot of reasons to hide from each other, but you shouldn't. Fake or otherwise, the only way this relationship is going to work is if you trust each other. And the only way you'll be able to prove it's working is by looking at each other the way you did just now."

"You don't want us to practice kissing?" I ask. The question surprises *me* more than it seems to surprise anyone else. I wince, looking at Bonnie before I stand alongside Clyde.

Clyde grins up at me. "I think you two can work that part out without me. Your relationship needs authenticity, not big-screen watchability. There's a big difference between a choreographed kiss and a real one."

"That's true," Jonah agrees, though no one asked for his opinion.

I raise an eyebrow and look at Bonnie for confirmation.

"He's right," she says with a shrug. I don't know if that makes me feel better or worse. "There's nothing romantic about an on-screen kiss."

"Unless you're already dating your costar," Jonah adds. "Right, Bon?"

He had better be talking about Derek right now.

Thankfully, Bonnie shakes her head. "Even then, every little move is usually laid out in a specific way and practiced about a million times. Spontaneity is what makes a real kiss so much better."

Spontaneity. Got it. If I want my kiss with Bonnie to look and feel real, we can't plan for it to happen. I rub my hands on my thighs as I process that. I eventually got used to kissing Shelby without a whole bunch of lead up to it, but *eventually* is the key word there. I don't have *eventually* with Bonnie. Houston's wedding is next week, which doesn't give me a lot of prep time. Ideally, I'll have a chance to kiss her before then so I'm not fumbling through it in front of an audience.

Why couldn't Jonah have waited just a few more seconds before he interrupted? I was on a roll. But at the same time, it's probably a good thing he stopped me. I'd prefer my first kiss with Bonnie to not have witnesses.

Clyde wraps his bony fingers around my arm, tugging me down so I'm closer to his level. "You have to be willing to let your guard down," he says softly. "And let go of the fear that has been holding you back for so long. I promise it will be worth it."

With a wink and a nod, he shuffles to the door and slowly makes his way down the steps outside. He seems to know more about me than he lets on, but I'm weirdly okay with it.

"Well, I'm going to go get some lunch," Jonah says, glancing between the two of us before following Clyde.

Bonnie steps forward to continue the procession out of the trailer. "I should check on the—"

"Lunch," I say, almost sharply. I step in front of her, tempted to grab her hand in case it helps get my point across. "You should get some lunch, Bonnie. You didn't have breakfast this morning."

She frowns. "But the—"

"Kasey is looking over the script. She and I have that covered. That's not your job. Your job is to give your best to Gabrielle, and you can't do that if you're not giving your mind and body a chance to rest."

For a moment, she almost looks angry as she stares me down. I'm currently blocking her way out of the trailer, and I plan to keep it that way until she agrees to eat something, even if I have to find Eli and convince him to drag her to the catering tent. But then she lets her hard expression fall and looks like she's on the verge of tears again.

"Okay," she says, her voice small. "Will you come with me?"

I hold out my hand, and a flash of something runs through me when she touches me. Something I haven't felt in four years.

Yeah, I'm in trouble.

CHAPTER SIXTEEN

BONNIE

When Eli and I first show up at Hank's house to pick him up for the wedding, I almost wonder if we're in the wrong place. While I know Hank lives alone and probably doesn't need much space, this cottage-like house is almost literally in the middle of nowhere, with no other houses in sight. It looks like the perfect location for a horror film, particularly with the large spider's web in the corner of the porch and no other signs of life anywhere.

As Eli turns off the SUV's engine, he looks back at me with a clear question in his eyes.

I shrug. "This is where he said to pick him up." And it's probably a sign that I need to try to get more sleep because I'm imagining all sorts of horrible things waiting to greet me as soon as I step outside the car.

I have spent every second of my free time the last several days with Hank, but looking at his house, it feels like I don't know much about him. Whenever I wasn't filming, I was sitting and talking with Hank, mostly inside my trailer even though we should have been out in a place where pictures could surface of our relationship. I really just wanted to keep him for myself because being around him is so easy.

But I still haven't been able to open up to him and tell him more of my fears and worries, and I'm pretty sure he's been holding back because of it. He almost didn't tell me his address, saying he could meet us on the production lot, and his suggestion stung. On the drive over here, I told myself that I have to trust this man.

It's not as easy now that I'm looking at his creepy house.

Eli grunts. "I'd rather not leave you here while I go up to the house." Apparently I'm not the only one imagining horrible things.

Nodding, I undo my seatbelt and put on my best smile, hoping it puts him at ease. "We can go get Hank together." This isn't helping my case when I promised Eli that he was the only security I needed on this drive, considering he thinks I might get murdered if he leaves me in the car alone. But I wanted Hank to feel comfortable. I'm lucky he offered to come to the wedding in the first place, and I think a whole security team would freak him out.

Granted, the team will be at the hotel, but we don't need them for the *drive*.

We walk to the door slowly, Eli just behind me, and I can't help but look up at the spider warily when we pass underneath it. The thing is huge and seems to be watching me like it might make me its next meal if I don't remain on my guard.

The door opens before I can knock, thankfully revealing Hank on the other side. "Hi," he says, eyes darting between us. "Everything okay?"

I point upward. "You have a spider."

"A Gasteracantha cancriformis," Eli adds, though I have no idea what he just said.

Hank grins the most natural smile I've seen on him all week. "Yeah, she is. That's Heather."

Though my jaw drops, I try to remain somewhat dignified as I look up at the terrifying spider again. I had no idea spiders could be so brightly colored, nor that they could be so spiky, bulbous, and...horrifying. It looks like a cross between an albino crab and a demon. "*That's* Heather?" I ask breathlessly. One of his five friends.

Chuckling, Hank steps back and opens the door for us. "Yeah. She's a great listener, in case you ever need someone to talk to."

"Unlike you, I have human friends for that." I clap a hand to my mouth in horror. "That sounded horrible. I'm so sorry. I know you have friends. It's just—Eli knows—I don't like spiders."

I'm so glad to step inside and have something else to occupy my thoughts as I take in the small space that Hank calls home.

Though tiny, the house is incredibly charming. Ahead of us is a quaint little kitchen and dining table, a perfect size for a man on his own. Hank's desk is to my right, placed in front of the window, and it probably has incredible views throughout the year. Beyond it is an old armchair that looks well-loved, followed by twin bookcases that are stuffed to the brim with books old and new. Between the bookshelves is a narrow hallway that I assume leads to a bedroom or two. The whole place is old, rustic, and incredibly Hank.

Hank watches me with unveiled curiosity in his eyes.

I smile. "This house suits you."

The smile he gives back to me is warm and comfortable, just like his home. "I think I may have come to suit the house over the last few years, but it's peaceful here."

"Now I need to see what your bedroom looks like." I move toward the hallway, only to be stopped by Hank.

He grimaces. "Sorry. You can... It's the room on the right. Just...don't go in the one on the left."

I know I shouldn't ask, but I can't help it. "What's in the room on the left?" When he turns a deep shade of red, guilt turns me to humor. "Is that where you keep all the bodies of the victims you base your books on?" Yeesh, that was bad.

And it kills Hank's good mood. He looks behind him, eyes fixed on the door to the left. "Shelby's studio," he murmurs. "I haven't...I haven't gone in there since..."

"Oh." Now I feel extra bad, and Hank looks so miserable that I can't help but throw my arms around his shoulders. "I'm so sorry, Hank. That must have been so hard to have that looming over you all these years."

Thankfully, he hugs me back, and it's even tighter than the hug he gave me when we first met. He's holding me like a man who is used to holding his world together and doesn't know how to let go.

"You don't have to come with me," I whisper, knowing this trip is going to be hard on him. Houston's wedding shouldn't be too bad, but I can't imagine how Hank will handle LA. He couldn't even handle his own town, passing out from the anxiety when he caught sight of his neighbors watching him. "Or I can have a driver take you back here from Sun City, if you still want to go to the wedding."

"I want to be with you." His reply comes soft but firm, and my heart seems to do a flip in my chest. "Wherever you need me."

I want to be with you. He may not think much of those words, but I have a feeling they are going to be on repeat in my mind the whole weekend.

Until I was stuck in a car with him for two hours, I never would have guessed Hank could talk nonstop. Even when we've hung out in my trailer, he's been more of a listener than a talker, so I thought I would have to spend the whole time prying information out of him with question after question. But as soon as I asked him what he did for a living before he started writing…

Hank McAllister the literature professor made an appearance and didn't shut up for almost two hours straight.

I didn't mind. In fact, I kind of loved it. He started talking about what he used to teach as an adjunct professor at the University of Denver and which courses were his favorite, and I sat and listened in awe because I felt like I was getting another glimpse of the man he was before grief wore him down. When we pull up in front of the hotel in Sun City, I'm genuinely disappointed that we don't have another two hours to go because there's something so beautiful about this version of Hank.

My one innocuous question seemed to bring more life back into the man than I've seen thus far, and I don't want that to go away. Who knew Shakespeare and literary theory could be so attractive?

I didn't, and dang this man is beautiful.

When Eli stops the car, Hank looks out the window in surprise. "We're here?"

I laugh. "I'm guessing you lost track of time in your lectures too."

Though color warms his face, he grins at me. "I doubted Shelby's insistence that I should go into teaching at first, but there's something fascinating about the human experience told through narrative. I'm sure you get that, being an actor."

Eli climbs out of the car and opens the back to start pulling out our luggage, but I'm still determined to keep this conversation going as long as I can.

"I never really thought of it that way," I say, "but yeah. There's something almost magical about storytelling. When I was a kid, I made up all kinds of stories and adventures. My stuffed animals went through a lot of drama, but it kept the loneliness at bay."

Hank takes hold of my hand. "Were you ever close with your parents? I know you said they worked a lot, but now?"

I hadn't meant to bring up my lonely childhood, neither now nor when we were talking to Clyde the other day, but after spending the last couple of hours seeing deep into Hank's soul while he talked about his favorite books and themes, I can't help but want to mirror his openness. If talking about his passion can help him rise above his heartache, maybe I can find a way to rise above mine.

Hank makes me want to trust him. To get close to him. To *hope*.

I take a deep breath and look out the window. Eli's standing by the door of the SUV, waiting for us to decide we're ready to go in, so I don't have much time. "They did their best when I was little. We didn't have a lot of money, so working was a necessity."

Hank frowns. "And now?"

I shrug. "Now, I think they don't know any other way to live. I've tried to give them everything they could ever need, but their jobs tend to come first. They're not bad parents, they're just..."

"They don't see how incredible their daughter is." His frown deepens. "They don't see you at all, do they?"

Before I can react to his insight, Eli opens the door. "Sorry, Ms. Aiken, but we should get you inside."

From the looks of the slowly growing crowd gathering on the sidewalk outside the doors, someone either recognized Eli or got a tip that I would be here, so he's right.

Hank squeezes my hand. "I'm not going to push you to talk," he says gently, "but I'm here if you want to." Then he glances at the many phones pointed toward us and seems to reconsider, his eyebrows pulling low.

"Just ignore all of them," I tell him, prepping myself with the same advice. "People will probably shout questions at you, but we can keep walking, even if you feel bad about passing them by."

"Oh, I won't feel bad."

I laugh. "It might be a good idea to smile if you can, but no pressure. Ready?"

"We'll see."

He steps out first, prompting a couple of screams and a loudly growing buzz of conversation among the little crowd, and then he reaches for my hand to help me out. I tuck my arm through his while people shout my name as well as his, and we follow Eli into the hotel lobby. All in all, it wasn't as bad as I thought it might be, and the concierge is ready to show us to our rooms.

I'm never going to tell Hank this, but it took a lot of begging and bribery on Trevor's end to secure a second room for Hank. The hotel is the swankiest in Sun City, and with all of Houston's wedding guests booked here for the weekend, the place is packed full. Despite the false nature of our relationship, Derek and I always shared a suite because it helped keep up the ruse. Plus, hotels always have strange sounds and weird lights, so having a friend nearby makes it easier to sleep at night.

I figured Hank wouldn't be as comfortable with the proximity, so I made sure he has his own room, no matter what it costs me. It's next to mine, which will hopefully ease my peace of mind but still offer him privacy.

We're halfway across the lobby when a familiar voice shouts my name. "Bonnie! You came!"

Excitement rushes through me as I catch sight of Houston Briggs hurrying toward me. "Hou!"

He wraps me up in a huge hug when he reaches me, lifting me off my feet. It's more enthusiastic than I would have expected, but the excited greeting fills me with warmth. Maybe our relationship didn't last, but I'm glad we managed to stay friends.

When he sets me back on my feet, he takes me in with his bright blue eyes. "Wow," he breathes. "You look great."

"And you look happy," I reply. He really does. He's always been a good-natured guy, especially when we were dating and he was in his athletic prime, but he looks different now. He still has the same messy blond hair and mischievous grin, but he looks settled and fulfilled. He looks *complete*. "I guess you figured out the complications?"

That gets a laugh out of him. When I last saw him in person, he was having a rough go of things with his soon-to-be-wife and seemed ready to give up on the relationship because things had gotten complicated. Seeing his obvious happiness, I'm glad he stuck it out.

"Yeah, I did," he says. "Speaking of…" He looks behind him, where a small group of people have been watching our exchange, and gestures for all of them to join him. I recognize his two sisters and his older brother, each of whom has a significant other on his or her arm, but it's the blonde in front who catches my eye. I've never met her, but it's clear she's the bride based on the way Houston smiles at her.

I can't stop my own smile. "Darcy! I'm so glad I finally get to meet you." I pull her into my arms, only realizing she might not be a hugger after I've already given her a good squeeze because she stands rather stiff. I take a step back, feeling the heat rise in my face. "Um. Sorry."

Darcy glances at Houston, then at Houston's family behind her, before she smiles at me. "No, it's totally fine. I just wasn't expecting…you're *Bonnie Aiken*. And you just hugged me."

I laugh. "Girl, you're marrying one of the best pitchers this country has seen in years. I'm small potatoes compared to him."

"Not true," Houston argues. "And I'm not pitching anymore. Anyway, you remember my siblings?"

I grin at Micah, his younger sister, and pull her into a hug that she happily returns. "It's so good to see you again, Micah! And Fischer!" I wave at the man behind her, since he's not easily accessible for a hug. I only met him once, but I remember well the way he was madly in love with Micah even though she had no idea. "I hear you two tied the knot last fall. Congratulations!"

Houston's twin sister gets a hug next. "Brooklyn!" She's my favorite of Houston's siblings, though I will never admit it out loud.

"Hello again, Bonnie," she says, her smile warm. "This is my husband, Jordan."

Jordan shakes my hand with enthusiasm. "Is Liam staying out of trouble?"

His question knocks some of the wind out of my sails. "Liam?"

He chuckles. "I was his publicist before Ethan."

"Oh! You're that Jordan! What a small world!" My smile returns as the unease ebbs. My friends and I look out for each other, but clearly I don't need to be on my guard around any of Houston's family. "Kasey has been a good influence," I tell him.

Houston takes my hand and nudges me around to the other side of the group. "You remember my older brother, Chad?"

Chad gives me a nod, but his eyes are on something behind me. He looks both shocked and confused, and I wonder what...

"You're here!" The woman who was standing next to Chad bounces on the balls of her feet, like she's brimming with energy as she looks at the same thing as Chad. With a frown, Chad takes the baby she's holding, and as soon as she's free, she rushes forward, ignoring me entirely as she passes me to get to Hank.

Oh my goodness, Hank!

Somehow, I forgot my pretend boyfriend in my excitement, and I feel terrible about abandoning him. Thank goodness for the woman who noticed him. As I watch her wrap him up in a hug he happily returns, I assume she's the last of Hank's five friends, Hope. If I remember right, he said she's Chad's wife.

I turn a smile to Chad. "You have a baby."

Though he clearly wants to go greet Hank, who kept off to the side on his own, Chad returns my smile and looks down at the bundle in his arms. She looks like she's only a few months old, and she is absolutely darling. "This is Moira. But we call her Mo."

"Can I hold her?"

Though he seems to debate for a moment, Chad carefully hands off his daughter and then follows his wife to go talk to Hank, leaving me with Houston and Darcy as the rest of the Briggs family makes their way to the elevators.

"I'm really glad you're here, Bon," Houston says, and he clearly means it. He wraps his arm around Darcy's shoulders, his smile wide and comfortable. Thankfully, Darcy seems to have relaxed as well as she leans into his side. Even knowing nothing about her, I can tell they're perfect for each other.

Mo coos in my arms and pulls my attention back to her and her hazel eyes peering up at me with interest. I haven't had the chance to spend a lot of time around babies, and I'm not sure I'm going to be able to give her back to her parents. She's so precious.

I sigh. Today has been a good day. "I'm glad you invited me, Hou. I know we didn't date for long, but I like to think we're friends. Darcy, you found yourself the best of men."

She grins up at him. "I know I did."

"I'm surprised you managed to bring Hank with you," Houston says, looking over to where Hank is talking to Chad and Hope. "From what I've heard about him, he's not really the type to leave his house."

He's not, but agreeing feels like I'm saying Hank's private nature is a bad thing. "Honestly, I'm lucky he offered to come with me. I was going to feel like I stuck out like a sore thumb if I came without a date."

Darcy laughs. "I don't think it's possible for you to be a sore anything. My sister doesn't have a date either."

"Where is Carissa, anyway?" Houston asks, looking around the lobby. "She disappeared before dinner was even over." His eyes lock on the group of people by the doors. The crowd has grown considerably and has probably taken all sorts of pictures and videos. The only thing holding them back is Eli, who is starting to look overwhelmed. The rest of my security must not be here yet.

Considering the size of this crowd, I probably shouldn't have hugged Houston so enthusiastically, but I couldn't help it. Hank and I are going to have to do something before we head to our rooms to make sure no one has reason to think I'm here to ditch Hank and break up Houston's wedding. That would be a disaster, no matter how untrue it would be.

"I think she went up to her room to video chat with her 'not-a-boyfriend,'" Darcy says with air quotes.

Houston rolls his eyes. "They're so dating, no matter what she says."

"One hundred percent," Darcy says. "Anyway, you must be tired from your drive, Bonnie. Don't let us keep you from settling in! If you'd like, you're welcome to join my bachelorette party tonight. It's just me, Carissa, and Houston's sisters, so it's not going to be anything special, and we won't be leaving the hotel so you won't have to worry about cameras."

I know she's inviting me out of obligation, but I still feel incredibly grateful for her friendliness. "I would love that, though I should make sure Hank won't feel abandoned."

"He's welcome to join the guys," Houston says, shrugging. "My old teammates are going to try to kidnap me and take me out drinking, so we're going to be hiding out in the hotel too and hope Chad is enough to scare them off."

I laugh. "Thanks, Hou. I'll let Hank know, and I'll text you."

They head to the elevators, Houston waving at the crowd and garnering some delighted squeals from the ladies while Darcy rolls her eyes at him.

I hurry to Hank's side and shuffle the baby in my arms when she squirms.

"Oh, I can take her," Hope says, and there's clear distress in her voice. "You don't have to—"

"I am not ready to give her up yet," I return with a laugh. "She's so darling, isn't she, Hank?"

His eyes dart toward the crowd at the other end of the lobby, and then he puts his hand on my shoulder and leans in to get a better look at Mo. He's a genius, and these pictures are going to be way more viral than anything I did with Houston.

I look up at him, and something shifts inside me when I see the smile on his face as he brushes his hand over the baby's soft hair. I wonder if he and Shelby planned to have kids. After what I experienced during the drive, I know he would be the type of father who tells the best sort of bedtime stories. Who is so gentle but also the fiercest of cheerleaders and defenders. I've never really imagined myself with a family, but if I ever did…

Hank would be a good choice of partner.

Fear grips my heart, sudden and strong, and I drop my gaze before my imagination runs away with itself. Liking Hank is one thing. Imagining myself actually settling down and having a family with him? That's looking for disaster and heartbreak. History has proven that that kind of life has never been for me.

"We should probably go before Eli gets stampeded by our fans," I mutter, holding the baby out to Hope. "Thank you for letting me hold her, and it's so nice to meet you. Hank talks highly of you both."

Turning red, he ducks his head for a second before looking at Hope and Chad. "For the record, I've said very little."

"You're two of his five friends," I argue. "That's nothing to sneeze at."

Hank snorts. "You're not making me sound great, Bonnie."

"One of those friends is a spider," I continue, failing to fight my grin.

Hank actually laughs out loud, which seems to confuse Hope and Chad, like they've never seen him laugh before. "We should go," he says, tucking my arm through his and pulling me toward the elevators to follow the others.

Before the elevator doors close, I meet Chad's gaze and have no idea what to make of his expression. He looks both amazed and concerned, two things that don't generally go together, and I have no idea what to do with that.

HOLLYWOOD HOT SCOOP

Bonnie's Baby Blues

SCOOPERS, I DON'T KNOW what to say that isn't already said in this picture. I mean...*Henry's smile. Bonnie's yearning. The baby!* Now, before you go thinking there's a secret Mini Dennie out there—I'm sure we can all agree Derek and Bonnie would have had the most adorable children—or even a Benrie baby, this cute bundle of joy is the niece of former Red-Tails pitcher, Houston Briggs. But that doesn't change the fact that Bonnie and Henry are both clearly baby-hungry.

There's still a lot to learn about our new favorite man of mystery, but no one can look at that face of his and see anything but a man in love. He doesn't have to be looking at Bonnie for us to know this man wants her to have his babies. And Bonnie! While you, like me, might have thought Bonnie was never going to settle down, it seems our leading lady has finally found her forever man. I'm getting teary-eyed just looking at them.

If Derek wasn't heartbroken before, he's sure to be now that he has no chance of winning Bonnie's love back. If anyone knows how to get in touch with the heartthrob hero, I am more than ready to hold him while he cries. I'm sure I'm not the only one!

We're keeping an eye out for any drama this weekend, because Bonnie and Houston were looking pretty chummy. Who do you think would win in a fight between the mystery writer and the retired pitcher? Henry may not have Houston's size, but it's the quiet ones who end up more dangerous in the end. Or will there be a catfight between the starlet and the virtually unknown Darcy Paxton? Vote below!

Make sure you hit that subscribe button because we are going to do everything we can to get all the insider scoops at the Briggs-Paxton wedding this weekend. Maybe these two couples will get into a brawl of epic proportions. Maybe Bonnie and Houston will rekindle the old flame and run away together. Or maybe Henry will get inspired to turn his casual relationship with Bonnie into something more permanent so he can get himself a miniature McAllister. *wink wink* XO

<PICTURE NO LONGER AVAILABLE>

EDIT: Sorry, Scoopers! We realized that the little Briggs baby deserves some privacy, so we've uploaded a new picture that does not show her face like the last one. Never fear! You can still get your fill of Bonnie and Henry's expressions, and you'll just have to take our word for it that Houston's niece is adorable. XO

Chapter Seventeen

HANK

"Okay, but if you can figure out how to force them to take down the picture, you can probably figure out who's behind the site, right?" Houston is pacing in front of his brother, an almost murderous look in his eyes. "You couldn't have forced them to take down the article entirely?"

Chad sighs, settling deeper into his armchair as he watches Houston wear a hole in the rug. Little Mo is sound asleep in Chad's arms. "I did what I could, Texas. I'm lucky I got them to agree to take down the photo that had my infant daughter's face."

The men of the wedding party have taken up residence in a sort of lounge in the hotel, and though I was tempted to ignore the invitation to join them, coming here was probably better than holing up in my hotel suite and pretending I was fine letting Bonnie go off with the women. It's not that I think she'll be in any danger, and Chad's family are all good people so they'll treat Bonnie well.

But a *Hot Scoop* article just dropped, and it wasn't great. I have no idea if Bonnie has seen it or if she's too busy enjoying the hotel spa, but I can't imagine how she might feel about what the article said.

I'm not sure how *I* feel. I have Liam to thank for knowing about the article—he texted me the link as soon as it appeared—and there are so many things about this one that have hit me harder than the others.

"Houston, you *have* to stop pacing," Jordan complains. "You're making me dizzy. I know that article sounded bad, but it could have been a lot worse. Everything will be fine."

Houston turns his sharp gaze to me. "*You're* awfully calm about this whole thing."

I'm not, but I'm doing my best to keep the panic out of my expression. It's as much the implications of the article as it is the realization that some of it might not be as inaccurate as previous articles have been. Obviously not the fighting Houston part, but... I haven't specifically thought about starting a family with Bonnie, but I do know my thoughts and feelings are heading in that direction. Slowly, but still.

My baby steps toward healing have been picking up speed at an alarming rate.

This article's insinuation that Bonnie and I are in this thing deep enough to be thinking about children is making *me* dizzy, and it is taking everything in me not to let my thoughts stray there. I'm still getting to the affection part of this relationship. It's dangerous to let my mind wander beyond that.

I look at Chad. "Did you get any useful information about *Hot Scoop*?"

Grimacing, he shakes his head. "I'm genuinely impressed by how well they keep their identities hidden. I guarantee it's multiple people, and they're not afraid to use any resource they can get their hands on."

"*Hot Scoop* has been a thorn in the sides of anyone of moderate fame in California and beyond," Jordan adds. "The PR firm I worked for is one of the best in the country, but even they couldn't get any leverage on the site."

That doesn't help my anxiety on the subject, but it's not anything I didn't expect. "I hope Bonnie is handling this one okay," I say quietly. "It was overall positive, but this goes beyond most invasions of privacy I've seen."

Jordan snorts. "You should get out more. I got to deal with Liam's bare butt making an appearance all over the internet, and that seems worse."

"From the little I know about Liam Connolly," Kit throws in, "I think he might disagree." Apparently Kit is married to one of Houston's many step-siblings, and when Kit showed up at the hotel right as we were heading to the lounge, Houston nearly tackled him with excitement. His happiness was short-lived because Liam sent me the *Hot Scoop* article only a few minutes later.

I look at Houston, watching him as he sinks into a chair. "You know Bonnie better than I do," I say slowly. While that may be true, it doesn't mean I like it. How can I get her to trust me the way she trusted Houston? She must have trusted him, considering their relationship was the only real one she's had. "How do you think she's handling this? What about Darcy?"

He shrugs and runs a hand through his hair, leaning his head against the back of his chair. I know this isn't how he planned to spend his bachelor party, but I'm glad to know he's a good enough human to worry about the effect of this article. "I'm sure Darcy is fine. She's stronger than anyone I know and is probably laughing about all of this. As for Bonnie..."

He sighs heavily. "She's never been the kind of person to see that sort of future with anyone. It's why dating her was so easy, because I wasn't that kind of person either at the time. I honestly haven't talked to her much since we broke up, just a message here and there, but I've never seen her look at…" His eyes jump to me. "She's never looked at anyone like she looked at you in that photo. This one might be closer to the truth than she'd like."

Our relationship isn't real. If there's anyone I can tell, it's this group. But the words stick in my throat. I'm not sure if it's because I don't want to break Bonnie's confidence or be in breach of contract, or if it's because those words are starting to feel less true. At least on my end, the feelings that bubble up inside me whenever I see her aren't fake.

I was actually looking *forward* to this weekend, in part so I could see Chad and Hope—and their three kids—but mostly because I eagerly left my house every day to spend whatever time with Bonnie that I could. It became less of an obligation and more of a *need* to be around her and learn more about who she is. She might not be willing to give me a full view of the woman she is beneath the surface, but I've been catching glimpses and hanging on her every word, no matter how insignificant.

And even now, after only an hour or so apart from her, I *miss* her. In a way I've only ever missed one person before.

"Hank?" Chad's voice is soft, but there is an unmistakable question in the way he says my name. He's wondering if I'm okay.

I meet his gaze and furrow my brow. It's like he can read my thoughts. "How did you know?"

He smiles, clearly understanding my vague question. "I think that's a question you should be asking yourself, Hank. You've been through this before."

Though the others look at me in curiosity, I ignore them. Chad's right, and this isn't the first time I've started to feel something stronger than simple interest. But everything with Shelby was easy. She was unafraid of love, which meant she fell hard and fast, even if I still don't know why she picked me. And she was so easy to love in return because she made me feel safe. Wanted. *Needed.*

With the fame that surrounds Bonnie and her life, it's hard to feel safe. Things like speculation on whether or not she wants a baby—my baby—are going to follow her as long as she continues to pursue her career path. And it's impossible to know if she'll ever want me because this relationship is, as far as I know, far from real. And needed? This woman is so hell-bent on helping everyone around her that she makes anyone else feel superfluous, not to mention her wealth, personal security, influential friends...

What could she possibly need from me outside of being a piece of arm candy?

"Houston," Kit says, rolling his eyes, "seriously, you need to relax or Darcy is going to kill us when you show up at your wedding tomorrow looking like death warmed over."

Houston scoffs. "But—"

"I genuinely think Bonnie will be fine," Jordan says, "and that article is way better than anything they could have said if they got a photo of the way Hank was glaring at you when he and Bonnie first arrived."

I choke. "The way I what?"

"Yeah," Fischer says, speaking up for the first time. He's been a quiet observer of all of this so far, which seems to be his way. "They could have had all sorts of fun with something like that."

"Why were you glaring at me?" Houston looks like I just told him I enjoy drowning puppies. "We don't even know each other."

I don't have an answer, so Chad replies for me. "Because you and Bonnie were all sorts of cozy. The article had it right about that."

Houston huffs another short laugh, looking at everyone as if he might get more of an explanation. Does he really not know how their reunion looked? "That's just how Bonnie is," he says, clearly on the defensive. He turns to me. "I mean, *you* know."

I don't know. Not really. She hugged me when we first met, but there's a difference between hugging your favorite author and launching yourself at an ex. I don't want to antagonize the man the night before his wedding, but I do need to set some boundaries. As much for his bride's sake as for Bonnie's.

"Her public image is all over the map right now," I say, my voice soft but with an edge I can't avoid. "And the internet would love to turn this weekend into a scandal if they get the chance. It would be best for everyone if you and Bonnie keep your distance from each other, no matter how friendly you both are."

"But Bonnie needs—"

"I've got Bonnie." A sudden rush of nerves from knowing just how big tomorrow's ceremony will be floods through me, but I fight down the anxiety. I'm going to have to get over my well-developed fear of crowds if I'm going to be of any use to Bonnie. I force a smile and stand. "All you need to worry about tomorrow is marrying the love of your life."

Houston doesn't reply, and though there's still an undercurrent of worry in his eyes, the moment I mention Darcy, he seems to relax.

I nod toward the other men. "I'm going to turn in. Thanks for letting me join for a bit, and don't have too much fun tonight."

Chad's chuckle follows me out the door and into the hallway.

For being a fully booked hotel, it's surprisingly quiet, and I debate going back to my room or exploring a bit. The last time I stayed in a place this nice was on my honeymoon, and the only reason we could afford it was because Shelby's parents footed the bill. They thought twenty-one was too young for her to get married but were supportive all the same and wanted us to enjoy ourselves.

Still standing in the hallway, I pull my phone out of my pocket and frown at it. I haven't talked to them since the funeral, thinking it was easier to keep my distance. But they lost their only daughter when Shelby died. Maybe we could have been helping each other through it. I still remember her father's phone number, and it would be easy to send a text. Check in.

I don't know how long I stand there and debate with myself, but I am more than grateful when Bonnie's voice cuts through my back-and-forth and gives me an excuse to chicken out. "Oh, Hank! I didn't expect to see you until later."

My whole body relaxes at the sight of her, which is a new sensation I could get used to. She's always so happy and sweet, brightening every room she's in. Whether or not she might feel the same way I'm beginning to, I'm glad to have her in my life for now.

"Hey." I almost roll my eyes at the single word that comes out of my mouth. "I thought you'd still be at the spa with the girls."

Particularly because she's wearing a fluffy white bathrobe and fuzzy slippers, her dark hair pulled back into a braid and her face devoid of makeup.

She's beautiful.

Bonnie smiles and steps closer. "Fran called me and told me about the new *Hot Scoop* article."

Though she doesn't look upset or worried, I take her hand anyway. Just in case. "You okay?"

She nods. "It could have been a lot worse, and Fran is thrilled that it's so positive. Are *you* okay? There was a lot of talk about you in this one."

"If it helps you, then I'm fine with it."

Red colors her cheek, brighter than I've ever seen it, and her eyes slip down to our clasped hands. "I'm sorry for abandoning you earlier. It's been so long since I last saw Houston, and I wasn't thinking."

Is she worried about my feelings or worried that she could have damaged our pretend relationship? I can't decide, and I'm not about to ask. In the grand scheme of things, it doesn't matter.

I feel that lie deep in my belly. It matters more than I want it to. "I was heading back to my suite to try to get some writing done," I say to change the subject. "I finally made some headway over the last few days."

"Can…" Bonnie bites her lip and looks around the empty corridor, turning an even deeper shade of red. "Can I join you? I have a couple of scripts my agent wants me to look over before I get to LA, so I won't bother you or anything, but I don't want to be…"

"Alone?" I finish for her. "Me neither, which is a strange sensation."

She grins. "Want to come hang out in my suite with me?"

I'm not sure how well I'll be able to focus on Gabrielle's story when the living embodiment of her is sitting next to me, but I don't think I could ever force Bonnie to be on her own. Anyone she might spend time with tonight is at the spa. Besides, I would be a fool to waste a chance to get to know her better, even if it is simply by watching her read a script.

"I would like that," I tell her, squeezing her hand. "And maybe you can help me brainstorm the book's climax."

Her eyes go so wide that it's almost comical. "Really? Oh, Hank, you have no idea how much I would love that."

Laughing, I lift her hand and kiss her knuckles. "Maybe, with your help, this book will turn out okay after all."

And maybe I won't get my heart broken again when all this is over, though that one feels a lot less likely.

CHAPTER EIGHTEEN

BONNIE

WHEN I OPEN MY eyes, I'm not sure at first where I am. I was dreaming about a sunset over a glittering lake surrounded by huge pines and towering mountains. It was more peaceful than anywhere I've ever been, and I desperately want to go back.

The last thing I remember before falling asleep was texting my friends about the most recent *Hot Scoop* article. No one seemed to be able to decide if this one was good or bad, but Derek was unusually quiet in the chat. I half expected him to start texting me individually, but he never did.

My pillow moves, waking me up the rest of the way as I become fully aware of my surroundings. Or, more accurately, who is surrounding me.

When I started getting sleepy, I cuddled up against Hank, and I have never been this comfortable in my life. With my head on his chest and his left arm wrapped snugly around my shoulders, I feel like he's protecting me from bad dreams. He's still in the spot he was before I fell asleep, sitting propped up against the headboard of my bed and writing in a leather-bound notebook because he doesn't own a laptop.

I shift, and his pen stops moving. "Bonnie?" he whispers.

As much as I want to look up into his face, I don't want to move and break this calm that sits between us. "How long was I asleep?"

His hand, which is wrapped around my arm, lifts as he checks his watch. Warmth spreads through me when his hand returns to its place like it belongs against my skin. "A couple of hours."

"Really?"

"You were out pretty fast, and I didn't want to disturb you and head to my room, so I—"

"Don't go." My hand splays across his torso before he can move, my fingers making little wrinkles in his t-shirt. I've only ever seen Hank in sweaters and flannel, and I like the pajama version of him. He feels...warm. Safe. Seeing him dressed down like this, it feels like he's here to stay. "How's your book coming?"

His chuckle rumbles through him. "Better than I expected, though I have no idea how it's going to end. This book has been elusive in a way none of the others have."

His fingers start dancing across the skin of my arm, and for a moment that's all I can focus on. For how resistant he was to being a part of this relationship in the beginning, he seems to have settled into it nicely. I know Fran made him join me with the chemistry coach, Clyde, but none of this right now can benefit the public's opinion. We're entirely alone.

And while I have always been comfortable with Derek, who is easily my closest friend and confidant, I never felt this way with him when we hung out alone. I love him, but even with me he keeps things tamped down and hidden because...I don't know why. Maybe he thinks having real human emotions is a weakness, and he hates weakness with a passion.

Or maybe he just doesn't know what he wants so he doesn't let himself ache for anything or enjoy what he has.

But Hank? Hank has never been afraid to tell me exactly what he's feeling, and I think I've taken that for granted so far.

It also terrifies me, and instinct says I should retreat before I start letting myself believe that I can keep this man. For once, I don't want to follow instinct. I want to stay right where I am.

So when I open my mouth, disappointment floods through me at the words I speak. "Did you used to sit in bed like this with Shelby?" Why would I bring her up? *Now?* So much for ignoring instinct.

Just as I expected, Hank tenses, but it doesn't take long for him to relax again. His fingers come to a stop on my arm, but he doesn't move away. "Yeah," he says after a moment. He tucks his pen into the notebook and sets it on the end table. I hope he doesn't mean to leave now that I've stupidly brought up his late wife. "She was more of a night owl than me because of late-night shows at her gallery, but she liked being next to me whenever I planned lectures." He takes a deep breath and lets it out slowly. "She had a bad habit of distracting me."

"How would she... Oh." I cut myself off as heat blossoms on my cheeks when I realize what he likely means. I can't say that I blame Shelby for looking at this adorable man and wanting to appreciate him fully. He may not be Hollywood's standard of masculinity—not like Derek—but his softness and steadiness are plenty attractive. Maybe a little *too* attractive.

I sit up, reluctantly pulling myself out from under Hank's arm because I have ruined the moment. "I should let you go to bed." Now that I can actually see him, he looks exhausted, so maybe it's a good thing to put some distance between us. If I was asleep for a couple of hours, that's a couple hours of sleep that *he* didn't get. "Oh, Hank, you should have woken me so you could have—"

"Bonnie." Smiling, he stands and picks up his notebook. "I'm fine. You needed to sleep more than I did. See you in the morning for break-fast?"

Though I nod, the only thing I want to do right now is ask him to stay. But I keep my mouth shut and watch him disappear through the door between our suites.

Then I'm alone.

My thoughts aren't going to be quiet any time soon, so I dig my phone out of the blankets and send a text to Cole, hoping for a distraction.

Rugby season has started, so there's a chance he's somewhere else in the country getting ready for a match tomorrow, but I'm hoping he's at home.

His text comes only a minute later.

That fills me with both relief and worry. Relief because Cole knew exactly what I was really asking, and worry because he must have also recognized Derek was being unusually quiet.

What does he mean by that? Cole isn't one to throw words out just because. He's the least talkative of all of us, and he's gotten even quieter since his girlfriend dumped him.

Too curious not to, I send another text.

Oh. Right. I curl my fingers around my phone as I snuggle deeper into my covers. *It's not real.* It's never been real. But I think I might want that to change, and I have no idea how to do real. With Houston, it was easy because we were both looking for company more than anything. But I don't want Hank in my life just because he's a warm body and a way to boost my public image.

It's only been a few minutes since he went to his suite, and I already miss him.

I must have been quiet for too long because Cole texts again before I can reply.

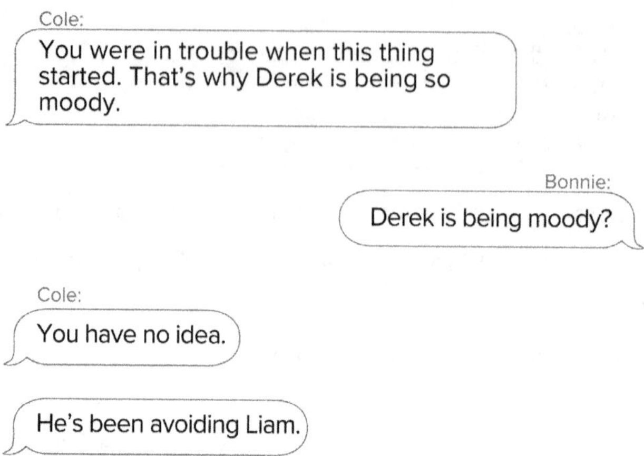

Derek never avoids any of us. I'm pretty sure he's got some internal timer that makes sure he gives us all equal attention, and he has a soft spot for Liam to begin with. (I mean, who doesn't? It's impossible to dislike Liam.)

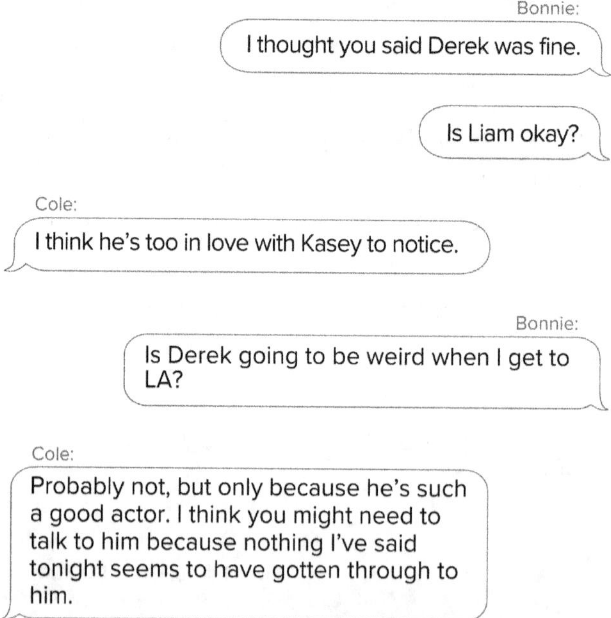

If Cole, who has known Derek longer than any of us, can't get through to Derek, I'm not sure what he thinks I'll be able to do. I love Derek, and we got especially close over the year and a half that we pretended to be a couple, but that doesn't mean I know him better than our other friends do.

Another text comes in from Cole, and I sigh.

Cole:
I shouldn't have said anything. I'll get Derek out of his funk. You have fun at the wedding.

For the next hour, I try not to think about a gloomy grump trying to cheer up a man who is always so calm that it's impossible to know what he's really feeling. Everything about that feels disastrous. I don't do a very good job at distracting myself, and the clock ticks later and later.

If I want to have even a chance at falling asleep, I can't be by myself.

Tugging the duvet off the bed and wrapping it around myself, I creep to the door that separates my suite from Hank's. His lights are off, so he's probably sound asleep and doesn't need me invading his privacy even more than I already have tonight.

I knock anyway.

Worst case scenario, he doesn't hear me and I spend the night going through the scripts I'm supposed to read this weekend. Best case, he—

A light flickers to life, glowing gold beneath the door. I unlock my side only moments before Hank opens the door.

"Bonnie?" he blinks at me, glasses askew, and does his best to stifle a yawn. His hair sticks up on one end, giving him an almost boyish look. "Is everything okay?"

Guilt pools in my belly. I feel like I'm standing in my parents' doorway and telling them I had a nightmare, all the while knowing they needed their sleep because they both had early shifts. "I shouldn't have woken you. I'm so sorry. Go back to sleep. I'll just—"

He grabs my hand, keeping me from sprinting back to my bed in shame. "Bonnie."

The concern in his eyes pulls me forward until I press myself against him, desperate for him to hold me the same way he did when I got caught in the harness. As his arms wrap around me, just as I'd hoped, I can't stop the emotion that rises into my throat. I feel *so safe*.

I'm almost *thirty*. I shouldn't be crying about a man hugging me. But Hank's fingers tangle up in my hair as he holds me tighter, and I've never felt this seen before. No one has ever noticed my fears and insecurities the way Hank does. Not even Derek.

"I can't sleep," I say quietly. "But I feel awful for waking you up."

Hank pulls away just enough to get a good look at my face—more specifically my tears—and then he glances at his suite behind him. "Do...do you want to come sleep with me? *Just* sleep," he adds.

I blush to match the red that rises up his neck. I wasn't thinking about anything more than that. "I do want that," I admit. "But I don't want to disturb you. You're used to being alone, and I—"

"I wasn't sleeping well either." Rubbing the back of his neck, he takes a step back to make room for me to come inside. "I haven't slept somewhere new in four years, except when I got snowed in with Hope and Chad during a huge storm, and they were..." He clears his throat. "I didn't sleep well that night either."

Holding back a giggle, I take a tentative step into his suite. I'm still cocooned in the duvet from my bed, which is probably going to be my best line of defense in keeping things platonic, even if I'd rather not. "I should warn you that I'm a cuddler."

He chuckles and leads the way to the king-size bed. "I'm aware."

"I'm also afraid of the dark."

"Why?"

I sit on the edge of the bed, surprised by the question. I don't often admit the fear—I can usually ignore it if I tell myself that I'm playing the role of someone who isn't afraid. But I don't think anyone has ever asked *why* I don't like the dark.

I wait until Hank sits on the other side of the bed before I say anything. "Because sometimes my parents worked double shifts so I was home by myself late at night, and I couldn't stop imagining things creeping around in the shadows. I have a pretty strong imagination, in case you didn't know."

Chuckling, he stretches out on the bed and wraps an arm around the pillow behind him. His left hand, I notice, sits on the mattress between us, fingers splayed out. "Does it make you feel better if I tell you that I've freaked myself out more times than I can count when I'm writing at night? Sometimes I forget Gabrielle isn't real."

"But she is real, kind of." I curl up into a ball and force myself to ignore his easily accessible hand. I'm fortunate that he's letting me sleep next to him; he doesn't need me crowding his bubble too. "You said Gabrielle is based on Shelby, right?"

He nods, eyes fixed on the ceiling now. "Maybe that's why this book is so hard to end," he mutters.

Even though he asked if I would help brainstorm tonight, I was pretty much asleep the whole time he was writing. I have no idea what's happening in the book or where Gabrielle might be heading, but there's something in Hank's expression that makes me nervous again.

"Do you ever think about writing books that aren't Gabrielle Frost books?" I ask. I can't decide how I want him to answer that question.

He looks at me, purses his lips, and then he takes off his glasses and sets them on the side table. He turns off the light, throwing the room into darkness, and when he settles back on the bed, his fingers find mine and hold on tight. Like he's trying to hold on to something else. "Sometimes," he whispers into the darkness. "But I'm worried what will happen when I do."

I'm worried too, but not about Hank's books. I'm worried I like him more than I should, and I'm terrified of what tomorrow is going to bring.

CE CREAM

CHAPTER NINETEEN

BONNIE

It's been a long time since I sat around and did nothing, which probably explains why Eli checked in on me to make sure I was feeling okay when I told him he had the morning off. But Hank suggested we order in breakfast instead of going down to the hotel restaurant, and I was more than happy to oblige. The morning evolved into afternoon, and I was next to the man up until about an hour ago when I reluctantly returned to my suite to get ready for the wedding.

Nothing momentous happened last night. When I woke, Hank was already up and scribbling in his notebook again. Whether we cuddled during the night or not, I have no idea, but I feel more rested than I have in a long time.

Looking at myself in the mirror, I can almost see a change in me. It's subtle, but I feel like there's more life in my eyes than I've seen in a while. Hank is good for me.

When I go to do my makeup, I wish I could go without but know what the tabloids would do with any pictures that surfaced. I never minded that part of my life before now, but today I wish I could simply have fun and not worry about how I'm being perceived every second of the day. I wish I could just exist for myself for once.

I keep my makeup minimal, only doing my eyes and letting my freckles be out in full force today. Hank likes my freckles, and I want to give him every reason to like me today.

Just before I shimmy into my dress—a silky, sage green spring dress that cuts low in the front and hangs long and free in the back—my phone vibrates on the vanity beside me. *Derek.*

Derek:

> Have fun today, Bonnie. Tell Houston congrats for me.

I purse my lips. Either Cole managed to get through to him last night, or Derek is pretending everything is fine. It could go either way.

Bonnie:

> I wish you could have come with me.

Derek:

> It's better that I didn't.

> I hope you and Hank have a good time.

Every romantic movie I've been in is telling me that Derek is jealous, but that doesn't make any sense. In the eighteen months I was Derek's pretend girlfriend, he never once gave me any signs that he wanted our relationship to be real. He performed our breakup scene exactly as Fran wanted him to without any arguments. He knew I was terrified of making any long-term attachments, so why would he...

I lift my eyes to the mirror, staring at the renewed worry in my expression. Whatever life I had a moment ago is gone. "Derek has always wanted a family," I mutter to my reflection.

That picture of you holding a baby spooked him. That's what Cole said.

What if...what if Derek never showed interest because he was so certain I would never want something like that with him? And now that there's speculation that I might...

Another text comes in before I can fully ponder that thought.

Derek:

> Sometime while you're in LA, will you check on Cole? He found out from Hot Scoop last night that Sage is dating someone from his old team, and I don't think he's taking it well. I think you can talk him out of a downward spiral.

I nearly throw my phone across the room but settle for tossing it onto the bed instead. What is with my friends suddenly deciding they need to keep secrets from each other and do everything indirectly? Cole wants me to talk to Derek, Derek wants me to talk to Cole, Kasey and Liam are in their own little happy world and oblivious to what's happening around them. At least I know Freya is being open with me as she continues to complain about her endless stream of bodyguard candidates. But Derek hasn't said anything to me about being in a bad mood, and Cole didn't bother mentioning his girlfriend moving on with someone from his old football team, and I hate that we're all falling into the bad habit of keeping our feelings to ourselves because it's easier than being open and risking the world exploiting that vulnerability.

Fully frustrated and not especially in a wedding mood, I tug my dress on and reluctantly slide into my heels. Would Darcy find it rude if I end up barefoot for most of the reception after the ceremony? Right now, I'm too annoyed to care about presentation.

A gentle knock sounds on the door between suites, and the calm that washes over me is almost instant. Leaving my phone behind, I hurry to the adjoining door and pull it open.

"No rush," Hank says, fiddling with his lopsided tie, "but the ceremony is starting in a few..." His words drop off as soon as he looks up, his jaw going slack.

I've spent enough time in designer gowns to be used to gaping looks, but there's something about Hank's gentle awe that buries itself deep inside my chest, like a ball of warmth that fills me to the brim with pleasure.

He slowly turns more and more red as he takes me in, eyes trailing over each aspect of my dress. When his gaze reaches mine again, his expression is full of nothing but admiration. "Wow," he breathes. "You look..." He swallows. "Even more beautiful than normal, which I didn't think was possible."

That would be a great thing to say with people watching. The fact that he's saying it when we're alone gives me some hope that my growing feelings aren't one-sided.

"You clean up pretty nice yourself," I say and tug his tie loose so I can retie it. "Though, I'm guessing you haven't had many reasons to wear a tie in the last few years."

He shakes his head. "Not since the funeral."

My hands grow still halfway through the knot, though it's not like I forgot about what happened to his wife. It's still such a crazy thing to think about. "Do you think you'll ever find out what happened to her?"

Another shake of his head. "The trail went cold, and it wasn't worth it for the police to keep looking into it." Before I can say anything, he brushes his finger across my cheek and elicits a blush on my skin. "Bonnie, you are entirely breathtaking."

I can see the deflection for what it is. No Shelby talk right now, which is fine by me. Finishing up his tie, I gently tug it tight and then straighten his glasses as well, just to give me something to do that will keep me close to him. "Are you ready to face the wedding guests? If you're next to me, they're going to be giving you a lot of attention."

To my complete surprise, Hank leans in until our noses brush, stealing my breath. "As long as I have *your* attention, I'll be fine."

Oh, he has it. He absolutely has it.

CE CREAM

Chapter Twenty

HANK

Breathe in.

Breathe out.

In.

Out.

Honestly, I don't pay much attention to the ceremony because I'm too busy ignoring all the people who are trying not to crane their necks and stare at us where we sit in the back. Every time I accidentally make eye contact with someone, my anxiety shoots up higher, leaving my body tense and my chest tight.

I don't know why I thought I could handle this. There are more people in this hotel ballroom than I've ever seen in Laketown at once outside of the county fair, which I avoided even when Shelby was alive.

If the sight of my neighbors is enough to make me pass out, it's a miracle I'm still breathing right now.

Partway through the ceremony, Bonnie takes my hand and squeezes it. "You okay?" she whispers, leaning in close.

I spent the night breathing in her sweet scent and talking myself into thinking I could have this. Could have her. This morning, I drank in every second she sat next to me and made little comments about the scripts she was reading. Up until half an hour ago, when we stepped into the ballroom and a couple hundred people stared at us until the ceremony began, I thought maybe I was ready to open my heart again.

If I can't sit in a friend's wedding without panicking, how am I supposed to be a part of a celebrity's life? This attention is far from atypical when it comes to Bonnie's everyday life.

She squeezes again. "My friend Liam has been talking about proposing to his girlfriend for the last four months and keeps chickening out, so I get the feeling it's going to be a long time before I go to another wedding. This is nice."

I shift closer, grateful for the distraction. "I met Liam when I talked to Kasey about the screenplay. He seems...like a lot." That, plus the dozen texts he has sent over the last few days, none of which I've responded to, and I have little faith in the two of us becoming close. I don't know if I have that kind of patience.

Bonnie snickers loud enough that it pulls a few gazes our way, though she doesn't seem to notice. "Liam *is* a lot. But he's one of the best people I know, and if you're around him long enough, he's impossible not to love."

"I'll take your word for it." Right now, I can't imagine being around *anyone*. Except her. She's never too much.

I don't know how she's been the first person I've met since Shelby's death who didn't make me nervous, but I've enjoyed her company since the day we ran into each other. Not as much the circumstances that come with her, but Bonnie herself?

I wrap my arm around her shoulders and kiss her forehead at the same time Houston kisses his new wife. The applause of the wedding guests feels like a cheer for me, for being brave enough to do more than hold Bonnie's hand. I haven't forgotten Fran's instruction to fully kiss Bonnie at some point this weekend, but I don't want Bonnie to think I'm only kissing her because I've been told to.

At some point, I need to open my stupid mouth and tell her that I am starting to have real feelings for her. She deserves to know, even if our relationship never goes anywhere.

Before I can even think about working up the courage to mention something now, while the wedding party is outside taking photos before the reception begins, Bonnie gets swarmed.

It starts with a bunch of big and burly men that I assume are Houston's old baseball teammates. Eli and a couple more men who must be extra security start wrangling the crowd into a semi-controlled line, but it's Bonnie who holds my focus. She greets many of the players by name, giving them hugs and asking how the spring training has been. As it so often is, her smile is wide and warm, and even when she doesn't know a person's name, she's just as friendly as she is with those she does know.

I may not love how easily I'm forgotten as she greets her fans, but I can't help but stand and watch in fascination as Bonnie Aiken proves why she deserves a place among the greats. I pull out my phone and start recording. I imagine this could be a great side of Bonnie to show the world. I'll send it to Trevor so he can forward it to Fran (who will never have my phone number if I can manage it).

But even as I film, there's a part of me that hates how quickly I've fallen into the idea that someone always is and always should be watching. If Bonnie wasn't so concerned about her public image right now, I would let her enjoy this moment in peace instead of making it possible for her friendliness to be broadcasted if Fran decides that it might help. I only end up taking a few short videos before I find a seat out of the way to watch Bonnie make her way through the line of fans.

It's maybe twenty minutes later—the longest twenty minutes I've endured in a long time—when I notice the change. It's so subtle that not even Eli seems to have caught it, but Bonnie's shoulders grow tense. Her smile turns forced. There's an anxiety in her eyes that wasn't there a moment ago, and I don't think it has anything to do with the woman she's currently talking to.

It's a look I know well, and I scramble to my feet and make my way to her side, tucking my arm around her waist and leaning in close. "Bonnie," I say, just loud enough for the nearest people to hear, "I'm afraid I'm going to have to whisk you away."

Though the people in line groan, Bonnie relaxes into me. "Already?" she says as she turns her gaze to meet mine. There's a sort of pleading in her eyes that's easy to understand. Under no circumstances am I allowed to let her argue that she should get through the whole line.

I never would have guessed it, but Bonnie has a social threshold.

Though I'm no actor, I try to make myself look chagrined by imagining the way I used to have to tell Shelby to stop painting and go to bed. A pang of sadness hits me in the gut, but I ignore it. For once, Bonnie needs *me*. "I know you want to stay and talk to everyone, but you have that..." Why does my brain suddenly go blank?

Panic crosses Bonnie's face before she fixes her smile and pats my cheek. "Right! I almost forgot about the call. Thank you, darling."

A few women in the crowd *aww* over the epithet, nearly sparking a wave of anxiety in me. I was doing pretty well, but now the attention is on *me*.

Swallowing, I shift my position so Bonnie and I are facing each other rather than side to side. I'm hoping it'll be easier if I don't see the crowd. "How do you do it?" I murmur, though this is hardly the time for a conversation like this. "How do you handle so much notice when you don't love the attention?"

While she may have been giving me all the signals of needing an escape, she still seems surprised by my question, her eyebrows pulling low as she stares at me with her blue-green eyes. Pink touches her cheeks but, beyond that, her freckles are in full view today. I can't stop myself from tracing their path with the tip of my finger.

Bonnie's lips part as she exhales. "How do you see me?" she whispers back. It's not an answer to my question, but I can be patient. Maybe something in her technique can help me so I'm less terrified of the possibility of this becoming my life.

I smile. "It's impossible not to see you, Bonnie."

"Can we go?"

I nod and slip my hand into hers, hyper aware of every point of contact in my fingers. Her hand is cool in mine, her grip tight, and I don't think anything in the world could get me to let go right now. The only reason I look away from her is to make eye contact with Eli, who nods and starts leading the way out a side door while the other two guards keep the disappointed crowd at bay.

Bonnie fixes on a smile and waves behind her as we follow Eli's hulking figure. "I'm so sorry I can't stay and meet you all!" she calls back.

"They're going to be at the reception," I remind her.

"I know, but..." Biting the corner of her lip, she gives me a blushing smile. "Is it bad that I would rather spend the evening with you instead of greeting fans?"

A strange sense of triumph runs through me, and I can't stop my grin. "Not bad at all. You can take a break now and then, you know."

As Eli leads us down a brightly lit corridor and into a similar lounge to the one I was in last night with the guys, Bonnie heads straight for a sofa and sinks into it with a heavy sigh, pulling me down with her. We end up pressed against each other, which I don't mind in the slightest.

The bodyguard takes up his post by the door, trying to stay far enough away to give us some privacy but too close to not overhear anything we might say.

Looks like my confessions will have to wait. Eli seems like a cool guy, if quiet, but I don't especially want him to hear me fumble through what I want to say to Bonnie.

"I don't remember the last time I actually had a break," Bonnie says once she gets settled. I can't imagine her dress is very comfortable, flattering as it is, but we won't have long before the dinner and reception begin out in the gardens behind the hotel, so it wouldn't make sense for her to change.

Not that I want her to change. She is truly breathtaking, and my eyes keep straying to the smooth skin left bare by the silky fabric. It's been a long time since I felt any sort of attraction like this, and every time I look at the plunging neckline that ends at a point just below her sternum, I feel like a teenage boy full of raging hormones. It's a bad combination with my growing interest in Bonnie as a person, and now that we're alone...

My heart starts pounding in my chest, leaving me feeling restless. Unsettled. *Nervous.*

Swallowing, I glance at Eli before turning my attention to Bonnie's hand clasped in mine. "You don't get breaks in between movies?" Maybe, if I focus on the conversation, I can stop thinking about how much I want to kiss Bonnie before the night is over.

Bonnie shrugs and rests her head on my shoulder. "I mean, I get breaks from filming. But from performing? Acting? It's pretty much nonstop unless I want to stay at home."

"Which you don't," I guess, though she's never said as much.

She nods. "Honestly, I'm almost never at my apartment. I tend to stick with whomever I'm dating at the time, and if I'm not with my boyfriend, I'm with one of my friends. I had a room at Derek's almost six months before Fran decided we should become a couple."

As far as I can tell, Derek is a good guy, but I still get a bad taste in my mouth every time I think about him. I'll likely end up meeting him tomorrow when Bonnie and I get to Los Angeles, and I'll be better able to get a read on his relationship with Bonnie. Eighteen months is a long time to be in a fake relationship, so I would be shocked if Derek didn't fall at least a little bit in love with Bonnie.

As long as those feelings are buried and dead, I can rest easy knowing Bonnie only thinks of him as a dear friend.

I rest my cheek on her head and start running my thumb along hers. "A couple of weeks ago, I would have wholeheartedly disagreed with you and said being alone is the best way to live."

Her grip tightens. "And now?"

Now I wish we had gone up to one of our suites instead of hanging out down here. "I'm starting to warm up to the idea of having someone else around," I say quietly. "You, in particular."

Her breath hitches. "Hank McAllister, are you saying I've cured you of your agoraphobia?"

I chuckle, remember how certain the set nurse, Boyd, was that I was suffering from more than social anxiety. "I think you have, Bonnie Aiken." But what I really want to say is *I'm falling in love with you so quickly that I don't think there's any stopping it.*

After losing Shelby, I didn't think I would ever be able to open my heart again. And while it's still terrifying to risk the pain of loss again, Bonnie has to be worth that risk. Everything I know about her, little though it may be, tells me that the chance to love her is a chance to experience something close to heaven.

I'm just about to throw away all my inhibitions and tell her everything, even with Eli here, when the door opens. Eli shifts to block whoever is on the other side, but the woman quickly realizes the room isn't empty and stops in her tracks.

"Oops! Sorry, I didn't think anyone would be in here." With her blonde curls and bridesmaid dress, she's clearly Darcy's sister, though I can't remember her name. She takes a step back to leave, but then her eyes catch on Bonnie and go wide. "Oh! Now I'm extra sorry for interrupting. I saw the way everyone crowded around you when the ceremony ended. Don't let me bother you."

"Wait!" Bonnie nods at Eli, who steps aside. "You can come in if you need a breather. It's Carissa, right?"

Carissa grins. "You remember me from last night?" She glances at Eli and gives him a wide berth as she slips into the room, sitting in a chair across from our couch. "I hope we didn't scare you off."

Bonnie shakes her head, though she's still resting it on my shoulder so the movement is limited. "I was just tired." Though she fell asleep fairly quickly, she left the bachelorette party early to hang out with *me*. "Did I miss anything good?"

Carissa shakes her head, loose curls bouncing. "Not really. Hope fell asleep about twenty minutes after you left, and Darcy wanted to get good sleep before today, so it was mostly just Brooklyn and me, and she's not especially chatty. It's okay, though. It was still fun to be around Houston's family, and I've never had a chance to have a spa experience like that. I figured I would take advantage of Houston paying for it, you know?"

Houston's twin might not be chatty, but Carissa clearly is. Bonnie's body language is still relaxed, so I don't think she minds, but I'm ready to find her a new hiding place if I need to.

"Are you from St. Louis, like Darcy?" Bonnie asks.

Carissa does another wild shake of her head. "No, we actually grew up in Philadelphia. I thought about finding a job in Missouri so I could see my sister more, but that was before I met..." She bites the insides of her lips, red coloring her face. I wonder what that's about. "Anyway, I'm glad Darcy and Houston are finally tying the knot. They've been dating *forever.*"

I frown. "It's only been a year and a half."

She shrugs. "Okay, so maybe that's not forever, but Houston has been talking about marriage pretty much since they started dating, so I don't know why they dragged it out this long. He knew what he wanted, and my sister isn't one to waste time on something that isn't going to pan out."

Bonnie goes tense, and though I can feel her trying to relax beside me, she's clearly not managing it well. "I don't know if I would say dating is a waste of time," she says. Her words are quiet and breathy, though I don't think it's enough of a change that Carissa notices. *I* notice, and I can't help but wonder what's going through her head. Who is she thinking about?

Carissa purses her lips and looks down at the phone she pulls out of her purse. "If you know, you know. You know?"

"Yeah," I say at the same time Bonnie says, "No."

She lifts her head and looks at me, and I get hit with a sudden realization. Bonnie has *never* been in love. She has no idea how something like this feels. What if... I barely let myself entertain the thought. What if she's falling for me and doesn't know it? I hate how much hope that gives me, but I'm going to cling to it as long as I can.

"Was that how it was for you and..." She stops herself, glancing at Carissa.

Thankfully, Carissa seems too interested in whatever she's typing to have heard Bonnie's question.

I smile, though there's nothing happy about the expression. Bonnie always seems to bring up my wife in our most intimate moments. I don't want to talk about Shelby. Not when I'm realizing I'm going to have to make the first move if I ever want something to happen with Bonnie. It'll take courage I haven't felt in a long time to tell her how I feel about her, but I can't afford to waffle any more. If I do, I'll lose her. "It was almost instantaneous with Shelby," I say, keeping my voice low. I will answer Bonnie's questions, but eventually she'll need to know that my thoughts are on her.

Not on Shelby.

"How did you meet?" Bonnie asks.

"At a frat party."

She snorts. "You? At a frat party?"

"Technically, I was out on the back porch *avoiding* the frat party."

"That makes more sense. I bet Shelby took one look at you and knew you weren't like the guys inside."

My smile feels more natural now as I think about how young I was. How naive. That day was so long ago. "I was trying to do the assigned reading for one of my classes, and she decided she needed to join in, and..." I shrug. "I don't know. The world didn't look the same after that. I found her on campus the next day and carried her books for her."

"You did *not*."

I chuckle. "I did. Being raised by my grandmother instilled a bit of old-fashioned chivalry in me. Shelby thought it was the sweetest gesture anyone had ever done for her and ended up ditching class so we could hide in the trees and..." And maybe I shouldn't finish that sentence.

Bonnie's grin turns wicked. "Did you make out in the bushes, Hank? Was that your first kiss with Shelby?"

I shake my head, knowing she'll have a hard time believing me. I haven't exactly been Casanova. But once I know I want something, I'm not afraid to go for it. At least, I used to be that way. Maybe I can be that way again. I let my gaze drift to Bonnie's mouth, wondering how it would feel to kiss her, as I mutter, "No, that was the second."

She gasps. "You kissed the night you met?"

"Yeah."

"Oh." She seems to wilt for a second, but then she smiles her actor smile and turns to Carissa. Is she...jealous? I probably shouldn't consider that a triumph, but I do. "Carissa, I hear you've got a man back home."

Carissa's head snaps up at the same time she stuffs her phone behind her, as if we might try to see whatever she was doing. "What? Oh. Not really. We're just...it's not really a thing."

Her crimson blush says otherwise. She's a grown woman—I'd guess she's somewhere in her mid-twenties—so I have no idea why she would think she needs to hide a relationship. My writer brain starts filling in the blanks with all the wrong things, but Carissa doesn't seem like the type of person to be in a relationship with a married man or a convict on the run. Granted, I know nothing about her, and I know next to nothing about her sister, but I do know Chad.

And I highly doubt Chad would let his brother marry into a family without doing a thorough check on all of them.

I need to not let my imagination get away from me, so I make a show of checking my watch. "Dinner should be starting soon, shouldn't it?"

"They were almost done with pictures when I left," Carissa confirms. She seems wildly grateful for a change in topic, relaxing in her seat again. "Darcy added the two of you to the family table, by the way, so you're not going to have to worry about crazy fans trying to talk to you while you eat. Just me." She throws on a sheepish smile that makes her more endearing than she has been so far.

Bonnie sits up straight, putting distance between us that I don't want. "I'll have to make sure we thank her. She really didn't need to do that."

Eli coughs over by the door but says nothing.

Carissa glances behind her, eyeing the big bodyguard. "Does it ever get tiring, having to have someone around for protection all the time? I can't imagine how hard it must be to have people constantly pay attention to you. Is it totally exhausting?"

Bonnie laughs. "Yeah, but it's not as bad when you have the right people with you. People who see the real you."

When her head slips onto my shoulder again, my heart resumes its racing from before, pounding so wildly that I'm sure Bonnie can hear it. I know what I want. But am I brave enough to go for it? If I'm not, this thing between us is going to end.

Carissa hops to her feet, a little smirk on her face as she studies us for a moment. "For what it's worth, you two seem to be the right people for each other. I don't buy into tabloid stuff, but from what I've seen of you guys, you make a really great couple. I hope it works out."

Me too, Carissa. Me too.

Chapter Twenty-One

BONNIE

BEING AN ONLY CHILD of working parents, I've always wondered what it would be like to have siblings or even a tight-knit family. It's one part of acting that I've never quite been able to grasp because it's not something I've seen, and not even my friends can help me. Derek is an only child and isn't close to his parents, who divorced when he was a preteen. Liam was raised by a single mom. Cole lost his mom as a baby and only has his dad and grandfather in his life. Though Freya has two younger brothers, being royals sort of negates their claim on having a so-called "typical" family.

Sitting with Houston's family at dinner is like a crash course on family dynamics, though they seem to have pretty healthy relationships from what I can tell. Brooklyn, Houston's twin, isn't nearly as talkative as her brother but manages to roast him quite thoroughly in her speech, ending it all with the highest praise. Chad does pretty much the same thing, though most of his teasing stories are from when Houston was little because Chad, who is significantly older than Houston, practically raised his younger siblings. He starts crying at the end of his speech, and Houston tears up too, though they both start laughing about it a second later. Micah, true to her sunny personality, has nothing but good things to say about her brother, and she practically has stars in her eyes as she wishes him a happy life with his new bride. They all clearly love each other and would do anything for one another.

I wonder if my parents would have had more kids if they could have afforded it. How different would my life have been if I'd had someone else to play with? Being imaginative isn't entirely a solo activity, so maybe I would have still made up stories and acted them out, but would it have become my entire personality like it is now?

It's almost terrifying to think of a life other than my own, which is irony at its finest. My whole job is pretending I'm living a different life, and I really don't want to deal with a mid-life crisis right now. Not when I'm finally in the role of a lifetime and on the cusp of becoming something I've dreamed of my whole life.

When Carissa gets up to toast her sister and new brother-in-law, I take hold of Hank's hand and try to find some confidence from his hold. Honestly, I haven't wanted to let go all evening, though I'm sure he's getting sick of me by this point since we haven't been apart since last night. Even my favorite extrovert, Liam, generally can't handle me for longer than twelve hours or so. But Hank hasn't made any moves to get some space.

Though he keeps his eyes on Carissa, Hank leans closer to me. "Everything okay?"

Suddenly I'm both blushing and on the verge of tears, and I try to cover the ridiculousness by taking a sip of water. I've never had anyone understand me as well as Hank seems to. It's making it difficult to sit still in my seat and focus on the wedding toasts. Do I deserve this? Do I deserve him? This relationship isn't real, but what if it was? What if we were simply here to celebrate a mutual friend and enjoy ourselves rather than being under scrutiny for something that isn't real?

I clear my throat and pretend I'm just a regular wedding guest with my regular friend next to me. My friend who somehow reads my body language and understands the things I don't say. My friend who has given up his privacy and free time to help me. My friend who held my hand all night, who looks amazing in a suit, who keeps giving me looks that aren't quite platonic every time his eyes stray to my dress.

Those looks have been giving me life through this wedding dinner out in the gardens outside the hotel. I am so ready to dance with this man and hold him close and maybe tell him how much I want to keep him, even if that's terrifying.

I smile, glad when Hank relaxes next to me. I'm pretty sure he has figured out when my smiles are real, which is just another thing to love about... My smile falters. Love? Did I really just think that?

Based on the way my heart starts up a frantic rhythm, I definitely thought about love. I haven't known Hank long enough to actually be in love with him—I don't even know what love feels like—but I think I took a hard fall in that direction last night.

What if I mess it up? What if it falls apart like everything else seems to and leaves me heartbroken?

Hank frowns. "Bonnie?"

I can't bear to look at him right now, so I look at Houston instead, trying to sort through my thoughts as tears well up in my eyes. I know I realized last night that I want this relationship to be real, but that's not the same as falling in love. My relationship with Houston was real, but I never loved him. I never looked at him the way Darcy is looking at him while he gives his own speech, like he is everything good in the world.

I've never been brave enough to want something that will last.

Ugh, why am I crying over this? Hank looking at me with attraction should be a good thing! He has played the perfect boyfriend today, and that can't all be fake. There has to be a part of him that likes me enough to consider this thing between us turning into more than a contract. Right? I shouldn't be thinking of all the ways it can go wrong.

The other guests start applauding, signaling the end of Houston's speech, and somewhere an orchestra starts playing. Houston helps Darcy to her feet, kissing her soundly to more applause, and they lead the way to another section of the gardens, where I'm hoping there's a dance floor and with it an excuse to hold Hank close the rest of the night and let him shut out the world for me so I can stop thinking myself into a spiral.

Hank's worried look doesn't falter as we sit and wait for the other guests to get up first, and he's just so downright adorable that it hurts to look at him. How is he so perfect? He's *too* perfect.

I'm going to ruin him. No matter how much I want something real with him, I don't know how to get close to someone. To open my heart enough to let them in. My own friends barely know anything about me, and I have no room to complain about Derek keeping things from me when I'm the exact same.

I picked a life of fame because I knew it would give me an excuse to hide my real feelings.

What if that fame means I'll never be able to have something real? Hank can't want my life. To constantly be watched and scrutinized and judged for being human. How can I ask him to be a part of that when I know he wants something quiet?

"Bonnie, you're worrying me," Hank says, and he sounds so genuinely concerned that it makes my heart throb.

I can't handle it. Tugging my hand free, I slip from my chair and dart into the gardens, feet crunching on the gravel pathway as I go. I don't even know where I'm going, and I know Eli is going to be hot on my heels, but I need space from Hank until I can figure out—

"Bonnie!" So much for space. Hank is right behind me, catching up quickly because he's not in heels. Though he doesn't touch me, his anguished voice pulls me to a stop anyway. "What happened? What did I do?"

I almost laugh, and though I search for my best escape, I can't bring myself to go anywhere. I feel pulled toward him like a magnet. "You didn't—"

"I'm doing my best not to think you're crying because of Houston, but I'm failing. He caused this or I did, and I don't like either of those options."

I've never heard him talk this forcefully, and I can't help but look at him. His breaths are ragged and his eyes are wild, and there's still that hint of desire behind his pained expression, like he can't help how he feels when he looks at me. That's not the kind of thing a person can easily act.

"You think I'm hung up on Houston?" I whisper. My voice is so much smaller than his, but it's about all I have the strength for. All of this is too much.

It's this place. The garden teems with flowers of all shapes and sizes, a kaleidoscope of color buzzing with bees in the golden light of sunset coming off the red hills beyond the city. The aroma of dinner melds with the floral air surrounding me, carried by the breeze. It may be March, but Sun City always holds the warmth of summer and a peaceful kind of life that I've never found in Los Angeles.

It's the most beautiful place I've ever seen, and Hank stands in the middle of it all. I've felt that peace with him. That warmth. It's like he carries it with him everywhere he goes.

He runs a hand through his hair and scoffs. I've never seen him this ruffled. "So I'm the problem," he guesses. "I thought we... What did I do wrong?"

Movement behind him catches my eye, but it's just Eli. He seems to be taking in the situation, but he doesn't get any closer once he realizes

I'm safe. I'm both grateful and annoyed that he won't get between me and this perfect man to save me from these feelings that feel too big.

Shaking my head, I start pacing because it gives me a reason to not look at Hank. I'm worried that if I do, I'll break. My heart is already pounding, my hands shaking as I fight the urge to throw myself into his arms where I know I'll feel safe and protected. "You didn't do anything wrong, Hank. I promise."

"Okay." There is anything but acceptance in that word. "I know it's been a while since I dated, but I'm pretty sure running away from your date isn't a sign that things are going well."

I groan. He's not getting it. "This isn't a real date!" I wince, looking around to make sure there isn't anyone nearby to overhear us. Eli does the same. But then my eyes land on Hank again, and his expression leaves me frozen. There's so much happening in his eyes, everything from hurt and frustration to determination and hope. *Desire.*

He takes a single step forward, and that one step lights a fire beneath me, warming me from my core outward until I'm convinced the flowers around me might catch the flames. "What if it were real?" he asks, taking another step.

I swallow. "This date?"

He nods with the next step. "This date. This relationship. What if..." His eyes slide down my dress again, agonizingly slowly, and then fix on my mouth before rising back up to meet my eyes. A fire burns in his gaze to match the burning in my chest. "Bonnie, I don't want to pretend anymore. Please tell me you don't either."

I shake my head. It's about the only thing I can manage because he just said words I didn't realize I was desperate for him to say.

Hank's determination slips as he furrows his brow, his steps faltering. "What does that mean?"

I shake my head again, even though I know that isn't clearing anything up. "Hank..." His name comes out in a whisper. If I say what I want to say, I don't know what will happen. I don't know how this will end, and that's terrifying. There's no script for a relationship with a man I never planned for. I swallow. "I don't want to pretend."

He exhales, and then he's taking hold of me and bringing his mouth to mine.

I melt. There's no other word for it. Something about Hank's kiss changes my entire state of being until I'm nothing but a part of him, melded to him in a way I've never been before. He kisses with confidence, but not in a commanding way. It's...honest. His lips move against mine like he's trying to say everything he can't say with words, and *I melt.*

Gripping the lapels of his jacket, I respond to his unspoken words and add my own, asking for more. Hank obliges, tucking his fingers into my hair at the back of my neck and tilting my head to the perfect angle as he deepens the kiss, turning me into molten lava. Forget melting. Now I'm combusting. I can't get enough, and every place Hank touches leaves a brand behind until I'm burning all over, and I stuff my hands into his hair to anchor myself.

What was I so afraid of? This is utter bliss.

I don't know who breaks away first, but neither of us speaks as we stand in the middle of an empty corner of the garden, straining for air in the coming twilight. Hank seems determined to keep both hands on me, though he can't decide where. He moves from my waist to my arms to my face and back again, almost like he's trying to convince himself that I'm real.

I chuckle when I look up and see his glasses askew. If I hadn't been so caught off guard by the intensity in that kiss, I might have removed them for him. Instead, I straighten them and laugh when he doesn't even open his eyes.

"Thank you," he breathes, though I don't know if he's talking about his glasses or that kiss. He seems just as overcome as I am.

I busy myself by fixing his hair, which I thoroughly destroyed, because otherwise I'll start kissing him again, and...I feel like we need to take things slowly. I was panicking about a relationship just a few minutes ago.

Hank catches my hand and presses it between both of his. "I hate that I'm asking this, but...how was that?"

Grinning, I bite my lip and love the way Hank's eyes immediately drop to track the movement. "I very much enjoyed that."

He groans and covers my mouth with his again with a kiss no less scorching than the last one, his fingers gripping my waist and keeping me close. When he pulls away, his eyes are shut tight.

He almost looks like he's in pain. "I'm..." He presses his forehead to mine while he catches his breath. "Bonnie, I'm worried this isn't going to be easy for me." A tear slips from his eye, sliding down his cheek as a shudder runs through him. But he doesn't let go of me, which says more than any words could. "I have spent so long protecting my heart that I've forgotten how to share it. But I'm trying."

I love how honest he always is. I don't love how he's still hurting this much and there's nothing I can do to ease that pain.

I brush the tear away as my own tears threaten to spill over. "Hank, we don't have to rush this. In fact, I would rather we didn't. I'm...reality is terrifying." Just like admitting any of this out loud is terrifying. "I don't know how to be in something real."

Opening his eyes, he chuckles and presses a kiss to my forehead. I don't know how, but he somehow manages to set me on fire with that touch just as much as he did with the sizzling kisses before. "No one does. We just have to..." He takes a breath and lets it out slowly. "Take it one day at a time. Shelby used to say..." He takes another breath, and this one seems harder than the last.

I tuck my arms into his suit jacket and pull him close, tucking my head against his neck. I don't know if this is helping or not, but I want to be as close to him as I can. "You don't have to tell me, Hank." I would almost rather he didn't, but a part of me is wildly curious to know how that sentence ends.

To my delight, Hank returns the embrace with enthusiasm, wrapping me up tight and pressing his face into my hair. "She used to say life is wasted if it's lived in fear. I don't want to waste any more of my life, Bonnie. Dance with me?"

I nod and let him lead me by the hand to the other side of the garden, where the reception is in full swing. Shelby is right. I have lived too much of life being afraid. Afraid to be seen and known and rejected. But as Hank pulls me into his arms and slowly sways with me at the edge of the dance floor, I can't help but think about how I have no idea how to not be afraid.

And I don't know how I can be enough for Hank. I want to be, but that doesn't mean I'm capable.

When we eventually go up to our suites, Hank gives me a simple but heated goodnight kiss. He doesn't invite me into his room, and I don't invite him into mine. I think we both know we need to take our time with this.

My phone is still sitting on my bed, and though I'm tempted to set it aside and leave it all until morning, I check my notifications anyway, noticing with a grimace that the battery is almost dead. Unease starts working its way through me when I see the many texts from my friends and several missed calls from both Trevor and Fran, some of which came in only a few minutes ago.

It's the text from Derek that I open.

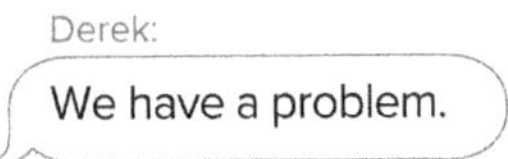

He included a link to a *Hollywood Hot Scoop* article, and I already know I'm not going to like what I find. I get just a glimpse of the headline before my phone dies, but it's enough to tell me I'm in trouble.

The Relationship Ruse: Benrie was Fake the Whole Time?

Hollywood Hot Scoop

The Relationship Ruse: Benrie was Fake the Whole Time?

While we're no strangers to publicity stunts disguised as relationships, this one hits harder than most. Yes, Scoopers, you read that right. Bonnie Aiken and Henry McAllister *were never actually dating*. It was all just a ploy to get Bonnie some positive press after she so callously tossed Derek Riley to the curb.

I know what you're thinking, and this Scooper was just as convinced as you were that Bonnie might have found her forever fella, but if you go back and look at it all with an unbiased eye, it's easy to spot drama for drama's sake. The tense ice cream date, the heroic rescue, the radio silence, and the carefully planned baby photo op. Tonight's Briggs-Paxton wedding was what put the final nail in the coffin when Bonnie staged a tearful exit after throwing jealous, mournful looks toward Houston Briggs, a man she hasn't dated in almost two years.

I was hoping Bonnie was one of the good ones, but it turns out she's just another attention-seeker hoping to use simple minds for her own gain. Too bad that isn't us. We've confirmed that her relationship with oil mogul Nathan Sanchez was also staged, and Seahawk Jeremy O'Hara dropped some heavy hints that his time spent with Bonnie wasn't entirely romantic. We can only assume the rest of them were phony as well, though anyone who has seen Derek Riley the last couple of days can tell he's genuinely heartbroken. I'm thinking he had no idea his relationship with the starlet wasn't real.

So what's the real truth here? I'm of the opinion that Bonnie has lately turned to a new tactic and put her acting chops to use, fooling these unsuspecting men into thinking she's really in love with them. We can't deny Bonnie has talent, but it seems she's using her skills both on and off the screen. Was Houston Briggs duped as well? How about McAllister? Or were they in on it with her?

We've done some digging into our favorite mystery author, and you'll never believe what we've found lurking in Henry's past. We're *dying* to tell you, and the shocking truth might actually *kill* you, but that will have to wait for another day.

What do you think? Did Henry know Bonnie was a fake, or was he a part of the scheme as well? We know he's got a flair for writing about detailed *murders*, but could he plot something less sinister but just as devious? Let us know in the comments below! And be sure to subscribe because you're not going to want to miss our shocking discovery about Henry's original murder mystery girl. XO

CHAPTER TWENTY-TWO

BONNIE

HANK HAS BEEN QUIET all morning. Not that I blame him. It has only been fifteen hours since the *Hot Scoop* article dropped, but they have been the most stressful fifteen hours of my life. I didn't sleep a minute, but neither did I turn my phone back on after plugging it in. I just sat wrapped in a blanket, trying my best to think of a way to fix everything. Trying to turn back time. Trying to understand why nothing good can ever last.

I only looked at my phone when the sun rose and I realized my friends were probably desperate to hear from me. I read the article, texted my friends to tell them I was fine and would see them in LA after I met with my publicist, and then I went back to wallowing.

Now Hank and I are sitting in a private sky lounge at LAX, waiting for Eli to secure a different way out of the airport because somehow everyone seems to have figured out that I'm here, and they all want a good look at the liar.

I'm amazed Hank still came with me. He has every reason to abandon me and go back to his quiet life, though I don't think it will ever be the same as it was. When I told him that I could face Los Angeles on my own, after I realized he had already seen the article, he simply shook his head and led the way out to the car without giving a passing glance to the crowds gathered on either side of the hotel door.

He was silent during the flight, and he's silent now, and the only indication I have of anything he might be feeling is the tremble in his hands that he can't quite hide. He's terrified, and I don't think it's all from the impending crowd outside.

I have no idea what *Hot Scoop* is going to say about Shelby, but with the hints they were throwing out, I can't imagine it will be anything good. So help me, if they start blaming Hank for her murder, I don't care what laws I have to break to take that website down for good. I would rather lose everything I've built than let Hank carry the weight of an accusation like that.

Eli comes back into the lounge, and based on his dejected expression, we're going to have to walk through the mob to get to the car.

I let out a sigh. "This is your last chance, Hank. You can go back home and say goodbye to all of this. It's okay. This was never part of the contract."

Dropping his elbows to his knees, he huffs out a single laugh and rubs his eyes beneath his glasses. I don't know how much sleep he got last night, but I'm guessing it wasn't much.

"Seriously," I say. "You can—"

"A sensationalized tabloid article doesn't change how I feel about you, Bonnie." He turns his head to look at me, his expression hard. "Do you really think so little of me?"

His question catches me off guard. "What? No, I think the world of you, which is why I don't want to—"

"You think I could spend the last couple of weeks learning who you are and then turn around and pretend you aren't someone worth knowing." That wasn't a question, and he clenches his jaw before he stands and tucks his messenger bag over his shoulder. He spent most of the four-hour flight writing in his notebook, and I can't help but wonder how much of the next Gabrielle Frost book is in that bag. Or was he not working on the book at all?

He sighs, shaking his head and running a hand through his hair. "I said this wasn't going to be easy, and *Hot Scoop* is apparently going to make that statement truer than I'd like. But I'm tired of living in fear, and my feelings for you run deeper than a fake relationship that never felt fake to begin with. Do you believe me?" He holds out his hand, and though his fingers are still trembling, the determination in his eyes outweighs any fear he may be feeling.

I want to take his hand, I really do, but I can't guarantee things are going to go in our favor. Fran wasn't happy when I talked to her this morning, and I can only imagine the fury she's going to be in when we get to her downtown office.

"Hank," I say weakly, "what if—"

"Aren't you tired of letting everyone else tell you how to live your life?" His eyebrows pull low as he studies me, but it's the warmth in his brown eyes that pulls me in and brings my hand up to meet his.

Everything about him has always been so warm, and he's right. This relationship hasn't actually felt fake, even when I tried to convince myself that it wasn't real. All of my relationships before were cool and calculated, everything planned and scripted. But Hank? Every moment with Hank has been nothing like I've ever felt before, like he is a sunny day and I've been in an air conditioned room for too long. I feel *alive* with Hank in a way I've never been.

As our hands entwine, his fingers are just as reassuring as his gaze, and I feel like I can breathe now that I know he won't abandon me today. Eventually he'll realize that being in my life is more trouble than it's worth, maybe even later today when everything continues to crumble, but at least for now I can pretend he—

"Bonnie." His voice comes out almost sharp, but it's still gentle. He's always gentle. "One day at a time."

I nod. I can give him a day. I want to give him so much more, but experience has taught me not to hope for too much for myself. It's easier to make sure everyone else is happy because my actions are the only thing I can control.

Though his expression is still hard, he pulls me close and gently touches a brief kiss to my lips. It's as comforting as it is a reminder of what he told me yesterday, and I take courage in his unwavering strength. When I first met this man, I never would have guessed he could be this solid and sturdy, but Hank is likely the strongest man I know.

"This is going to be rough," I warn him, holding him close enough that I can steal another bolstering kiss before we go face the masses.

He smiles, his hand tightening around mine. "I've been through worse."

His next kiss is more like it was last night, enough to get lost in. While a lounge at the airport isn't the most romantic of places, it's so much better than walking through a crowd of angry used-to-be-fans.

"Can we just run away?" I ask against his mouth.

I feel his smile on my lips. "Trust me. It doesn't make the problems go away."

"I guess you would know."

Chuckling, he takes a step back. "Are you ready? How do you want to handle the crowd?"

I stand up straight, calling on every ounce of confidence I have. "Together. This relationship isn't fake, no matter what they all think."

"Do you want me to kiss you?"

Though I know he's asking if we should kiss in front of our audience, I can't help but tease him. "Hank, if you don't know how to read the signs, especially after last night, I may need to set you up with another session with Clyde."

He rolls his eyes, but then he leans in and captures my mouth, just as I wanted him to. His hands move to cradle my head, and I tug him as close as I can get him, determined to enjoy this as long as I can before everything falls apart.

Eli has to clear his throat to get our attention again, or we might have stayed here forever.

Hank takes hold of one of my hands again and smiles at me. "I'll follow your lead, Bonnie." He's not trembling anymore, and I hope he stays that way. I hope we can get each other through whatever is waiting for us outside those doors.

The crowd bursts into a flurry of questions and comments as soon as we pass through the doors and into the California sunshine. Airport security is keeping them back, but the flashing cameras and shouted questions are still as overwhelming as ever. My instinct is to run away, as it always is, but I take a deep breath and don't stop walking until one particular question stands out from the others.

"How is filming going for the Frost movie?"

Hank and I both turn toward the man who asked the question, our steps slowing in unison. Everyone else quiets down, though it won't last for long.

Before I can come up with a diplomatic answer that won't give anything away, Hank speaks first.

"No one could have been a better choice to play Gabrielle than Bonnie," he says. He keeps his voice low, which forces everyone to remain quiet. I don't know if he's doing that on purpose or if he's just nervous, but he seems to have taken command of the entire crowd, which isn't easy to do. "I was worried that the adaptation would fall flat, but Bonnie has been crucial in bringing life to something so near to my heart."

"Is that why you started up this fake relationship?" someone else asks. I don't see who.

Hank must have seen because he narrows his eyes on someone in the crowd. "There was never anything fake about my feelings for Bonnie."

Several people throw out questions at once, though they're all along the same lines and all directed at me. *Is any of this real?* They all know I'm going to say yes, regardless of the truth, and that is what Fran would want me to say. In fact, Fran wouldn't want me standing here talking to reporters at all. But even though my publicist has always been good for me, Hank is right. I'm tired of letting everyone else decide my life for me.

"It wasn't real," I say boldly. A hush runs through the crowd again, and I turn my gaze to Hank. He seems to be holding his breath, waiting to see what I'll say. I smile. "Not at first, anyway. But as I've come to know Henry, I've started to realize there are more important things than public opinion." Before I can say anything else, Hank uses a finger to turn my face toward his and catches my mouth with a soft kiss, one that I meet with the same enthusiasm I did in the lounge. The cameras start flashing like crazy, and while Hank isn't quite as relaxed as he was before, he still matches me beat for beat.

A moment later, Eli ushers us into the waiting SUV and shuts the door behind us, closing off the frenetic energy of the crowd.

"I think I could get used to that if it always ends in a kiss," Hank says. He's shell-shocked, but one corner of his lips is pulled up in an amused smile.

I laugh and pull him toward me, determined to take advantage of this time alone while we've got it.

Chapter Twenty-Three

Hank

It's NOT LIKE I ever missed Denver after leaving. I always liked the quiet of Laketown better than the city, but Shelby wouldn't have survived being in a small town for longer than a week or two at a time. She was always too big for the small life. I did enjoy teaching college classes, which I couldn't have done in Laketown, but otherwise the only thing keeping me in the city was my wife.

Stuck in the traffic of downtown LA, I'm not sure anything could convince me to live here. Not even Bonnie, though she's done a good job of trying. Trevor wasn't kidding when he said Bonnie is a kisser, and I'm not complaining in the slightest.

I only wish Eli wasn't stuck in the front seat, forced to pretend he has no idea what's happening in the back.

Last night, after I found the article, I did a lot of thinking. A lot of feeling too. It was a good thing I was alone, or Bonnie might have decided I was too messed up to be worth her time. But the longer I spent with my thoughts and emotions, the more I realized I don't want to lose what we've built together, small though it may be. No matter what happens, I've made my decision about what I want in life, and I'm going to fight for it. Fight for *her*.

I just have to hope I'm strong enough to *keep* fighting. I have a feeling Bonnie is going to need as much convincing as I do, which means my work is cut out for me.

When we finally reach Fran's office building, my will to speak to the publicist is at an all-time low. While I do have her to thank for forcing me into Bonnie's sphere, I can only imagine what she might have waiting for us. Either she'll push us to make our relationship more public than I'll be comfortable with, or she'll tell Bonnie she needs to move on and find a different shmuck to play house with.

I just want Bonnie to be able to live her life. Preferably with me in it. I still don't know what it's going to look like, and I know it won't be easy. But the best things in life never are.

Fran is waiting for us in her massive office, her gaze stormy and her manicured nails tapping on her glass desk as we approach. The wall behind her is entirely made out of windows, and this office is high enough that anyone with a fear of heights probably hates coming in here. I notice with a frown that the chairs we sit in are considerably lower than they need to be, forcing us to look up at Fran rather than sit across from her as equals.

She may be good at her job, but this whole setup is giving me villain vibes.

"Bonnie," Fran says once we're settled. "Mr. McAllister. How was your flight?" The question is rougher than it needs to be, like she intends it to be an expression of her displeasure. It seems to be working on

Bonnie, who sinks deeper in her seat, but I won't let Fran intimidate me. This is just like dealing with Mariah, my agent, though I'm not convinced Fran has *my* best interest at heart.

I grab hold of Bonnie's hand and smile. "Uneventful. Thankfully."

"Mm hmm." Fran resumes her nail tapping, glancing between us from behind her cat-eye glasses. If she had a fluffy white cat to stroke, she would be comically terrifying. "Mr. McAllister, I seem to remember giving you very specific instructions on how to handle the wedding."

She isn't calling me Henry, which must be her way of furthering her superiority. Or maybe she just doesn't like me.

My smile grows because the feeling is mutual. "Technically, I did exactly what you asked me to. I just didn't do it in front of a camera." Bonnie tenses, looking over at me, and I can almost feel her wariness. She must know I'm talking about our kiss, and I don't want her to think I did it because I was told to. So I keep talking. "My very real affections for Bonnie are not something I wanted her to learn about along with everyone else. She deserved to know first."

Fran's expression hardens even more. "And now everyone is questioning the verity of this relationship, thanks to your little misconception of being honorable."

"I think you mean veracity," I reply calmly. "Besides, I think Bonnie handled that *Hot Scoop* article pretty well already."

Fran's stoicism cracks, making way for a mixture of confusion and alarm. Her eyes dart to her computer, but she turns her focus to Bonnie. "What does he mean?"

Bonnie shrugs. "We talked to some reporters this morning as we were leaving the airport."

Fran turns pale, and she scrambles to type something out on her keyboard. "Why would you... Bonnie, you know what I say about talking to people when we haven't made a plan!"

Bonnie shrinks. "I know, but..." She trails off and retreats the same way she did with Beckett. I hate seeing her defeated like this.

"She didn't say anything that wasn't true," I argue for her. "And I think the people there appreciated the honesty. I know I enjoyed it." I wink at Bonnie, which is something I've never done. I'm pretty sure I make a mess of it because Bonnie bites the inside of her lips and looks like she might start laughing.

I fight a smile. "Hold off on the winking thing?" I guess under my breath.

She snickers. "It was cute," she whispers back.

"*Cute* isn't what I was going for."

"Either way, it's working."

"Oh," Fran says, pulling our attention back to her as she scrolls on her computer. "Okay, well, you seem to have appeased people. It's the impending *Hot Scoop* bombshell that will be harder to spin."

My stomach does a flip, leaving me nauseous. I've been trying not to think about the hints they dropped last night about Shelby—Bonnie is great for distraction—but I'm pretty sure the murder is going to be out in the open soon. It was on the news when it happened, so it's no secret, but no one outside Denver cared about a random art curator whose murder was never solved.

That's likely about to change.

I won't be able to hide from it anymore, and while that's terrifying, it doesn't feel like a knife in my gut like it used to. Falling for Bonnie, learning to let go of my fears and pains, has been easier than I thought it would be, and as long as she doesn't leave me to face it all on my own, I think I'll be okay.

I might even be okay without her, but that's not the direction I want things to go.

"Is there anything we can do to stop them from bringing up Hank's wife?" Bonnie asks.

Fran's eyebrows shoot up. "You have a wife?"

I frown. "You didn't do your own research after all those hints they dropped last night?" I thought that was part of her job.

She chuckles. "Henry, darling, I don't work for you."

My jaw drops. Is she serious? "But you know they're going to bring Bonnie into it, and you *do* work for her."

"Yes, which means I should ask again. You have a wife? Because that causes complications that I would rather not—"

"My wife was murdered four years ago," I snap, rising to my feet. I should probably be alarmed by how easily those words come out, but I'm too angry to care right now. "And that's something you should have figured out before you ever put so much faith in me when it comes to your client. Did you know *anything* about me before you attached me to Bonnie? Or did you just take the easy way out when the internet picked me as her next fling?"

Fran stares at me, her mouth in a little O, but I don't think I've ruffled her as much as I would like. "Murdered?" she says, one eyebrow lifting high in interest. "And Bonnie is playing a homicide detective from one of your books. Oh, this is good. This is really good. We can work with—"

"No," Bonnie says. She gets up and stands next to me so the pair of us are now looking down at the publicist. "We're not going to exploit his pain just because you think it will make a good story."

Fran *tsks*. "Bonnie, sweetie, you know we have to use everything we—"

"I said no!" Bonnie looks almost furious, and I hate how attractive it makes her. Well, I don't *hate* it, but I probably shouldn't be this tempted to grab her and kiss her until she can't breathe. That's something better saved for later, when we don't have an audience.

But it *will* be happening later.

Fran seems to study Bonnie for a moment, and then she rolls her eyes. Clearly she doesn't see Bonnie's assertion as something she needs to worry about. I didn't like this woman from the beginning, and I especially don't like her now. "Bonnie," she croons.

"Francine Romero, you have a lot of nerve," a deep voice says from the hallway. It precedes a man I don't particularly want to see right now as he stomps into the office followed by Fran's harried assistant, who likely tried to stop him from barging in.

Fran jumps to her feet in alarm. "Derek!"

Derek doesn't stop walking until he is on the other side of her desk and looming over her, backed by the bright light of the windows. "It was *your* idea for Bonnie and me to start dating. *Your* idea for us to break up. *Your* idea to force her into this stupid fake thing she has with McAllister, and now your next *brilliant* idea is to have Bonnie *stage a torrid affair with me?* Are you out of your mind?"

"What?" Bonnie says, though it's more of a squeak.

Derek growls as he forces Fran back into her seat by stepping into her space. I hate to admit it, but he's genuinely intimidating, and I can see why he's cast in the roles of spies and superheroes. If I didn't know better, I would think this man is more than just an actor. "You are incompetent," he snarls. "You are unprofessional. You care more about your paycheck than you do your clients who rely on you to keep their lives relatively normal, and I'm done. Bonnie can keep you if she wants, but I won't have any part in your cheap gimmicks anymore."

I curse under my breath. I was so ready to dislike the man forever, but he just flipped my aversion to admiration in a single angry speech.

Before anyone can say anything, another person comes barreling into the room, out of breath and panting. I recognize Liam, though I'm glad he's wearing a shirt this time around. "No!" he mourns as he looks around the room. "Did I miss you firing her? Your stupid security wouldn't let me in, and I had to make a run for it." He says that last part to Fran as he rests his hands on his knees and tries to breathe.

She scowls. "That's because you're not my client."

He points at Derek with a mischievous grin. "Neither is he, so are you going to have him thrown out? Because I wouldn't recommend it. There are a whole lot of paps outside hoping for something juicy, and I don't think there's a person in the world who would side with you over Derek Riley. So keep that in mind when you think about trying to ruin him after all this is said and done." He stands up straight, pressing a hand to his ribs as he keeps trying to breathe like normal. "And the same goes for Bonnie. She deserves better than what you've given her, so you'd better watch your step."

Dang it, now I like Liam too. I guess I shouldn't have expected Bonnie to have friends who weren't worth knowing, even if they do text excessively.

Fran scoffs. "I'll admit I'm disappointed, Mr. Riley, but I can see there will be no changing your mind. If you will kindly exit the premises, I have business to discuss with my *clients*."

"I'm not your client," I say immediately. While I'm grateful Derek was able to get under Fran's skin, I feel like I need to step up my game and help Bonnie however I can. "You made that very clear. But I'm not about to leave Bonnie by herself if she intends to stay."

"Neither are we," Liam adds.

"The choice is up to you, Bonnie," Derek says. "You do what you think is best for you, and we will stand behind you."

"Always," Liam says.

Forever, I want to finish, though the thought shocks me into silence. Do I mean that?

I think I might.

To my pleasure, Bonnie looks at me instead of either of her friends. "What do you think?" she asks quietly. "Fran has gotten me to where I am today, and she knows who I am and what I need."

I shake my head. "She knows who you were when you were nineteen. You're allowed to grow into someone new, and what worked before doesn't necessarily work now. But if you're not ready for something new, I'm sure she'll be better going forward." I say that last part loud enough for Fran to hear, just in case.

Tears well up in Bonnie's eyes, but she's smiling. I hope that means I said the right thing. "You see me," she whispers, and then she leans up on her toes and kisses me.

We seriously need to stop doing this in front of an audience. Self-consciousness holds me back, especially with Derek as a witness. But there's also a small, cavemanish part of me that wants to prove to him that what I have with Bonnie is real, so after the initial shock, I lean heavier into the kiss than I should.

When Bonnie pulls away, she looks dazed but speaks with confidence. "Fran, I think this is where you and I part ways, but I wish you the best."

Fran's jaw drops. "You can't mean that. Derek is one thing. He, at least, is smart enough to take care of himself, but you can barely—"

"Enough!" Bonnie says at the same time I step forward to defend her. The word comes out so sharply that it catches me off guard and leaves me speechless. Bonnie doesn't share that problem. "Are you really surprised that I would fire you when you spend so much of your energy trying to tear me down? Fran, you can't honestly expect people to stay with you when you're always using them to make yourself look better."

Scoffing, Fran touches her fingertips to her desk and leans forward. "You were *nothing* before I found you," she seethes.

Bonnie lifts her chin. "I may not have been well known, but I was *never* nothing. Yes, you helped my career, but any publicist could have done what you did. I don't want to waste any time with someone who thinks so little of me when I know I'm better than that. I clearly thought better of *you* than I should have."

As Fran sputters something incoherent, I grab Bonnie's hand, completely in awe of this woman and the growth she's made since the day we met. Bonnie squeezes back, tighter than I expected, and when she inhales, her breath stutters into her lungs, like she's terrified of the words that just left her mouth.

Time to leave.

It only takes a tug from me to break Bonnie from her stiff stance, and then she's leading the way out of the room. Derek and Liam are close behind us, and no one says anything until we get into the elevator.

Liam clears his throat, looking back at Bonnie. "That was the coolest thing I've ever seen, Bon."

"That was amazing," I agree. "*You* were amazing."

After smiling at me, Bonnie puts her hand on Liam's arm. "Thanks for defending me." She looks at Derek. "Both of you."

"Are you kidding?" Liam says. "I've been dying for an opportunity to go to bat for you since the day we met, but you never give me a chance."

Eyes shining, she pulls him into a one-armed hug that he returns with enthusiasm.

"But you're not actually going to go without a publicist, are you?" Liam asks as he pulls away.

Bonnie snorts, her shoulders relaxing. "Oh, no way. I was hoping your guy had an opening."

Liam grins. "Ethan's the best there is. I'm sure he'd be happy to take you on. You too," he says to Derek.

Derek grunts, his jaw tight as he turns to glance between Bonnie and me. "So this is real?" he asks, nodding down to our clasped hands. I can't tell what he thinks about it, though he doesn't seem happy.

Bonnie nods and draws closer to me. "It's real."

"It always was," I add.

Derek meets my gaze and seems to study me until the elevator stops and the door slides open to the lobby. "Good," he says, but then he has to turn his focus to the crowd gathered at the doors. Eli and a couple other security guys are waiting for us, but it's still a fight to get out to the waiting SUV. All four of us climb inside, the men moving to the back so Bonnie and I can take the middle seats.

"That's going to bring up some fun questions," Liam says once we're on our way. He both looks and sounds amused, which hopefully means he wasn't being sarcastic about the 'fun' part.

Derek shakes his head. "Does nothing bother you?"

"Plenty of things bother me," Liam replies, leaning his arms on the back of our seat so he's right in between Bonnie and me. "Like people not texting me back." I wince, but he keeps talking, "The trick is learning how to fight back when it comes to *Hot Scoop*. They can smell fear. But ever since Kasey did her whole 'Liam is awesome' spiel, they haven't been able to get any traction when it comes to the two of us."

I look at Bonnie, hoping she'll explain.

She smiles. "Kasey basically fought fire with fire, but that's not going to be easy with us. Especially because we still don't know what they're going to say about your wife."

"Wife?" Derek and Liam say at the same time.

I groan. "*Late* wife. You really should lead with that part, Bonnie."

"Oh good," Liam says. "I thought I was going to have to punch you. But sorry about your wife. That's rough."

It is rough, but it's getting easier every day. I'm healing, and it's all thanks to Bonnie. Despite the two men behind us, I lift Bonnie's hand and press a kiss to her knuckles, trying to tell her with my eyes that I am so glad I have her in my life.

Now I just have to figure out how to make this all work for both of us. It won't be easy, but I'm going to give this everything I've got. Though she can take care of herself, Bonnie deserves a man who will fight for her, and I intend to be that man.

Chapter Twenty-Four

BONNIE

Liam and Derek have been talking non-stop during the drive from downtown LA to Derek's house in Malibu. That's normal for Liam, but after my text conversation with Cole, I expected Derek to still be at least a little moody. Instead, he's smiling and rolling his eyes, no sign of a mask in sight. I've known Derek long enough that I can tell when he's acting, and he isn't.

Now I'm more confused than anything.

Hank has been quiet, but that seems as normal as Liam being loud. I fully plan to have a long—and private—conversation with him later, but right now I need to rid myself of as many problems as I can so I don't have as much to deal with. Fran was one of those problems, even if I didn't realize it until we met with her. Cole is another.

"How is Cole doing with the whole Sage disaster?" I ask during a lull, turning in my seat so I can get a good look at Liam's and Derek's faces.

Liam wrinkles his nose in disgust, which isn't very reassuring. "Sage is a four-letter word."

Derek sighs. "He's hanging out with his dad tonight, or I would have made him come with us so he's not alone. I think he's taking the news harder than he wants us to think."

"It's been five months since she dumped him," I complain. "Does he still think he has a chance?"

Derek shrugs. "Even if Sage ever wants to get back together with him, he should really consider declining and moving on. He can do what he wants, but Sage was never good for him. He needs someone who..." He frowns and looks at Liam. "Honestly, he needs someone like this dork but with better self-control."

Liam grins. "Aww, you think I'm a dork? Kasey will be so happy to know you agree with her!"

Derek rolls his eyes, but his smile is wide. "Case in point. Cole needs someone who isn't afraid to express herself and show him how she feels. Sage was too much like him. Kept things too close to the vest."

Derek is probably right, and Cole is stubborn. "I'll try to talk to him," I mutter, though I have no idea when. "By the way, Cole was worried about *you*."

Derek grumbles. "I know. But he had it wrong."

"You mean you're not heartbroken about my feelings for Hank?" I take hold of Hank's hand, just in case he thinks I'm not serious about those feelings. I'm probably going to have to fill him in on the situation with Cole so he doesn't spend the rest of the weekend feeling clueless, but I kind of love that he's content to simply listen. I meet his gaze for half a second and feel the warmth of his attention all the way down to my toes.

"Honestly," Derek says, "I *am* heartbroken, but not for the reasons you think." He sits forward, nodding at Hank before fixing his deep blue eyes on me. "I'm sad that I let our relationship hold you back from finding something real. I suspected you were ready, but..."

My heart throbs. Derek always did know me better than I know myself. "But what?"

"*I* wasn't ready. I was so worried you would get hurt again, but seeing you with Hank..." He sighs, sitting back in his seat again. "I realized I was in your way for a long time instead of helping you. I hated that."

Liam pats his chest. "Not everyone can be perfect all the time."

"Or ever," Derek shoots back.

"Speak for yourself."

Hank leans in close, and though I'm pretty sure he planned to say something, he seems to get distracted for a second and instead brushes a kiss against my lips. He smiles, his eyes closed as he touches his thumb to my bottom lip. "Sometimes I'm convinced *you're* perfect," he murmurs.

I bite my lip where he touched it, tempted to squeal with happiness even though his line was totally cheesy. I don't know how we got here, but I'm not complaining. "I'm not perfect," I murmur back. "But I love that you think I am. Only sometimes?"

He shrugs and kisses me again. "I like to think I'm a realist."

"Says the man who writes murder mysteries."

"All of those mysteries are based on true events," he argues.

"Oh," Liam says, the word pulling us apart. "Okay, can we talk about that?"

"Talk about what?" Derek asks, since I'm too busy glaring at Liam for interrupting.

"Murder."

Derek groans. "If you're about to tell us you think another one of your neighbors has murdered his wife, then—"

"No! The new neighborhood scandals have all been about paint colors and landscaping choices, which is so painfully dull that I'm tempted to move to somewhere more interesting. No, I mean that whole part of the last *Hot Scoop* story." He points at Hank. "You're not secretly a serial killer writing about his own murders, are you?"

Hank grimaces. "That's what you got out of the article?"

Shrugging, Liam leans his arms on the back of our seat again. "They were heavily hinting *something*, and even my publicist thinks they're on to something real or they wouldn't risk the potential discrediting from spreading something too outlandish."

Hank's grip tightens around mine, his face turning pale, and he seems to be tongue-tied from Liam's questioning.

"Hank hasn't murdered anyone," I say sharply. Then I look at him. "You haven't, have you?"

He gives me a look of such confusion and insult that I can't help but laugh.

"Can I tell them about Shelby? You can say no." When he nods, I turn back to the boys in the backseat. "Hank's wife was murdered, and the case went cold. They never figured out who did it."

Liam whistles low. "Ouch. Sorry."

Derek, on the other hand, looks thoughtful. Liam likes to joke that Derek is secretly a world-class spy because he always seems to have the right connections to fix problems or find answers, and I'm pretty sure his mind is spinning, searching for a way he can help. I'm not sure how he could do anything about a four-year-old cold case, but I'm not about to stop him from trying.

"*Hot Scoop* probably found one of the old news stories," I continue. "I just hope they don't try to turn it against Hank somehow."

Liam, now resting his chin on his arms, shrugs and glances between us. "You might need to be more worried about yourself, Bon. The internet loves Hank."

Hank and I both wince, though I have no idea if we're thinking the same thing. "I don't like the idea of my past doing damage to your future," he says quietly, and then he turns to Liam. "Is there anything we can do? Fight fire with fire, so to speak?"

Apparently we *were* thinking the same thing. It seems our lives are intertwined whether we want them to be or not, so I'm glad this is something we've both chosen.

"Jensen," Derek says suddenly, calling up to his driver. "We need to go back to Santa Monica."

"Why?" Liam and I ask at the same time.

"Where to, sir?" Jensen asks, ever the professional. He's already turning around despite having no more idea of our destination than I do. I swear, Derek's staff treat him like royalty more than Freya's do sometimes.

Derek lifts his phone to his ear. "Félicie."

"Oo, we're going fancy tonight?" Liam grins. "Kasey is going to regret ditching me to hang with her friend."

Hank looks at me, brow furrowed, and I chuckle. I forget that he isn't familiar with our world.

As Derek tells his assistant to get us a table at the high-end restaurant, I smile at Hank. "Félicie is one of the most expensive restaurants in the country."

Hank's eyes go wide. "And why are we going there?"

"Because Derek seems to think we need to be out in public tonight."

"And a burger place isn't public?"

"Different kind of public," Liam offers brightly. "Apparently we need to be seen by the right people. Derek, better make the reservation for five. Kasey will kill me if she misses this." He grabs his own phone, probably to call his girlfriend and inform her of the impromptu plan for the night.

"Scratch that. Five. Thanks, Margo." Derek ends his call and looks at Hank, his expression warm and open. "The *two of you* need to be seen by the right people. Preferably before *Hot Scoop* releases your wife's story. They dropped another hint post just before we got to Fran's office, so they're going to stretch anticipation as long as they can, which should hopefully buy us just enough time to get ahead of it."

"And how is eating at an obscenely expensive restaurant supposed to get ahead of a story about my wife?" Hank asks.

His hand is trembling again, and I worry he won't trust Derek enough to agree to the plan, whatever it ends up being. He's nervous in front of regular people, and I doubt he'll be any better in front of the high-end crowd. The last time I ate at Félicie, it was mostly full of celebrities and politicians.

Derek still looks distant, like his plan isn't fully in place yet. "So far, you've only been seen in photos captured on the fly and in secret. Nothing intentional."

I think I know where he's going with this. "You want us to show the world that my life is carrying on as normal," I guess. "And that we planned this dinner ages ago. Félicie is impossible to get into on a whim."

"Unless you're Derek Riley," Liam says with a chuckle, though he's still on the phone, which quickly pulls his attention back. "No, you can't show up in sweatpants, Kase."

"He makes a good point," I say and frown at my comfortable travel clothes. I don't look like a slob, but neither am I dressed for the likes of Félicie. "We'll have to stop at my apartment so I can change, but that won't help Hank."

Derek shakes his head, a mischievous grin on his face. "Or you could go shopping."

I practically hear Hank gulp. I know he's probably going to hate it, but it will be a great way to act like a true couple who aren't worried about whatever nonsense *Hollywood Hot Scoop* is teasing. Besides, I love shopping.

"You are a genius, Derek Riley," I say and reach back to pat his cheek.

Though he rolls his eyes, I can tell he's glad he found a way to help. Tonight's adventure may not do much to curb the interest in the gossip, but I hope it will at least solidify my connection to Hank. If we can get our peers to believe the relationship is real, it will be that much easier to convince the rest of the world. And maybe then they'll finally leave me alone.

It worked for Liam when his good guy image was in danger, and I hope it will work now. Those of us who carry the burden of fame have to look out for each other, after all.

"Don't worry," I tell Hank, squeezing his hand. "I won't leave your side. I promise."

CE CREAM

Chapter Twenty-Five

HANK

Bonnie lied to me. Less than forty-five minutes after she promised not to leave my side, she abandoned me to take Kasey into a dress boutique, and now I'm stuck standing with my arms out wide while a man with a head of neon blue hair measures every inch of me. Every. Inch.

Liam seems to find my discomfort amusing, and Derek is too busy on his phone to notice how often I look toward the door and my line of escape. Bonnie once thought I didn't like to be touched, and at the time I thought she was wrong. As a tape measure passes between my legs, I'm rethinking that stance.

"I take it you've never been fitted for a suit," Liam says, laughter in his voice as he watches from a chair.

I clench my jaw and shake my head.

"What did you wear when you got married?"

"Whatever I found on the rack that fit," I grumble.

The blue-haired man gasps and says something in French. I have no idea what he says, but I hear his offense clear as day.

Derek glances up and *replies* to the man in French, prompting rapid back-and-forth that is full of amusement on Derek's side and frustration on Blue's. Which is definitely not the tailor's name, but that's what I'm calling him in my head.

I look at Liam, my eyebrows low. "He speaks French?" I know Derek can hear me, but my capacity for social niceties pretty much dropped to zero when Blue ran a hand down my rear end. I don't even know what he might have been measuring at that point.

Liam smirks. "Honestly, I don't think there's anything Derek *can't* do."

"I don't know carpentry," Derek mutters, returning to his phone.

I genuinely don't know if that was a joke or a true statement of the one skill he doesn't have, and I'm too intimidated to ask.

"Jean-Paul will make you look like you belong at Bonnie's side," Liam says. "Just for tonight, and then you can go back to your professor look. People seem to love that."

Jean-Paul's continued muttering makes it clear that he is not to be counted among "people." He shuffles toward a velvet curtain that leads into another room, making notes on his tablet as he goes.

I immediately sink onto a chair between Liam and Derek. "I don't even want to think about how much this is going to cost."

Liam scoffs. "Oh, we've got you covered."

"No, I..." I cringe. "I can afford it. I'm a *New York Times* bestselling author, so..." I usually hate bringing up my wealth—with nowhere to go and my house paid for, it has been collecting exponentially for the last two years—but I feel so out of place next to these two men. Especially Derek. Liam, at least, could pass as any guy on the street in his t-shirt and jeans, but everything about Derek screams wealth and privilege. And *influence*. He has the look of someone who knows he can get anything he wants in life, so it's a good thing he's not a terrible human.

"It just seems superfluous," I finish, dropping my elbows onto my knees. Today has been exhausting, and it's nowhere near over. I am going to do everything I can to fix things for Bonnie and show her that we can be good together, but I'm desperate for the night to be a short one.

Liam puts his arm around my shoulders. "Can I be honest with you, Hank?"

"I'm afraid to say yes."

Derek chuckles, still focused on his phone.

Liam takes my comment as agreement and plows forward. "You are not at all what I pictured for Bonnie."

I swallow. "This is exactly why I was afraid."

"No, I mean that as a good thing!"

"Then keep talking, Connolly," Derek says, shaking his head. He's smiling, so he must think Liam has a valid point to make.

Liam huffs a sigh of frustration, but I have yet to see him anything but happy. "See, the kind of guy I imagined Bonnie would be with was more like Derek."

My heart sinks, and it feels like the weight of it pulls the rest of me down with it. "Oh."

"You're making it worse," Derek warns.

Liam groans. "I didn't mean like... Okay. Trying again. Since I've known Bonnie, she's never been the kind of person to get attached romantically, so I could never picture her perfect partner. I just had her past relationships as examples, and they were all the kinds of guys who are used to getting their way. So I thought that was what Bonnie wanted."

Feeling nauseous, I lean forward and look at Derek. "Are you hearing anything positive in this?"

Derek smirks. "Give him a second. He'll get there eventually."

"Yeah," Liam agrees. "What I'm saying is you are so different from all those guys, my man Derek included, that I think you're the one who just might stick. Bonnie has seemed so different today in the best way. I think she needs someone like you to help her feel confident."

She needs someone like me.

"She needs someone who wasn't picked for her, you know?" Liam adds.

"I don't think she's ever felt like she's been someone's first choice," I say quietly. I don't even know if that's true, but saying it out loud to the people who know her best might help me prove Liam's theory true. I want Bonnie to need me. I want her to know that no matter what, I will be there for her. That I'll *choose* her.

"She wasn't the first choice for Gabrielle," Derek says after a moment.

Liam frowns. "What? She never said that."

Shrugging, Derek slips his phone into his pocket. "They signed a more experienced actor first, but she found out she was pregnant and decided to drop out, so they went with Bonnie instead. And I don't think the director kept his disappointment a secret."

Liam swears under his breath. "That sucks."

If I am ever around Beckett again, I'm going to have a hard time resisting the urge to punch the director in the nose. "But she's perfect for Gabrielle," I growl.

"She's also way better than most of the actors I know," Derek says, "but Hollywood has never been kind to women. They see what they want to see."

"And Bonnie is beautiful," Liam adds. He laughs when I raise an eyebrow at him, holding up his hands in surrender. "Easy, Prof. My heart is happily promised to Kasey. I just mean there are a lot of people who are too stupid to look past her face and see the talent underneath."

Now I understand why she had to get my help in convincing Beckett to rework the script. If he wasn't happy about her being there in the first place, he probably hated her trying to mess with his movie. But it's going to do so much better with Bonnie's input.

"I can't decide if I want the movie to flop to spite the director or if I want it to blow expectations out of the water for Bonnie's sake," I mumble right as Jean-Paul returns with three suits in tow, though I have no idea how he could have them so quickly. Apparently he already had measurements for Derek and Liam, so they get to skip the poking and prodding I had to endure. I don't even want to imagine how many suits these two men already own, and yet they're perfectly happy to be buying another.

They live in a different world from me, and I can't help but think about how poorly I fit within it. Within Bonnie's world.

"Sounds like the girls have found their weapons for the night and are heading to a salon, but they shouldn't be long," Liam says after checking his phone. "So, gentlemen, are we ready for our night on the town?" He looks right at me, his eyebrows high in expectation.

My anxiety rises, but I nod. For Bonnie, I'll do just about anything. Even if I still don't know how we're going to make this work, I want to try. That alone is a miracle unto itself, and I'm not about to throw it away.

When Liam said we were going fancy, I didn't realize we would be taking a limo to the restaurant. It feels...excessive. But after reluctantly agreeing to hit up a barber, who was as exasperated by the state of my self-cut hair as Jean-Paul was by my lack of fashion, I have no energy left to argue against anything that may or may not happen tonight.

I just want to be next to Bonnie. Beyond that, I don't really care.

The limo pulls up outside the salon, and I step out first. I might be a little desperate for a moment away from Liam, who seems like a good man but is excessively cheerful and chatty. Though I like him, I stand by my assessment of Liam being "a lot."

I'll take his texts over his non-stop conversation.

As I lean against the side of the limo and take in a deep breath of city air, a pang of homesickness hits me harder than I expect. Outside of vacations, I spent my whole life in Denver up until Shelby's death, but I got used to the mountain air over the last few years. Used to the stillness of my empty lane. Bonnie's life is probably never still.

I press a hand to my heart, hoping to calm the anxiety that hasn't gone away all day.

We can make this work. Somehow.

Derek climbs out of the limo, shutting Liam inside as he comes to stand next to me. His bodyguard also joins us, standing a few feet away, but I'm okay with that. As soon as Derek showed his face, people started to take notice, pointing our way and pulling out their phones.

"I suggest smiling," Derek says calmly. He has an easy, content expression on his face as he leans against the car. It's not a full smile, but it's enough to show anyone who's looking that he's in a good mood.

I do my best to match him. "Thank you. For all of this."

He shrugs. "Bonnie is one of my best friends," he says, as if that explains everything. It does to a point, but there's still an unanswered question hanging between us.

He said he was heartbroken because he thought he was holding her back, but I have to know. "Was she ever more than a friend?"

Derek looks at me, his eyebrows lifting ever so slightly. It's such a subtle expression, not something any of the passersby might notice, but I have a feeling he wants me to know what he's feeling. At least some of it. "Honestly?" He lets out a breath. "I don't know. I knew what she wanted—or rather what she *didn't* want—so I never let myself entertain the idea."

"But if you had?"

"She's Bonnie Aiken." He chuckles, tapping his heel against the tire of the limo. "I would have fallen in love with her in a heartbeat if I'd let myself."

That shouldn't make me feel better, but it does. A little. "Well," I say with a casualness I don't feel, "I'm glad you never let yourself."

Derek's chuckle becomes a full-blown laugh. "You're good for her, Hank. I hope it all works out."

The growing crowd around us starts buzzing with energy and conversation, and at first I think it's because Liam just slipped out of the limo. But then movement catches my eye, and I look toward the entrance to the salon right as Bonnie and Kasey, flanked by Eli, make their way toward us.

My jaw drops.

I won't lie; I didn't think I could be more attracted to Bonnie than I was at Houston's wedding. But as she glides toward me in a navy-blue dress that hugs her thighs, my mouth goes dry. My fingers turn numb. My heart tries to pound out of my chest. I'm vaguely aware of Liam sweeping Kasey into his arms and giving her an unabashed kiss, but my whole focus is on Bonnie.

I force myself the last few steps forward, still taking in the pure elegance of her gown. The collar is high on this one, and I'm disappointed about that. But then she gets close enough that I can pull her into my arms, and my hands find bare skin at her back. There goes the numbness, replaced by vivid sensation in each of my nerve endings as her smooth skin spreads heat from my fingers to my toes.

My anxiety is gone, replaced by pure attraction.

Bonnie grips the lapels of my suit, her cheeks pink and her smile wide. "I thought you might like this one," she whispers as a shiver runs through her from my touch. I don't know if she's cold or if it's a shiver of pleasure, but I can't bring myself to let go. "And look at you! All fancy."

I reply to her comment with a kiss, one without inhibition because it's all gone now. I don't even care that two dozen people are crowded around us and watching without shame. I am almost desperate to show this woman how much I want to be a part of her life, and not just because she's more beautiful than anyone I know. She has an internal beauty that is so much brighter than the outer, and I wish the world could see that part of her.

I wish the world knew the woman I'm coming to love.

Derek clears his throat, breaking us apart, and I have to fight the glare I want to throw at him. He looks like he might start laughing as he nods toward his bodyguard, who holds the door of the limo open. "We do have a reservation to get to," he reminds us.

Bonnie wipes lipstick from my mouth with a tissue she pulled from her clutch, laughter in her eyes. "Let's have fun tonight," she whispers.

I nod, though right now I'm thinking 'fun' should involve more kisses like the one we just shared. Why in the world was I so resistant to taking that step in our relationship? Each kiss has been better than the last. "Just how long will I be required to share you with your friends tonight?" I ask quietly as we make our way to the limo. Derek slips inside, leaving the two of us alone for a moment. "I am willing to do whatever will help you the most tonight, but Derek has a bad habit of interrupting us just when things are getting good. I'm pretty sure we were well on our way to selling this relationship."

Bonnie's eyes sparkle as she laughs and presses her hands to my cheeks. "Where is this coming from?" she asks. "When I met you, it seemed everything I did terrified you. What changed?"

I know we're still being watched, and that should be enough to send me into a panic. But with Bonnie right in front of me, she's the only thing I can see. Apparently I didn't need to shut myself off from the world. I just needed someone who could shut the world out for me. "*I* changed," I whisper. "Because of you. That first time we met, when you hugged me, something inside me healed. You brought me back to life, Bonnie."

Though tears glisten in her eyes, Bonnie is nothing but smiles as she leans up and kisses me again. Based on their cheers, the crowd around us seems to appreciate our inability to stay away from each other, and who am I to deny them?

The limo window rolls down, and it's Liam this time who clears his throat. "Okay, lovebirds," he says through laughter. "I'm glad you like each other, but I'm starving. If you make us miss this reservation, so help me..."

"You'll what?" Bonnie asks, still clinging to me. "Honestly, it's a miracle we got you out of the house in the first place, Liam Connolly."

Kasey pokes her head out as well. She's pretty much on top of Liam as she leans on his shoulders. "It's not his fault he likes me more than he likes all of you. He's going on tour soon, and I refuse to waste any of the time I get with him before he goes."

From the little I know about Kasey, she's still fairly new to this famous life, but she doesn't seem to mind the way the crowd whispers and giggles about what she said. I can almost imagine the sorts of things *Hollywood Hot Scoop* might say about her, but she and Liam really do seem to have freed themselves from the tabloids' hold. They're living their lives how they want to and clearly thriving.

I look at Bonnie, who grins and sticks her tongue out at Kasey, and I wonder if we could do that. If there is some way for us to get out from under the scrutiny of the internet and simply live our lives the way we want to. I'm not one hundred percent sure what that would look like for Bonnie, and my own ideals have been shifting since the day I met her.

I don't know how long I can last if everything I do is dictated by someone's twisted idea of news. I don't know how long *Bonnie* can last. But I know we can figure this out together.

"Chop chop!" Liam says, rolling the window back up.

Bonnie sighs. "I guess we should go."

"If we have to." But I kiss her again, to show her just how reluctant I am to share her attention.

Chapter Twenty-Six

Bonnie

Dinner is more fun than I've had in a long time, and I'm not sure I can credit all of the entertainment to my friends. They're always amusing, but it's the man next to me who really gets me going. For the most part, Hank is still just as quiet as ever, letting Liam and Kasey control the conversation, but about halfway through our meal he starts making little comments under his breath that have me choking on my food when they make me laugh.

He has always had a subtle sense of humor, but this is something different. It feels like he's settling in, getting relaxed, and letting the old Hank make an appearance, like he did on the drive to Sun City or when we were arguing about his characters in the ice cream parlor. If this is what he was like before Shelby died, I wish I could have known him back then.

Before loss and grief suppressed the man he truly is.

"I still can't believe you actually thought your neighbor murdered his wife," Derek says, rolling his eyes.

Liam groans in outrage. "You weren't there!"

"Even I thought something sketchy was going on," Kasey says. "Like, who complains about their sick and dying dog for weeks on end?"

"Someone who has to clean up after said sick and dying dog," Hank mutters. He shifts in his seat, leaning back and putting his arm on the chair back behind me so he looks like he's never been more relaxed in his life. Liam sits that way all the time and is doing it now across from us, but I don't think I've ever seen Derek in a position like that. He is always on his best behavior when out in public, like he's been in the public eye for so long that he forgets how to be human.

Hank does not have that problem, and he keeps pulling eyes in our direction as other patrons fail to hide their curiosity. That's what we get for sitting at a table in the middle of the restaurant, but Derek thought it best if we were surrounded. I think Hank's relaxed look is going to do wonders for our public image.

Unable to help myself, I reach over and untie Hank's bowtie, letting it hang loose on his chest. "The easygoing look is working for you," I explain when his eyes meet mine in question.

He catches my hand before I can pull it away, lifting it to his lips so he can kiss the base of my wrist. "You are entirely beautiful," he replies.

It's another unexpected side effect from the shift in our relationship. Where before Clyde had to force compliments out of him, Hank now seems unafraid to say everything he's thinking. Well, not *everything*. The hungry look in his eyes is saying a lot more than his mouth, making me shiver.

Noticing the shiver, Hank moves his arm from my chair to my back. The warmth of his hand leaves a searing brand on my skin where he touches, which is enough to make me want to call it a night. But then his fingers shift, working their way down my spine until his hand is around my waist, tucked beneath the fabric of my dress. *Oh.* Okay, maybe choosing this dress was a bad idea because Hank seems to like it a little too much.

I might like his touch a little too much.

"Everything okay, Bonnie?" Liam asks. He looks like he's ready to burst into laughter, so he probably knows exactly why my face is on fire right now.

I throw a subtle glare toward Hank, but we have too many witnesses for me to give his boldness a proper response. But oh, how I want to. I take a massive bite of cheesecake instead, though I've already eaten my allotted calorie count for the next century with tonight's dinner. If I didn't have that interview with Derek in the morning, I would be hitting up his home gym first thing to counteract tonight's indulgence.

And maybe to try to curb my growing attraction to Hank McAllister.

I might combust in my seat with the way his fingers are playing on my skin, and his little smirk tells me he knows it. He starts trailing little circles with one of his fingers, and I'm pretty sure I'm going to fall apart in the middle of the restaurant. Who knew a tiny touch could be so powerful?

"You know," Liam says, thankfully taking the attention off of me, "we probably should have found you a date tonight, Derek. Evened out the numbers."

Derek rolls his eyes, though part of his focus is on Hank's arm behind me. He has that look in his eyes that he always gets when he's being protective of one of his friends, though I don't know what he could see in Hank that would warrant his sudden wariness. I'm thoroughly enjoying myself, though now I wish we were somewhere more private.

"I did *not* need a date, Connolly," Derek mutters.

"But it would have helped show everyone that you're not actually heartbroken by your breakup with Bonnie," Liam argues.

"Maybe."

"What about your new assistant? She would have happily stepped in as your date."

Derek actually growls at that one. "Don't start."

Liam snickers. "But she is so *attentive*."

I frown, looking between the two of them. "Did Margo do something?"

"No," Derek says at the same time Liam coughs out, "Not in so many words."

"Oh, there's a story there," Kasey says, just as interested as I am.

Derek rolls his eyes. "There is not—"

"Margo totally hit on him this morning!" Liam interrupts. "Wasn't even a little bit subtle, though it's not like we can blame her when she's working with this specimen day in and day out." He waves a hand over Derek, who looks like he might get up and walk away before this conversation gets too far.

"How is that not doing something?" Hank asks. Even he seems intrigued by this new topic.

Groaning, Derek takes a large gulp of water, glaring at Liam the whole time. "She didn't *hit on* me."

"She told you that if you're ever feeling lonely, she's just a phone call away," Liam argues. "You can call it what you want, but that's pretty obvious."

"That feels like a blatant misuse of her position," I mutter, suddenly thankful that Trevor has never once treated me as anything but a boss. In fact, I should probably give Trevor a raise for being a perfectly aloof yet competent assistant. When I see him in the morning, I'll be sure to tell him that's my plan.

Derek shrugs. "I don't think she meant it how it sounds. And she's a really good assistant." He drops his voice and adds, "She got us a table here without any prior notice, and I've lost track of the number of other miracles she's worked over the last few months. I'm keeping her."

"Even if she hits on you?" Liam asks. "She seems the persistent sort."

"I can handle her, Connolly. Drop it."

He shouldn't have to *handle* anything. I've dealt with my fair share of nonsense with my career, but Derek endures everything I do times ten. Who's looking out for him while he looks out for all of us?

Hank's hand starts traveling along my back again, making me realize I've gone tense. "You good?" he asks quietly, sitting forward.

I can't help but lean into him, grateful when he turns his touch into a side hug. I'm still not used to how well he sees me and notices when something is wrong. "I'm fine." He doesn't believe me, but I won't admit to anything else while we're with my friends. "It's been a long day."

Hank meets Derek's gaze and lifts an eyebrow. I'm assuming he's asking if we've done enough to counteract *Hot Scoop*'s momentum, but he's smart enough to not say anything out loud.

Derek purses his lips, glancing around the restaurant with an air of casualness. Not many people seem to be paying attention to us like they were when our meal started, which hopefully means we've lost any real interest. We're just a group of friends and couples out for dinner. "We have that gig in the morning," he says after a moment. "Probably best if we turn in early."

"I'm in the mood for more dessert," Liam says as he wraps an arm around Kasey. "You three go on without us."

Kasey rolls her eyes but seems thrilled about his suggestion. "I don't know where you put it all, Liam." She pats his stomach, shaking her head.

He chuckles and leans in to kiss her. "You can help me work it off later."

The kiss, I'm guessing, is two-fold. He clearly enjoys kissing his girlfriend, but it also provides a small measure of distraction as the rest of us rise from our seats and move to the exit. We'll still be noticed, but hopefully anyone who might pass along photos or intel will be too focused on

Liam's unfiltered affection for Kasey to realize we're disappearing into the night.

The air outside is moderately cool, so I lean into Hank as we fall in step behind our bodyguards. He tucks me up against his side, and I'm pretty sure he kisses the top of my head, which will make for a great photo if anyone caught it. There are fewer paparazzi around than I expected, but a few flashes still greet us as we reach the limo.

Eli opens the door, and I slip inside, followed by Hank. Derek, on the other hand, remains on the sidewalk. He leans his arm against the frame to look in at us and smiles. "It'll look better if you leave on your own," he explains. "You're welcome to your room as always, Bon, and I had the staff prepare a guest room for Hank as well."

I sigh, overwhelmed with gratitude for this man who has always been so good to me. My apartment is closer, but it only has one bedroom. I want Hank to have space if he needs it. "Derek, you are one in a million."

Chuckling, he shakes his head. "I hope tonight helped." Then he shuts the door, leaving me alone with Hank for the first time all day.

I immediately kick off my shoes and snuggle up next to him. "Finally."

He laughs. "As much as I wanted to hate Derek, I can't do it."

Alarm shoots through me. "Why would you ever want to hate him?"

"Because he got to hold you like this long before I did."

Derek never held me quite like this. At least, not outside of public events, and even then he never touched me the way Hank does. Hank has returned his hand to my waist, his fingers pressing against my ribs in the most tantalizing way. There were times I thought Derek's interactions with me were more than that of a friend pretending to be a boyfriend, but he never made me feel the way Hank does.

Wrapping my arm around Hank's torso inside his jacket, I breathe in his clean scent and shake my head. "Keep on like this, McAllister, and I'll probably forget Derek ever existed."

His hold grows tighter, pulling me closer. "How did you first meet him?"

"Derek?"

He hums.

Memories of that first day on set come flooding back, though it's not like I ever forgot. Because of Derek, I met Liam, Cole, and Freya, and their friendships have been the only thing keeping me afloat in this crazy world of fame. "We were in a movie together. Derek was the lead, and I was an unnamed side character."

"That's hard to believe," he murmurs, pressing another kiss to the top of my head.

I snort a laugh. "I've really only been famous as an actor since meeting Derek. Before that, I was just the token pretty girl hired to add flair to a movie or boost the image of whoever I was dating." Hank doesn't have a comment for that, and I don't expect him to. But it's weird to think about those days. "I was a nobody for six years, and then this big Hollywood star accidentally spilled his coffee all over me."

Hank stiffens. "Derek...spilled his coffee on you? *That's* how you met?"

"I haven't told you the best part. He did it on purpose."

"What?!" Hank actually growls, which isn't a sound I thought he would ever make, and it is far more attractive than it should be.

As he starts mumbling insults under his breath, I shift until I'm on his lap, which shuts him right up. This was a bad idea, given how much easier this will make kissing him, but I clearly said the wrong thing and got him all worked up over something he doesn't need to worry about. I need him to listen.

"Let me tell the story," I say, pressing a hand to his cheek.

He nods slowly, eyes fixed on me.

I grin. "Derek spilled his coffee on me because earlier that day he witnessed a run-in between me and the female lead, a woman who was...let's just say she isn't the nicest human in the world. She went off on me after we filmed one scene because, according to her, I was stealing the spotlight from her even though my role was purely background. Not even a speaking part. She told me I would never amount to anything and I should kiss my acting career goodbye because no one was going to hire me. Derek didn't like that."

"I'm failing to see how spilling coffee on you fixes anything," Hank grumbles.

I snicker. "You are seriously cute when you're protective."

"Again with the cute," he says and leans forward to kiss me.

I press a hand over his mouth. "Can I finish?"

"Tell your story faster."

Biting my lip, which only seems to rile him up more, I debate if it's actually worth finishing this story. But I don't want him to think poorly of Derek if I'm going to keep him around, which I really want to do. I like impatient Hank, and the temptation to kiss him is growing stronger, so I get to the point of my little tale.

"The way Derek explained it, he never would have been able to get close enough to have a conversation with me without creating some sort of justification because his costar was...possessive? He couldn't even talk to the women on the production staff without Miss Perfect showing up and demanding his time. So he spilled his coffee on me as he walked past during a break and insisted on helping me clean up."

Hank groans. "You do know that this is sounding a lot like how Gabrielle met the movie critic in book two, right? Only, their version of 'clean up' was a little more...clothesless."

We both blush, and suddenly I realize I shouldn't be surprised that Hank is as good at kissing as he is. His books have plenty of steam, and he must have gotten that from somewhere.

I clear my throat and run my hand through his shorter hair. Liam and Derek went all out with tonight's display. Hank looks amazing, but I kind of miss the scruffy author look he usually has. "Derek just wanted to talk. He wanted to make sure I was okay after the verbal assault, and when I told him I was totally fine, he pushed until I admitted that her words had really gutted me. Then he told me that I was a phenomenal actor because he almost believed me when I said I wasn't hurt, and he said it was okay to show emotion in real life as well as in my acting."

Derek had been so kind in a way no one in Hollywood had been before that point. Six years of doing everything I could to feel like I might actually belong in this career I had dreamed for myself, and he was the first to give me a spark of hope.

"Next thing I knew," I continue, "my side character role suddenly had a speaking part that wasn't in the original script. The female lead was furious, but Derek spent the rest of filming keeping her busy so she couldn't give me any more problems. And a month after that shoot, I got a call to audition for a lead role in a romantic comedy. My agent almost died of shock when I got the part, and that movie did way better than anyone expected. Derek showed up at the premiere, which generated a lot of buzz, and he invited me to his house a few weeks later because he 'wanted help looking over some scripts.'" I throw that last part in air quotes.

Hank's jaw grows tight. "Is that when you started up your *fake* relationship?"

Oh, he is adorable when he's jealous. "That's when I made my first friend in Hollywood," I say, going back to playing with his hair. "He introduced me to Cole, who was playing in the NFL for the Oregon Badgers at the time but often came down to California to see his dad, and then I met Freya when she visited Derek on one of her diplomatic business trips to the US. A few months later, he adopted Liam into the group. It took over two years of us being friends before Fran had the brilliant idea to make us more."

Hank reaches up, tucking a curl of hair behind my ear. "So you owe everything to Derek," he mutters. His expression is one of resignation, like he knows he'll never measure up to the man. A lot of people get that look when they meet Derek, but Hank doesn't need to be one of them.

Smiling, I lean closer and touch the softest of kisses to Hank's lips. "I do owe a lot to Derek. But my life is not the same as it was a month ago—*I'm* not the same—and I owe that entirely to you." Pulling his glasses from his face, I tuck them away for safekeeping, and then I kiss the bridge of his nose. "You have made me confident, Henry McAllister." I kiss his cheek. "You see me in a way no one has ever seen me before." I kiss his chin. "You..."

I pause as familiar fear grips my heart. I have only ever known a life on my own. Yes, I have the most amazing friends, but they have their own lives. They can only share so much of mine with me. Like Liam, they're all going to find that person who makes them feel like their life is so much more complete, and I will be secondary.

"You make me think I could be someone's first choice," I whisper, though admitting it out loud is terrifying. Gripping the lapel of his jacket, I close my eyes and try not to let my mind tell me that this thing with Hank is just as temporary as all the others. That sooner or later he's going to realize our worlds don't mix and he would rather go back to the life where he is comfortable because he didn't choose this. Not at first.

"Bonnie." His whisper fills the dim space with so much emotion that I open my eyes again. He looks different without his glasses, but he's the most handsome man I've ever known. He swallows as he takes me in with his warm brown eyes. "Bonnie, I know it might be hard to believe, considering the way I was when we met. I was broken. And you fixed me." He brushes his fingers against my temple, leaving a trail of heat. "But I need you to know that my reasons for wanting to be with you have nothing to do with what you've done for me. It's because of who you are. I don't make decisions lightly, and when I do, it takes a lot to change my mind. So believe me when I say that if given the choice between having you in my life and going back to the quiet I lived in before I met you, I would choose you. Every. Single. Day."

Then he kisses me, his mouth warm and hungry and full of so much passion and emotion that my heart aches to experience all of him. I've never felt the way I feel about him, and with each kiss I fall deeper into whatever this is. I want to be as close to him as I possibly can and never be without him. Hank seems to want the same thing, holding me flush against his body as he soundly and thoroughly kisses me in the back of the dark limo.

I am very, very glad that the drive to Derek's house is a long one.

CE CREAM

chapter twenty-seven

Bonnie

"I'M GOING TO BE honest with you both." Ethan, my new publicist, settles in the chair that will be occupied by our interviewer in a few minutes. He looks between Derek and me, his expression hard but not in a cold way. It's obvious he's going to do his best to make sure things don't get worse. "Fran made a mess of things, and it's not going to be easy to clean it up."

I resist the urge to sigh dramatically. When Derek called Ethan this morning and asked if he would meet with us before our interview, I had high hopes for things turning around. Ethan talked to us for a few minutes when he arrived, getting the full scope of the situation, and then he was on the phone while we went through makeup and wardrobe. I'm not loving the fact that he already looks tired.

"Did last night do anything to help?" I ask, practically holding my breath as I wait for his response.

Ethan offers me a small smile. "I think so, but it's hard to say anything for sure until *Hot Scoop* posts another story. If the two of you are okay with it, I'm going to record some of this interview and post it to socials. There's no question that Jimmy is going to ask you about your relationship with Hank, so I want you to be as honest as you can be without mentioning the origins of the relationship."

I frown. "But I already told the world that it was fake."

Though his mouth tightens, Ethan keeps his expression fairly soft. "I know. But I think from this point onward, it will be better to keep the attention on the relationship as it is now. Not how it started. We want to control what we can."

That makes sense, even if I don't like hiding the truth more than I already have.

I must be broadcasting my thoughts all over my face because Derek takes hold of my hand and squeezes. "I think he's right, Bon. And Hank said himself that it was always real on his end. Maybe it was Fran's idea to push the two of you together, but I don't think it was ever fake. Not even for you."

Warmth spreads through me as I think about waking up in Hank's arms this morning. Like at the hotel, Hank let me come into his room and sleep next to him even though I've never had a hard time sleeping at Derek's house. There's something so calming about being in his embrace, like listening to his heartbeat keeps all my fears at bay. When I'm with Hank, I don't worry about being ignored or forgotten. I don't worry about being passed over.

I would choose you. Every. Single. Day. His words have been on repeat since last night in the limo.

"If I could," Ethan says, pulling my attention back to him, "I would like to talk to Hank as well. Not only will his actions—good or bad—affect you, Bonnie, but I get the sense that he could use someone on his team."

Nodding, I grab my phone from where it's tucked under my leg and shoot a quick text to Hank. He's hanging out with Liam and Cole this morning, but I'm hoping he's near his phone. "He's a very private person," I tell Ethan, "so I want to make sure he's okay with you having his number before I give it to you." I made that mistake once by giving it to Derek and the rest of my friends, and I don't want to betray Hank's trust again.

He answers quickly, and I can't stop the grin that spreads across my face.

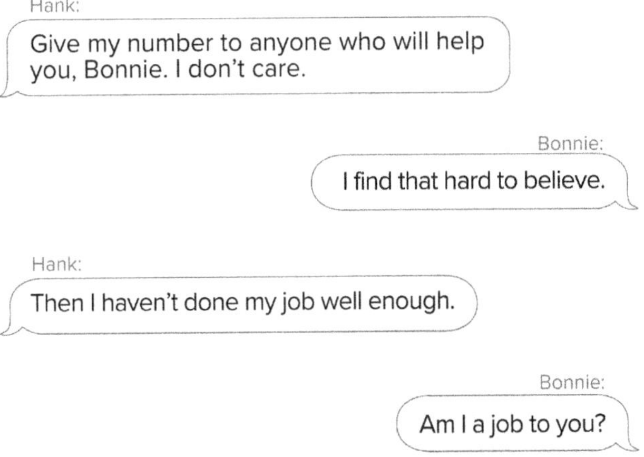

I snort a laugh that is half amusement and half to try to cover up the wild blush that fills my face with heat. As cheesy as that line was, I feel it in my core. "Here's his number," I tell Ethan, sending him Hank's contact card.

"Thanks." Ethan's smile looks a lot more natural now. I've only inter-acted with him a little before now, and usually when Liam is in some sort of trouble, so it's nice to know he isn't uptight like Fran was. "You look happy, Bonnie."

Letting out a sigh of contentment, I nod. "Hank makes me happy."

"That's what the world should know." Still smiling, he turns to Derek. "Derek, do you need any direction for this interview? I'm hoping Jimmy sticks to talking about the movie, but any reporter worth his salt is going to follow public interest. He's likely going to talk about the breakup."

Derek looks at me for a second before shaking his head. "I've got it covered."

We get ten minutes into the interview before Jimmy shifts the conversation to our dating lives. "I have to ask," he says, looking between us. "Has the breakup made the job difficult for you two?"

I meet Derek's gaze, reading his thoughts in his eyes, and I nod once. I'm happy to let him take this one, especially because Ethan is standing behind Jimmy's chair with his phone trained on us.

"Honestly," Derek says, still looking at me, "Bonnie and I came to the natural conclusion that we're better as friends. That's how things started, and that's how they're going to stay. I hold Bonnie near to my heart and wish her the best in everything she does, just as I do all my friends."

Jimmy looks at me, but it almost seems like his next question isn't the one he planned to ask. His words come out more hesitant than he's been so far. "How are you doing with all of this attention on your love life?"

My eyebrows shoot up at the same time Ethan's do. That's not the kind of question I was expecting. I take a second to sort through my thoughts and then smile. Might as well say the truth. "I picked a life that will never truly be private, but I think part of the reason I like Henry as much as I do is because he doesn't expect me to be anything but who I am. He lets me be real and doesn't judge my quirks and insecurities. It's hard to let myself feel human sometimes, but not when I'm with Henry. He makes everything easier, you know?"

Jimmy nods, giving me a smile, and then he turns the conversation back to our movie.

By the time the interview wraps up, I'm feeling even more at ease than I was before. I didn't think that was possible. But it feels like no matter what *Hot Scoop* might say about my relationship with Hank, it won't change my opinion of him. He is good for me, and I want to make things work between us.

I think I finally understand why Kasey and Liam don't care what the tabloids say about them. They love each other too much to let anything get between them.

"I'm going to try to get a peek at what *Hot Scoop* might say about Hank's story," Ethan says as we head for the car. "They're not all that fond of me after the Liam stuff last fall, but I have a few contacts who have been trying to get close to the site."

"You're setting up spies?" Derek asks with a chuckle.

Ethan shrugs. "They've clearly got them. Why shouldn't we? You guys deserve to live your lives without having to watch your every move."

I pull him into a hug, ignoring the way he goes stiff as soon as I touch him. I'm hoping he's just surprised and not against hugs because I have a feeling I'm going to want to hug this man a lot in the future. He's a million times better than Fran. "Thank you."

He splutters something about it being his job, his face growing red, and then he heads for the parking lot.

Derek and I climb into the waiting SUV, and though we don't say anything during the drive to Malibu, I'm pretty sure we're both feeling the relief of being able to breathe again.

Cole looks miserable. He's sitting on Derek's back porch with a book, but I don't think he's actually seeing what he's reading because his gaze is distant.

In the chair beside him, Hank is writing in his notebook, but he looks up as soon as I step through the back door. The smile that spreads across his face feels like it warms up all of California. "How did it go?" he asks, and the sound of his voice rouses Cole from whatever thoughts he was lost in, pulling his eyes up from his book.

Though my heart reaches out to Cole, filling me with a need to talk to him and see how much he's hurting, I've missed Hank in the hours I've been away this morning, and I can't ignore the draw of his smile. As he sets his notebook on the armrest of his chair, I slide onto his lap and greet him with an eager kiss. Reluctantly, I keep it mostly tame despite the sparks of attraction that build as my lips explore his.

Pulling away and chuckling at the soft groan of protest that comes from Hank's throat, I press my palm to his cheek and smile. "I think it went really well, and Ethan is going to try to soften things with *Hot Scoop*. Did he call you?"

He nods. "I like him so much more than Fran."

"Me too. Where's Liam?"

"He decided we were boring and he would rather hang out with Kasey."

Sounds right. If he doesn't put a ring on her finger soon, I'm going to question his sanity. "How were things here?"

Hank glances at Cole, whose dark eyes stare back at him. "Fine." There's a lot of weight to that word, which almost comes out as a question, and I can't help but turn to Cole with a raised eyebrow.

He groans and rolls his eyes. "I shouted at your boyfriend. I've already apologized."

A surge of protectiveness rises in my chest. Tucking my arm around Hank, I curl up close to him as if that might protect him from Cole's grumpiness. "Why did you shout at Hank?"

Hank snickers. "I deserved it."

"I highly doubt that."

"I told him I know how he feels, even though it's not true."

My arms reflexively tighten around him even more, and I glare at Cole. "His wife was *murdered*," I say sharply.

"I know that." At least Cole looks chagrined as he drops his gaze to the cement, but I can almost feel his anger still simmering under the surface as he clenches his jaw tight. He's not usually an angry person, so it's weird to see him like this.

Hank presses a kiss to my forehead. "I shouldn't have said what I did," he says quietly. "I knew Shelby loved me up until the end. I don't know how it feels to have someone *choose* to leave."

"Oh." I relax. "I guess I hadn't thought of it that way."

Sighing heavily, Cole runs a hand through his dark hair and shakes his head. "I still shouldn't have yelled at him," he mutters, still looking at the patio floor. "It's just..." He's tense, muscles flexing with every stiff movement and making him look panther-like. But a panther in a cage. For most of the time I've known him, Cole has always been calm and relaxed outside of his games. His breakup really did a number on him, and I've hated watching him get all twisted up until he's almost unrecognizable.

"Derek said something about Sage dating one of your old teammates," I say softly. I don't want to reopen the wounds, but I need to know that Cole is going to be okay. That my friend is still in there somewhere. *Something* needs to snap him out of this funk.

He nods slowly. "Not just a teammate. He was my best friend before I left the team."

I wince. *Yikes*. No wonder he's tense. "Oh, Cole, I'm—"

"I don't need your pity, Bonnie." Getting to his feet, he looks at the two of us snuggled in our chair and sighs. Maybe I shouldn't have been so eager to get close to Hank when I know Cole is still struggling with his breakup, but it's too late now. "I'll be fine. Eventually. Once I stop feeling like she's dating Javi to get back at me somehow. Don't let me darken your day."

"Cole!" I shout before he can take more than a couple of steps toward the door. When he looks back at me, I give him a sad smile. "If you ever need to talk, I'm here."

He matches my expression. "I know. Thanks, Bon." His eyes flit to Hank, and his smile shifts into something warmer. Closer to the smile I'm used to, complete with a bit of mischief. "Don't think I won't do more than yell at you if you hurt her, McAllister."

I gasp as Hank chuckles beneath me. "Did you just threaten my boyfriend?"

Cole folds his massive rugby arms. "Maybe."

"Wow."

It's such a brotherly gesture that tears well up in my eyes. Derek has always defended me, but I never realized how much Liam and Cole have always had my back just as much. They are far more than friends, and my fears that they might leave me behind were clearly ridiculous.

We're family. That's never going to change.

"Please don't leave," I tell Cole. Though he showed some life just now, I don't think he should be alone today, even if he wants to be. I wish Freya were here; she can usually get him to relax when no one else can. But I'll do my best to fill in for her while she helps run her country.

Though I can see his reluctance competing with his natural inclination to please the people he cares about, Cole nods and heads back inside. Hopefully to go find Derek, who has several scripts to run through today but will give Cole his full attention without hesitation. They've been friends long enough that Derek would do anything for Cole.

Once Hank and I are alone, I let myself fully relax into his hold and breathe in his clean scent. "I missed you." It sounds crazy, given how short a time we've been apart, but I've gotten too used to having him around so entirely.

His fingers trace a path along my arm, his touch featherlight. "I missed you too."

I smile into his neck and close my eyes. "Are you sure you're okay after Cole yelled at you? And threatened you?"

He chuckles. "The threat is to be expected. And I yelled at plenty of people in my day. Heartbreak has a strong hold, even when you wish it didn't."

"I hope I never have to experience that." As soon as the words leave my mouth, I tense up and stop breathing. I basically just said that I never want to break up with Hank because there is no doubt in my mind that I would be heartbroken if I did.

Hank is quiet for a long moment, his hand still stroking my arm. When he speaks, his voice is soft. Tentative. "What does your dream life look like, Bonnie?"

It would be so easy to lie and tell him that I'm living it. I'm filming a movie adapted from my favorite book. I have the most amazing friends who help me be true to myself. I am dating a man who makes me feel wanted and treasured. But my dream life?

"I don't know," I say after a long moment. "My dreams have always been changing. When I was a little girl, I wanted my parents to treat me like I was more than an obligation or an afterthought. When I got older and realized that was never going to happen, I found a career that would help me be remembered because I was so afraid of being forgotten. After I met Derek and his friends, that was less of a fear, and I wanted to be valued for more than my looks. I wanted to prove that I was talented and skilled. I think I'm getting there."

Hank tucks my hair behind my ear. "And now? What is your next dream?"

How do I even put it into words? I lift my head up so I can look at him. "Do you remember what you asked me at the airport? And the meadow? And even on set before that?"

Though his eyebrows pull low, he nods. "I asked if you were tired of letting everyone else tell you how to live."

"I am so tired." I hate that my eyes fill with tears, but it feels like the world is suddenly weighing down on me as I really let myself think about his question. What do I actually want in life? "When I was a kid, no one told me what to do, and it was so lonely. When I got hired for my first movie, there was always someone telling me where to go and what to do, and all I felt was relief. I leaned so heavily into that that I think I went too far in that direction and gave up any autonomy I had. And now I don't…"

I take a deep breath, terrified of the words that want to spill out of me. "I don't even know what I want for myself, Hank, and I still rely so much on other people." Panic fills my chest, hot and heavy, as my thoughts start to spiral. "But I want you! I know that. You are the only thing in my life that is certain, and as terrified as I am of losing you, more than anything I want you to be happy. I don't want you to feel as helpless as I've felt for so long. So if you don't want to deal with this ridiculous public life I've been thrown into, then I'll—"

Pressing his hand to my cheek, Hank catches my mouth in a fervent kiss that not only silences my words but also the fears that spiked while I was rambling. His thumb rubs my cheek, his other hand wraps around my waist, and he kisses me like a man who knows exactly what he wants.

"I told you," he whispers against my mouth. "I will always choose you."

I believe him. And while there are so many things about my life that are still unknown, especially when it comes to how it will look in the future, I know for sure that Hank McAllister is the one choice I will never regret.

HOLLYWOOD HOT SCOOP

The Wild Mystery of the Mystery Writer's Murdered Wife

SCOOPERS, HAVE WE GOT a crazy story for you! I know you're all dying for the dirty details after that doozy of a headline, but first we need to talk about the elephant in the room. No, we're not talking about Liam Connolly's weird soda habits—*why order it if you're not going to touch it*? We're talking about the absolute adorability that is Benrie!

I know we were all concerned about the truth of their relationship, but there's no faking this kind of heat. Not even for a Hollywood heavy hitter like Bonnie Aiken. Check out the slideshow below for a whole smorgasbord of snapshots from Bonnie and Henry's night on the town, taken by many of our wonderful patrons! (Want to see your photos featured? Check out our paid plan on our website here to become an Insider Scooper.) Henry is clearly besotted, and we've never seen our favorite leading lady look at anyone the way she looks at her poetic paramour.

Love is in the air in Los Angeles!

And that just makes today's true story all the more tragic. Buckle up, readers, and grab your tissues. As we've discovered, this isn't the first time

Henry McAllister has given his heart to someone, and he lost his first love in the most heartbreaking of ways. That's right, Scoopers. Shelby McAllister, Henry's wife of six years, was the victim of an unsolved crime four years ago and lost her life, leaving our mystery writer a widower without closure. Very little is known about Shelby's murder, but we here at *Hot Scoop* have all the gruesome details.

Keep reading to get the full story!

chapter twenty-eight

Hank

It feels strange to be back in Laketown on Tuesday afternoon. It shouldn't, given the sheer amount of time I've spent here over the last four years, but I'm not the same man I was when I left. And it's not just me. Bonnie said something similar about herself on Sunday night as we made the drive to Derek's Malibu house. The house that was, I'll be honest, opulent to the extreme.

I have no idea why a man needs that much space for himself, but spending a night in a guest room bigger than my entire house really put into perspective the level of fame and wealth Derek has. When taking that into account, plus an afternoon spent watching Derek pace shirtless on his back patio while chatting on the phone in full Russian with who knows who, it's clear that Bonnie actually feels something for me if she's willing to pass on him to be with me. So I guess that's nice.

If anyone fits the definition of a manly man, Derek does.

Speaking of manly men... After reluctantly dropping Bonnie off at her trailer, I stop by June's hardware store before coming back to my house so I can fill her in on everything that happened in Sun City and Los Angeles. June appropriately freaks out and asks a million questions, as if she thinks maybe I've been forced into acting differently. I'm glad for her concern, but I can only handle her skepticism for so long before I tell her that I will see her on Thursday when she delivers my groceries, which seems to calm her down.

It's at that point that she tells me she and Jonah discovered someone sabotaging the film production after yet another thing went wrong on set. They're now in a tentative relationship, which is a story I'm going to need to hear at some point.

Now I'm home, and I've been apart from Bonnie for less than an hour and already feel an ache in my chest where she belongs. That's probably why I'm still standing on my porch instead of going inside to shower and settle back into routine. It's a routine I don't actually know if I can go back to because it all feels wrong. I have the end of my novel to type out and probably a million emails to ignore, but I've been staring at my door for the last five minutes as if I'm worried I'm going to find a dead body inside.

Hot Scoop would love that. Their last story, posted yesterday afternoon, was rather tame, and I stopped reading halfway through because I didn't care what they had to say. But they would probably enjoy another murder mystery in my life, and I'm tempted to set something up so they can keep pretending they're doing some great work by sharing information that doesn't need to be shared. Maybe June would be up for pretending to be dead. Give her a little excitement in her quiet life, though she already seems to have found that with Jonah.

"Okay, this is getting ridiculous," I tell myself and grab the door handle.

But that's when I realize what feels off, and I look up at the corner of the porch where a broken and dirty web sits empty.

"Heather?" Alarm shoots through me as I search the awning for any sign of my spider friend. She's nowhere to be found, and I even search the whole exterior of my house to no avail.

Maybe it's a bad sign that I'm this attached to a little spider, but there's a physical pain in my chest as I try not to think about what might have happened to her. She's been living on my porch for months, and to think she's gone...

This loss feels far stronger than it should, and I push open my door before I dwell too much on my attachment to the arachnid. Maybe a shower will help clear my head. But when I get inside, everything still feels wrong, and my anxiety starts to spike as I take in the little space. It's all so small. And I don't just mean compared to Derek's mansion. This house is *tiny*. It's the kind of place someone comes to visit for a week, not somewhere to spend all his time.

It's also...dusty. Like no one has been here in months.

"Please tell me it wasn't always like this," I say to the house in general, knowing there's no one here to answer.

There has never been anyone here, and I think that's the problem.

I can't be alone anymore.

Gripping my bag tighter, I make my way to my bedroom to at least unpack and get cleaned up, but my feet slow halfway there of their own accord. Right in front of the door to the second bedroom. I almost can't bring myself to look at the block of wood separating me from Shelby's studio, but neither can I keep walking down the hallway. I'm frozen in place. Frozen in time. Not sure what I need to do.

So I grab my phone and send a text with shaking fingers.

Hank:

Heather is gone.

Thankfully, the response comes almost immediately.

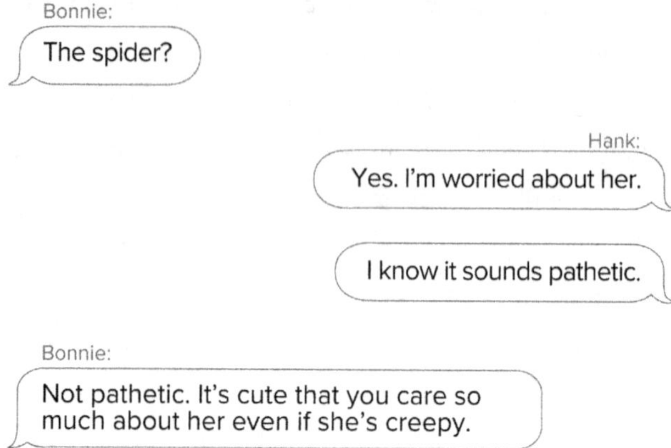

I chuckle, appreciating the levity when I'm on the verge of spiraling.

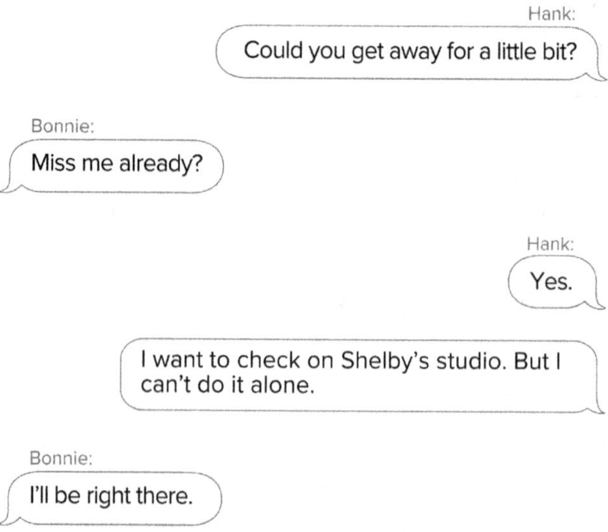

And she is. I only have to wait fifteen minutes before she's walking through my door. I haven't moved from my spot in the hallway, my bag sitting by my feet and my eyes locked on the studio door. I can't even pull my eyes away to look at Bonnie until she takes hold of my hand.

"Whoa, Hank, your hand is freezing." She cups my fingers between both her hands and lifts them to her mouth to blow warm air. "You don't have to do this if you're not ready."

"I think Heather was..." Okay, this is *really* going to sound crazy. "I think she was here to help me move forward from Shelby." Yep, that sounds as stupid as it feels, but I haven't been able to think about anything else for the last fifteen minutes. Even though Bonnie hasn't said anything, I keep talking because I need someone else to understand what I'm feeling right now. "Heather showed up right when I started writing this latest Gabrielle Frost book. And she was the first one I willingly told about what happened to Shelby. It was when I was talking to her that I realized I needed to try harder with you and let someone else in. And now that Heather has disappeared..."

I press a hand over my heart, hoping I can keep it from beating right out of my chest. "It feels like Shelby is really, truly gone."

"Oh, Hank." Bonnie hugs my arm, but she seems to decide that it isn't enough and wraps her arms around my torso, pulling me into a tight embrace. It's her hug that breaks me, like knowing that she's here to hold me together gives me permission to let all the pain out.

And I fall apart, sobbing in the middle of a narrow, dim hallway as my loss tears through me and leaves me shredded and raw. She's gone. The woman who changed my life, gave me hope, made me feel real love for the first time is *gone*. And I can never get her back.

How can anyone survive a pain this acute?

It could be an hour or it could be just a couple of minutes, but eventually my grief runs dry. The cracks start to close. I feel empty, but I also feel like I've finally let go of a burden that has dragged me down for so long and left me trudging through life under its weight. I've still been clinging so hard to the life I knew, but it's time to finally let it go.

Time to move forward.

I need to let go of Bonnie too—physically. I can't keep her here forever, and she still has a movie to finish.

A murder to solve.

I'm not sure how to feel about the idea that I've fallen for the woman who is putting my late wife to rest, but I have. She sparked life back into my soul and made me want to live again, not just because I want to be with her but because she helped me feel love again.

Love.

With that word filling my whole being, I tilt my head back and dry my eyes with my sleeve, noticing with a pang that Bonnie was crying right along with me. I didn't want her to cry, but it makes me love her all the more. "I haven't scared you off yet?" I ask, my voice as raw as my heart.

She shakes her head. "Not even a little bit."

I might if I tell her that I love her. It feels ridiculous and impossible to think I have fallen this far this quickly, but I knew I loved Shelby within less than a week of meeting her. For me, love is the sort of thing that creeps up on me and grabs me from behind, which is a really terrible metaphor when I think about how I nearly killed Gabrielle with a phone charger from behind in this last book.

Last book. Standing here with Bonnie in my arms, I suddenly know how the book is going to end.

"I think I'm ready," I say, switching from our embrace to holding her hand far tighter than she'd probably like me to. "At least, I hope I'm ready. I've never been good at goodbyes."

Bonnie squeezes my fingers, her smile small but warm. "I'm here as long as you need me, Hank. I've got nowhere to be."

"You have a movie to film," I argue.

"It can wait."

Turning to meet her gaze, I search for any sign that she might only be saying that to bolster my spirit, but I know better than to think I'll find any deception. Over the last couple of days, I got an insider look into Bonnie's life and the way she interacts with the people she's closest to. Bonnie was so sweet and gentle with Cole even though he clearly hated being coddled. Watching Bonnie laugh with Derek as he cooked dinner for the whole group that night dispelled any lingering fears that she harbored any romantic feelings for him. Even meeting Freya again over a video chat showed me just how much Bonnie cares for people because Freya seemed to relax more the longer she vented to Bonnie, who had great advice for her.

Bonnie is almost never disingenuous. She wouldn't be now.

Holding tightly to her hand, I lean down and press my lips to hers. "Thank you," I whisper, and then I grasp the doorknob and push it open.

The door creaks from disuse, and it's almost comical how much dust rises in the air from the breeze it creates. It's four years of untouched time, and both of us cough as we take our first steps inside. Sun streams in through the windows, and a part of me wishes I had known the curtains were open because anything in here is probably ruined from so many months of exposure.

"Wow, she was..." Bonnie frowns as she takes in the chaotic space. "Prolific."

I laugh. It's the last thing I expected to do when coming into this room, which only makes me laugh more until I almost can't breathe.

Bonnie is being generous. The room is filled to the brim with canvases and easels and random art projects that don't even make sense. At one point Shelby decided she was going to become a potter, so there's a wheel in the corner that she only used once because she was always too drawn to oil paints, and there's a whole box of yarn from the time she decided to take up crochet but got too frustrated with the process. Literally every surface is loaded with something, whether it be supplies or works in progress or cups that long ago held paint water.

"She was a mess," I say once I stop laughing. "It drove me crazy, so I allowed her this room to use however she'd like so her mess didn't extend to the rest of the house. It was even worse in Denver. She had the whole garage."

Though I don't want to let go of Bonnie's hand, I need both my hands to lift up a fallen canvas and set it on the easel it fell from. It's a half-finished painting of Laketown in the fall. She probably took a reference photo standing right in the middle of Main Street, and I can only imagine how many times she nearly got run over to get the perfect angles.

Just behind it is a complete painting of Shelby's childhood home, one full of warmth and nostalgia in the obvious time she took to make it perfect. I take a picture of it, and though I hesitate for a moment, I send it to her parents before I can talk myself out of it. Whether or not they respond, they would probably love to have this one. If nothing else, they deserve to know it exists. They deserve a lot of things I didn't give them in my grief.

It's time to fix that.

"She was amazing," Bonnie says, looking through a stack of canvases leaning against the far wall. "You said she was a curator, right? Did she ever sell any of these or put them in the gallery?"

I move to her side and wrap her up, pulling her against me. I thought it would be difficult coming in here, but now that I'm getting a flood of memories of Shelby sitting hunched on a stool while she painted, I just feel sad for letting all of this stay locked up and unseen for so long. "No, she never shared anything she painted," I say. "That's not to say I didn't push her to hang some of her pieces in the gallery to try to make some space. She painted for the sake of painting, and that was fine by her."

"Is that...?" Bonnie points to a painting sitting halfway tucked behind a blank canvas. "Did she repaint a Monet?"

I chuckle. It's still unsettling to feel so happy in this room, but I'm going to credit it all to the woman in my arms. "She spent almost all summer on that the year before she died. I think she was trying to see how close she could get it? She and her coworker were having a contest to see if they could fool the other, though I don't know if they ever got to the testing stage. It was where I got the idea for the forgeries in the book."

Bonnie spins around so she's facing me. "We didn't really talk about the *Hot Scoop* article after it dropped yesterday. How are you doing?"

I shrug. "I barely read it. Not the second half, anyway. I just wanted to make sure things were good with you."

Grinning, she leans up and kisses the tip of my nose. "As long as you're around, I think things will be great. The internet loves you. And the way you look at me."

"And how do I look at you?"

Pink splashes across her cheeks. Mixed with her smile, it's a truly beautiful sight. And I say that while surrounded by my late wife's incredible artwork. I shouldn't be able to stand here so easily and think about how much I've come to love someone new, but it almost feels like Shelby is trying to tell me that just because the sun has set on something spectacular, it doesn't mean I won't find equal beauty in the sunrise.

Bonnie bites her lip. "You look at me like you've found something you thought you'd lost. Like you were living in black and white and now you're seeing color. Like the sun has come out after a month of rain."

"And here I thought I was the writer," I murmur, brushing my nose against hers. "With you and Kasey around, I might as well retire now."

"But what about Gabrielle?"

"Gabrielle is ready to live a quiet life with Captain Stacey."

Gasping, Bonnie takes a step back. Much to my irritation. "You're ending the series," she guesses, and I can't tell if she loves or hates that idea. My agent isn't going to like it, but I'll be sure to tell Mariah I don't intend to stop writing. It will just be something new. "But if you finish with Gabrielle, what's next?"

She's too far away. Reaching out, I grab hold of her shirt to tug her back into my arms. "You tell me," I say and cover her mouth with mine.

Bonnie giggles into the kiss, which makes it difficult to do it justice, and then she leans away just long enough to say, "You saw me an hour ago, McAllister."

"Too long ago," I complain before kissing her again. I take a step forward, nudging her backward, and though we have to navigate paintings and a papier-mâché donkey, I manage to get her up against the door. I lean into her, wanting to get the most out of this kiss because this is the first time we've been alone since...ever. Even when we were in the limo after our fancy dinner date, there was a driver and bodyguard up front and only a glass partition between us and them. Derek's house was full of people. Now...

Now I want to show Bonnie just how much I've come to appreciate her in my life, and I intend to take my time.

My phone buzzes in my pocket between us, making me jump backward like I've been burned. Bonnie laughs breathlessly, but I'm considering tossing the stupid thing out the window because I don't see a reason why it needs to exist anymore. Outside of being used to contact Bonnie, who will hopefully not be far away from me very often, the phone is useless.

It's an unknown number calling me, which probably means it's not something I'm going to want to answer, but I do it anyway. "Who is this?"

"Hello, Hank," a familiar voice says.

My anger flickers. "Chad?"

"Why did you unplug your landline? I've been trying to reach you for over an hour."

I don't like the sound of that, and dread fills my belly as I reluctantly step back to give Bonnie some space. "What's going on? And how did you get this number?"

"Do you really want an answer to that?"

I groan because he's right. I don't want to know.

"Anyway," Chad says, "I'm calling to let you know that I'll be in Laketown tomorrow."

"Okay?"

"And I'm bringing a detective from Denver with me."

I sink onto a nearby stool as my energy disappears. Those words had the same effect as dousing me in ice water. "Why?" I breathe, though I think I know the answer.

Bonnie steps over to me and puts her arm around me. She might not know what I'm hearing on the other end of the line, but she can clearly see my distress. I'm grateful for her support, and I flip the phone to speaker so she can know why I'm suddenly dizzy.

Chad takes a long time to respond, like he knows how much I'm struggling. "They found him, Hank. Shelby's killer."

Bonnie gasps, but I feel numb. "It's been four years," I rasp.

"Yeah, and a widely read website just broadcasted the story to the world. That stirs things up. I'll tell you about it tomorrow, but I wanted to give you a heads up. Maybe some time to prepare yourself."

I never told Chad about Shelby, and I don't think he first learned about her through *Hollywood Hot Scoop*. It's a testament to his friendship that he never pressed for details, even though I'm sure he wanted them.

"Thanks," I choke out and hang up.

Bonnie shifts so she's standing in front of me, her hands locked around mine. "What do you need, Hank? Is this development a good one or a bad one?"

I meet her eyes, desperately latching onto the comfort I see there. "I don't know," I admit.

"Do you wish he hadn't warned you?"

"Yes. But also no. I..." I shake my head. "I don't think there's any good way to go about something like this. I should be glad they found him, right?"

She shrugs. "Maybe. But it also seemed like you were ready to let her go, and now you can't. Not until tomorrow, anyway."

I take a breath, holding it in my lungs as my heart pounds an uneven rhythm in my chest. I'm pretty sure I won't be able to sleep tonight. Not with this anxiety leaving me feeling like I'm teetering on the edge of a cliff.

Bonnie squeezes my hands. "Hank? What can I do?"

"Stay," I whisper back.

She nods, and I pull her into my arms, resting my face into the crook of her neck because she's the only thing that can keep me from falling. As long as she's here, I'll be okay.

CHAPTER TWENTY-NINE

BONNIE

"Freya, I need you to listen to me very carefully. What I'm about to tell you is not to leave this room."

Freya snorts, looking around her. "Which room? Mine or yours? Where are you, anyway?"

I glance down the hall, though this house is so tiny that I would have noticed if Hank had left the bedroom. He was still asleep when I crept out here to video call Freya, and I hope he stays that way as long as possible. He's pretty worked up over the impending conversation with the Denver detective who's coming sometime this morning.

I've cloistered myself in the kitchen, which is really just a counter-top and sink. It's adorable but suffocating. I don't know how Hank spent four years in this space.

"I'm..." I need to talk loud enough that she'll hear me, but I'm worried that Hank will hear me talking to her and come out instead of getting badly needed rest. I wish I had headphones, but I didn't exactly come prepared. I'm currently wearing Hank's pajamas, which are excessively comfortable but far too big on me. "I'm in Hank's house."

Freya squeals, forcing me to turn down the volume as she starts saying something in Candoran, which I absolutely cannot understand. It has a lot of English influence, but it's the Scandinavian roots that are lost on me. Still, I'm glad I have someone to talk to, even if I'm confused by her current circumstances. She's in her bedroom, which is unusual for this time of day. It's in the afternoon for her, and I'm lucky she answered in the first place. Usually she's in council meetings.

"Bonnie," she says, moving her phone closer to her face. "I know you have said that your relationship is real, but I did not realize you would be—"

"I'm in love with him, Freya."

That shuts her right up. It shuts me up too because those words are terrifying. But it's the truth.

After another double-check that Hank's bedroom door is closed, I keep talking. "It *hurts* when I'm not with him. Is that normal?"

She shrugs. "I have not experienced romantic love, as you know, but I..." She stops, her eyes fixing on something over her phone, and then she lets out a very un-princesslike curse. "Oh, he has found me." She scrambles off her bed, and the image blurs until everything goes dark.

I furrow my eyebrows, waiting for an explanation. I don't get one. "Um. Freya? Is everything okay?

She whispers her reply. "I am convinced my current buffoon of a bodyguard is aware that I intend to dismiss him, and he has therefore decided he must be at my side at all times to prove his competence."

"Are you hiding in your closet?"

"Yes, well, it is not like your closet, which can barely hold a ball gown let alone a—"

"I think you have things backwards, Peach. He should be the reason you *don't* have to hide from anyone."

She lets out a heavy sigh. "I know this, *vennen min*. Unfortunately, Anders does not."

I snicker. "You'll find the right fit eventually."

She mutters something that sounds like a prayer. "I certainly hope you are right. Now, if we can get back to your Hank. Cole tells me he is very attentive. I love this for you."

Sighing, I sit on the edge of the counter and rest my back against Hank's lone cabinet. "He's the best man I've ever known."

"And you are scared because...?"

"I never said I was scared."

I wish I could see more than just a dim outline of Freya, but I'm pretty sure she rolls her eyes. "You did not have to. I know you, Bonnie. And I can see that you are wanting to give this a try, which is so good. I have wanted nothing but happiness for you, and it warms my heart to see you letting yourself feel. You have not told him?"

I shake my head. "How is someone supposed to tell another person something like that?"

"It is only three words."

"But those three words are huge. Besides, he just found out that his wife's killer was found after four years. This isn't exactly a great time to tell him that I'm in love with him."

"You love me?" a deep voice replies.

I squeak in alarm and fumble with my phone, my thumb accidentally hitting the power button and ending the call. "Hank!"

He's standing at the edge of the hallway leading to the bedrooms, bleary-eyed and tousle-haired in plaid pajamas to match mine. But there's a look of hope in his eyes that sets a fire in my belly.

I nod. "I do."

He exhales, swallows, and then he crosses the room in four quick strides, gathering me up in a hug that surpasses all other hugs. I don't know how he always manages to convey so much in such a simple hold, but I never want him to let go. Since I'm still on the counter, I wrap my legs around him to keep him close and dig my fingers into his hair.

"I love you too," he says. "I wanted to tell you last night, but..."

He did tell me. Maybe not in words, but he kept his arms around me all night, holding me close as we lay together in the darkness. We did nothing but listen to each other breathe until we fell asleep, but every second I spend with this man is a second where I feel more loved than I've ever felt in my life.

"I love you, Bonnie," he whispers again, and they're the best words I've ever heard.

We spend the next hour making breakfast together—well, Hank makes breakfast because I've lost my cooking skills over the last several years—and doing everything we can to talk about anything that isn't Shelby or *Hot Scoop* or the fact that I should be on set right now but am here with him while Eli pretends I'm sick in my trailer. We speculate about Cole, who refused to talk about Sage while we were in LA and spent a long time gazing out the window at the ocean as if trying to figure out what he's supposed to do next. We talk about Freya and her bodyguard predicament, and Hank jokes that the next one will be an attractive man with perfect teeth and a flirty personality because that's what happens in all the princess books he claims he doesn't read.

It all feels nice. Comfortable. While this house is still far too small, it is quickly starting to feel like home, and I don't know what to do about that. The only thing I do know is I love Hank and desperately want to be wherever he is.

The knock on the door comes right as we're drying the last of the dishes, and the tension seeps right back into Hank's shoulders. He seems too afraid to go open the door, but I don't think I can do this for him. If it were me, I would want closure, but I also have no idea how it feels to lose someone the way Hank did. I can only hope I'm of some use to him.

After a deep breath, he steps to the door and pulls it open. "Chad."

"Hank. This is Detective Perez."

Hank steps aside to let the two men into the house, looking pale. But the detective seems like a nice man, and hopefully he'll deliver the news kindly. Hank clears his throat, looking around the space. "I don't have any chairs except these," he mutters, gesturing to his desk chair, which doubles as a dining chair, and an armchair that tried to swallow me and my omelet. Apparently the chair was Shelby's, and she loved its lumpiness, though I have no idea how.

Chad smiles grimly, meeting my eyes for a second. "It's okay," he tells Hank. "The two of you can sit. We'll stand."

"This shouldn't take long," Detective Perez agrees.

I wait until Hank looks at me, and then I move to his side and take his hand. He settles in the armchair and pulls me with him so I'm on his lap and his arms are tucked around me. If this is where he wants me, this is where I'll stay.

"You found the person who...?" He can't even finish the question because his voice breaks.

Perez nods. "As I'm sure you're aware, there has been a lot of talk about your wife's case the last couple of days, and we had a sudden influx of calls from people who thought they had pertinent information. Most of it was nonsense and hearsay, but then I got a call from Briggs."

Chad steps forward. He looks a lot like Houston, but there's a hardness about him that always made me curious about where it came from. Houston told me he was a private investigator, which explains why he's here. It probably also explains his tough exterior. "One of my old clients called me up Monday night," he says. "She bought a painting from the

Denver Fine Art Collective not long after Shelby's death, and when the *Hot Scoop* article dropped, she got..." He looks at Perez and scratches his chin, a question in his eyes.

Perez chuckles. "Paranoid?"

"That's probably the best way to put it. Apparently she's a fan of yours, and she called in an art expert to verify her acquisition. He determined it was a forgery."

"Shelby's gallery sold her a fake?" I ask in surprise.

Hank's arms tighten around me. "And we're sure this 'expert' is really an expert?" he asks.

Chad and Perez share a glance. "I don't think you can get better than the King of Art," Chad says with a shrug. "Adam Munroe is one of the top dealers in the country, and I've used him a few times to help with cases."

"He's known for catching forgeries," Perez adds. "Especially over the last few years. In fact, the Art Collective flew him in from San Francisco yesterday morning, and he found six other fakes in their collection."

I feel something shift in Hank, though he doesn't move. I can almost hear his mind working behind me. "What does this have to do with my wife?" But his question almost isn't a question.

Chad must see something in his eyes because he smiles. "You're smart," he says with a shrug. "I think you've already figured it out."

"My wife is a huge fan of your books, by the way," Perez throws in, though I'm not sure now is the right time. "She thinks you're brilliant."

Twisting in my seat so I can see Hank's face, I'm shocked to find him almost scowling. "What am I missing?" I ask.

Hank shifts me off his lap so he can stand and start pacing. "They talked to her," he says to the floor. "They talked to all of them, and no one..."

Chad folds his arms. "No one knew any of the pieces were switched out. The owner said everything was accounted for, and in a gallery that size, there was no reason to look closely at any of the artwork when nothing was missing. So it was never a point of interest."

Hank stops. There's a fire in his eyes now, like a long-dead ember has been reawakened. "Kelli authenticated the fake painting before the sale, didn't she?"

Chad and Perez both nod.

"So there could be any number of forgeries out there because she's their top expert and confirms everything that comes through the door."

Another nod.

Hank growls as something else clicks into place, though I still have no idea what's going on or who they're talking about. "Shelby's death was an accident, wasn't it?"

Though Chad nods, Perez clears his throat. "Well," the detective says, glancing between the two men. "It's not easy to *accidentally* stab someone, especially after tying them up and dragging them several blocks away."

"*But she wasn't supposed to die,*" Hank replies, and his anger makes way for a heart wrenching cry. "If she had showed up twenty minutes later..."

Chad grimaces. "She probably would still be alive," he says softly.

"Wait!" I jump to my feet as I finally catch up, though I'll never admit I started mentally running through the plot of Hank's book because everything was starting to sound familiar. The murdered curator, the forgeries made by her coworker, the real paintings being switched out for the fakes... "Hank, are you telling me you actually solved Shelby's murder without realizing it?"

Hank runs a hand through his hair, his eyes on Chad and the detective. "It was Kelli?" he asks weakly, talking about the other curator at Shelby's gallery. "Truly?"

Perez confirms it with a nod. "We brought her in yesterday afternoon, and she confessed to the forgeries."

"She enlisted an ex-boyfriend to help swap the fakes for the real deal," Chad says, "and Kelli said Shelby arrived for her shift early and saw something she wasn't supposed to see. The boyfriend panicked and grabbed her. Kelli moved Shelby's car across town to shift suspicion."

"She wanted us to tell you that she never wanted Shelby to get hurt," Perez says with a shrug. "She's still an accessory to murder, but take that as you will."

Hank returns to the chair, sinking back into it with an exhausted sigh. Hanging his head like he is, he looks almost as broken as the chair he's in, and I don't know how to help him. So I turn to Chad.

"Did you read Hank's first book?"

He nods, his eyes still on Hank. "You had it all figured out, Hank. You just didn't know it."

Perez shifts his weight, like he's suddenly uncomfortable. "Maybe we should have paid closer attention to your version of it all, Mr. McAllister."

Hank looks up and nearly smiles. "I don't think the desperate imagination of a grieving man counts as evidence, Detective."

"Kelli told us how to find Mike Johnson, her ex. He was brought in less than an hour later, and he confessed to his part in the whole thing."

Chad lowers his voice as he adds to the detective's statement. "They're both going to be locked up for a long time, Hank. Shelby will finally get justice."

Hank lets out his breath, and for a moment he looks completely lost. Like he doesn't know what to do now that it's over. But then he looks up, tears shining in his eyes. "Thank you," he says to Detective Perez. He struggles out of the chair as he turns his gaze to Chad. "Both of you." Unlike the detective, who gets a brief handshake, Chad gets a hug.

With that, the two men head out into the appropriately drizzly morning and leave me alone with Hank once more.

I'm still dumbfounded that Hank's fictional book ended up following so closely to the truth. It's going to take some time to process that. "Hank, you *solved* Shelby's murder. That's incredible!"

He shakes his head. "That was coincidence."

"Honestly, at this point I'm not sure I believe in coincidence."

He meets my eyes, a wrinkle forming between his eyebrows as he silently questions my meaning.

I gesture between us. "This? There's no way this *just happened*. Call me crazy, but I feel like you and I were meant to meet, Hank McAllister."

The little smile that curls up the corners of his lips is the first sign of happiness that I've seen since Chad called yesterday, and relief shoots through me. "You think this was fate?" he asks.

I shrug. "Stranger things have happened."

"You mean like Kasey showing up on Liam's doorstep?"

Snickering, I nod and start making my way to him. "Exactly. If they can find each other through a food delivery app, is it so crazy to think fate had a hand in bringing me to you? Think about it." I grab his hand just in case he might start arguing before I really get going. "You wrote a book that just happened to be a bestseller."

He wrinkles his nose. "I like to think talent had something to do with that."

"Someone just happened to like it enough to turn it into a screenplay."

"A calculated business move," he argues, his smile growing.

"Beckett just happened to be chosen to direct it, and he picked, well, not me, but—"

"I intend to make sure Beckett knows he's an idiot for not choosing you first, by the way," Hank growls.

I'm liking this new growly side of him, and I pull him closer with a grin. "His first choice *just happened* to get pregnant and retire to focus on her family. And the studio *just happened* to choose your hometown for the filming."

Hank groans. "And you *just happened* to be a fan of mine and came looking for me right as I was running away?"

"Exactly!" I'm smiling so wide now that it almost hurts. "If I had been thirty seconds later, we would have missed each other."

I expect him to smile, but he frowns instead, his eyes jumping to the coat rack in the corner. There's a familiar umbrella sitting there, bright red with white polka dots. It's just like the one Gabrielle has in the books. "The day that we met," he says slowly, "I was going to leave the meeting with Beckett ten minutes earlier than I did."

I feel like I should hold my breath. "Why didn't you?"

"Because something in me said I needed to stay a little longer. Almost like a voice in my head telling me to wait a few more minutes."

I gasp, my heart picking up speed. "Why did you listen?"

He sighs. "It felt like Shelby, and I was desperate to hold on to that feeling. That's really why I was running from Beckett's tent. When the feeling went away, it felt like I was losing her again. So I ran." His teary eyes trace my face as he finally smiles again. "I ran into you."

As I wrap myself in Hank's hold, I think about my own life and what led *me* here. I think about my parents doing their best but inadvertently making me feel like I had no worth. No reason to be given love. I think about Derek being the first person to really see how desperate I was to be known and valued and the chance he gave me. The *family* he gave me. I wouldn't trade my friends for the world, but what if things had been different?

"There is so much I would have missed out on," I say out loud, even though Hank hasn't been a part of my thoughts and probably has no idea what I'm talking about. "Maybe I was *meant* to be born to working parents who didn't have the capacity to love me the way I wanted them to. I might never have found you otherwise."

Hank's arms pull tighter around me. "Bonnie, everyone deserves to feel loved. Especially you."

"That's the thing. I *do* feel loved. And even if I didn't, I..." I take a long, deep breath as a feeling of peace settles over me. "I never loved myself. That should have been a good place to start. It took me a while, but I've finally figured that part out. No matter who else may or may not love me, *I* love me."

"That's a big thing, Bonnie. And for the record..." He presses a kiss to the top of my head. "I love you too. I always will."

I grab his collar and tug his mouth down to mine, letting all the emotions of the morning melt away as we kiss. I have a few weeks left of filming, but after that I won't have an excuse to stay in Laketown. I have no idea what our future is going to look like, but I know one thing with everything in me:

I am absolutely in love with this man, and I don't intend to ever let him go. Especially not today. Today is for us and us alone.

CE CREAM

EPILOGUE

HANK

Two and a half years later

"Henry David McAllister, there is no way you're carrying me over this threshold when I am the size of a blimp." Bonnie folds her arms, clearly determined to win this argument I didn't know we were going to have.

My eyes drop to her rotund belly. "But it's tradition," I say with a pout.

Her stance doesn't change, though I can see her resolve breaking the longer we stand here on the porch. "But *why* is it a tradition?" she asks. "I thought that was just a newlywed thing, and that isn't us. Besides." She splays her hands across her stomach. "I am like fifty pounds heavier than normal. And you're not that strong."

"Hey," I complain. "I've been working out."

"Lifting a baby carrier with a bag of flour in it is not working out, Hank."

"Tell that to my arms." I flex, though I am well aware that there's not much there. I *am* stronger, and I'm feeling confident in my abilities to carry our child as soon as he arrives. Or she. We still don't know the gender, which is driving me crazy, but Bonnie wanted it to be a surprise.

I point to the door to the Laketown house, which is sitting wide open because my wife refuses to let me pick her up. "I first carried you across this threshold two years ago after our honeymoon," I tell her, as if she doesn't remember. "I carried you across the threshold when we bought the house in LA. *And* the one in London." That house might be my favorite, but only because my latest series is set in London and it's a lot easier to write about the gloomy weather when you're in it, rather than basking in the heat of sunny Southern California.

Bonnie gestures to the house in front of us. "This house isn't new," she reminds me. "And we're only staying here for a week before we go back to California. I'm not having this baby in the middle of nowhere."

I wrap my hands around her belly and sigh. "She just doesn't understand," I tell our unborn child.

Bonnie laughs. "I really don't, Hank."

"The house might not be new," I agree, "but everything inside?"

Bonnie's expression shifts to one of curiosity, and she tries to take a step inside.

I shift into the doorway and shake my head. "Tradition," I insist.

Sighing, she looks down at her stomach and waves her hands in resignation. "Fine. But if you drop me, I'm telling Cole."

The threat lands as she intended, though I'll never admit it to Cole. He might be one of the nicest people I know, but the man is built like an ox. Unlike me. He would pulverize me.

It takes some huffing and puffing, but I manage to lift Bonnie into my arms and step through the doorway, putting her down on the other side. It's more a testament of my lack of muscle than it is her weight, no matter what she says. "Was that so difficult?" I ask, breathless.

Bonnie laughs and pats my cheek. "You tell me." But then she gets her first look at the front room, and her eyes go wide. "Hank! When did you do all this?"

I grin broadly, probably a bit too proud of my handiwork, which includes a couple of couches and a slightly bigger dining table with *multiple* chairs. And she hasn't even seen the second bedroom yet. It took forever to go through all of the art supplies and canvases with Shelby's parents, but we donated whatever paints were still good and sent the finished paintings to the gallery where Shelby worked. Most of them, anyway. I kept a few of my favorites for myself and hung them up around the house.

"Remember when you and Derek flew up to Alaska for that charity thing?" I ask.

Bonnie nods. "A year ago?" Then it clicks, and her eyebrows shoot high. As if she knows what's waiting for her, she waddles over to the second bedroom and nearly screams when she sees the setup. "Hank! You did this all the way back then? But I wasn't even..."

I wrap her up in my arms, kissing the base of her neck as we gaze into the sunlit nursery together. This room is my favorite. "I guess I was feeling hopeful."

Bonnie starts crying, which has happened a lot while she's been pregnant. "I love it, Hank. But you know I'm not delivering our baby here."

"I know. But this way we'll be prepared for the next one."

Bonnie laughs. "I have that drama I'm filming next year, and then Kasey keeps telling me she wants me to be in the movie she's writing right now. It might be a while before I have time for another baby."

"I know that too." Though, I'm going to do my best to persuade her otherwise. She has to do the hard work up front, but I'm more than willing to give up writing time to look after the kids while she takes the world by storm. She's so in demand that I'm pretty sure some studios have been trying over the last few months to cast her in pregnant roles just so they can have her in their movies in the interim.

Ever since the wild success of the first Gabrielle Frost movie and its sequel, she has turned down everything but the roles that really interest her, for which I am extremely grateful. I love watching her act, but I love more when she's with me.

Leaning into me, Bonnie sighs with contentment as she continues to look around the polka-dotted room. "This house is too small for a family, Hank," she says after a while.

I'm hoping that means she's expecting a big family, just like I am. We haven't come to any conclusions about what our family is going to look like, deciding it is best to simply see where life takes us. "Mm," I murmur, kissing her temple. "I suppose that means we'll need something bigger for our summer vacations. But I couldn't decide on a floor plan for the new house, and the architect I hired really wasn't much help, so I—"

She twists to face me, taking a step back so there's some space between us. "Architect? You're not going to tear this place down, are you?"

"The fact that you're worried I might do something so horrible is really attractive. Is that weird?"

"Hank!"

"I bought the lot next door," I say with a shrug. "And the one next to that. Actually, we own the whole street except for Chad's house. I really shouldn't be in charge of finances when both of us are making so much money, but with our other houses in such busy areas, I thought we could use something more private."

Bonnie throws her arms around my shoulders, and though she's a lot harder to hold when she's blimp-sized, I hold her as tightly as I can. I always do.

"I love you," I tell her.

"We're having a girl," she replies.

I gasp. "You've known this whole time?" My mind starts spinning with images of a miniature version of Bonnie running around, and I can't picture anything more perfect. The next month of waiting is going to be agony.

I lean back so I can brush my finger along her freckled cheek. She grows more and more beautiful every day, though *Hot Scoop* thinks she'll hold on to her baby weight after our baby is born. What do they know? Just last week they posted a story about a two-year-old with the ability to see through time, so I think they're losing their touch. Besides, even if Bonnie doesn't lose the baby weight, she'll still be the most attractive person in the world. Call me biased, but there's no contest.

"What if we name her Gabrielle?" Bonnie says.

I barely hold back my snort of laughter. "That would be arrogant of us, don't you think? That name made us both more famous than we ought to be, though I hear it's a very kick-buttery name." Besides, Gabrielle will always make me think of Shelby, and that chapter of my life is over. I'm eager to keep living this new one.

"Well, what do *you* think we should name our daughter?" Bonnie asks, raising her eyebrows.

I grin. "I'll let you know when I meet her." And then I kiss my wife, savoring this moment just as I've savored every moment I have with Bonnie. I don't intend to take any second for granted.

The End

Also by Dana LeCheminant

Starstruck Love Stories

Moonstruck

Lovestruck

Dumbstruck

Thunderstruck

Awestruck

Wonderstruck

Love in Sun City

Kiss Me if You Can

She Likes It, Hey Micah

The Chad Next Door

Crossing the Brooklyn Briggs

Houston, We Have a Problem

Standalone Romances

For Butter or For Worse

The Fear of Falling

The Wonder Boys

Love on Camera

Love in Writing

Love on Display

Love in Disguise

Simple Love Stories (Sweet Love Stories)
Simplicity
Growing Young
Bittersweet Brews
In Front of Me
As Long as You Love Me
Dear Dalia
Let Go

Terms of Inheritance (Sweet Romance)
Forever You and Me
Holding On to Everything
A World without You
Love, Strictly Speaking

Historical Romances
The Thief and the Noble
A Twist of Christmas (part of The Holly and the Ivy anthology)
What Dreams May Come
This above All
Never Doubt I Love

About the Author

Dana LeCheminant writes sweet romantic comedies, heartwarming contemporary love stories, and swoony historical romances—with a twist. Known for putting a fresh spin on beloved tropes, she lets her characters lead the way, believing they always know their stories best. Her books are full of banter, emotion, and connection—all of the swoon without any spice. When she's not dreaming up her next twisty trope or emotional arc, she's hiking the remote Utah backcountry or cruising down rivers in search of new inspiration. Dana has been telling stories since before she could spell and has no plans to stop anytime soon.

Dana loves connecting with her readers!
You can find her on social media (**@authordanalecheminant**) and on her website, **lecheminantbooks.com**.

www.ingramcontent.com/pod-product-compliance
Lightning Source LLC
Chambersburg PA
CBHW071348300726

48976CB00006B/1806